DESTINY OUR CHOICE

DESTINY OUR CHOICE is a wide-ranging
novel of the English Civil War. At its centre
stands Henry Ireton, a prominent land-owner
from the county of Nottingham who chooses,
as a matter of principle, to follow the rising star
of Oliver Cromwell.

As the trial of battle and political intrigue
develops, Ireton's powerful mind and gift of
swift decision are seen to carry increasing
influence in high places. While he suffers from
the unrelenting hatred of Royalist and Leveller
alike, he wins the total trust of Cromwell and
Fairfax. Had the doomed king only chosen to
believe in Ireton's integrity and accepted his
plan for saving the monarchy, the tragedy of
his trial and execution might have been
averted. Human choice, or was it destiny,
decreed otherwise.

About the author

Destiny Our Choice is John Attenborough's third novel, following his highly acclaimed *One Man's Inheritance* and *The Priest's Story*. As well as these three novels, he is also the author of *A Living Memory*, 'a valuable slice of literary history' (*The Sunday Times*), which is a history of the publishing house of Hodder and Stoughton.

He lives in Kent.

Destiny Our Choice

A novel of Cromwell's England

John Attenborough

We make our Destiny our Choice

Andrew Marvell

CORONET BOOKS
Hodder and Stoughton

First published in Great Britain in
1987 by Hodder and Stoughton
Ltd.

Coronet edition 1988

British Library C.I.P.

Attenborough, John
    Destiny our choice: a novel of
Cromwell's England.
I. Title
823'.914[F]   PR6051.T74
    ISBN 0-340-42649-7

Printed and bound in Great Britain
for Hodder and Stoughton
Paperbacks, a division of Hodder
and Stoughton Ltd., Mill Road,
Dunton Green, Sevenoaks, Kent
TN13 2YA (Editorial Office: 47
Bedford Square, London WC1B
3DP) by Richard Clay Ltd.,
Bungay, Suffolk.

To the memory of
MY MOTHER

in happy recall of the days
that are past

Contents

Part One

The carefree young man
1624–1629

A stubborn and saucy fellow towards the Seniors and therefore his company was not at all wanting.

Anthony Wood, *Athene Oxonienses*

1

On a clear May morning in 1624 the great tenor bell of the parish church of St Mary the Virgin proclaimed to a sad, small world that Mr German Ireton was dead. The bell sounded and resounded across the fields surrounding the village of Attenborough. Its insistent monotone echoed in Toton and Chilwell. The grievous news hurried along the shallow ripples of the Erewash stream, past its marshy banks and into the broad waters of the Trent to the City of Nottingham five miles away.

There were, indeed, few people in that part of Nottinghamshire who did not mourn the death of German Ireton. A good farmer and sportsman, he was respected for his outspoken honesty of purpose by the old land-owning families in the county as well as by the lively merchants of Nottingham. In his own village of Attenborough he was known as one whose word was his bond – a good man and a good master. Those who worked his fields or served his household trusted him as their forebears had trusted the family ever since the day, some seventy years back, when a younger son of the Derbyshire Iretons had purchased the farm in Attenborough and set to work to restore its fortunes.

And now, the squire was dead before his time, 'taken by the Lord in His infinite mercy' as his contemporaries would say: and leaving his widow, Jane Ireton, to run the small estate and bring up the eight surviving children of the marriage.

At long last on this fine spring day, the funeral service and the committal proceedings came to an end, and the villagers and family servants waited silent and bareheaded in the Lady Cross field to the west of the ancient church as the mourners moved in sad procession from the graveside to the family home.

Most of the young Iretons attended the service, John and Matthew holding the hands of Mary and Sarah, all of them grave and a little self-conscious in clothes made specially for the occasion. The local landowners were also present in force – prominent among them members of the Charlton and Pewtrell families, the Owthorpe Hutchinsons, the fair-haired Thornhaugh from Fenton and Sandys from Scrooby – their carriages and horses neatly mustered on the far side of the green. But it was on the young man holding Jane Ireton's arm at the head of the procession that the onlookers' eyes chiefly rested.

In 1624, in the penultimate year of the reign of James I, Henry Ireton was only thirteen years of age, yet he already carried himself with a calm, adult dignity that deeply impressed the spectators at his father's funeral. They saw a young man with bright, intelligent eyes deep-set in a face unnaturally white, his dark hair falling gracefully over a white collar: a youth athlete in movement and already as tall as his mother. Could this really be young Henry Ireton, the lad the village had known since the day of his baptism in 1611? Harry with his love of hawking, his skill as a rider, his almost reckless courage – qualities which were oddly matched by his unusual sympathy for children and animals?

These villagers reckoned they knew the lad as well as they knew the old squire. And as the mourners entered the low-slung, square-windowed house beside the church they naturally turned to speculation about the boy's future.

'Looks every bit a soldier this morning,' said one of them. 'And that's not surprising seeing as 'ow 'e's been makin' enquiries about the local militia. Only the other day 'e was over Fenton way to see the Thornhaughs.'

'You don't know nothin',' interrupted Edward Brewster, the head groom to the Iretons who had taught Henry and his brothers all they knew about horses. 'Master 'Arry was over at Fenton to buy a young mare recommended by a friend. I should know, as I was there too.'

'And did 'e buy the mare, Mr Brewster?'

'Why, sure 'e did. I reckon 'e did right. But nothing I could say would 'ave stopped 'im. Once that lad makes up 'is mind, yer can't shake 'im.'

'Ay, that's what parson says,' the parish clerk chipped in. 'Learns everything mighty quick and is real obstinate in argument. Some days, long after 'is lessons, 'Arry will be disputin' with parson about all sorts of things in the Bible. And as often as not, young 'Arry outwits 'im too.'

The local people were right about the obstinate streak in the boy's character. Some held that it was derived from his father who could be extremely difficult if anybody tried to double-cross him. Indeed, such a man was unlikely ever to find forgiveness from Mr German Ireton. But those who were part of the Ireton household had good reason for knowing that Henry owed these characteristics, as well as his good looks, to the lady of the house. Jane Ireton had retained her youthful charm and figure despite her many confinements, and her mind was as sharp as the needles she used for her embroidery. She was better read than her husband and, unlike him and most of her neighbours, her reading extended beyond a knowledge of the Bible. In general she was well informed by correspondents about events occurring far beyond the Nottinghamshire boundaries. She knew, for instance, of the baneful influence George Villiers was exerting on the heir to the throne. And it was she who had decided to have her young family educated by the local parson rather than send them to the Nottingham Free School. In that way, she felt, she could keep an eye on their progress and a better check on what they were being taught.

The Rev. John Mather, on his side, was wise enough to treat Jane Ireton with the respect reserved for his intellectual equals; and he derived some happiness from the knowledge that on at least two occasions he had successfully defended the lady against her enemy, the Archdeacon of Nottingham. The latter, seeking to maintain a single state religion, did not approve of Jane Ireton's independent proclivities in matters of religious observances. In terms of the church liturgy which the archdeacon was charged to uphold, Mrs Ireton should have been 'churched' after each confinement and she and her family should not have insisted on standing when receiving Communion. But she argued forcibly that, in both cases, her attitude was totally justified by Scripture. In the end the worthy archdeacon was persuaded by the rector to give up arguing with such a formidable opponent, and be content with having her offences placed on record for the benefit of future generations.

A few weeks after German Ireton's funeral, Jane summoned the Rev. John Mather to the Ireton home to discuss young Henry's future.

It was time, she said, for her eldest son to receive a wider university education, something which would better equip him for leadership in the days ahead. She insisted that she was perfectly capable of managing the household and the farm until Henry came of age or found a wife. How soon would he be allowed into a university? And which university should it be?

The wise old rector watched Jane Ireton and his eyes shone with a certain pride as he considered his reply. 'Henry, Madam, has enough book learning to go to university tomorrow. That I can guarantee. But I doubt if he will gain entry into a good college before he is fifteen.'

'And what, pray, do you mean by a good college?' Jane Ireton demanded. 'Are you speaking of discipline or learning or sound religion?'

'I speak of all three,' Mr Mather replied, 'but especially the matter of religion. Most colleges at Oxford and Cambridge will adhere to the Rubrics of Queen Elizabeth's Established Church – but some more strictly than others. I have it in mind that Henry will expect to be allowed some latitude of thought. If I may say so, Madam, he seems to inherit your independent thinking.'

It was finally decided that John Mather should travel via Leicester and Banbury to visit his old friend Dr Ralph Kettel at Trinity College, Oxford; he would seek to have Henry enrolled as a Gentleman Commoner for entry to the College in 1626. Three weeks later the parson returned, his mission successfully accomplished, and none the worse for his tedious cross-country journey except for a streaming cold. Dr Kettel, he reported, had been most helpful. He was extremely proud of the college of which he had been president since the turn of the century. He had, to the parson's surprise, shown a marked interest in encouraging the entry of young gentlemen from the North of England.

'They're always more independent than the Londoners,' he kept on repeating. 'And north of the Thames is a natural catchment area for my college. Indeed, you must understand, my dear Mather, that on your journey you have been travelling since Banbury over land acquired and administered by our pious founder and his family. A small college, Sir, but our influence spreads far.'

'A somewhat eccentric scholar, would you say?' said Jane Ireton after hearing the rector's account of his mission.

'That, Madam, would be a fair description of Dr Kettel. He claims to be of sound Anglican belief but he also expresses a profound dislike for a certain William Laud at St John's College who seeks to impose on all of us a uniformity of religious practice which you would not approve. Moreover, as all Oxford knows, President Kettel prefers the company of the young gentlemen in his college to the dry-as-dust disputations of his older colleagues. I think Henry will find him a very stimulating tutor.'

So Jane Ireton's eldest boy was duly enrolled for entry to the College of the Sacred and Undivided Trinity in Oxford. Two years later, in 1626, he rode from his Nottinghamshire home, accompanied by Edward Brewster's son who would act as servant or batteler to his young master, with accommodation within the college.

2

On the day when young Henry Ireton was conducting the mourners from his father's grave to the modest Ireton home facing St Mary's church in Attenborough, Samuel Dowdswell was drinking himself silly in an ale-house at a village near Oxford.

His friends – and he still had them – assured him that no man had ever succeeded in drinking his way out of trouble: but his misfortunes compelled their sympathy. Three years earlier, the bad harvest of 1621 had brought hardship to many small-holders on the Oxford–Berkshire boundary, but most of them had survived with the help of friendly creditors and a modicum of luck.

Sam Dowdswell was less fortunate. His thirty-acre farm at South Leigh near Witney, which the Dowdswells had owned and cultivated since the early fifteenth century, lay alongside property owned by the Pope family. That wealthy clan, as many a farmer knew, was never satisfied with what it owned; its appetite for land was boundless. So, when Sam Dowdswell could not meet his debts, his farm was seized on the strength of a legal order obtained from the local Justices by the Pope family.

Who, indeed, could stand in the way of these upstart vultures from London? Ownership of land was the sure way to higher social standing, and Thomas Pope, having amassed a fortune from a lucrative government appointment, had been improving his status from the day that Henry VIII ordered the break-up of the great monastic estates.

As Treasurer of the Court of Augmentation of the King's Revenue, Thomas Pope was well placed to choose what land he wanted. Not content with building a house for himself on the site of the great Cluniac monastery of Bermondsey, he had made major investments in Oxford and Berkshire farms. It was indeed true that by 1621 Sir Thomas Pope's descendants could ride from Banbury to Oxford without leaving their own land.

Yet they still wanted the Dowdswell farm. And nobody, least of all a penniless yeoman, had the strength to fight their enclosures. The old Sir Thomas had, indeed, made some charitable amend by endowing the derelict Durham College in the middle of Oxford and renaming it the College of the Sacred and Undivided Trinity. But cynics noted that the chapel prayers for the pious 'founder and the Lady Elizabeth his wife deceased' did not extend to curbing their descendants' appetite for land.

Sam Dowdswell, as was to be expected from a man of good yeoman stock, refused point blank to have any dealings with the new claimants for the land his family had owned for generations. He tore up the order the agent presented to him and, aided by his son, bundled the wretched man off his farm. But it was a final and pointless act of defiance. If the Dowdswells were to retain their independence, Sam had no option but to leave South Leigh and find some other occupation in which he could remain his own master.

At first he struck lucky. Using his knowledge of horses to good advantage, he set up livery stables at Osney near Oxford, shrewdly relying on the young gentlemen of the university to provide him with his day-to-day livelihood. Meanwhile, he was confident that his old Witney friends would use his expertise when it came to buying a horse or having a brood mare served.

All might have worked well for Sam Dowdswell had he not been saddled with his wife, Rebecca. The latter had recently become a fervent member of one of those Anabaptist sects which were springing up all over the country. In her new-found enthusiasm she resented the move to Osney which took her away from her strict Baptist friends in Witney. She disliked the custom Sam was building up among the Oxford students with their parade of fine clothes and propensity for gambling. And her extreme puritan theology condemned horse-racing and other sporting activities supported by her husband's business as the work of the Devil.

Brooding over the Old Testament disasters of the Israelites whenever they deserted their ancestral faith, Rebecca nagged Sam constantly, and became increasingly censorious of her children – young Sam, who had turned eighteen, and his sister,

Maggie. God, as revealed to Rebecca, was a God of judgment. Love did not enter the equation. Her saving mission was to expose and punish the wicked of this world lest they be condemned to Hell-fire when they finally faced the Great Judge. She saw Sin on all sides – not least in her own home.

Within a year of moving from the farm at South Leigh, young Sam left home, driven out by his mother, he said, to seek his fortune in New England across the sea. Thus Sam Dowdswell was deprived of his chief helper and the heir to the new business he was creating. It was understandable that Sam blamed Rebecca for the loss of his son.

But worse was to follow. Maggie reacted differently to her mother's killjoy attitudes; or rather she looked for independence nearer home. At sixteen she was strikingly beautiful – a country girl with lively eyes and clear complexion, light of foot and possessed of a firm young body – and she adapted more easily than her brother to their change of fortune. Indeed, she enjoyed working at the stables, especially when, under Sam's tuition, she was allowed to exercise the horses. The company of the horses and of her father's stable lads was infinitely preferable to home life under Rebecca's stern, unforgiving eye.

Soon Maggie took to walking out in the long summer evenings. She needed fresh air, she said, after mucking out the stables all day, and she coupled it with a natural desire to meet the local girls of her own age.

But this display of independence roused her mother's worst suspicions. Maggie's absences were checked and her movements watched until, inevitably, Rebecca discovered her cuddling one of the stable boys in the fields behind the house.

In her fury the mother lost all control. White with anger and deaf to Maggie's protests of innocence, she seized the girl's wrist, dragged her struggling into the house and up the stairs, hurled her into her bedroom and locked the door.

Some sort of Devil-possession seemed to give Rebecca superhuman strength. Gasping for breath, she still managed to pour out a flow of vituperation loaded with biblical quotations: 'Delilah . . . Gomer . . . oh, may God forgive your wickedness

... yes, I've been watching you these past weeks ... fornication, that most deadly sin ... must be punished ... a prostitute's punishment ... a public whipping ... a shaved head.' Rebecca was still uttering a confusion of threats as she descended the stairs and re-entered the kitchen. When Sam Dowdswell lurched back from the ale-house later that night, his wild-eyed wife was waiting for him. Had he not been drinking with his friends, he might have attempted to reason with the woman, or at least to calm her rage. As it was, he listened half dazed to Rebecca's hysterical assertions.

'Maggie must be punished,' she told her husband. 'A thrashing she'll never forget ... and that's your responsibility, Samuel Dowdswell.'

She handed him a leather belt. Together they unlocked the door of Maggie's room where the girl was lying on her bed. In a moment her wrists and ankles were tied and Rebecca pulled away the slip that covered her.

Maggie cried to her father, 'Mother is lying. I've done nothing wrong.'

The girl's words only served to increase Rebecca's anger. She spoke in a harsh toneless voice as if she were a judge delivering sentence. 'So now she calls me a liar, does she? Lay on, Dowdswell. A stroke for each year of her sinful life.'

Maggie screamed as the first blow fell on her naked body, and her eyes turned to her father, pleading for pity. What she saw made her scream before he struck a second time. There was no pity in Sam Dowdswell's eyes ... no sadness ... no mercy ... She glimpsed a man who, in his drunken state, was taking a sadistic pleasure in beating her. The father Maggie loved had become a beast.

Long after her hands and wrists were untied Maggie lay on the bed writhing from the welts across her thighs and back. From time to time a small, pathetic whimper escaped her lips. But at last she lay silent. Her head turned so that her eyes pierced the darkness of the surrounding walls and focussed on the savagery and injustice of what had been done to her. She was obsessed by the memory of the white-faced, dominating Rebecca and her father's manic eyes.

But at some point in the long night a new resolution took

hold of her. A new courage was born. 'I'll show them,' she kept repeating to herself, 'I'll show them,' and at length fell into a troubled sleep. By morning light her decision was firm. Come what may, she'd follow her brother into a wider world and live her life away from a home that had become the Hell to which her dissenting mother was for ever referring.

About ten o'clock next morning Maggie Dowdswell stole away from the stables while her father was involved in a complicated deal with a Witney farmer, and started walking stiffly down the high road to Oxford. She hardly noticed that the sun was shining out of a clear blue sky, or that the birds were filling the air with their mating calls. Nature paid no heed to the girl's misery. But soon she was jerked out of her solitary thinking by a friendly carter who overtook her and offered her a lift into Oxford.

'You for the city, young lady?' the man asked kindly. 'I can take you as far as the Mitre in High Street, if that'll suit you.' Maggie smiled her thanks and took her seat by his side. She said nothing, looking straight ahead over the horse's ears. But her silence worried her companion. He inspected her more closely.

'Seems you might be hidin' somethin',' he said. 'Would you be runnin' away from trouble, by any chance?' The girl brushed away a tear. 'Now don't you cry,' he added. 'It's a lovely day and you're too pretty to be weepin'. Just tell me what it's all about.'

Thereupon Maggie confided that she had been most cruelly treated by her mistress and was forced to find new employment. No, she wasn't afraid of hard work, she said. All she wanted was a kind mistress who'd give her food and accommodation. Could the carter make any suggestions?

'Why, of course I can,' the good man replied. 'They're always wantin' extra help at the Mitre. And a niece of mine, name of Betsie, says it's good fun working there. Smarten yourself up, lass, and leave the rest to me.'

On reaching the Mitre he bustled into the kitchen quarters which opened off the inn yard and re-emerged with an impressive middle-aged woman who studied Maggie carefully as she stood beside the cart. Apparently satisfied with her inspection, she had a quick word with the girl and engaged her on a temporary basis. Maggie understood she was to help Betsie in serving the customers and would be accommodated in Betsie's upstairs room.

Back in Osney, Sam and Rebecca Dowdswell were scarcely on speaking terms. Sam was filled with a hopeless remorse. 'I should never have done it, never have done it,' he kept repeating. 'I should have stood up to Rebecca. That stable lad's a good boy – swears 'e never interfered with our Maggie. Just a little honest courting, like all the young 'uns get up to. And now Maggie's gone. She won't come back, I know her. She won't come back as long as this dissenting she-cat rules the roost. I doubt the hurt will ever be healed.'

Rebecca, on the other hand, remained totally unrepentant. 'We did right, Sam Dowdswell,' was all she'd say. 'Never doubt it. We did right. We did our duty as we've been commanded. And if our children have left our home, we accept it as the Lord's Will. Whom he loveth he also makes to suffer.'

The uneasy partnership continued another twelve months, with Sam grimly working at the stables and Rebecca poring over her Bible or praying at a little Dissenter's Assembly in Osney. But neither her obstinate will nor her narrow faith could save Rebecca from the plague that struck the county in the winter of 1621. She died after a mercifully short illness and was buried at Witney, her hands clasping the Bible even in death.

Sam alone remained at Osney. He could not find it in himself to grieve for Rebecca. He was no hypocrite. All he could do was to stick to his work, cursing his misfortunes and drinking too much. Yet sometimes in his loneliness he remembered Maggie. Serving in Oxford, he'd been told. But why should she return to him? Hadn't he driven her away? And hadn't she inherited the independent spirit on which he and his ancestors prided themselves? The same thoughts chased each other again and again through Sam Dowdswell's mind. And one evening, when he returned fuddled with drink, he surprised himself by kneeling as he'd been taught to do as a child.

'Bring her back to me, dear Lord. I've done wickedly, I know. But forgive me . . . please forgive. And please persuade Maggie to come back.'

3

The friendship between Betsie and Maggie flourished from the first hours of their acquaintance. Both were young and pretty, and the city girl's good nature and sense of humour evoked a quick and warm response from the younger girl.

On that first night at the Mitre the two girls were undressing together in the shared servants' bedroom on the top floor of the hostelry when Betsie caught sight of the marks on Maggie's body. The country girl turned away in embarrassment, but Betsie's horrified eyes were large with sympathy.

'Easy, love. Easy now,' she said. 'Don't turn away. I won't 'urt you. Let Betsie 'ave a good look.' The older girl touched Maggie's back carefully. 'Gawd, you've been in trouble, you 'ave. Received a public whippin', 'ave you, in front of a pack of gloatin' self-righteous citizens? You been a bad girl, Maggie? It don't mean nothin' to me, but don't let the old dragon know.'

Maggie shook her head in dumb misery. 'No,' she stammered. 'No, she doesn't know a thing. But, Betsie, I want to explain . . .'

The city girl broke in, speaking half to herself and half to her companion, 'No, Maggie, no. You keep quiet. Questions and answers don't 'elp nobody. It's 'appened – and that's that. But, by 'Eaven, I'd like to get my 'ands on the swine that did it – and that's a silly thing to say, too. Best thing you and me can do, Maggie, is to try and forget it together.'

Betsie crept down to the kitchen and returned with a kettle of hot water. She took off Maggie's shift very gently, stood her naked on a towel in the middle of the room, and bathed her body with great tenderness. Next she produced some ointment and applied it to Maggie's back. Finally she wrapped the girl in another towel, settled her into bed and kissed her on the forehead.

'There, Maggie, there you are, love. Whatever your worries, they'll be safe with me. Parson up at the big University Church in High Street says there's nothing in this world that love won't heal. Let's 'ope 'e's right.'

Betsie blew out the candle. But she stayed awake until she was sure that Maggie slept.

Gradually Maggie's back healed. It was not long before she was giggling with Betsie over the mannerisms of the different customers in the dining room. The Mitre catered for a wide range of visitors – overnight travellers as well as senior members of the university and a few of the wealthier students. Sometimes the girls received special instructions, as when the diminutive Dr Laud from St John's College was entertaining three high dignitaries from the royal palace in Whitehall. Occasionally, some well-known Oxford worthy would make a rather grand entry and Mrs Wotherspoon – to give the Dragon her true name – would take personal charge of the service.

On one occasion Maggie found herself serving the celebrated Dr Ralph Kettel. The eccentric President of Trinity was in his most jovial mood. 'Thank you, Madam,' he boomed in answer to Mrs Wotherspoon's welcome, 'thank you for your enquiry as to my health. You find me, I am happy to say, in excellent spirits. I have finally tired out all the lawyers in Oxford, and my lease from the Provost of Oriel for that parcel of land in Broad Street is sealed, signed and delivered this very day. My architect is already planning the finest house you may ever see in this university city. Kettel Hall we'll call it, Madam; and you will stand amazed at its magnificence. The moment, I suggest, calls for celebration – roast duck and the finest claret in your cellar.'

The big man's piercing grey eyes swept the room, well aware that his size and eccentricity of dress made him conspicuous. 'I see, Madam, that Miss Betsie has a charming new helper – a country girl by the looks of her. Perhaps one of them might be permitted to serve the food and the other open the bottle. Delightful . . . very pretty . . . But let them be warned, Madam, in what peril they stand. I do not refer to myself nor to the young men in my charge, but to the sons of Belial and the hosts of Midian that swarm in our midst. Welshmen, too,' the old president added as an afterthought, chuckling and pointing a fork towards Jesus College.

Betsie chattered about Dr Kettel after the girls finished their work. 'They say he's a fine scholar,' she told Maggie, 'but he's different from the other grandees . . . says openly he prefers the company of the gentlemen of his own college to all the learned professors who spend day and night arguing about the wording of the prayer book.'

'And 'e's nice to serve, too,' she continued. 'Always seems pleased to see us. Sometimes 'e gives you a friendly tap on the bottom as well as a tip – but nothing offensive, you understand. Not like some of the gentry as gets too saucy.'

Suddenly Betsie realised that Maggie was taking her rather too seriously. 'No need to worry, love. I'll point out the nasty ones that want to look at you straight through the bodice. They're easy to spot and the Dragon don't stand no nonsense from them, I can tell you. Any trouble, and she has 'em turned out into the street, quick as lightning.'

Betsie was no virgin. She made the point explicitly one night, thinking to put Maggie at her ease. The two girls were sharing one bed, cuddling together to keep warm, when Betsie said, 'I've never asked what you've been up to, Maggie. But you should know I've enjoyed a lover or two, since I came here. Mind you, I'm particular. None of them stinking drovers from the market for me. I wouldn't touch them with the wrong end of a punt-pole. Let the women in the town pleasure them and take their money. A man's no use to me if he can't make love sober. And 'ere's another thing, Maggie. Don't you get caught in bed with one of the guests or the Dragon will send you packing before you know what's 'appened.'

'But Betsie,' Maggie protested. 'You don't understand. I've never taken a lover. I did nothing to deserve that whipping. Cross my heart. I'm not what you think I am.'

It was then that Betsie discovered that Maggie really was telling the truth. There was a pause in the conversation, until Betsie continued. 'Look, love,' she whispered, 'it might be time for you to learn a bit. After all, what's a university for?' She gave a little laugh and held Maggie closer. 'Tell you what . . . we'll take a walk beside the Cherwell one day. We might even go boating.' She squeezed Maggie's hand. 'Who knows? We might catch a fish or two . . . And we'd play the fish like anglers do,' she added dreamily. But Maggie with a little smile on her face was already asleep in Betsie's arms.

On the following Sunday the sun was shining bright with expectation as the two girls crossed the meadows and reached the Cherwell about a mile upstream from Magdalen Bridge. Both were hatless and wearing full-skirted dresses cut low at the shoulder. Their hair, Betsie's fair and Maggie's dark, was drawn off the face into a knot behind, with ringlets at the sides to match the fashion of the day. They were not exactly dressed for a cross-country walk. But as they raised their skirts to save them from trailing in the grass, their shapely ankles were most gracefully exposed. It was fairly certain that any young man, sculling or punting at his leisure, would take a second look at the two girls sitting under the willows.

Indeed, hardly had the girls settled themselves on the river bank before two lads, with much shouting and splashing, reversed their boat to have another look.

Betsie nudged Maggie in the ribs. 'Not them two, love. I know 'em, they're a bad lot. Talk rude and act rude. When they call, you keep quiet – or look the other way. Then we'll get up very dignified, and let 'em see we're moving further up the river. That shows we don't like the look of them, see?'

A few minutes later Betsie squeezed Maggie's hand. 'That's the fish we'll play,' she said, pointing to a young man some fifty yards away who appeared to be reading a book in a moored punt.

'Betsie, he's studying,' Maggie protested.

But Betsie knew better. ''E may 'ave meant to do some reading, love, but his eyes 'ave decided we're easier to look at than 'is Latin texts. I've been watching 'im. You wait 'ere a moment.'

Betsie walked slowly along the bank until she was level with the studious young man. 'Excuse me, Sir,' she began, with a charming hesitancy in her voice, 'I hope I'm not bothering you but I wonder if you be returning to the bridge before Evensong. My friend's a little tired and would be grateful for a lift.' How easily Betsie landed her catch.

A few moments later, the older girl was beckoning Maggie to join her. Indeed, she was already in the boat and holding it steady when the young man braced himself to lift Maggie off the bank. Somehow, Betsie manoeuvred the boat so that Maggie had to jump for it. The young man stood firm with Maggie safely in his arms.

Amidst many apologies and much laughter, the introductions started: I'm Betsie, I'm Maggie. I'm Thomas Martin, but Tom is what my friends call me. So he had friends, had he? And he was studying at Magdalen College, was he? Last year at Oxford and Final exams in seven weeks' time? Oh dear. And did he live in college? No, Tom said, he lived in rented rooms in the High. Kind old landlady, too. He offered some lemonade and sweet biscuits to the two girls. By the time they reached Magdalen Bridge on the return journey, an al fresco meal had been arranged for the following Sunday when Tom would bring a friend to join them.

So the affair began, and so it prospered. Eighteen-year-old Tom Martin, with a studious side to him that added dignity to his youthful charm, found himself bewitched by Maggie's bright eyes and smile of invitation. Supposing it rained, he said, would she like to see his rooms? But of course, came the diffident answer, that would make a pleasant change from her stuffy room at the Mitre. But supposing the sun shone, could they not go riding together provided Tom could hire a couple of horses?

Tom Martin looked so surprised that Maggie burst out laughing. 'Look, Tom,' she said, 'there's no need to ask why I'm working at the Mitre. But I can tell you that my family knows as much about horses as any Kentish gentleman, and we've owned land in this part of England long before the church lands were carved up to make money for the king and his friends.'

Tom accepted the country girl's challenge. There came a day when Margaret Dowdswell of South Leigh rode out of Oxford at the side of Thomas Martin from the Cray Valley in north Kent. Here was no case of a rich young man stooping to befriend a poor girl. The young lovers, crossing Magdalen Bridge and making for the high ground beyond Headington, rode as equals under the sun, each enchanted by the other. They cantered over the open fields till they found a group of beeches topping a small hill that overlooked the city. There Tom tethered the horses while Maggie spread out the packed lunch. Then, with the meal completed, they lay together side by side, very excited, knowing they were going to consummate their love for the first time. Neither was ever sure who made the first move. But the boy was very gentle and the girl welcomed him to herself without embarrassment. Afterwards they remained close together, sometimes sleeping, sometimes whispering their love as if sharing a secret joy that nobody should disturb. Only the horses, cropping the grass beside them, served as a reminder that, sooner or later, lovers must return from enchantment to a real world where joy and suffering, wealth and poverty, also lie side by side.

Headington was the first of many meetings. Tom's joke about the rain became a cryptic invitation for the two young lovers. A note would arrive at the Mitre and be handed to Maggie: 'I'll be waiting for you after dinner – corner of the Turl and the High. I think it's going to rain all night but I'll look after you. Tom.' And at some hour between ten and midnight the conspirators would leave the inn and hurry arm in arm along the street to Tom Martin's rooms. Early next morning Maggie would return as secretly as she had departed, creeping up the stairs to the shared room at the top of the house. Through sleepy, half-closed eyes Betsie would watch her companion hop into the second bed, without a care in the world.

'You be careful, Maggie,' she said. 'You're getting too fond of Tom Martin. 'E'll go back 'ome when term ends, you know, and then where will you be?'

Maggie sighed but the little half smile never left her face. 'Yes, Betsie, we'll both be very sad, but we have agreed together that our love is for the present, not the future.'

Halfway through July, the young lovers rode for the last time on the hills above Headington. They looked down to the spires and towers of Oxford. They lay together in passionate farewell and they cried when they parted – Tom to his acres in Kent and Maggie to her serving at the Mitre. Yet neither was truly sad. They accepted the inevitability of departure as old people gradually come to accept the inevitability of death. Tom and Maggie would go their separate ways, united for ever by the shared memory of first love in high summer.

Three months later Maggie told Betsie she was going to have a baby.

'I know it,' said the older girl. 'I've been watching you, you know; and I've been wondering 'ow we're going to get rid of it. There's a woman, I know . . .'

Maggie interrupted, 'Betsie, you don't understand. I want the baby. It's going to be the most beautiful baby – it's all planned. And once it's safely delivered I'm going to go back to my father. No, I won't tell him about Tom, but he'll know his daughter has given birth to a baby as good as any Dowdswell that ever was born. Those enclosures may have deprived our family of its birthright, but not of its history. I said I'd show him, and so I will.'

Betsie stood amazed. Maggie seemed transformed. Proud, not anxious; happy, not sad; confident, not fearful. She seemed unaware of the problems that lay ahead. She'd even planned the future.

'You will help, won't you, Betsie? We'll persuade the Dragon to let me go on working here as long as possible. And then, when the baby's due, we'll find somebody who'll help me. Now, that uncle of yours' – Maggie's scheme had already taken shape – 'that uncle who lives out at Witney and gave me a lift when I left home, hasn't he got a nice wife, Betsie? I'm sure he has, and they've got no children, have they? Now, if they could give me house room till me and the baby were strong again . . . What do you think, Betsie?'

And so it was arranged. Early in 1622 Maggie gave birth to a baby boy at the home of Betsie's uncle and aunt in Witney. They were good people and insisted on Maggie staying with them until the baby was baptised and christened in the name of Martin Dowdswell.

Back in Oxford, the Dragon had not been unhelpful – her kindness, according to Betsie, being partly due to Dr Kettel's unexpected intervention. Noticing Maggie's absence from the dining room, the president had been informed by Mrs Wotherspoon in a hushed voice that the unfortunate girl was 'in trouble'.

'Nonsense,' the old doctor had replied. 'Some of the greatest men in history have been bastard born. Who are we, Madam, to know whom God will favour in this earthly life? Since Miss

Maggie is with child it is our Christian duty to help her rather than indulge in pious but pointless condemnation.'

True to his sentiment, the old doctor arranged for a costly set of baby clothes to be conveyed to Maggie by Betsie. 'And remember, Miss Betsie,' he concluded, 'if the girl needs further help, I rely on you to tell me.'

A few months later Betsie was able to confirm to Dr Kettel that Maggie and her baby had rejoined Samuel Dowdswell at Osney. She and her uncle had, in fact, been responsible for arranging the first meeting between father and daughter. They had found Sam sober and penitent. He made no excuses for himself.

'I drove Maggie away,' he said. 'It was I who did her wrong. It's for me to repent, not her. You ask her to forgive me and I'll make a home for her and the baby.'

4

On Michaelmas Day 1626 Henry Ireton and Tom Brewster entered Oxford on horseback, accompanied on their easy-paced ninety-mile journey by a couple of packhorses. Tom was five years older than his fifteen-year-old master, but neither young man had travelled so far afield before.

In the mellow light of September they studied the lie of the land with farmers' eyes They were surprised by the size of the flocks and the many breeds of cattle they saw on their journey. They noted the frequent alternation of meadow and woodland and the undulating ground south of Leicester. They descended to Banbury and the water meadows of the Cherwell, crossing the myriad streams which would one day hamper the progress of an artillery train and aid the escape of a royal fugitive.

They made their youthful comparisons – Leicester as big as Nottingham, but no river to match the Trent; Banbury with a market square more spacious, but a castle no match for Newark's mighty fortress; trees in profusion, but nothing to equal the oaks of Sherwood forest. These Nottingham lads had clear standards of measurement.

But when they reached Oxford all comparisons ceased. No place or community known to the travellers could match the stone spires and buildings which were to be central to their lives for the next three years. In a state of wonder and expectancy they turned out of the Banbury Road into Broad Street and dismounted outside the entrance gates to the Trinity parklands. Henry Ireton had entered a new world.

The college porter assured Mr Ireton that he was expected and had been allocated rooms next to the old college library, with an adjoining room for his servant. Temporary stabling could be provided by the college – the porter pointed Brewster to some outbuildings lying back from the street where the packhorses could be off-loaded. And would Mr Ireton be pleased to attend the President's Lodging at five o'clock that same evening.

As the chimes of Oxford struck the hour Henry Ireton, his dark hair brushed, hands and nails spotless, and a clean linen collar showing neatly over his doublet, was ushered into the president's study.

He found Dr Kettel in his most expansive mood. The president's sprawling frame was magnified by an academic gown half falling from his shoulders, and his arms appeared to embrace the desk at which he was seated. The low ceiling of the room, its woodwork lightened by an exquisite vine-leaf motif painted in gold, only served to emphasise the bigness of the man.

His size contrasted powerfully with the slim young gentleman-commoner whom he beckoned to a chair on the other side of the desk. But Henry was chiefly aware of the piercing grey eyes boring into him.

So they were meeting at last, the president began, and complimented Henry on his time-keeping. Yes, he knew all about Mr Ireton from reports reaching him through his old friend, the rector of St Mary the Virgin at Attenborough. He trusted Mr Ireton would enjoy his studies and steer clear of trouble.

'There are no rules in my college, Mr Ireton. But if you break any of them, we send you home at once. Is that clearly understood?'

The old man chuckled at his joke and suddenly added, 'A question about your servant, Mr Ireton. Name of Brewster, I think. A local Nottingham boy, isn't he? Related, I suppose, to that celebrated Dissenter, Edward Brewster, who lived at Scrooby until he and his friends set off for America in the *Mayflower*?'

Henry bridled. 'Thomas Brewster, Sir, is the son of our head stableman at Attenborough. He has, I believe, an uncle of the same name in the American colonies. But my family does not employ a man because of his relatives – nor yet for his religious beliefs. Brewster travels with me because he volunteered to do so, and because I judge him to be totally honest and totally dependable. Would you not agree that such qualities are more important than questions concerning bishops and prayer books? However, I should add that, like his father, he's a first-class judge of a horse. And like your friend, the rector of Attenborough, he is a man of Independent religious belief.'

Henry looked the old president straight in his keen grey eyes, and the student and the scholar liked what they saw. Raising himself from his chair with ponderous difficulty, Dr Kettel came round the desk and put his arm round Henry's shoulders.

'Well spoken, young man,' he said. 'Well spoken, indeed. I'm sure we shall understand each other very well and enjoy each other's company over the next few years.'

But there was more to come. Standing beside him, the president grasped a large pair of scissors which Henry had previously noticed lying beside a selection of quill pens and other writing impedimenta.

'You are surprised to see these scissors?' demanded Dr Kettel, waving them aloft and snapping them open and shut with the dexterity of a professional barber. 'Pray, be reassured, Mr Ireton. Your hair is most excellently trimmed and will, I trust, never require attention from my scissors. But should you, by some stray chance, be tempted to follow the fancy of certain young gentlemen in this university and allow your locks to trail below your shoulders, then beware, Mr Ireton ... beware ... or, *snick, snack*, and my scissors will remove the cause of offence.'

'I see you smile, young man' – the old man's kindly eyes took stock of the lad before him – 'and quite right, too. Life at your age should not be taken too seriously. Even at my time of life I retain some slight appetite for laughter. But my scissors have a serious purpose, too' – and he opened and shut them decisively. 'I take the view that Oxford is no place for courtiers; nor yet a stage for those foolish masques which, according to my latest intelligence from Whitehall, are the chief diversion of King Charles and his young French consort during their waking hours. I intend to keep this college as a dwelling place for men, not peacocks.'

The old man was still smiling as Henry closed the door.

The new gentleman-commoner had no intention of wasting his next three years at Oxford. He was a dutiful son and fully aware of Jane Ireton's hopes. Since he was modest about his natural intelligence he acquired many friends who also admired his good looks and sporting proclivities. It was his tutors in college who first realised that young Henry Ireton from the County of Nottingham was endowed with exceptional gifts, both in presenting a case and in demolishing other people's arguments. Here, surely, was a lawyer in the making – a judge, perhaps, or a Member of Parliament or the king's Privy Council. Dr Kettel, that shrewd judge of young men in his care, foretold a glittering future for the latest member of the college.

This optimistic view of Henry Ireton's potential received powerful reinforcement towards the end of his first year at the university. Like every educated family in the land, and like every don and undergraduate in the two universities of Oxford and Cambridge, Henry was reasonably well versed in matters theological. In his home village of Attenborough the Iretons and the parish priest had for many years agreed to a form of worship which laid more stress on preaching and the truth of the scriptures than on the forms of worship evolved by the Elizabethan Church Settlement. The Iretons did not like the prayer book which was being foisted on them by royal decree. Nor did they like the rule of bishops which reminded them too closely of the corrupt old order which the Reformation had swept away. They saw no special merit in uniformity, but they thought little about it since the Independent Ireton view was generally accepted without argument in the village, and the Archdeacon of Nottingham had long ceased to demand their conformity.

It was only after a term at Oxford that Henry Ireton discovered the depth and extent of contrary opinions among his fellow students – and the conviction with which these opinions were held. There were Scotsmen who embraced a Presbyterian form of church government and would have nothing to do with episcopacy. There were young men who believed, with the king and Bishop Laud, that England's salvation depended on universal and strict adherence to a prayer book and a national church governed by bishops under the headship of the king. There were Anabaptists to be found, more in the town than in the colleges of the university, who were already turning fundamentalist beliefs into revolutionary demands for greater political freedom. There were undergraduates from Roman Catholic families who were openly declaring their allegiance to Rome now that the young queen was surrounded by spiritual advisers brought from France with orders, as many believed, to bring England back under papal rule.

One such member of the college was Edward Ford who came of an old Sussex family and was a few years senior to Henry Ireton. The two men held a high opinion of each other, and remained on excellent terms so long as they avoided theological argument. But in the seventeenth century, theological argument was unavoidable, and since both men expressed themselves well in debate, they tended to attract an undergraduate audience which, by shouts or answering catcalls, was calculated to raise the temperature of debate to boiling point.

One of these noisy arguments was raging in the Trinity gardens when the president marched out of his Lodging to investigate the disturbance. The moment he was spotted there was an ominous hush. The two speakers were tongue tied until Dr Kettel ordered them to continue the debate. He would be interested, he assured them, to hear their exposition.

Edward Ford and Henry Ireton stuttered on, turn and turn about, with arguments that had now lost half their point and all their sparkle. The fire had gone out of them and soon the president called a halt, telling them that their knowledge of the scriptures was sadly deficient. Next day they would each receive an annotated Bible for which they would be charged. These arrived early the following morning, with the president's compliments. In both volumes a similar slip had been inserted at Psalm 133: 'Behold how good and how pleasant it is for brethren to dwell together in unity.' On each slip the president had written in his atrocious handwriting:

In verse one, *for* Unity *read* Trinity.

I prefer this reading.

Ralph Kettel

On that day a lasting friendship was forged between Edward Ford and Henry Ireton. The president had enjoyed his joke and made his point. The Bibles were cheap at the price.

5

While Henry Ireton was adapting himself to the routine of college life and the eccentricities of the President of Trinity, the Dowdswells – father, daughter and grandson – were settling into the give-and-take of a shared home at Osney.

The presence of the four-year-old Martin had long since successfully repaired the brittle relationship between Maggie and her father, for both took a pride in the little boy's progress, and he was often left with his grandfather while Maggie went to market.

Betsie, who had played a considerable part in the family reconciliation, confirmed to her friends at the Mitre that Maggie and her small son were in good health and well cared for. She also noted, with more than passing interest, that Sam Dowdswell's visits to the local ale-house were now less frequent and less prolonged. Not surprisingly, this information reached the long ears of Dr Kettel who, on his occasional visits to the Mitre, always questioned Betsie about Maggie's progress. It was not, therefore, surprising that when Tom Brewster enquired about stabling for Mr Ireton's thoroughbred mare, the college porter at the Trinity Lodge assured him that the president recommended Mr Dowdswell's establishment at Osney.

For a countryman, the lure of the country is irresistible. How better to escape the dangerous, dank humours of low-lying Oxford than by filling the lungs with the purer air of Boar's Hill? How better to enjoy the open fields and the contours of the little hills that dictate the course of Thames and Windrush and Cherwell than from the saddle of a good horse?

With his merlin caged in the mews at Attenborough, Henry made riding his chief leisure occupation at the university. At first his stocky little mare, Lady Jane, was ridden by Brewster from Osney to the college gates, where Henry would join various cross-country excursions organised by his fellow students – especially by Edward Ford. But after Edward's return to his Sussex home, the routine changed.

Perhaps Henry felt the need for solitude in his final year at the university. Perhaps he tired of his fellow students' chatter. Perhaps he sought the companionship of rougher down-to-earth types such as he knew in his home village and now rediscovered at Sam Dowdswell's stables. But certain it is that once Henry Ireton's lectures finished for the day, he found it more satisfying to make his own way to Osney and exercise his mare on the open land west of the university city.

He and Tom Brewster would often take their horses up to the high ground of Cumnor and Boar's Hill. Sometimes, accompanied by Sam Dowdswell and his daughter, they would exercise the horses as far as Witney and Eynsham. It was on one such ride that Henry Ireton uncovered the circumstances in which the Dowdswell family had been deprived of its small-holding at South Leigh.

'That is wrong,' he told Sam, 'totally unjust. If I'd been here at the time, I would have fought your case for you in the courts. But now?' He shrugged his shoulders, as if to dismiss the matter from his mind. Indeed Sam urged him to do so.

'Nay,' he said, 'I'm better suited at Osney. I'm more use to my friends, keeping an eye on their horses. Don't you worry about us, Mr Henry.'

But young Henry Ireton *did* worry about them. 'Sam Dowdswell,' he told Tom Brewster as they returned to Oxford, 'may make more money in his present job; but what about Maggie? What about little Martin? That boy has as good a right as anybody to possess the land his family once owned. We need more men in England with a real stake in their own property. The last thing I want to see is the build-up of bigger and bigger estates run by the minions of absentee landlords – probably wasting their income on fine clothes and pomposities at Whitehall and Nonsuch and Theobalds. That's the sort of thing that happens in France.'

Tom Brewster was not too sure what his master was talking about, since he did not recognise the names of the royal residences. But like his father he reckoned that what an Ireton did was good and what an Ireton said made sense. He made the point to his fellow servants at Trinity and also to Maggie

Dowdswell to whom he was greatly attracted. In this way the girl became vaguely aware of Henry Ireton's social conscience. Somehow, she was sure, Henry could be persuaded to help young Martin reach the goal she'd set for him even before he was born. Woman-like (Delilah-ish her late mother would have said), she made a point of being present when Henry visited the stables. She was delighted to see the warmth of the welcome little Martin gave the young student from Trinity. Soon she and Henry were discussing how the boy could best be equipped to win back his place among the yeomen farmers of England.

'It's not just a question of making enough money to buy a few acres of good farming land,' Henry told Maggie. 'The boy will need education and confidence if he is to stand up to stronger neighbours and win their respect. That's what we have to secure for young Martin.'

In this last year at the university Henry, a natural teacher, began to give the six-year-old regular lessons in the Dowdswell home before returning to college. As to Maggie Dowdswell, his relationship with her was totally uncomplicated, and it might have remained that way but for Sam Dowdswell's boast to his friends at some local celebration that he could produce a horse from his stables to match any horse in the district.

To prove it, Sam was prepared to back his fancy over a four-mile cross-country course, and soon it was common knowledge in Witncy and Eynsham that a steeplechase had been arranged for the Saturday after Easter. The course would start at the butter market in Witney and finish in South Leigh. Palm Sunday was named as the closing date for entries, which should be notified to the publican at the Mason's Arms, South Leigh.

It was less widely known that Sam Dowdswell's boast was a secret challenge to his long-standing enemy – the agent of the Pope family estates who had been responsible for the Dowdswell eviction from the farm at South Leigh. He was well aware that this agent, William Sanderson, was hunting the country regularly and boasting both about his horse and his prowess as a rider.

Now at last Sam was presented with the chance for which he had long been waiting. Only recently, he had acquired a strong bay gelding from Leicester – sixteen hands and a sure-footed jumper – and, knowing every inch of the ground over which the race was to be run, he was totally confident in his ability to ride the winner. Three weeks before the race Dowdswell was being quoted at three to one, with Sanderson at fives and the field at fifteen.

And then, in the course of a routine gallop, the bay went lame with a back tendon giving trouble and a nasty cut on the near hind. A careful examination of the wound was enough to show that Sam's horse could not possibly be ready for a stiff cross-country course by the Saturday after Easter.

Dowdswell cursed his misfortune and scratched the bay. He remained in a state of total despair until Maggie reminded him that his original challenge concerned a horse from his stables, and not a horse in his ownership. Why not persuade young Henry Ireton to chance his arm with Lady Jane? Tom Brewster, whom she had consulted, was confident of the little mare's staying power and Mr Henry was, in Brewster's words, born to the saddle. It was already known that, in addition to an assortment of local gentry and yeomen farmers, two entries had reached the Mason's Arms from Magdalen College and one from Christ Church. So Henry, by nature a tough competitor, was soon persuaded, and confident that Lady Jane would acquit herself well.

Once the entry form was completed Sam Dowdswell took control. Twice he walked the course with Henry, pointing out the special characteristics of the twenty jumps and three streams the riders would encounter. 'Memorise each one exactly, Mr Harry. There's a nasty one here by Plaxton's covert, with a ditch on the far side; and you could be wise to skirt that bit of plough before you reach the grassland approaching the first water jump. Most riders will go for the cattle crossing, but it's terrible sticky down there and I reckon Lady Jane can jump the stream a little higher up where the take-off is firmer.'

The instruction was thorough, and summed up by the older man's final words of advice. 'Don't try to lead from the start, Mr Harry. Once you're clear of Witney pick your own course. Every jump will be marked by a white flag, and the only rule is that you have to jump to the right of each flag. The gates are easy enough. It's the hedges that cause trouble: they are mighty uneven and most riders will race for the low points. But you've got a wonderful jumper in Lady Jane. You'll do better to make your own course, Mr Harry, and keep well away from the long-striding heavyweights.'

At a quarter to two on the day of the race the little party emerged from the inn yard at Witney – with Brewster holding the leading rein and Henry Ireton in the saddle, looking totally relaxed. A few bystanders raised a cheer.

Then as horse and rider approached the starting point at the butter market, a whisper of excitement ran through the crowd: Who's that young fellow with the keen eyes and dark hair? See him, over there on his own: white breeches, black boots and hard black hat – yes, that's the lad, wearing a red cravat under his riding habit. Dowdswell's entry, ain't he? The little chestnut mare, with the white blaze and the three white socks? Caw, she's a beauty, a real thoroughbred, looks a picture . . . But strong enough to last the course? Not very likely. And that young whipper-snapper in the saddle? He's a bit green for a punishing run like this, ain't he? The punters admired, but doubted; and the odds against Lady Jane were quoted at twenty-five to one.

Suddenly, the chattering and the laughter ceased. An expectant hush spread through the crowd thronging the butter market. The starter, looking very official, called the riders to order, marshalled them in a rough line and, at last, after much jostling and manoeuvring, lowered his flag.

They were off – a clattering of hooves away down the street with Henry Ireton keeping Lady Jane well away from the leading competitors. Soon the riders were turning off the Oxford road into the fields and racing towards the first jump.

As Lady Jane cleared the first thorn hedge Henry felt an extraordinary sense of exhilaration. The little mare never turned her head, her ears were pricked forward as if she knew for sure that something very important was afoot that day. The rider's only problem was to hold her back until the field got sorted out.

Lady Jane continued to perform perfectly and Henry's confidence grew. By the twelfth jump – the awkward hedge and hidden ditch at Plaxton's covert – the contest was effectively reduced to five runners, with one of the lads from Magdalen in the lead, closely followed by two farmers and William Sanderson on the big roan.

It was time for Lady Jane to challenge the leading group. Henry took her carefully downhill towards the first stream, noting that the four riders ahead of him were making for the cattle crossing. He jumped the water twenty yards upstream as Sam had suggested, and with mounting excitement saw that he'd made up a lot of ground on the leaders.

Seven jumps later – and it looked like a two-horse race as he and Sanderson moved up a stiff slope from the third and final water jump. One more hedge, and then the sprint to the winning post.

But would the little mare last the pace? For the first time Henry sensed she was tiring. Now, indeed, was the time to show the skills old Brewster had taught him as a boy. Keeping well to the left of Sanderson's big roan, he made for a gap in the hedge hard by an overgrown thorn. He was talking all the time to Lady Jane. 'One more jump, little lady – and you can show off your pace on the level. Come along, my beauty – come along. No mistake now, take it carefully.'

Perhaps the boy was overconfident. Perhaps he was too concerned with his own mount. Suddenly he realised that Sanderson was cutting across his course and making for the same gap. Henry was in a risk-all situation. Too late to change direction, he urged the little mare forward, kept his head down and took the low jump as close to the thorn bush as he dared, with Sanderson thundering along on his right and yelling at him to keep clear.

Henry hardly knew what happened next except that Lady Jane landed miraculously with him clinging to her neck and the roan crashing into the hedge to the right of the gap. Thorn had ripped the sleeve of Henry's jacket, his left shoulder felt numb and his left thigh was scratched and bleeding. But, somehow, he regained his seat, and Lady Jane recovered her stride. By luck or the grace of God they had escaped disaster and now at last they were clear of the field and racing to victory with the cheers of the South Leigh supporters willing them past the winning post.

Henry eased up as he crossed the finishing line and leant

forward to give Lady Jane a reassuring pat. He was hardly aware of the cheering spectators, of the kerchiefs waving, of Sam Dowdswell rushing forward with Maggie close behind, accompanied by Tom Brewster who had hacked back from Witney to see the finish.

Henry was talking to himself, his lips moving   Must get a grip . . . forget the blood and the torn coat   dismount with dignity . .   show the onlookers that winning a tough point-to-point is all part of a normal day's work for any member of the Ireton family . . .

But it didn't happen like that. Henry just managed to get his riding boots clear of the stirrups before falling, totally exhausted, into Sam Dowdswell's arms. Somehow, the Dowdswells managed to part a way through the excited crowd and reach the safety of the inn while Brewster threw a blanket over Lady Jane and led her away to her stall, crooning to her in a language which only horses and horse-lovers understand.

Upstairs, in a bedroom put at their disposal by the inn-keeper, Sam and Maggie stripped off Henry's clothes and examined his lacerated leg. A quick inspection, a quick call for hot water.

Maggie whispered to Sam, 'This is my job, Father. You get downstairs and celebrate the Dowdswell stables' victory. It's your big day, too. We'll join you when Harry is cleaned up,' and the girl bent to her task, wondering at the whiteness of the boy's skin and the strength of his body.

Soon, in the room below, Sam was the centre of a happy band of supporters with the other riders joining in the celebrations – all except Sanderson who had retired with a black eye and a flaming temper.

But Henry knew nothing of this. He lay half naked on the bed, his eyes closed, conscious only of Maggie bathing his leg and left arm. He opened his eyes and asked about Lady Jane – was she hurt? Maggie assured him his horse was in Tom Brewster's safe hands. And Sanderson? Maggie kissed him on the forehead and told him not to worry – the agent would survive, more's the pity! And clothes? Be quiet, Harry. We'll find you some clothes and get you back to Oxford in due course. Please stop worrying. Lie back and rest.

The questioning ceased. His body relaxed. The hint of a

smile lit his face. He was alive to the girl's touch, alive to her voice. His right hand reached out to hers . . .

Suddenly a heavy footfall sounded on the stairs and Maggie was aware of Dr Kettel towering over her and the young man lying on the bed. She started back, but was reassured by the old man's smile.

'So, Miss Maggie, you've taken charge of my gentleman-commoner, have you? I can see you are a very good nurse, and it's well known that daredevils like Harry have all the luck. Nevertheless, I think it will be best if I now take over responsibility for our Mr Ireton and convey him back to Oxford in my carriage. There, I will get my physician to examine him and confirm that no bones are broken. Meanwhile, if you and your father can borrow some clothes for the young man, I should be deeply obliged. I would prefer to have my travelling companion properly clothed when I re-enter Oxford.'

From his great height Dr Kettel smiled down on the girl. 'No need to look scared, Miss Maggie. You've done well – very well. But once you and your father have borrowed some clothes, I think you should find young Brewster and make sure the horse is well cared for. After all, it was the little mare that won the race. Good-lookers, both of them. A marvellous horse and a superb rider. Lady Jane is a bit like us. She'd also do a lot for Henry Ireton, eh?'

Dr Kettel chuckled to himself as Maggie hurried away. Two hours later he and his gentleman-commoner left the Mason's Arms together in the new presidential carriage. But before leaving, the president took Sam Dowdswell aside and made a final observation.

'I'll be deeply obliged, Mr Dowdswell, if you will take this note and collect my winnings from that rascal at Witney. You will see that I succeeded in placing my bet on Lady Jane at twenty-five to one, and I shall be most happy for you to use the money for a Dowdswell family celebration. I'm not, you must understand, a gambler by nature.' The president was in his most genial mood. 'But the college servants were talking so loudly about Mr Ireton's prospects that I felt it incumbent upon me to support our Trinity entry. And now back to Oxford.'

Dr Kettel waved farewell. As he left the inn, he was murmuring to himself, 'My gentleman-commoner from Nottingham . charm as well as courage . . a natural winner . . if I'm any judge of these things.'

6

William Sanderson was not the only angry person in the hours
that followed the Witney steeplechase. Maggie Dowdswell felt
all the anger of a child whose favourite toy has been confiscated
by an unreasonable adult. She aimed a savage kick at the
newel post by the foot of the stairs and hurt her toe in doing
so. Why should that silly old fool of a president interfere? He'd
said she was a good nurse, hadn't he? Couldn't he trust her to
take care of Harry out here at South Leigh? Why rush him
back to Oxford along that miserable, bumpy road? Surely, he
could have spent the night in comfort at the Mason's Arms.
Life was really most unjust.

Somehow she managed to pull herself together and force
her way through the crowd downstairs to pass Dr Kettel's
requests to her father. But that was where duty ended. She
was in no mood for the boisterous jokes of her father's friends.
The noise and the laughter and the drinking were intolerable.
Making her way unobtrusively to a side door, Maggie escaped
from the hot overcrowded room into the twilight of a fine April
evening.

No longer did she attempt to hold back her tears of self-pity,
but soon she began to shiver with cold. She was miserable out
there without a cloak over her light dress, and there was no
warmth in the stars. She looked up to the sky. Surely, she
thought, God might have helped her.

Still sobbing, she wandered to the back of the inn; at least
she would find warmth in the stables. Yes, she remembered
now, Harry's little mare had been taken there after the race.
Lady Jane would understand why she was crying, and a horse
would be better company than those noisy fellows swilling ale
back in the Mason's Arms.

She peeped over the stable door and made out the shape of
Lady Jane standing still and peaceful in the darkness. Then she
noticed Tom Brewster bent low beside the horse, apparently
applying some sort of salve to the animal's near flank.

All the time Tom was talking as if to an old friend. 'Steady, girl . . easy does it . . . you run a lovely race, milady . . . No, I won't leave you . . . o'course I won't.'

The lad seemed absorbed in his task but some sixth sense must have alerted him to Maggie's presence at the stable door. Without stopping his work, he said, ' 'Ello, Miss Maggie. Want to see 'ow this little lady's farin'? Come inside, love. Lady Jane will be pleased to see you, won't you, my beautiful?'

Tom straightened his back and held out an arm to guide the girl into the stable. 'My, but you're mighty cold,' he said, gripping her hand, 'and you've been cryin' too, or I'm much mistaken. There shouldn't be no tears on a day like this. Come over 'ere, lass, and make yourself comfortable on the rug in the corner. I'm finished with Lady Jane for the night, but plan to keep 'er company. That's 'ow Mr 'Arry would like it and I don't suppose your dad needs me to join the celebrations. E's got a lot o' friends, 'as your dad.'

Tom led Maggie across to the rug. He pulled out a handkerchief and gently wiped the girl's eyes as he might have done for a hurt child. He took off his jerkin and rolled it up for a pillow – a silent invitation, silently accepted.

The girl lay down gratefully and without diffidence, her head resting on the jerkin. There was something reassuring about Tom Brewster. Warmth returned to her body and her mood changed.

There was warmth, too, in her voice and her eyes were bright as she looked up at Tom and pulled him down beside her. 'Thank you, Tom,' she said, 'you're a good man . . . you understand.' On the night of the Witney steeplechase, Maggie fell asleep cradled in Tom Brewster's arms. For both of them it had been a long day.

At Osney, Betsie waited anxiously for Sam Dowdswell's return. She'd been happy enough to spend her free day from the Mitre with young Martin Dowdswell while the rest of the family travelled their respective roads to Witney and South Leigh. Indeed, she had grown very fond of the little boy. At five years old he was a delightful companion. The two of them had played dominoes before supper and Betsie had noticed how quickly he counted the numbers on each stone. He was going to be a smart lad – and no mistake. Then he'd proudly shown her the Bible which Henry Ireton had given him. He'd even read to her the story of the child Samuel, assuring her between many hesitations that, according to Uncle Harry, this story explained why his grandfather was called Sam.

Now supper was finished and Martin safely tucked up in his little bed in the upstairs room which he shared with his mother. Betsie had lit the candles hours since, in the big room downstairs and still she waited, half asleep, in the chair beside the stove.

Well after midnight she awoke to the raucous noise of Sam Dowdswell singing his way home. He opened the door with a bang and rushed up to her – the victor returning in triumph. He lifted her high in the air and danced twice round the room before collapsing into the big chair with Betsie on his lap. Protest was useless. Sam was a powerful chap and he held her firmly in his arms.

'We've won, Betsie girl,' he said, running his hand through her fair hair and giving her a smacking kiss. 'By Heaven, you should have been there. The boy was magnificent, I tell you ... magnificent ... rode that bastard Sanderson into a thorn hedge ... magnificent's the word for it. And he nursed the little mare round that course to the winning post with a skill I'd never have expected in a boy of his age.'

Stopping the flow of slurred superlatives, Betsie at last persuaded Sam to make less noise or he'd wake young Martin. And anyway, where was Maggie?

Sam looked up with a start. 'Maggie? What's this you're telling me, Betsie? Thought she'd come back earlier ... wasn't anywhere to be seen when we left ...' Poor Sam, he might be far from sober, but in his fuddled mind hateful memories were inexorably stirring. 'Mustn't lose her again ... couldn't bear it,' he muttered. 'You do something, Betsie ... you know her better than I do. You go find her.'

He let Betsie free, tried to get up and slumped back into the chair. With a smile, part affectionate and part amused, the girl covered him with a rug, kissed him on the forehead, put another log on the fire, and blew out the candle. Best let Sam Dowdswell sleep where he lies, she thought, and tiptoed her way to Maggie's bed in the room where her other charge was still peacefully sleeping.

As to Maggie, she could wait till sunrise. Betsie smiled to herself, remembering the old days at the Mitre. She wouldn't be surprised to find our Maggie returning with Tom Brewster and Lady Jane some time tomorrow. No, she wouldn't be a bit surprised.

And Sam? Betsie lay on her back, her long legs at full stretch, looking up at the ceiling from Maggie's bed: Sam's a dear chap at heart, she thought, but he'll do better when he has a woman to love him as well as look after him. And you can't have more than one woman in a house this size, my girl ... Maggie or Betsie? Maggie and Tom? Betsie and Sam? And what about young Martin? Oh, stop asking questions you can't answer. You're tired, Betsie. Why worry about the future? Tomorrow will look after itself – it always does. The girl's eyes closed and she too slept as peacefully as the little boy beside her.

Back in Oxford, on the morning after the race, Henry Ireton woke from a long sleep. He was in unfamiliar surroundings. His eyes opened slowly, confirming that he was lying on a luxurious four-poster bed in a low-ceilinged room. The heavily embroidered curtains round the bed had been drawn back and a hint of morning sunshine filtered through the lattice of a small window set close to the eaves. Somewhere outside a blackbird was in full song.

His questing eyes lighted on a hand-bell placed on a bedside table. He was about to reach for it when Simon, the president's manservant, shuffled to the bed from the far corner of the room.

'Well, well, well,' observed the old man, looking hard at Henry. 'So you're back in the land of the living, eh? 'Ad a good sound sleep, I'd say. Never stirred, Mr Ireton, since we gave you a bowl of soup last night, though I reckon it's the posset Dr Kettel made you swallow that sent you off into the land of dreams. 'E knows a thing or two about physic, does our president.

'And where am I, do I 'ear you say? The answer, young Sir, is that you're enjoying the privilege of a nice rest in the best

49

guest-bedroom the president can offer you. Now, don't you do nothing till I report to Dr Kettel.'

The servant moved away, shutting the great oak door quietly behind him. Five minutes later the president was stooping over the bed, his hand resting lightly on Harry's forehead.

'And how does it feel on the morning after?' he asked.

'You mean my shoulder, Sir?'

'No, no, no, young man. We'll soon put your shoulder straight. I mean, how does it feel to know you've ridden that blackguard Sanderson into the hedge? No need to worry about him. We saw his disgusting tactics from where we were standing, close by the finishing post. Plain for all to see . . . Hearts in mouth, I can tell you, until your little mare came through the gap with you clinging to the animal's neck. I don't suppose you'll win every race like that. Still, you made a lot of friends yesterday, young man, as well as a bit of money for Sam Dowdswell.'

The old president paused and his rasping voice dropped in tone as if he were talking to himself. 'And to be honest, you made the President of Trinity rather proud of his gentleman-commoner. A winner on his first outing . . . and only eighteen . . . where will the next performance take place?'

Suddenly, as his manner was, the president switched to a more business-like note. 'Now as to this shoulder of yours and the lacerations on your leg. You're in luck, let me tell you. An old friend of mine, Dr Mayerne, is in the city staying with little Laud round at St John's. I've persuaded him to visit you before he returns to London.

'Never heard of Sir Theodore Mayerne, young man? Well, let me further your education.' And the president proceeded to give Harry a quick description of the great doctor: A French exile . . . Reformed religion . . . born Geneva . . . educated Heidelberg and Montpellier . . . lives in London but honoured as a Doctor of Medicine by this university . . . physician to the king and his young queen . . . a specialist in curing the ague, a complaint that afflicts Cambridge as well as Oxford, my friend . . . likes the contents of my cellar . . and rather fancies his Latin.

The president ended his catalogue of the doctor's achievements but added with a laugh, 'Mind you, I don't think he'll speak Latin in my presence. His syntax is hardly in the classical tradition.'

At midday Sir Theodore arrived at Trinity to examine the patient. First he looked at the lacerated thigh. Then he felt Henry's shoulder very carefully. As his sensitive hands pressed on the collarbone, his eyes watched the patient for any signs of discomfort. Finally, he turned to Dr Kettel.

'No break, my friend, only serious bruising. But the young man's left arm should be trussed in a sling for two weeks, and that means no riding and no journeys over these damnable English roads. The prescription is for peace and quiet while the shoulder mends and the leg wounds heal. Luckily, they are beautifully clean.'

The doctor turned to Henry. 'I bid you farewell for the present, young man. Meanwhile I have suggested to the president that you remain in college. May you make good use of your enforced stay in Oxford.' The great man bowed and left the room to dine with the president.

Tom Brewster, who had returned to his duties in college, was instructed to ride to Attenborough carrying a letter from Dr Kettel to Mrs Ireton, which explained why the president had decided to keep Henry in Oxford until he sat for his final exams in June. But the letter also suggested that a period spent with lawyers in London should be regarded as an essential part of Henry's education: 'Your son, Madam, has in my view an exceptional intellect. Whatever the future holds for him, whether as a landowner or as a spokesman in the great affairs of state, his mind can only be stimulated by the discipline which the Law provides and by contact with the men to whom the Inns of Court give birth.'

One evening Dr Kettel expanded his ideas to Henry in considerable detail. The old man and the student had dined well – a rich game soup, smoked eel, spiced duckling in a wine sauce, and a tart of apricots, the whole feast accompanied by the best Bordeaux from the presidential cellar. It was common knowledge in Oxford that Dr Kettel took immense pleasure in the joys of the table and Henry was idly wondering how his mother would react to this excess of academic luxury when the president broached the subject of Henry's future.

There was a third university, he said, a natural extension to the instruction available at Oxford or Cambridge: and that third university was situated at the Inns of Court in London. A complete knowledge of the Law was more important than it had ever been. Every man of property needed to understand – and sometimes to defend – his rights of tenure. The buying and selling of land must be properly documented and that should never be left to the rascals who contrived absurd delays and profited from the ignorance of their clients. Moreover – and here the old president looked searchingly at his young companion – 'Who is to say, Harry, where destiny is pointing your course? Suppose, for instance, you become a Member of Parliament, suppose you want to see to its conclusion some cause close to your heart, suppose you want to reform the law itself, suppose you feel called to right some great wrong, how will you succeed unless you possess the knowledge and expertise of an Eliot, a Hampden or a Pym?'

Was it on that evening that Henry Ireton decided to absent himself still longer from his Nottingham inheritance? Or was it Jane Ireton's response to Dr Kettel that settled the next phase of her eldest son's life?

Henry was never sure who or what caused him to study Law in London before finally returning to enjoy his inheritance at Attenborough. But certain it is that within a few months of being duly accredited with a Bachelor of Arts degree from Oxford University, Henry Ireton arrived in London to take up residence in the Middle Temple.

7

By mid-July 1629 all the young men had left Oxford – some to return to their studies at Michaelmas, some to marry and enjoy their fathers' acres, and some to seek fame and fortune in a wider world. The university was deserted except for the college servants, and at Trinity the president dined alone.

He sat hunched in his chair at the head of the long dining table in the President's Lodging, enjoying the last of the Burgundy. In a benevolent mood induced by his excellent meal, he considered how well the college silver appeared by candlelight, and how well Simm cared for him and his possessions. Yes, he was truly grateful for the old servant's constant and unobtrusive loyalty. He was well aware of the man hovering in the shadows by the door leading to the kitchen, silently awaiting his final instructions.

Suddenly, the president's rasping voice broke the silence. 'No need to hang around, you old rascal. Just fetch me the brandy and the chess board. Then get yourself to bed. You can clear the table in the morning.'

A few minutes later the chessmen stood in array before him, but Dr Ralph Kettel's mind continued to range over his past record and present performance. Thirty years ago he'd been elected president of this college – way back in the last years of Good Queen Bess (that's the way he thought now about the old termagant). A mean inheritance, he remembered, despite the extent of Sir Thomas Pope's endowments. Buildings in disrepair and students as idle as any in Oxford – God alone knew how they'd been allowed entry! Well, he'd changed all that, shored up the old Durham library, built a new hall and rounded off the Broad Street frontage by building Kettel Hall.

More important, he'd used his own methods to set a new and higher standard for the young men under his tutelage. Not, like some of his lickspittle colleagues, by bowing and scraping to courtiers in Whitehall . . . Ugh! The president belched happily. Oh no, he'd pressed into his service his friends among the parish priests of England, men of the calibre of old John Mather. They were better equipped than courtiers to choose the Trinity intake.

And now? His eyes took in his present surroundings – the gentle light from the candles in their silver candlesticks illuminating the polished table and the glass decanter beside him, and tactfully leaving in shadow the indifferent portrait of his predecessor.

His long predatory arm stretched for an apple from a finely-wrought fruit bowl, recently presented to him by young Edward Ford. A Sussex man, wasn't he? Owned a lot of land down there, came from a 'recusant' family and – to his credit – proud of it. Recommended, if he remembered rightly, by old Barton who'd clung too publicly to his Rome allegiance and suffered for it – silly, obstinate fellow. In matters of religious belief, the president followed the main stream of the Elizabethan Settlement, though the thought of little Laud with his 'Thou Shalt and Thou Shalt not' annoyed him every time he looked from his garden at neighbouring St John's . . . Come, come, Mr President, forget these prelatical arguments, he admonished himself. Enjoy the last of the wine and apply yourself to the future of Henry Ireton which is your immediate problem.

As he peeled his apple his eyes returned to the chessmen: Ah yes, we have a presidential problem on our hands. And Dr Kettel swept his plate to one side, replaced it with the chess board, finished his Burgundy and poured himself a generous brandy.

Carelessly he ranged the chessmen haphazard on the board. Now . . . he picked up and replaced the Black King . . . that's me: can't move far but the pieces revolve round me. The White King? That must be Sam Dowdswell, the horse-coper. A dear man, but no will of his own, governed by women . . . He fingered the White Queen, reflected a moment and then said firmly, 'Miss Betsie, this is your rôle: it's high time you found a partner.'

With lightning speed he moved the White Queen across the board to capture the Black Queen, who stood exposed in a vulnerable position. 'I'm very sorry, Miss Maggie,' he murmured, surveying the Black Queen. 'I'm very fond of you and

I know you'll be disappointed. But in this game the men under my command have no place for you. Perhaps, your moment will come. Who shall say?'

More chessmen assumed human personality. A Black Bishop, John Mather, was removed from the board: A pity, grumbled the president, your death makes my task much harder. However, we can still win the day. And Henry Ireton and his mother were duly installed as the two Black Rooks.

Other chessmen acquired new names. On the black side, a prominent Middle Temple lawyer and Sir Theodore Mayerne On the white side, Mrs Wotherspoon, the hated Pope family agent William Sanderson, and a defecting Maggie downgraded and transformed into an isolated White Pawn.

The president was clearly enjoying his private game. He fingered two Knights, one black and one white – a couple of eccentric rovers, eh? Tom Brewster, eh? And little Martin? Deep in thought, he took another bite of apple and came to a swift conclusion.

A sort of inspired madness seemed to direct his great hands. The Black Knight, Tom Brewster, captured the White Pawn, Maggie. Brewster in turn was removed from the board by the White Queen, Betsie. The two Black Rooks advanced relentlessly on both flanks. One of them – it must have been Henry Ireton – swept William Sanderson aside en route. The White Queen, out of position after capturing Tom Brewster, proved unable to ward off the threat of the advancing Ireton Rooks . . . Check and Mate, called the president, and swept the chessmen off the board – all of them except the White Queen.

He smiled as he contemplated the piece resting in the palm of his hand: You're a clever woman, Miss Betsie, as well as a pretty one. You've been on my side all the time, haven't you? *You* let those Ireton Rooks win the game on purpose, eh? Good girl. I don't doubt but you are pleased at the result. You'll be happy, married to Sam Dowdswell. And you'll make him happy too, but only if Tom Brewster captures Maggie, eh? Just as he did in the game.

You're asking me a question, Miss Betsie? What have we done with the little boy, the White Knight? Ah, that's a very sensible point you make. Which way should we have made him move?

The president frowned. 'Women.' He mouthed the word without affection. Women, even good women, always causing complications . . . always asking questions. He poured himself a final brandy, and his mind shot off at a tangent.

Keep clear of women, Harry Ireton. Consider the trouble they cause. Helen, launching a thousand ships and wrecking the civilised world. Delilah sapping Samson's strength. Messalina, disgusting woman, bathing in asses' milk and bringing a great empire into contempt. And today, young man, down there in London where you'll soon be learning the Law, you'll find a chit of a French girl queening it in Whitehall. The king you hold in honour stands bewitched, letting her fill the court with hireling priests from Rome and women who flaunt their religion to the great disharmony of the kingdom . . . hardly a word of English among them . . . and the queen a wilful child born of Medici mendacity and Navarre bravado . . .

The president suddenly halted his tumbling thoughts. He looked again at the White Queen, still resting in his hand: Don't worry, Betsie, about an old man's prejudice. All women, I grant you, play a necessary part in the procreation of the race; and you, Betsie, have a special part to play in my plans. But you must understand that some men with a capacity for leadership run better on their own . . . No, no, no, I'm not thinking of a celibate president but of certain young men who have been in my charge. For some of them I foresee a place in tomorrow's history books. Such men must not be held back by pretty young women before their careers can open out. You understand, don't you?

That very attractive lass, Maggie Dowdswell, longs to possess Harry Ireton and longs to be possessed by him. Oh yes, Miss Betsie, there was no mistaking the longing in Maggie's eyes in that bedroom at the Mason's Arms. Young Harry reminded her, didn't he, of the lad at Magdalen who sired young Martin. I take you into my confidence, Miss Betsie. I shall need your help.

The old man stared again at the White Queen in his hand. Perhaps he had drunk more brandy than was his custom, but his mind was crystal clear.

So you still worry about the little boy, Miss Betsy? Suppose we persuade Tom Brewster to take service in Trinity and suppose he marries Maggie Dowdswell, won't it be right for Tom to take Martin into his care?

No? You still look doubtful, Miss Betsie. Do you know something of which I'm ignorant? I grant you that all women, good or bad, clever or silly, like to keep their own secrets. Just tell me, please, what further refinement my plan requires.

But not, I think, at this late hour The president replaced the White Queen with the rest of the chessmen, snuffed the guttering candles in the silver candlesticks and took himself to bed. In the morning he would seek further inspiration.

The following evening Ralph Kettel appeared in the doorway of the dining room at the Mitre Inn. He stood stock still surveying the length and breadth of it, knowing that he had made an entry which any leading actor might have envied. The diners were immediately conscious of his presence and whispered his identity to each other.

Mrs Wotherspoon hastened across the room to greet him. 'A very pleasant surprise, Mr President, and luckily we have your usual table available' – a welcome which was doubly inaccurate since, earlier in the day, Simon had made the president's intentions pellucidly clear to the lady. Still, the president enjoyed these little deceptions and there at his chosen table stood Betsie, happily unaware of her rôle as the White Queen.

A brief discussion followed. What did Mrs Wotherspoon recommend this evening? Berkshire broth and roast capon followed by the fruit tart? Excellent. And to accompany the meal, a dry white wine from Aquitaine, followed by a glass of Madeira to round off the meal. And Miss Betsie to attend me? Very charming. Thank you, Madam, for your consideration.

It was not until Betsie had served the main course that the president asked her to stay beside him as he sought her advice on a difficult problem.

'Young Henry Ireton,' he began a little hesitantly. 'Mr Dowdswell will be sorry to learn he's off to London, eh? Must have done the stable a lot of good, saddling the winner of the Witney Steeplechase. But I forget . . . you missed the race, didn't you?'

'That's right, Sir. I agreed to look after Maggie's little boy at Osney while the others went with Mr Ireton to South Leigh.'

'Of course, Betsie, I should have remembered. It was Maggie who accompanied Mr Dowdswell and Tom Brewster on the great day. Actually, I have news for the Dowdswells. I've asked Tom to work in the college next term . . . very fond of Oxford he is, and has no taste for London. That's something you might like to pass to the family. They're keeping well, I hope?'

Betsie remained silent, wondering where the tortuous old man was leading her. He must be coming round to Henry Ireton or young Martin. Then she said, 'The Dowdswells are all well, thank you Sir. Except of course for Maggie's anxiety about little Martin's schooling. The lad is thoroughly put out now that he receives no lessons from Mr Ireton. Such a bright little boy, too.'

'So Mr Ireton's been giving the boy lessons, Miss Betsie? This is news to me. Maggie's quite right. The boy's schooling must not be neglected.'

'But, Sir, there's no cause for anxiety. Mr Ireton has promised Maggie he'll see that Martin is educated as a yeoman's son should be educated.'

'Promised, so you say? And how, pray, can he keep his promise while he's working at the courts of law in London and Martin is resident at Osney?'

'I don't rightly know, Sir. Nor does Maggie. But she says – and Tom Brewster says – that Mr Ireton always keeps his promises.'

'Really? Very touching.' The president looked into the clear blue eyes of the girl standing demurely at his side. She was a clever one, too. 'Would Martin, then, need to leave home? How would he react to such a notion – or Maggie for that matter?'

'It's something only Maggie can answer, Sir. But I doubt if she'll marry until Martin is off her hands. And really, it would be better for her to marry, don't you think?'

'Yes, Miss Betsie. Yes.' The old man gave her a friendly tap on the bottom. 'Now run away, Miss, and find me that glass of Madeira, will you? You've given me quite enough food for thought this evening.'

So that's the way of it, thought the president. Maggie doesn't marry till Martin gets his yeoman's education. Betsie can't marry Sam until Maggie and Martin leave the Dowdswell home. And they are all certain that Henry Ireton will keep his promise. Well, that goes for me, too. But Maggie must not be allowed to think she can ensure Martin's future by marrying Henry. Oh dear me, no. That move has no place in the presidential strategy. So . . . will the boy be sent to London or Nottingham? Either way, Henry will need his family's help if he is to keep his promise. Why on earth do young men get carried away like this? Social justice? It's never been fair since Jacob deceived Esau. Still, our young man has a very objective as well as a decisive mind. And where does his heart lie? The president looked away from the table as if searching for inspiration. Then he said to himself: At present, I believe, the only woman he loves is his mother.

8

Henry Ireton's move to London was still three months distant. First he must return to his family at Attenborough, and this he longed to do. It would be good to make sure that his mother had no problems in administering the Ireton property. It would be fun to see more of his brothers and sisters, to renew acquaintance with local friends, to ride again with old Brewster, to waste a few hours observing the bird-life on the stretch of water behind St Mary's church.

But at this precise moment he found little joy in the homeward journey. Turning out of Oxford on to the Banbury Road, he became increasingly aware of a barrier building up between himself and Tom Brewster. The two young men had nothing to say to each other as they travelled the familiar, ill-kept road.

Henry was by nature and upbringing a tough character – essentially practical, conscious of his ability but not in any sense boastful. Perhaps he was a bit of a fatalist. Though he had loved his three carefree years at Oxford, he was not the sort of lad to spend much time in looking back over his shoulder. His present concern lay with the future and the next step in his career. He had few regrets about the past and no anxiety about tomorrow.

By contrast, Tom Brewster was a worried man. He could not work out what lay before him at the end of the journey. Studiously guiding his horse clear of the pot-holes and wheel-ruts of the road, he remained in a state of indeterminate silence, unaware of the passing scene or of his companion's presence.

Henry, who had never seen Tom in such a miserable mood, wondered what on earth had hit him so hard? Was he sad at leaving Lady Jane in Osney where she was to be served by a first-class stallion in Sam Dowdswell's ownership? No, Harry couldn't believe it. Theirs had been a joint decision. They'd parted with the little mare easily enough – a final pat, a handful of oats, and 'Good luck, Milady' from Tom. Her future, they both knew, lay safely in Sam Dowdswell's hands. And there was ample compensation in the two fine horses they were riding – part of an exchange arrangement they had concluded with Sam.

So, had Tom's black mood some link with the college, where over the past three years both of them had made a host of friends among the students and college servants? Or had Tom been affected by a somewhat flowery valedictory speech from the old president who had looked forward to seeing them both again in future years? No, such civilities were no more than a pleasant formality though, come to think of it, the president had taken unusual care to include Tom Brewster in his farewell. But surely to goodness Tom knew his stay in Oxford was limited to Harry's three years of residence? So, why the sadness?

Henry's mind turned to the day they had said goodbye to the Dowdswells at the little house in Osney. He thought of Sam with great affection – a fine man and a friend to whom he would be happy to trust his life as well as his horse. He remembered that final firm handshake – the seal of a fair bargain and a mark of gratitude to one who had helped his business prosper. It seemed like a pledge of loyalty which would be binding on both of them. But there was also Maggie standing beside her father and making no attempt to hide her grief at their departure; and worst of all, little Martin crying his eyes out. Henry distrusted emotion, as his mother did. It could cloud your judgment all too easily. But he still had the little boy's words in his ears: 'Who will teach me now? When will I see Uncle Harry again? How far away is London?'

Forget it, Henry. You're trying to examine Tom Brewster's mind – not your own. Cut out the memory of the dark-haired Maggie with her sparkling, daring eyes and capable hands. She's never been more to you than a girl who joined you on the rides along the ridge of Cumnor Hill and nursed you for a few minutes at South Leigh. If she's still on your mind, consider rather your promise to help Martin to regain the yeoman status that Maggie's father lost so many years ago.

Gradually, the miles slipped away. The two riders had passed Banbury and Dunchurch and were approaching Lutterworth before the thought of Martin recurred to Henry. Yes, of course, he would keep his promise to give the lad a chance in life. The Iretons always kept their promises, even 'to their own hurt'; and he recited to himself the fifteenth psalm which his father had made him learn by heart long ago. He smiled to himself at the memory though it didn't solve the problem. Maybe he'd quoted the psalm as a tribute to John Wycliffe who, long ago, had caused such offence to the Establishment that he had been banished from the councils of Church and nation to end his days in this country living of Lutterworth. Perhaps Wycliffe's exile was part of God's purpose. Otherwise, how would he have completed his translation of the Bible? On a silent journey, the traveller easily turns to speculation.

Turning into the stableyard of the inn in the main street of Lutterworth, Henry still had no idea how to help Martin. Nor could he explain his companion's morose behaviour on the journey.

At dinner that evening, Henry put the question straight to his companion: Why so silent, Tom? Why so short of cheer?

No, there was nothing wrong – nothing at all, Tom replied, but he spoke without conviction. Little by little as the meal progressed, the truth was coaxed out of him.

First, there was Tom's worry about London. He hoped Mr Harry would understand, but he had no wish to live in London. Understand? Good Heavens, Tom, there will be plenty of people to look after me in the Middle Temple. And there'll be a big choice of jobs for you on the Ireton farms.

But Tom's worry did not end there. He confessed he was not seeking a job in Attenborough, but wanted to strike out on his own. Once he'd seen Harry back with his family, he planned to make a new start.

'Fine,' said Harry. 'But how and where?'

'Well,' Tom replied a little hesitantly. 'Well Mr Harry, I ain't been doing nothing behind your back. But while you was staying in the President's Lodgings before your exams, the old gentleman had a word with me, see? Said he needed me in the college – wanted me to take over the stables and keep an eye on those idle chaps that hang around the college, doing too little and eating too much. Think about the idea, says he. There's no hurry. First see Mr Ireton safely home to his family. Then make up your mind. And if you decide to return to Oxford, be sure there's a good job waiting for you. I shan't offer the post to anyone else before Michaelmas. So that's the way of it, if you see what I mean.'

Henry Ireton burst out laughing and clapped Tom on the back. 'Cunning old Kettel. Knows a good man when he sees one, eh? Cheer up, man. Take the job and enjoy it. You'll do the president proud, of course you will. And maybe you'll keep an eye on Lady Jane? I'd like that.'

'You're sure you and Mrs Ireton won't mind?'

'Of course not, Tom. I'll talk to Mother. All you need to do is to persuade your father to let you out of his sight again.'

The two young men laughed. Next day they rode the forty miles to Attenborough with hardly a care in the world and their eyes fixed on the future. But Harry still found it hard to understand Tom's diffidence and hesitation. The lawyer in him doubted whether he had heard the whole truth in the inn at Lutterworth. Unprompted, his thoughts returned to Sam Dowdswell's daughter

Jane Ireton also had a problem on her mind. Hardly had her eldest son washed and changed out of his dust-laden travelling clothes before he was asked by a servant to join his mother in the ground-floor room which she had appropriated for her own use after her husband's death.

The resemblance between mother and son was immediately apparent – the fine features, the bright penetrating eyes, the dark hair, the easy carriage and, most noticeably, the unassuming air of authority that seemed natural to both of them. Mrs Ireton greeted her son with evident delight, beckoned him to a seat beside her and then, in her direct down-to-earth way, turned at once to the subject that was troubling her. Now that Oxford was behind him, Henry was clearly to be treated as head of the Ireton family.

Eight growing children, she told Harry, were more than the Ireton home could reasonably hold. It had been different when his father had been alive. Then, with something of a squeeze, the children could be packed into two rooms with the latest arrival at her side in the big double room. Perhaps they should be grateful to God that Death had deprived her of three babies, who now lay secure in their innocence under the shadow of St Mary's church.

But what of the future? Did Henry realise that Mary and Sarah were no longer children? Probably not. Brothers were slow to notice such transformations, until they suddenly woke up to the fact that the family could boast two of the loveliest young women in the County of Nottingham.

And there was her second son, John. He was being difficult. He had no wish for a university degree and no inclination to interest himself in farming or any other country pursuit. Then, quite apart from his small sister, the needs of Matthew, Thomas and Clement must be considered. What would Henry advise?

The latter looked around the room his mother had made her own. His eyes noted the exquisite embroidery lying across an elegant table by the window seat. They moved to the small, almost feminine, desk covered with farm accounts but surmounted by a vase of roses freshly picked from the garden. What a brave, splendid person his mother was.

He leant over and kissed her lightly on the forehead. Then he stood towering above her, his hands clasped, his lips breaking into a smile. He addressed her with mock severity, assuming a ridiculous donnish voice distinctly reminiscent of Dr Kettel's rasping timbre. 'No plans, Mrs Ireton? No plans at all? This is most reprehensible. No ideas, now you have lost your chief of staff at the rectory? The situation must be remedied forthwith.'

Jane Ireton began to laugh too. 'Let me tell you, Henry Ireton, Bachelor of Arts in the University of Oxford, that I am a poor helpless woman, awaiting your learned and considered judgment. It is true that in your absence I have relied on the advice of the late rector. I expect his successor, Mr Gervase Dodson, will be equally helpful. Certainly he's a fine preacher, knows his Bible and can prepare a boy for the university as well as John Mather prepared you. But friendship is not built in a day. From now on, I'm relying on you.'

Henry stooped to kiss his mother again – one could not fail to notice the mutual understanding and love that united them. He must, he told her, make a few calls, see some old friends and make acquaintance with the new rector. Then within twenty-four hours, the Ireton Oracle would speak! With that, he bowed himself out of the room and Jane Ireton returned to her embroidery. Her sensitive face was relaxed and untroubled. Henry would not fail her.

Henry's first call was to the stables. He found old Edward Brewster casting his expert eye over the horses taken over in part exchange from Sam Dowdswell's stables. 'Not a bad bargain, Mr Harry, not bad at all. I've always held there's nothing like two for the price of one, eh? But what's this I hear about you licking the Oxfordshire gentry at Witney? Young Tom tells me the little mare did us proud . . . wish I'd been there to see the race. Made some new friends, too, or so I hear. Sounds as if Oxford has more than men of learning to recommend it.'

Henry smiled. The old chap would talk till twilight if he were given the chance. But there were other folk to visit, and so it was agreed they'd ride together in the morning and try out the Dowdswell horses on a visit to Fenton where Henry's friend, Francis Thornhaugh, lived.

Next, Henry called on the new rector. It was a change to find a young man replacing his old tutor who had almost become a village institution. But he took to the new man, Gervase Dodson, who gave him a very clear account of the progress of the Ireton children.

'Start with brother John,' said Dodson. 'Clever at figures, very clever. But determined to get away from Attenborough and chance his arm as a merchant in the City of London. Matthew? Well, he's a natural scholar . . . should certainly go forward to Oxford or Cambridge in two years' time. Tom? No need to worry about him. He's a real charmer, never short of friends. I guess he'll rest happy in the local life round here. And so will Clement who hardly leaves Tom's side.

'You ask about the girls, Mr Ireton?' The priest paused for a moment. 'I think your mother can best bring you up to date with their progress, but it would not surprise me to find Mary and Sarah leaving home in the next few years. They certainly won't lack for suitors.'

Henry thanked Gervase Dodson for his help and sauntered back to the Ireton home where he found Thomas and Clement trying to repair an ostringer's old glove which they needed for a kestrel they'd acquired. 'Show us how it goes,' they pleaded. Soon Harry was showing his two younger brothers how to work the heavy leather with needle and thread. Hawking was the sport he loved best. He'd fly his merlin again as soon as he was back from Fenton.

The next morning, accompanied by Edward Brewster, Henry called on Francis Thornhaugh. The two young men were good friends as well as neighbours, and about the same age. though Francis was not entering Magdalen College, Oxford until the following year.

His family was in closer touch with the county than the Iretons were – and Francis was already active in recruiting for the county militia. 'You never know, Harry, when we may be needed, with the roads so damnably dangerous and civil authority so feeble. I hope you'll join us when you finish with the lawyers in London.'

Harry agreed to consider the idea, but added that, after his recent journey from Loughborough, he was more concerned with the poor condition of the country roads than the danger of highwaymen on the way to London. Then he told Francis of his mother's preoccupations.

Francis laughed. 'Excuse my mirth, Harry, but you take life too seriously. I hold your mother in great respect but I doubt whether she need worry about your sisters. John Bainbrigge, over from Lockington, already has his eye on Mary, is sure she wants him and will be willing to look after the children of his two earlier marriages. I'm told he only waits to know whether he applies to you or your mother before making a firm proposal. And, of course, with his possessions he won't be difficult about a dowry.

'And Sarah? Why not take her to London, Harry? Let her see the big world you're set to enter. She'll keep you from getting too serious with your law books. She has a good mind, you know, and she'll be glad to get away from Nottingham – or so I think. As for marriage, she won't accept any man she doesn't choose for herself. But once she comes to a decision, she'll prove as obstinate as you. So go to it, Harry. Pay my respects to Mrs Ireton but don't let your mother or Sarah know who is the author of your grand strategy.'

Riding home in the afternoon of this lovely summer day,

Henry Ireton pondered on Francis' advice. With every mile he liked it more, especially as it fitted so well with Gervase Dodson's suggestions. And Sarah would be a marvellous companion if he could persuade her to join him. They'd choose suitable apartments near the law courts. They'd explore the great city together from the Tower of London to the Palace of Whitehall, from Greenwich to Gravesend . . . His youthful imagination carried him to Canterbury and Dover . . . to Surrey and Hampshire . . . Yes, he must talk with Sarah and his mother the moment he reached Attenborough.

He and Edward Brewster were walking their horses the final quarter mile to the stables when the older man broke into Harry's train of thought. It seemed that Tom Brewster was causing his father a certain anxiety.

'You know what's in his mind, Mr Harry. Don't want to join you in London. Don't want to help me with the horses here. Says he's fixed up with a good job in the college. But there's more to it than that, Sir, or my name's not Brewster. There must be a girl in it. So I says to Tom, "Come out with the truth, lad, if you want any help from me." And sure enough, the truth came tumbling out of him. A girl called Maggie, daughter of this Mr Dowdswell – she's the draw, Mr Harry, and Tom's determined to win her. But when I ask how she feels about him, Tom begins to hesitate.' Old Brewster was clearly embarrassed. 'Tom thinks . . . he thinks . . . she may be sweet on you.'

They were already in the stableyard and unsaddling the horses before Henry had a chance to allay the old man's anxieties. 'Rest easy, my friend. Of course I know Maggie Dowdswell – as pretty a girl as you'd find in Oxfordshire. But I'm not thinking of taking up with Maggie – or anybody else. It's up to Tom to win Maggie, if he can. There's no problem here' – and Henry tapped his heart. 'I've only one commitment to Maggie Dowdswell and that concerns a little boy called Martin. Tom knows all about him. And Tom knows, as you do, that I'll keep my promise to her about young Martin. You may both have to help me keep my promise – but that's another matter. As for Tom and Maggie, it's a great idea Send Tom to Oxford with your blessing and mine. I reckon

67

Maggie's an Oxford prize that's well worth winning. And if Tom wins, you won't be disappointed, my friend, and I shall be truly delighted.'

9

Henry and Sarah Ireton stood hand in hand beside the parlour window of their new home. Their mother had given her approval to Henry's London plan. And now, on this first day since their arrival in the capital, they gazed in excited wonder at the multifarious traffic on the Thames as, yesterday, they had gazed with equal amazement from Highgate Hill on the panorama of the great city stretching out before them.

Brother and sister, now aged nineteen and seventeen, had travelled post from Nottingham, changing horses at successive staging points. The state service had operated with remarkable efficiency once they had reached the Great North Road at Grantham, and they had been well satisfied with the condition of the post horses they had hired.

They had travelled leisurely southwards, spending the first night at Stamford where the Burleighs continued to be the power in the land, and the second night at Hitchin. Thence, after crossing the Cecils' vast estate at Hatfield, they had reined their horses at the top of Highgate Hill to stare at London for the first time.

Henry informed his sister – he was always fascinated by statistics – that the population of London had risen from seventy-five thousand in the days of Queen Elizabeth to a figure in excess of two hundred and fifty thousand today. 'Imagine it, Sarah. A city's population more than trebled in a hundred years – it's almost incredible.'

'And now,' replied his down-to-earth sister, 'we are on the point of increasing the numbers by two insignificant digits – two more souls to be added to the thousands who have been drawn from the country to this great city in search of employment, enlightenment, and wealth if lucky.'

The prelude to adventure was behind them. Side by side they rode the last few miles into the heart of London, wondering what they would find on arrival. Would they in due course be numbered among the lucky ones?

They need not have worried. Nothing had been left to chance. On reaching the post house hard by Temple Bar, they had been met by a Mr Joseph Shipley acting on instructions received, apparently, from Sir Theodore Mayerne. Joe had conducted them to his house overlooking the river, where they had been introduced to Mrs Shipley and reunited with their baggage previously collected from the carrier by Joe.

As Hannah Shipley served dinner on the evening of their arrival, Harry and Sarah managed to learn more about their landlord and his lady. Joe proved to be a licensed Thames waterman who had often been of service to Sir Theodore. He was a man proud of his calling, and without an enemy in the world save for the new hackney carriage proprietors who were, it seemed, threatening to take over the watermen's traditional short-run custom.

Perhaps this reduction in the watermen's clientele provided one reason for the Shipleys to let part of their commodious three-storey house to lodgers such as Sarah and Harry. But it was also true that their two surviving children had left the family home – the married son to set up his own business in Greenwich, and the daughter to accompany her husband on one of the new Londonderry settlements recently sponsored by the livery companies of London.

Certainly the Shipleys' house, strategically situated to the west of the Middle Temple boundary, exactly met the needs of the young Iretons. As they watched the thriving business of the river they thought themselves the luckiest and happiest people in the whole of London. They resolved to make it clear to Joe and Hannah that they would like to be treated as part of the household, and not as superior people separated by some class partition from the good people to whom they paid their monthly rent. That might not be the style adopted by London's high society – but it was the way of the Iretons from Nottingham.

They were arguing how best to set out on their discovery of London when a commotion at the front door announced Sir Theodore Mayerne's arrival:

A routine visit, my dear Mrs Shipley . . . just to satisfy myself that your guests are safely installed . . . mustn't stay long . . . my chariot's blocking the approach to the river. Not yet started their exploration of London, you say? Then, if I may be permitted, I will see the young people before reporting to my old Oxford friend who charged me to arrange their London accommodation.

Preceded by Hannah Shipley, the doctor mounted the stairs to the first-floor living room. It was already familiar to him, with its rather heavy wooden chairs and cupboards, its single table and bookshelf, the darkness of the low-ceilinged room somewhat relieved by the light from the wide lattice window and the brightly coloured cushions covering the chairs and the window seat. He had come to know it well when assisting at the birth of the Shipley children, for he had made it a rule to select his patients from all classes of society. Indeed, he had been known to tell his students they could learn more about the causes of illness in the narrow lanes of a city than they could in noblemen's houses or the palaces of kings. It was as true of London as it was of Paris.

Before him, standing beside the young man he'd visited in Oxford, Sir Theodore beheld a girl of striking appearance. She possessed poise as well as beauty – her auburn hair lit by the sun, her fine features reminiscent of her older brother, except that her cheeks carried more colour and her mouth suggested a sense of humour that was all her own. There was intelligence here as well as charm.

And how, the doctor asked, would Sarah occupy her day while her brother slaved away for those dry-as-dust lawyers in the Middle Temple?

The young lady anticipated no problems. She would work in the kitchen and visit the markets with Mrs Shipley. Perhaps she would be privileged to meet Mrs Shipley's friends. She would hope to learn more about the ways of London from Mr Joseph Shipley whom she understood to be well-informed in such matters. She even hoped – and her bright eyes looked directly at Sir Theodore – she even hoped that one day she and her brother might find occasion to visit the Palace of Whitehall and Westminster Hall.

'So,' Sir Theodore interrupted, 'you also take an interest in the ways of the court and the workings of Parliament. Well, we must do what we can to meet your wishes. But I should warn you, young lady, that at present you are more likely to see King Charles in his fine carriage than Mr John Pym lecturing the Commons of England. And why? Because, Miss Sarah, His Majesty entertains no great love for Mr Pym and his colleagues. In fact, he fully intends to rule for the present without their help.'

Henry broke into the conversation. 'But how, Sir, can the King of England rule without Parliament? How, otherwise, can the Royal Exchequer pay for the continental adventures provoked by the Duke of Buckingham?'

Sir Theodore smiled. 'Well spoken, young Harry, well spoken. But you will find there are always ways and means available to the ruler who is subtle in his approach. There are always people ready to pay much gold for the king's favour. A scheming alderman, for instance, who fancies himself a knight, or a City guild which seeks the Royal Seal to give permanent authority to its monopoly trading rights. But who am I to say – a Frenchman by birth and only English by adoption? Though I make a livelihood from curing the ailments of English men and women, I do not pretend to understand the workings of their constitution. I can only tell you that, like the human body, it sometimes functions ill. Very ill, indeed,' he added, 'in a day when Buckingham has his throat slit by a Portsmouth matelot and Sir John Eliot languishes in the Tower for speaking too loud at Westminster.'

Sir Theodore turned to Henry. 'You'll doubtless learn more about these political problems, Henry, when you eat your dinners in the Middle Temple. Meanwhile, your sister must not be allowed to take London life too seriously. Visit the bookshops by St Paul's, my dear, and sample their wares. Get Joe to ferry you across the river and visit the Globe theatre for a Shakespeare play – the actors perform better in Southwark than they do in Shoreditch. And don't let yourself be tied to the streets of London. Cross the river and travel south to Sussex and east to Kent.'

The famous doctor joined them for a moment by the window and looked across to the Southwark staithes at the far end of London Bridge, and beyond to the high ground of Kent. 'Yes,' he said as he took his leave, 'if you wish for a long life, my children, seek the pure air of the English countryside.'

* * *

There was still a week before Henry had agreed to report to the Middle Temple chambers of Master Chapman – a Common Law man in whom Dr Kettel placed confidence. The young Iretons greatly enjoyed their exploration of London.

They made themselves familiar with the narrow cobbled lanes of the City. They noticed how the wooden-framed houses, often rising to three storeys, kept the sunlight from the streets. Here and there they spotted brick buildings newly completed by builders from the Low Countries. They paused to look at the churches and the halls of the great livery companies.

They walked up Fleet Street towards St Paul's Cathedral – its Gothic splendour diminished by the loss of its spire from lightning. They bought some books at The Sign of the Sun in St Paul's churchyard and, returning to the Shipleys' house, held their noses as they hurried past the evil-smelling Fleet River – the effluent, it seemed, of all the filth of London. They thanked God that Sir Theodore had found them accommodation well away from that noisome stream.

They visited some of the local markets with Hannah Shipley: Clare or Newgate for meat and fish, Leadenhall for poultry, eggs and fresh vegetables. In the expanse of Cheapside, she told them, you could buy anything you wanted, provided you had the money. 'But it's good value,' said Hannah. 'You pay less in Cheapside than in the New Exchange near Somerset House or the King Street stalls off Whitehall. You'll find the top prices always follow the fashion.'

One afternoon Joe rowed them downriver to Greenwich, and on another weekend upstream to Hampton Court. The distant glimpse of the royal palaces made them long for the day when they would have a closer sight of the king and queen, riding perhaps in Whitehall or walking in the royal park of St James.

All too swiftly the week of sightseeing came to an end and Henry reported for duty in the Middle Temple. As his habit was, he gave himself entirely to his new calling. He undertook without question the menial tasks Master Chapman gave him, conveying documents to the courts of law, and studying ancient statutes and laws concerned with property in a dingy back office leading off Mr Chapman's fine room.

Sometimes Henry was despatched to Gray's Inn or Lincoln's

73

Inn to make appointments for his master. Sometimes he would travel up to Holborn where the scriveners prepared and copied deeds concerned with the ownership and sale of land. Henry enjoyed these visits for he found the scriveners to be men of education and understanding. One of them told him how he had learnt his skills from a Mr Milton, whose son, now studying at Cambridge, was reputed to be a man of outstanding scholarship.

It was on one such visit to Holborn that Henry encountered his old Oxford friend, Edward Ford: Edward . . . Harry . . . What brings you to London? The president? Don't believe you . . . must talk. Still talking, they agreed to stop for a meal and drink at The Blue Boar in Holborn where, over a twelve pence 'ordinary' they up-dated each other on their current activities.

Edward, it transpired, had on this occasion hurried to London because of a property dispute in Sussex. 'Can't make head or tail of it,' he said. 'But a learned fellow in Lincoln's Inn – name of Prynne – knows all the answers. Talk, talk, talk . . . it's almost impossible to stop him. Still, he knows the Law. And though he takes a poor view of the Old Religion, he's clever and honest enough to see that this rogue neighbour of mine is using my recusant status to bend the law for his own benefit. Anyway, the erudite Mr Prynne has fixed the blackguard well and truly,' and Edward tapped a cumbersome parchment sticking out of his coat pocket. 'Thanks to Mr Prynne I shall return tomorrow to Sussex, a happier man.'

'But Edward, you can't leave so soon. Come, at least, to see my lodgings. It's not a mile away, and I can give you a lovely view across the Thames.'

'To Southwark, you mean?'

'That's right. The other end of London Bridge whither the self-righteous aldermen of this city have banished the players and such rougher attractions as bear-baiting and the cock-pit. Look. Why not come to the play tonight? All the past week my sister has been begging me to take her. Joe Shipley will row us across. Come on. We'll take Mother Shipley too. Agreed?'

Three hours later, fortified by a glass of wine and Hannah's chicken pie, the party set forth from Temple Stairs, with pipe-smoking, bearded Joe bending to the oars. Henry sat on the port side of the boat beside the buxom Hannah, resplendent in her Sunday dress. Edward sat opposite, his neat pointed beard carefully trimmed, and wearing a wine-red doublet above fawn hose. And next to him sat Sarah.

The little party appeared no different from other happy, expectant boatloads of Londoners making for the play – it was to be William Shakespeare's *Romeo and Juliet*. But Harry, looking at his sister across the boat, suddenly realised he was looking at a new creation. This girl he'd known from childhood seemed transformed – head uncovered, hair slightly ruffled by the breeze, brown eyes alive and excited, blue velour cloak only half concealing the low-cut cream dress she'd bought in the fashionable New Exchange the previous week. Why, his sister, Sarah Ireton, might have been one of the queen's ladies-in-waiting emerging from Somerset House. No, that was an understatement. Her assurance suggested a princess . . . a queen. Could any man pass by without a second glance? Even Joe Shipley seemed to play the courtier as he gravely helped her from the boat to the landing stage.

After the play they emerged to find Joe heading the queue of watermen waiting for fares. Hannah thought the play lovely – quite carried away, she was. Henry secretly considered the plot ridiculous and the beauty of the words murdered by the actors' histrionics, but he gallantly played up to Hannah's enthusiasm and praised Joe for his skill in manoeuvring his boat to first place at the landing stage.

But Edward and Sarah spoke not a word. They sat side by side, his left hand lightly holding hers, his right arm clasped about her blue cloak as if for protection against the cool autumnal night. For all too short a time – the mere crossing of a river – they stayed close together, enchanted by some secret understanding that needed no language. It had all been said for them at the play.

It seemed only seconds before Joe moored the boat.

'Goodnight, Edward,' Sarah said, standing at the top of the Temple Stairs.

'Goodnight, my Juliet,' came the whispered reply, 'until we meet again.' And Edward Ford turned abruptly away. Without a backward glance he disappeared into the darkness of the City's streets.

Part Two

The scholar goes to war
1629–1646

Having had an education in the strictest way of
godliness, and being a man of good learning, great
understanding and other abilities, Henry Ireton was
the chief promoter of the Parliament interest in
Nottinghamshire.

Lucy Hutchinson, *Memoirs*

10

Within a week a letter addressed to Miss Sarah Ireton reached the Shipleys' house by special messenger.

Bold handwriting, strong expensive paper, a wax seal imprinted 'E. F.' – all this was noted by Mrs Shipley as she signed the receipt for delivery. She ran upstairs filled with romantic speculation: Sarah's first love-letter, I'll be bound. Oh, to watch her open it – her long delicate fingers breaking the seal, a blush rising to her cheeks, even a tear coursing down them! But no, Hannah, no. At such moments a young lady will wish to be left alone.

And so Hannah curbed her excitement – in and out of the first-floor room without lingering. 'A letter for you, Miss Sarah. Good news, I hope.' That was all she said, but: Yes, she was sure it would be right for her to delay her visit to the market just in case . . . you never know . . . sometimes young ladies like to share their secrets . . . and Henry won't be back from his law books till the evening . . .

Five minutes later Sarah came bounding down the stairs and flung herself into Mrs Shipley's arms: 'Hannah, darling Hannah, you'll never guess . . . the letter . . . it's from Edward . . . asks if he may see me again . . . do you think Henry can find time to take me to Sussex? How far is Hastings?' Sarah hugged Mrs Shipley as if, in her excitement, she must have something solid and reliable for support.

The letter in her hands had been most carefully written.

My dear Sarah,

I write to you immediately on my return to Sussex. I fear I was too silent as we crossed the Thames on that star-lit evening, and when we landed I could bear no company but yours. And so I hurried away from Henry and your two good friends. Even now, though I have so much to say, I lack the eloquence to interpret what I feel. I recall the play:

> Can I go forward when my heart is here?
> Turn back, dull earth, and find thy centre out.

And so may I ask you to persuade Harry to conduct you to this corner of England where my family have lived for so many, many years? Please, Juliet – Sarah – let me show my home to you. Please tell me you will journey here as soon as the spring flowers set the fields alight. And please forgive me for leaving you so abruptly when parting was such sweet sorrow.

The play is over, but the enchantment will stay with me for ever. I long to see you again.

Your devoted admirer,

Edward

'There, Sarah, there.' Mrs Shipley spoke as if she knew she was cast for the role of Juliet's nurse. 'Mr Ford is a fine gentleman – a very handsome young man, to be sure, and a good friend to your brother. But you must reflect, before you reply. And there's your mother to consult as well as your brother . . .'

Hannah kissed Sarah gently on the forehead and became once more the practical housewife. 'Come,' she said, 'you and I must walk quickly to Clare market, or the butchers' stall will be empty and we shall have no meat for the men's dinner.'

Between Henry and Sarah there were no secrets. Back from the Middle Temple, Henry was immediately told of Edward's letter. All day he had attended the Court of Chancery, listening to Master Chapman winning a difficult freehold property case for a City alderman. Indeed he was eager to tell his sister of the part he had played in furnishing his master with the necessary evidence. But he accepted that Sarah's letter from Edward Ford was much more exciting. And much more worrying too, he thought to himself as he listened to Sarah talking.

Sarah Ireton, daughter to that sturdy Nottingham Protestant, Mr German Ireton, being courted by a Papist? And taking this single letter so seriously? Henry had always been sensitive to Sarah's reactions and he was aware of the certainty as well as the excitement in his sister's voice. But in their world of arranged marriages and bargained dowries, could there really be a place for love at first sight? Was the romance of Romeo and Juliet more substantial than a poet's fancy? Perhaps he'd been too quick to criticise the absurdity of Shakespeare's plot.

Aloud, he told Sarah how happy he was for her. Edward, he agreed, was a good man: his best friend at Oxford and a member of one of the finest families in England. Still, it might be wise to return to Attenborough and tell their mother of Edward's interest before stepping too far into the future. If they left their heavy baggage in the Shipleys' care, they could reach home within the week.

It was only when they reached the Angel at Grantham that Henry referred to Edward's unwavering adherence to the Old Religion. The Ford family, he conceded, was hardly likely to be harassed in their home county of Sussex where they enjoyed a splendid reputation among the wealthy landowners, but the recusancy laws would effectively stop Edward from holding any public office and might involve him in fines and other legal disabilities. The fact that the Iretons were Independents who believed in toleration did not unhappily eliminate such problems.

Take, for instance, the present situation at the king's court. In casual talk with fellow law students, Henry had been made increasingly aware of the embers of political argument being fanned into a blaze by the religious stance of antagonists. At this very moment there was, he had been told, a battle royal in progress in the palace of Whitehall: Dr William Laud urging the king to make use of the prayer book compulsory in all places of worship, even among the Presbyterians of Scotland, while the queen, surrounded by her French priests, was openly criticising the bishop as a mean little red-faced man of lowly birth and little education. It might all be hearsay, but Master Chapman avowed that the king was unable to distinguish between the views of Henrietta Maria and his favourite counsellor. An unhappy court, indeed.

'But, Harry,' Sarah interrupted, 'how should the royal dilemma concern us? You and I know where the Iretons stand.

We believe in independence of religious belief – which means toleration of all true Christians provided their convictions do not lead them into traitorous alliance with England's enemies. Mother holds these views equally strongly – just think of the rows she and John Mather have had with the Laudian Archdeacon of Nottingham. And anyhow,' she added inconsequently, 'whatever anybody says, Edward and I are going to marry. You'll see.'

When Harry and Sarah reached home, Jane Ireton heard out her daughter's story with a certain amused resignation. At first she was surprised by the passionate conviction of a girl whom she had always regarded as the most level-headed of all her children. Who was this fine young gentleman, then, who had swept her away from reason? In her day, a story-book romance was not the way by which marriages were arranged. But Jane's eyes noted Sarah's animation, her ears heard the excitement in the girl's voice, and she had no doubt that this daughter of hers would stand by her convictions as obstinately as her elder brother. So, if Harry's Oxford friend was serious and Sarah was sure of his love, the marriage would go forward and, of course, it would have her blessing.

'Only,' she added, 'it may be wise to wait a little and celebrate the wedding in London rather than in Attenborough. The new rector, my dear, has already engaged himself to officiate at Mary's wedding to Mr Bainbrigge. While he is a man of fine intelligence, he holds highly critical views about the rule of Rome, and locally one must take account of his views.'

Jane kissed her daughter and asked her to find Henry so that she could discuss these matters with him as head of the family. Apart from ensuring Henry's presence at Mary's wedding his mother had, in fact, another matter for discussion, more urgent in her view than Sarah's romance.

'It's this little boy from Oxford,' she told Henry the moment he entered her room: Name of Martin Dowdswell . . . arrived in the village two days ago from Oxford . . . riding pillion to Tom Brewster . . . the pair of them sleeping in old Brewster's cottage and awaiting your arrival. Tom says you'll know the boy.'

'Know him? Why, of course I do, Mother. I'd intended to return to London by way of Oxford in order to see him. But it looks as if Tom has forestalled me – I wonder why.' And Henry told Jane Ireton of his quixotic promise to the boy's mother.

'I was angry, you see, that his family should be so unjustly dispossessed of land they'd farmed for centuries – and by an upstart land-grabbing court official from London. I told Martin's mother that the Dowdswells' yeoman status could only be recovered if the boy were properly educated and trained in farming. And in my spare time at Oxford I gave the boy his first lessons in reading, writing and arithmetic. That's the whole story. From what I've seen of Martin, I judge him to be very intelligent for his age. The question is not whether, but how, I keep the promise I made to Maggie Dowdswell.'

'The girl Tom hopes to marry?'

'That's the girl. I'll go and see Tom and little Martin without delay. But first, Mother, can we accommodate the boy in the village if Maggie really wishes to leave him with us?'

Jane Ireton was silent for a moment. Then she looked straight at Henry. 'Tell me one thing,' she said. 'Are you the boy's father?'

Henry smiled. He loved the directness of his mother's question. 'No, I give you my word. He was born years before I went to Oxford and Maggie has never told me or her own father who sired the child. But she's made it clear on many occasions that her lover was a man of breeding. She's proud too in her own way and certainly will not ask him for help even if she knows where he lives. All she wants is for Martin to be helped back into the land-owning class to which he belongs. I fancy she must be using Tom Brewster as her ambassador.'

'*All* she wants, Henry? You seem to be as headstrong in your promises as Sarah. It will be better, I think, for me to talk with Tom Brewster. Clearly you cannot take on this responsibility while you are working in London.'

Some hours later, Tom Brewster met Henry. Mrs Ireton had been more than helpful. Provided Tom's father and mother would provide the necessary accommodation she would arrange for Martin to accompany Thomas and Clement for schooling at the rectory. It would be limited, she said, to a trial period. If Martin was unhappy or misbehaved, he would be sent back to Oxford.

Tom Brewster was truly grateful to Mrs Ireton, but he added, 'You will keep an eye on him, Mr Harry, won't you? Martin thinks the world of you. And if you watch his progress, I'll return happy to Oxford.'

'And persuade Maggie to become Mrs Tom Brewster?'

'That's right, Mr Harry. She's promised to make a home with me in Oxford – but only when Martin's future is assured. Maggie knows I've found a good job with Dr Kettel and she really wants to make a fresh start. The fact is, Sam Dowdswell is set to marry Betsie from the Mitre; and Maggie knows Betsie well enough to be sure that there's only room for one woman in Sam Dowdswell's house.'

Over the Christmas holidays, Henry saw much of Martin – a sturdy seven-year-old, big for his age, and blessed with his mother's eyes and natural intelligence. Together they walked along the banks of the Erewash and Henry told Martin of the spring days ahead when birds would be returning in great numbers to the water meadows behind the house. They rode pillion to Nottingham and watched the skills of some travelling showmen and acrobats.

Martin was introduced to the younger Iretons. He appeared to experience no difficulty in making friends and he loved being with old Mrs Brewster whom he immediately regarded as the grandmother he had never known. All in all, Henry left Attenborough with the conviction that his mother's plan for Martin Dowdswell would cover the next two years while he completed his legal training in London.

11

Although Martin was safely lodged with the Brewsters, Henry was persuaded by Sarah to stay with his earlier plan and return to London by way of Oxford. It lengthened the journey by a week, but Sarah was insistent on seeing Oxford for herself and, if possible, on meeting the redoubtable Dr Ralph Kettel whose eccentricities had so frequently figured in the 'do-you-remember' small talk of Edward and Henry. Indeed, as brother and sister rode with Tom Brewster along the familiar road through Leicester and Banbury, the president was a frequent topic of conversation.

On reaching Oxford, Tom was asked to deliver a letter to the president inviting him to dine with the Iretons on the following evening. A prompt letter of acceptance was received at the Mitre where Henry and Sarah were staying. But when the great man arrived at the inn he insisted on acting as host. To Henry's surprise he took the greatest delight in escorting Sarah to his favourite table in the dining room. After consulting her about the meal, he continued to flatter her outrageously, directing much of his conversation at her.

'You tell me, young lady, you have met Edward Ford? A great friend of your brother, as I remember, provided they were not quarrelling about theology. Of course they didn't know what they were talking about, so I gave each of them a Bible to study.'

Henry laughed. 'Gave, did you say, Sir? As I remember it, Edward and I both had to pay for those Bibles and each was marked with your handwriting so that the bookshop value was greatly reduced.'

'Reduced, Henry? On the contrary. Although my script may be a trifle distinctive, that small correction to Psalm one hundred and thirty-three will assuredly enhance its value. And in any case, you will agree that it has drawn your attention to a verse of Scripture which should be memorised by anybody who seeks to exercise authority in this world of ours. Even you,

Miss Sarah, could be wise to heed it at a more domestic level.'

The president smiled as if enjoying a private joke, but he continued on a more serious note.

'"To dwell together in Unity" – a useful piece of advice, don't you think, for private as well as public life? A pity it's not better understood by the heads of our Oxford colleges – or for that matter, by our representatives in Parliament. But the latter are a bad-tempered lot, drawn mostly from the legal profession, isn't that so, Henry? They might do better to leave their law-books and study the psalms.'

Did the president wink at Henry or Sarah as he rose to leave? It was hard to say. When they thanked him for his hospitality, he gallantly replied that, on the contrary, he was in their debt for bringing Tom Brewster to Oxford.

'A most reliable young man, Henry. Persuaded old Dowdswell to sell me a couple of greys for my carriage at thirty pounds the pair. A real bargain, eh? I'm very pleased with Tom: he's a fine ornament to the College.' And the president lumbered off into the Turl, a huge cloak flapping from his broad shoulders.

'I like your president,' said Sarah. 'He could be a very good friend.'

In later life Henry Ireton came to regard these interim years, spent variously in London, Oxford and Nottinghamshire, as his last days of private freedom before Destiny laid its hold upon him. It was at this time that he first affected the carefully trimmed moustache and pointed beard, so fashionable with the court painters, which gave him the air of an aristocrat born to high command. Not that he would have accepted any suggestion that in these matters he was following the fashion of the court or even of the lawyers and men of letters whose London society he now began to enjoy. He was, from his early days, a man of simple tastes and clear mind – a very private person except within the circle of his own family.

And family affairs occupied much of his time. These years included Mary Ireton's marriage to Jack Bainbrigge in the parish church of St Mary – a brilliant occasion supported by the county families of Leicester and Nottingham, with dancing and music in the garden. John Ireton was successfully apprenticed to a cloth merchant in the City of London, and established in rented rooms in Essex Street within easy distance of the Shipleys' house. Matthew would be going to Magdalen College, Oxford, where Henry's friend Francis Thornhaugh was already a student. Tom was determined to be a soldier and seek service with the Swedish army, while Clement and Henry's youngest sister seemed happy to stay with their mother in the small sturdy wood-beamed house beside the church at Attenborough.

As to Edward Ford and Sarah, their romance raced to its fairy-tale conclusion, as if ordained by Heaven. Many further love-letters were exchanged, to the scarcely concealed joy of Hannah Shipley. In the springtime Henry and Sarah rode through the Weald to visit the Fords' Tudor mansion sited in a fold of the hills behind the old Cinque Port of Hastings. There Sarah's youthful charm stilled any religious doubts which, in other circumstances, might have troubled the Ford family.

Her courtship, Henry remembered, led to his first experience of a sea voyage, for Sarah persuaded Edward to organise their return to London on one of the ships of the family's coastal fleet. With Edward in command they had sailed up-channel on a light south-westerly breeze before rounding the North Foreland into the Thames estuary. They had disembarked at Gravesend as foreign dignitaries were wont to do, and taken horse to London. If only later voyages had been equally calm and uneventful!

Later that year, while inspecting some property near Grantham, Edward visited the Iretons in Attenborough and won Jane Ireton's approval to his marriage. Mrs Ireton recognised in him an admirable example of the land-owning, land-loving class to which the Iretons belonged; and she shrewdly appreciated that no liturgical or doctrinal differences would ever keep Sarah from the man of her choice. Married in a City church by an Anglican priest sympathetic to the Old Religion, Edward and Sarah were now living a blissfully happy life in Sussex.

The only disruptive element in the Ireton home proved to be young Martin Dowdswell. At first he seemed happy enough playing around the stables under old Brewster's eye, and endearing himself to Mrs Brewster. But in spite of his quick intelligence he hated the lessons at the rectory. He told the Brewsters, probably with reason, that the rector resented his presence in the schoolroom. Twice he managed to escape from this drudgery, once in the company of Clement Ireton – a misdemeanour for which each boy received a thrashing from Jane Ireton, followed by a three-day bread-and-water diet. That was for lying about their escapade, the one crime for which Mrs Ireton would accept no excuses.

Privately, however, she was convinced that Martin would be unhappy if he remained at Attenborough, and persuaded Henry that the boy needed the discipline and wider companionship of a city school. So it came about that Henry arranged for Martin to be lodged with the Shipleys and attend St Paul's School in London. It was, perhaps, Henry's first diplomatic success. To his relief, the boy showed no desire to return to Oxford, and for the next few years Joe and Hannah found enormous pleasure in caring for him and watching over his progress.

By the age of twelve, Martin had one consuming ambition – to be a soldier. Joe and Hannah always maintained that the lad's enthusiasm for the military life began on the day when they took him for a treat to watch the old Company of Archers performing their complicated drill at Moorfields. Certain it is that on Henry Ireton's next visit to London he was dragged off to the Artillery Garden by young Martin who had already acquired a considerable knowledge of the military art.

There was, of course, no standing army in England – nothing beyond the highly decorative Life Guards of the Sovereign, first established by King James and recently re-equipped by his son. Their scarlet uniforms were often to be seen within the precincts of Whitehall Palace. But the counties each supported their separate volunteer militia units and the City of London took especial pride in its six regiments of train bands. And the Artillery Garden was one of their training grounds.

To Henry's surprise, Martin was able to expatiate on the intricate drill formations practised by these volunteer soldiers: Double distance, twelve foot between rank and file; change to open order, that's arm to outstretched arm, Uncle Harry. And he knew all the postures for pikemen and musketeers. In fact, with Joe's help, he'd made himself a pike of eleven feet – the real thing, Uncle Harry, should be sixteen or seventeen feet, but it's a bit too long for practising pikeman's drill in Joe's house.

He had also pursued his new hobby far beyond the confines of the Honourable Artillery Company's Artillery Garden. In recent weeks he'd bought himself a copy of William Barriffe's *Military Discipline*. Paging through the book, Henry was amused to note that the author included criticism of the London train bands: 'making men file-leaders out of respect of favour the Officers bare unto them', or 'because one man hath a better buff-coat than another'. Here were mistakes which he and Francis Thornhaugh must be careful to avoid when organising the Nottingham militia.

Knowing that Thornhaugh's militia was mounted, Martin urged his guardian to purchase Cruso's *Military Instructions for the Cavalry* with its emphasis not only on discipline but also on the importance of uniform in building up the trooper's confidence in his squadron.

Hour after hour, Henry and Martin discussed different aspects of the *art militaire*, branching out into the theories evolved in the Netherlands Wars, and modified by the Swedish hero Gustavus Adolphus who, to the grief of Protestant Europe, had been killed in 1632 at the battle of Lützen. It was not long before Martin's enthusiasm had infected Henry Ireton.

'One day,' said Henry, 'one day, perhaps, you will have a chance to see service with the great European captains. Maybe, Martin, you will find a place in one of the famous Scottish regiments which the Swedes have praised so highly. But first you must finish your schooling . . .'

'And then you'll let me enrol with the Honourable Artillery Company?' This schoolboy knew all the answers. 'They'll accept me at fourteen, you know. A drill sergeant told me last week that he reckons I'm already big enough to join. Some of these Londoners are very small men.'

There, for the moment, the matter rested. But Henry told his brother John about Martin's ambitions, and John suggested that Martin would need to work in the City if he were to gain entry into the Honourable Artillery Company, which supplied officers to the train band regiments. Henry also realised that it was high time he acquainted Maggie and Sam Dowdswell with Martin's interest in soldiering.

In 1635 this preoccupation with Martin's ambitions and the other moves in the Ireton family were swept from Henry's mind by the appalling punishment imposed on William Prynne, the Lincoln's Inn lawyer who had given such good advice to Edward Ford.

Prynne was known as a wordy and conceited advocate, so opinionated and obsessed with his own cleverness that he had few friends. A somewhat lonely man, he had been using his leisure to write a series of pamphlets on subjects which bore only the vaguest of links with his legal practice. Whenever he put pen to paper in favour of certain principles he passionately held, such as the supremacy of the courts in upholding an Englishman's liberties, his words reflected his courtroom style: ridiculing his opponent's case with language guaranteed to foment a maximum of anger and resentment.

William Prynne was just beginning to enjoy his popularity as a pamphleteer when he launched a scathing attack on the youthful Roman Catholic queen, Henrietta Maria, accusing her of extravagance and frivolity in staging costly masques and plays at court while the king was dunning the City for cash to finance the cost of government.

Retribution was swift. Prynne was summoned before the King's Court of Star Chamber and received a sentence of fearful savagery – a fine of £3,000, the surrender of his Oxford degree, his person to be exposed in the pillory like a common criminal and his ears to be cropped.

The legal world and the City merchants were shocked and furious, and Henry Ireton fully shared this anger. Accompanied by Master Chapman he and many members of the Inns of Court went to view this most pitiful public spectacle – the wretched Prynne with his head and legs imprisoned in the stocks and his ears cruelly mutilated and bleeding, yet still shouting defiance and urging the silent bystanders to read his pamphlet. There was no jeering from the crowd – only pity for a brave man unjustly condemned. An act of royal vengeance, implemented by the king's counsellors, had caused this unloved lawyer to be hailed as a hero by the citizens of London.

Master Chapman rammed home the injustice of the verdict: 'Made, Henry, by a Royal Prerogative Court manipulated by the king's toadies, a court that should have been abolished a century ago, a court that has no standing in our legal system.'

But Henry needed no spur to his anger. In an age of cruel penalties he had seen something more terrible to him than a man's suffering. He had seen wickedness in high places, a confirmation of all that the preachers and lawyers and Members of Parliament had been proclaiming. With his own eyes he had witnessed an act of injustice perpetrated here in the centre of London by men who dared to claim the king's friendship. Such men, be they archbishop or clerk or belted earl, must be removed from the King's counsel. Henry Ireton was filled with the calculated anger of a Cato denouncing the enemies of his country. *Delenda est Carthago.* Such men must be destroyed. For the protection of the king's realm, Englishmen must be alerted to the danger.

Early the following morning the twenty-four-year-old crusader set out from London, completing the sixty-mile ride to Oxford within the day. His speed was a measure of Henry Ireton's resolution.

12

After the punishing ride from London, Henry slept without stirring in his room at the Mitre. But next morning his mind was working overtime as he dressed and descended the stairs for breakfast. The spectacle of Prynne's suffering had jolted him out of his carefree life. It was as if the gross injustice affected him personally. Was this something that he, Henry Ireton, was called to remedy? He could only hope that wise old Ralph Kettel would help him to clear his mind.

At ten o'clock he presented himself at the door of the President's Lodging and asked Simon whether his master could see him during the course of the day. A few minutes later the old servant shuffled back across the hall to confirm that the president would be happy to entertain Henry to dinner provided he could put up with the presence at table of a gentleman-commoner who was already booked to dine with the president.

'A very pleasant gentleman,' old Simon confided, 'name of Edmund Ludlow. He's out of Wiltshire, Sir, and very full of his own opinions, the president tells me. But perhaps that's no bad thing in a young man.'

Henry thanked Simon for his good offices, and after remarking how well he was looking, wandered across to the college stables where he surprised Tom Brewster grooming the president's carriage horses.

Tom straightened himself and gave Henry a delightful smile of welcome. 'My, it's great to see you again, Mr Harry. Straight from London, are you? With good news of Martin? Or are you here to admire the greys? A lovely pair – and no mistake. The president's the finest grandee in Oxford now.' Tom was clearly proud of his purchase from Sam Dowdswell. But he had further cause for pride.

'If you've a moment to spare, Sir, I can show you something more exciting than the president's horses. A baby, Mr Harry. We've got a baby. Maggie's given birth to a lovely little boy.

You must come and see them both. Betsie, what used to be at the Mitre, is over from Osney specially to see her. You remember Betsie? Well, she's got herself married to Sam, and now she's expecting a baby too. Things are very lively these days in Oxford.'

Tom handed the horses to a boy and conducted Henry past the lodge gates towards a small house owned by the college in Holywell. There they found Maggie and Betsie gazing into a little wooden cot at the latest addition to the Brewster family.

Maggie looked up. 'Harry Ireton!' she cried. 'What in the world brings you to Oxford? Don't tell me you've come to see our baby or me or Betsie! Still, now you've come, you'd better take a good look at the little chap.' And Maggie lifted the bundle out of the cot and thrust it into Henry's arms. 'Come now, don't look so serious – he won't bite you.'

She was laughing at his discomfiture, but paused for a moment to enquire about Martin. How tall was he? How was he doing at school? Henry reassured her, as he returned the baby to her care. Yes, Martin was big for his age, in excellent spirits, working hard and well cared for by Joe and Hannah Shipley, though he wouldn't recommend London for a health cure – overcrowded and noisy, the last place you or I would want to live. But he did bring exciting news about Martin. How would the Dowdswells react if Martin decided to become a soldier?

'A soldier?' Maggie's eyes were shining with excitement. 'A soldier? An officer? Why, Sam has always claimed that a Dowdswell fought at Agincourt. What do you say, Harry?'

'You don't need him at Osney?'

Betsie broke into the conversation. Sam's business, she said, was doing well. They would all love to see Martin at Osney, but with all his education it might be better for him to make his own life. And anyway – she looked down at her stomach and laughed – there won't be much room for him in a few weeks' time.

So, in the small house in Holywell, it was agreed that Martin should finish his schooling at St Paul's and then be apprenticed to a City merchant in order to qualify for membership of one of the six train band regiments of London. If, at the age of eighteen, Martin still wanted to be a soldier, Harry or his brother John would help him to join one of the Scots regiments fighting in Germany. If he changed his mind, he would still have a trade at his fingertips.

It was time for Betsie to return home and Tom Brewster showed her to the door. For a moment Harry and Maggie were left alone with the baby.

The girl turned and impulsively clutched his arm. 'I'll tell you something the others don't know. Martin's father came from a line of soldiers: and I gave Martin his father's surname. So, soldiering must be right for Martin too.' She put a finger to her lips. 'It's a secret, remember: just something that only you and I know.'

That same evening Henry Ireton dined with the president. Apart from the presence of Edmund Ludlow, nothing seemed to have changed from his student days. His eyes noted the polished surface of the long table, the college silver reflecting the soft light of the candles, the fine Dutch landscape dimly seen on the wall away from the log fire, old Simon alternately serving at table and then retiring to his post beside the door to the kitchen; and the whole scene dominated by the gangling old man, sitting – almost sprawling – at the head of the table, snapping and waving his hands as accompaniment to his conversation.

The meal had started with a brief introduction to Edmund and a joke about the republican proclivities of the Wiltshire Yeomanry which had brought a blush to the boy's cheeks. But now, with the main course served, fresh fruit on the table, the glasses filled and Simon dismissed, the president turned to Henry.

'Now, tell me Harry, what brings you so fast to Oxford, eh? Not just to admire my horses or the Brewsters' baby, I'll be bound?' The president swallowed a mouthful of capon and toyed with his wine glass as his piercing eyes focussed on Henry. As with all events within the college, the old man seemed very well informed.

'So what is worrying you? Is it the state of your soul? Or the state of the nation? Come, make out a case to me; and let Edmund act as jury.'

Henry was not too sure about the boundary between his

soul and the nation. All too often they seemed to be interlocked. But he answered the president's challenge by recounting the full story of William Prynne's humiliation and horrible punishment. He assured his host it was not simply the nature of the punishment which disgusted him – he had seen enough of stocks and street-whipping and public executions during his years in London. To Henry's mind it was a still greater outrage that this eminent Oxford scholar and lawyer should have been condemned by a Royal Prerogative Court without being allowed to plead his case before a jury and a legally appointed judge. And why? Because he had exercised the Englishman's right to free speech – in Prynne's case to criticise in writing the extravagance of this foolish French queen, a subject which was the talk of every ale-house in London. Henry's voice, normally musical and measured, was rising to an angry crescendo.

The president interrupted him. 'Easy, Harry, go easy. The Court of Star Chamber has been an instrument of royal power for hundreds of years. That earlier and most splendid queen, who ruled England when I was appointed president of this college, often made use of these Prerogative Courts, as did her father and grandfather before her. Why, then, has King Charles' practice become so unacceptable in recent years? That is the question you should set yourself to answer.'

Edmund Ludlow, red-faced and obstinate, was about to intervene with a tirade against the monarchical system when the president restrained him.

'No, Edmund, not now. For the moment, you are the jury and should only speak when you give your verdict, and let me remind you that in this capacity you need to control your prejudices. If you air your republican case in public as loudly as you did in the college gardens last Saturday, you will find yourself facing the same court and the same penalties as poor Mr Prynne. The fact that he is a distinguished Oxford scholar has proved to be no defence, as Henry Ireton has indicated.' Edmund Ludlow relapsed into sulky silence and the president resumed his 'tutorial'.

'Henry has made it clear that this Lincoln's Inn lawyer, Prynne, has been cruelly wronged.' Henry and 'the jury' nodded in agreement. 'But much more is at stake than one man's humiliation. Look at it like this. We are living in a world in which certain acts of government are causing men to question old loyalties. And each man's opinion hinges on his concept of personal freedom.'

The president thrust out his right hand to emphasise his points. 'First' – and he raised his index finger – 'what is to be the relationship between the Church and civil society? That is the question with which William Shakespeare grappled and, like his contemporaries, left unresolved. Do you insist on your own preferred form of Christian observance? Or do you obey the commands of a ruler who is officially Head of the English Church – and in these matters allows himself to be led by a narrow-minded and fanatical archbishop? Secondly' – and he pointed the second finger of his right hand – 'where does power ultimately reside? With the monarch who claims he inherits supreme power by divine right? With the Law which governs our actions now that the Church has been deprived of its political and legal rights in England, if not in Scotland? Or with Parliament as the executive hand which drafts our laws?

'I suspect you will both want to side with Parliament. Most of the young men in this university talk fine language about *vox populi*. But, my friends, to equate the voice of the people with our elected or hereditary Members of Parliament is so much clap-trap – and everybody should know it by the time he leaves this college. Parliament, as it presently exists at Westminster, is the squabbling voice of lawyers and land-owners, whether they come of aristocratic or yeoman stock. Either they represent their private interests or else areas of England that are derelict. They have little contact with the expanding towns where true power increasingly lies. More-over, the members of both Houses are, for the most part, convinced that each of them speaks with as much divine inspiration as His Majesty King Charles – and with much better sense. Unfortunately they cannot even resolve among themselves as to where they should draw the boundary line between the Church and the State. The more I hear of their arguments, the more I want to say to each of them "Sir, thou hast nothing to draw with, and the well is deep".'

The president, clearly delighted with his last sentence, emp-tied his glass, belched with satisfaction and poured himself a brandy. 'Well?' he said, turning to young Ludlow, 'how far would you accept my analysis?'

'I go all the way with you, Sir. But in theory I see no need for a king. As to our present monarch, I would hold that he spends too much of the nation's money on his queen, his court, his palaces, his hunting lodges and his paintings.'

'And you, Henry?'

'I would not go so far as Mr Ludlow, Sir. He used the phrase "in theory". But "in practice" I find that in that part of England which I know best, we honour the kingly office. We regard the monarchy as a treasure we have inherited from our history – something too precious to be destroyed. But no man of spirit will stand idle while his king is so controlled by evil counsellors that he deprives his subjects, without justification, of their freedom as well as their fortune.'

'Not stand idle, you say?' The president repeated. 'Not stand idle? So what will you do? Return to Nottingham or Wiltshire and brood on injustice? Or enter the lists and fight?'

The young men were silent. Ralph Kettel rose from the table. 'Edmund,' he said, 'has two years at Oxford before he comes to a decision. But for you, Harry, the question is more insistent. It demands an answer. Sleep on it tonight, and we'll talk tomorrow in the light of day.'

Henry Ireton was always swift to make decisions. Next morning he was back at the President's Lodgings, his mind made up.

'So you would enter the lists?' The president smiled. 'My friend, I never doubted your choice.' He looked with great affection on the young man pacing the Trinity gardens beside him. The fine features, the athlete's step, the warm heart and the self-reliant ice-cold mind – he had spotted Ireton's qualities of leadership years ago. His judgment had been right.

'Well, let me give you a little presidential advice,' he said. 'First, tell your mother how your mind is moving. And, when you return to London, choose your friends with care. Remember this old man's advice. If the king's advisers are to be removed, action can only come through Parliament. You must, therefore, mix with the people who matter at Westminster: John Pym, by far the most influential voice in the House; John

Hampden whose words and motives all men trust; Hazelrig, the hot-headed Holles, Edward Hyde and a few others. But take your time, Harry. Rome was not built in a day and you need to curb your impatience. Try to remember the words of your riding master: Look before you leap.'

The ungainly old man and his young protégé returned to the president's study. Standing by his desk, Ralph Kettel looked at Henry Ireton as he had once looked at him on the first day of his arrival in Oxford.

He grasped Harry's hand. 'May God be with you,' he said. 'I've never doubted your choice of action. And here's a letter which may help you on your way.'

They said goodbye. As Henry left the room he looked at the inscription. The extraordinary handwriting with its mixture of Greek and Roman characters was crowned with a blot of ink where the quill pen had protested against the powerful hand that held it. But the name of the addressee was clear. The letter was to be delivered personally to Sir Theodore Mayerne at his house in St Martin's Lane, London.

13

Henry Ireton took the slow road back to London.

Sometimes in later life, he wondered what *daemon* in the university city had prompted him to choose the leisurely route that crossed and recrossed the meandering Thames in preference to the more northerly Wickham road that had brought him so swiftly to Oxford.

Why, he asked himself as he ambled along the rough road, had he not first travelled north to speak with his mother as Dr Kettel had suggested? Had he feared to be diverted from his purpose by the peace of his mother's presence? Would he have been beguiled by the siren notes of the birds that inhabited the trees and water meadows behind St Mary's Church? Would he have found it impossible to resist the appeal of the broad acres that were his by right of inheritance?

Or did he, perhaps, need more time for decision? Certainly, he claimed that his thoughts were always most lucid and decisions most easily reached when riding alone in the country. And he was conscious of a strange premonition that the sealed letter he carried in his saddle bag might play some part in influencing his future career.

Or did he simply feel that his first priority lay with Martin? That, having fulfilled his promise to Maggie Dowdswell to educate her son, he should now get clear of his obligation, once and for all, by setting Martin on his path to an independent life?

As Henry rode through the Thames valley towards the capital his mind constantly reverted to Martin and so, by association, to those campaign manuals that Martin had shown him in the Shipleys' house.

At each successive change of horse he found himself judging the lie of the surrounding country in military terms. Oxford, Wallingford, Reading, Windsor – castles and bridges guarding the passage of the Thames, strongholds which had dictated the course of every campaign in middle England since the days of the Roman occupation.

How would the author of the *Art Militaire* read the options open to a commander in the field? Foot soldiers and those ponderous artillery trains drawn by a team of shire horses would move more easily if they avoided the Chiltern hills he'd traversed so swiftly on his post-haste ride to Oxford. Comparatively small garrisons would suffice to defend the Thames crossings. And with well-secured bases, cavalry could easily control the surrounding country or, if required, disrupt the movement of enemy transport. Riding through ideal cavalry country, Henry Ireton experienced a sense of elation.

He put all speculations behind him as he rode through Brentford, past Tyburn and the Holborn Stream, and on to the scriveners' offices by St Andrew's Church where he turned south towards the Shipleys' house near the Strand. He was back now in the real world – the noise and bustle of a great city. And Joe and Hannah were at home to welcome him.

They had news for him too. During his absence John Ireton had spoken to Martin and arranged for his cloth-trade indentures to be completed. And the Shipleys confirmed they would be happy for Martin to continue lodging with them after completing his final year at St Paul's School.

Joe also volunteered to deliver Dr Kettel's letter to Sir Theodore Mayerne. Joe hadn't seen the famous doctor for some time, he told Henry, but he liked to keep in touch with his regulars, especially Sir Theodore: He's got a lovely garden, you know, in St Martin's Lane . . . takes as much pride in his flowers as he does in his experiments . . . always inventing something or other in his back parlour, but the garden's the thing . . . a real picture in early summer . . . you ought to see it, Mr Harry.

A fortnight after Joe delivered the president's letter, Henry received a charming note from Sir Theodore, inviting him to join a gathering at his home, in the garden if weather permitted. Moreover, Henry was also invited to bring any other member of his family who might be in London 'including your school-boy protégé whose name Dr Kettel has mentioned in a recent letter. And don't let the lad be overawed by any grandees who may be present. Assure the young man, with the compliments of your doctor, that rich and poor look much the same, when stripped.' Henry smiled as he perused the letter a second time. This French exile really was a man after his own heart.

Guests were already perambulating in small groups in Sir Theodore's garden as Henry and John Ireton, together with Martin Dowdswell, were ushered through the hall and reception rooms to a terrace at the rear of the house. It was a warm evening with no breeze to disturb the trees or the guests. The newcomers looked down upon a garden which was indeed the picture Joe had foretold: a fig tree by the house, roses in full bloom with their fresh scent pervading the still air, peach trees trained against a south wall, and a knot garden leading to a mulberry tree at the far end. It was a lovely setting for a party in high summer.

The three young men had travelled from the Maypole in the Strand by hackney coach, determined to look their best on this first plunge into London society, and now as they emerged from the house curious eyes were directed towards them. Who were these surprise guests that the doctor was springing upon them?

Certainly their youthful good looks commanded attention as they stood, apparently calm and self-possessed, beside their host, looking down on the colourful scene before them. The trio were unfussily dressed – fine linen collars above dark green or wine-red jerkins with wide sleeves, and dark breeches, hose and buckled shoes. But each was, in his own way, distinctive.

In the centre stood Henry looking extremely handsome with his dark, deep-set eyes, white skin and neatly trimmed beard – surely the sort of young man to find favour at the king's court. His brother was on his right, clean-shaven and rather thick-set by comparison with Henry, but giving the same impression of youthful authority – another Ireton who would not be afraid of leadership. And on his left stood young Martin – still only thirteen years old but tall and strong, and easily distinguished by his red silk jerkin from the green-suited brothers.

Lady Carlisle was the first to spot the new arrivals and broke away from her companion in order to meet Sir Theodore as he descended the steps with his three guests.

'No, dear lady' – the doctor was very firm, knowing her

ladyship's predatory instincts as well as her limitless capacity for intrigue – 'I cannot permit you to take all my new friends under your wing at a single swoop. But let me introduce you to Mr Henry Ireton who is, I assure you, an authority on horse-racing, the state of the Law and the County of Nottingham. You, in turn, may be able to interest him in the paintings recently purchased from Italy by His Majesty. And perhaps, with the aid of Mr Pym, you may enlighten him on the world of politics, as seen from the twin viewpoints of Whitehall and Westminster?'

Sir Theodore smiled to himself as he moved away with John Ireton and Martin – Lady Carlisle was a strange character and the doctor often wondered what had brought her so close to John Pym.

However, he left the younger Ireton in the company of a City alderman and his wife before conducting Martin towards a man who was sitting alone, apparently absorbed in the activities of some musicians who were tuning their instruments in preparation for playing a recent composition by Thomas Tallis.

As Sir Theodore approached him, the solitary figure stood up and revealed himself to be a man of medium height, broad-shouldered, clean-shaven and somewhat carelessly dressed. It was hard to guess his age, for there was a fleck of grey in his hair and his forehead was lined as if he had been through a period of illness or deep mental anxiety. Yet Martin received the immediate impression that he was in the presence of a man of considerable physical strength – a countryman, perhaps, who might be out of sorts with the Society people around him. But a strong man without a doubt – a man in the prime of life whose age must be well short of forty.

'Oliver,' said Sir Theodore, 'I want you to meet this lad from St Paul's School whose guardian is also numbered among my clients. Martin, this is Mr Cromwell from the Isle of Ely and a Member of Parliament for Cambridge. I know you and Mr Ireton have a strong Oxford connection, but I trust you will bear with Mr Cromwell's native loyalties.' A servant was ordered to set wine and cold meat before them, while their host hastened away to attend his other guests.

The Member for Cambridge looked at Martin and began

to chuckle, well aware that the doctor's introductions were rarely made without purpose. He beckoned Martin to a seat and said in a friendly but unmusical voice, 'Thank the good Lord for your presence, young man. You may not know it, but you've rescued me from an evening of boredom which I only endure because of my gratitude to this great doctor who cured me of my Fenland fever. Gave me some Jesuit concoction from Brazil, I believe. But let's get away from illness. It's a subject as boring as Lady Carlisle's silly tittle-tattle about the queen. Come and sit down, Martin. Get started on one of these chicken pasties – I find them excellent. And tell me about yourself and this guardian of yours. What's his name, did you say?'

'Mr Henry Ireton, Sir, from the village of Attenborough near Nottingham. He's a graduate of Trinity College, Oxford, and a member of the Middle Temple.'

Martin looked shyly across the small table at his companion. The boy was conscious of searching grey eyes which lit up the rather heavy features of the man sitting beside him. The eyes were friendly and humorous and full of encouragement. Martin's shyness disappeared. Suddenly, it seemed the easiest thing in the world to tell Mr Cromwell everything he knew about Henry Ireton and his family, and everything he knew about his own family in Oxford. He even sketched in his personal hopes for a military career. Oliver Cromwell was a very good listener.

As Martin told the Ireton brothers when they were recounting their experiences to Joe and Hannah Shipley after their return from the party, he wouldn't mind seeing more of Mr Cromwell. He thought Henry might like him too! For Martin, it had been a memorable evening.

The Ireton brothers also had their stories to tell. John had received a bellyful of aldermanic indiscretions which reflected the City's increasing hostility to the king and his constant demands for money. Somebody – but not, of course, the alderman – must do something about it: ship money was the last straw. According to John Ireton's new City acquaintance, Hampden's refusal to pay ship money was all the more sensational because this big landowner from Buckinghamshire was as rich as Croesus. A matter of principle you see – not an inability to meet the demand. Such a stand had greatly impressed the alderman.

'As a matter of fact,' added Henry, 'Mr Hampden is a cousin of Martin's new-found friend. That's a scrap of information I collected from my big fat companion in a brief interval when he wasn't talking about himself and his latest speech in Parliament.'

Harry had been fascinated by John Pym's views on the powers of Parliament, but even more intrigued by his friendship with Lady Carlisle. 'Talk about Beauty and the Beast,' he said. 'Here was Beauty in the form of a lady, who dances daily attendance on the queen, fawning on this great shaggy commoner as if he possessed divine status. To be fair to Mr Pym, he really seems a formidable character. "The Ox" they call him behind his back. Some time ago, Master Chapman told me that this John Pym would soon become the most powerful voice in Westminster, and after talking with him I can well believe it. If His Majesty wants to govern his kingdom without the help of Parliament, he'll need to muzzle this particular ox or get badly gored. I wonder where Lady Carlisle stands in this matter.'

Next morning the three young men went about their respective business – Henry to Nottinghamshire, John to the Clothworkers' shop in the City and Martin to St Paul's School.

As for Joe, he repeated most of what he'd heard the previous evening to his friends up and down the river, while Hannah told him to curb his tongue and hoped that none of her menfolk would get themselves arrested for saying something indiscreet about the king's household.

When Henry reached home he found his mother serene and untroubled by the affairs of the outside world. She and her garden, the village of Attenborough and its rich farming land seemed a million miles away from the people he'd encountered at the house in St Martin's Lane.

It was clear that in these last few years Jane Ireton had assumed total control of the family estate. The tenant farmers respected her, and nothing but bad weather would upset the even tenor of sowing and harvest and the weaning of the lambs.

While she enjoyed good health it would be ridiculous for Henry to seek to share or reduce his mother's responsibilities.

For the moment, the home he loved could be no more than a temporary place of retreat. The summer days passed quickly enough. Henry visited the old Brewsters and told them of the little grandson he'd held in his arms in Oxford. He argued with the rector on matters theological but agreed with him that the rule of bishops was not a necessary part of the English Reformation. He spent many hours observing the birds that haunted the low-lying fields and trees beside the Erewash Stream. He spotted the regular all-the-year-round residents – childhood friends like the little grebe, the teal, the shoveller and the reed bunting. He noted with satisfaction the summer visitors – little ringed plovers, blackcap, willow warblers and the rest. Once he reported to his mother that he had spotted a yellow wagtail for the first time. And in the evenings he would return to tell Jane Ireton of his activities away from home – his meetings with Dr Kettel and the Dowdswells, of the Shipleys' kindness, of Martin's wish to be a soldier. Again and again, he would revert to the talk of the town which he and John had picked up in Sir Theodore Mayerne's garden.

Mrs Ireton listened to all he had to say with lively interest. Henry was her favourite son and she was sensitive to all his moods and enthusiasms. She was left in no doubt about his increasing concern for the liberty of the citizen and the threat to freedom of speech from the king's Prerogative Courts. Was not this new interest in public affairs the inevitable outcome of the education she had planned and provided for him? How could Henry find fulfilment within the limits of the country gentleman's life which had proved so satisfying to his father?

A wider world was calling. And now that his mind had been alerted by the persuasive voice of John Pym, it was merely a question as to whether he would prefer the local to the national stage.

Perhaps he would find himself a wife and interest himself in the county's affairs – the local militia for example, as Francis Thornhaugh had once suggested. Jane Ireton subtly tried to encourage the idea, only to find that her son's thinking would not allow for 'playing at soldiers'. Henry told his mother that Ireton's Troop of Horse, if it was to be formed, would comprise the best riders and the best horses in Nottinghamshire. Sixty men – officers and troopers – would carry out drill and field manoeuvres as prescribed in Martin Dowdswell's cavalry textbooks. They would be uniformly armed and uniformly dressed – buff coats and dark red breeches which brother John would supply. Promotion would be by merit, and not by birth or possessions. And, most important of all: there would be no theological arguments. The men he commanded would be tolerant men in the Independent tradition which the Ireton family had always upheld. It was a very comprehensive picture which Henry Ireton presented to his mother.

For three more years Henry's life continued to alternate between Nottingham, Oxford and London. Once he brought Martin Dowdswell to Attenborough and travelled to Oxford with him and old Mr and Mrs Brewster to see Tom and Maggie's little boy. Once, at his mother's request, be travelled to Sussex where Sarah had recently lost her first child. On another Oxford visit, he rode out to Osney to meet Sam and Betsie and their first child – also a boy. And always on these Oxford visits he called on old President Kettel.

But his mother noted sadly that Henry showed no inclination to marry, though he was by no means averse to female company. And she was beset by a disturbing sense of foreboding when, in the early summer of 1638, Henry announced that for the next six months it was his intention to lodge with the Shipleys in London.

14

The sun was shining out of a clear blue sky as Henry Ireton dismounted at the post house, north of Cheapside. He settled his account, joking about his dislike of London with the post boy who had ridden beside him over the last ten miles. They were good friends, these two, united by their understanding and care for the horses they rode: and Henry could count on similar friendships along the chain of post houses on the north road to Nottingham and the Wickham route to Oxford. They served to guarantee him the best available horse at the post-master's disposal – a matter of no small importance to a young man who was by nature a fast mover and lived in an age when mobility was best measured by a horse's stamina.

The two-day ride from his home had been uneventful, and Henry had no premonition of trouble as he set off on his short walk to the Shipleys' house. But at St Paul's he found his progress blocked by a great crowd of men and women pressing towards Fleet Street and the Strand. There was no way he could cross to the Temple or Thames-side. The mob was surging forward in an angry, dangerous mood. People were shouting abuse from the house windows of upper storeys overhanging the street. Somewhere, just ahead, could be seen a posse of soldiers moving in single file on each side of a horse-drawn cart – and this cart dragging a man chained by his arms to the tailboard . . . At each beat of a drum a short stock whip hissed across the wretched fellow's back . . . a back raw and bleeding . . .

What in God's name was afoot? Surely, no vagrant being whipped out of the parish by order of the local justices? This was an everyday event in the country – a routine punishment which sometimes provoked pity, sometimes ridicule, but never a crowd of this size.

A bystander enlightened him. 'It's John Lilburne, Sir. 'Onest John, they call 'im in the City. A cloth-worker 'e was, with a taste for writin' . . . Escaped arrest some time back when 'e'd written something our dear archbishop didn't appreciate.' The man spat to express his contempt for the king's chief adviser. 'Yes, they picked up our John when 'e returned from the Low Countries where 'e'd been 'iding to escape arrest. Thought 'is case 'ad all blown over . . . poor devil. Then 'e made matters worse by refusin' to plead before the court . . . demanded a citizens' jury or summ'at. I dunno the rights or wrongs of it, but this crowd don't like it, that's for sure . . . Poor chap. If 'e survives as far as Palace Yard, 'e'll be saluted as a bloody martyr, whether 'e ought to be or not.'

Whipped from the Fleet Prison to Westminster for claiming an Englishman's right to free speech? Here was savagery beyond all justice. The crowd's anger was contagious, but Henry Ireton was already infected. He pressed forward, burning with the same sense of outrage and blind fury that he'd felt at Prynne's sentence three years earlier. But now he needed no presidential advice. If the Star Chamber court imposed this sort of sentence, it must be closed for ever. London – no, all England – would demand it. And if Archbishop Laud was responsible for the decisions of these Prerogative Courts – or maybe the Earl of Strafford, recently returned from Ireland – then they must go too.

As Henry pushed his way forward one would have seen the glint of steel in his eyes, a new determination in the set of his chin. Youth had fled from him – the calm, intellectual features transformed into the face of a fighting man prepared for battle.

Suddenly he spotted Martin Dowdswell in front of the crowd and level with the soldiers. He was heading a band of City apprentices close to the horse-drawn cart, and looking as if he and his fellows might at any moment disrupt the procession. God almighty, the boy would be in real trouble if he was caught leading this City rabble . . . Henry forced his way through the crowd. Just beyond Somerset House, he managed to get a hand on the boy's shoulder . . .

'Steady, Martin,' he said. 'Easy now, take it easy.' He gripped the lad's arm and firmly inched his way to the side of the road. Martin was furious at being pulled away from the action, but his struggles were no match for Henry's strength. As the crowd surged on its way Henry managed to control his temper, speaking very quietly and slowly as if to a man out of his mind.

'I know how you feel,' he said. 'I really do. I'm of the same persuasion. So are many other men you trust . . John Pym, for instance. Yes, and Joe Shipley too. But to win this battle, we have to unite with those who are in a position to force the issue to a conclusion, and *not* join in a street riot which will only turn honest citizens into enemies.'

Not for a moment did Henry relax his grip on Martin's arm. The crowd swarmed past them, heading for the pillory at Westminster, and at last Henry was free to propel his man toward the Shipleys' house.

But there was to be a further diversion before they reached home. As Henry and Martin drew level with the main entrance to Somerset House, Lady Carlisle emerged, accompanied by a younger girl. Both of them were apparently intent on visiting the new fashion shops in the Strand. The older woman recognised the young men immediately.

'Why, if it isn't Mr Ireton?' she cried, nudging her companion. 'And where, Sir, have you been hiding these last few years? I thought we came to an understanding in Sir Theodore's garden that I would arrange for you to view the royal pictures and Sir Peter Paul Rubens' painted ceiling in the Banqueting House of the palace. Don't tell me, pray, that you have forgotten our conversation? Have you, perhaps, abandoned your legal career in favour of country life? Or do you find a new attraction in these rabble-rousers who seem to be gaining so many new adherents?'

Lucy Carlisle was enjoying her little moment and the girl at her side was not attempting to conceal her amusement at Henry Ireton's embarrassment.

But the latter, still gripping Martin firmly by the arm, would not allow the lady to have it all her own way: Of course, Madam he remembered the evening in St Martin's Lane as if it were yesterday . . . a most pleasurable occasion . . . and her Ladyship was in the company of Mr John Pym, was she not?

A woman dependent on the queen's favour does not like to have her name publicly coupled with the king's most dangerous enemy, even though she enjoys dabbling in politics. And it was Lucy Carlisle who was blushing now, as Henry blandly continued his apologies.

Serious concern about his family property, he assured Lady Carlisle, had detained him in Nottinghamshire, hence his regrettable failure to respond to her gracious invitation. Now he had come to London to ensure that his ward was keeping good company while apprenticed to a City cloth merchant – did Lady Carlisle notice a twinkle in Mr Ireton's eye? But he continued with a formal introduction – 'the Countess of Carlisle: Mr Martin Dowdswell'. Lady Carlisle might recall that Mr Ireton's ward was also present at Sir Theodore's reception. Perhaps he also might be permitted to accompany her Ladyship to see the royal pictures? 'Martin,' he added, 'is lodged by Temple Stairs with Sir Theodore's friends, Mr and Mrs Shipley – that is the house, Milady, where I also live when visiting the capital. It is but a few steps from Somerset House.'

The two young men and the two ladies from the queen's court parted on the best of terms: it could be agreed that honours were even. Two days later Lady Carlisle obtained a royal pass to permit her party of four to visit the galleries in the palaces of St James and Whitehall. The card of invitation, delivered to the Shipley's house, set out the names of those invited, from which it was learnt that Lady Carlisle would be accompanied by Miss Susanna Martin.

The royal pictures were indeed magnificent. On their way to St James', Lady Carlisle explained that the Surveyor of the King's Pictures would be conducting their party round the galleries. This Mr van der Doort was more knowledgeable about the pictures than anybody in the palace, save the king himself. But he was very sensitive about his command of the English language and they must be careful not to laugh at his Dutch accent nor show surprise if he lapsed into German or Italian, as he often did. Evidently he was a man of moods and strange affectations.

They found the little Dutchman duly waiting for them at the Tiltyard outside St James' Palace, and he led them at once to the gallery, apologising all the time for the overcrowding of the pictures. 'Diss galleria iss moch too foll,' he told them.

'*Troppo . . . troppo*, ever since Lanier bought Duke of Mantua's collection. *E molto Intendenti di Pittori* – dees fine Mounsier, but it voss baad to send by ship from Italy. Much damage . . . I tell king vee can never make good. *Ach*, it voss foolish. But now I show dee perfect ones, *hein?*'

He made them pause for some minutes before Titian's *Ecce Homo* and stopped them again to admire Van Dyck's great painting of King Charles riding through a triumphal arch. 'Not all great painters clever,' Mr van der Doort informed his listeners, 'but my countryman, Sir Anthony, ees vaary clever man. 'E imitate Titian and so make king look like great emperor *non e vero?* King vaary pleased.'

A scarcely concealed cynical smile crossed Mr van der Doort's face as the party left St James and were led by him across the Holbein gate over King Street, and so to the long gallery in the Palace of Whitehall.

Here they were confronted with a profusion of marvellous religious paintings: Correggio's *Holy Family*, Veronese's *Finding of Moses*, *John the Baptist* by Leonardo da Vinci, Mantegna's *Death of the Virgin* and Raphael's exquisite *La Perla*. The effect was overwhelming. Such a collection had never before been assembled in any European capital.

Mr van der Doort seemed almost overwhelmed by the extent of his responsibilities. 'You make second visit?' he enquired. 'Then I show you *Dutch Boy* by Holbein and Bruegel's *Three Soldiers*. Self-portraits, too, by Rembrandt and Rubens – all, you note, all from Low Countries – all great paintings from my own land. But 'Ees Majesty 'as *gusto* – taste, you say – only for dee Italians – grander, bigger. *Capito?*'

'One day Meester Inigo Jones will persuade king to send more paintings to Greenwich, Hampton Court, Oatlands and Windsor – so many, many palaces . . . all for one man.'

The little man rambled on, talking to himself as much as to his hearers. But suddenly his critical mood changed, as he announced, 'And now, ladies gentlemen, take quick look at great masterpiece ordered by king.'

They were approaching the entry to Inigo Jones' Banqueting House, and with a fine sense of theatre the Surveyor of the King's Pictures put a finger to his lips. 'Not a sound, plees . . . silence is commanded . . . king and queen at meal. But look up, plees, to ceiling.' And there, dwarfing the two small figures at the table in the centre of the hall, the visitors beheld the splendour of Sir Peter Paul Rubens' masterpiece – the apotheosis of James I surrounded by a fantastic allegory depicting the triumph of Wisdom and Plenty. The contrast between the artist's heavenly conception and the earthbound mortals at the dining table was inescapable.

Only a momentary sight of the Rubens' ceiling was permitted to the visitors before Mr van der Doort hurried them away to a private palace exit opening on to the riverside. There they left him, a strange lonely little man over-absorbed in his own responsibilities. Henry Ireton conducted his little party to Westminster Steps where the faithful Joe Shipley was waiting for them.

Lady Carlisle and Susanna were taken by surprise – were they not returning to Somerset House? Henry reassured them. 'But at once, Milady. Only I decided that a river journey might be more comfortable for the ladies than the jolting of a carriage.'

In a subtle way Henry had regained the initiative. As Joe Shipley made fast his boat against the queen's private landing steps at Somerset House, it was apparent that Lady Carlisle had greatly enjoyed her morning's expedition. For her it had provided a welcome diversion from the boredom of court routine, and already plans for seeing more of Mr Ireton were forming in her active mind. But Joe also noted that the younger lady thanked Martin most gracefully as he helped her out of the boat. Later, Hannah Shipley was informed by her husband that he wouldn't be greatly surprised if Martin saw more of the younger lady in the days ahead – about the same age, he reckoned, and uncommon pretty.

As for the ladies' escorts, each was, it seemed, absorbed in his own thoughts.

Martin had been deeply impressed by the luxury of the king's residence – splendour on a scale beyond his imagining. But crossing King Street he had also seen the pillory, now empty, where honest John Lilburne had suffered the public humiliation decreed by the Court of Star Chamber. Martin had already heard from his fellow apprentices of the man's incredible courage which had made him the hero of the London crowd. It was said in the King Street ale-houses that the buildings still echoed with Lilburne's denuciation of the king and his ministers. Somewhere in Martin's mind was a puzzle where the pieces did not fit – two 'opposites' that could not be reconciled. But why worry himself with such insoluble contradictions? He was young and handsome, and his most enduring memory of the day was the charming figure of Lady Carlisle's companion. Somehow and somewhere, he meant to meet her again.

Henry Ireton, however, was concerned with more mundane thoughts. How, he kept asking himself, could the king afford to spend so much money on these Dutch and Italian pictures at the same time that he was demanding that the City defray the cost of a silly war with Scotland – a war provoked by Archbishop Laud's attempt to impose the Rule of Bishops on the Presbyterian Church of Scotland? How could wise men be so foolish? Was it not time that the City and Parliament combined to say 'No' to the king?

While Henry was increasingly concerned with the political and religious problems of the nation, he could not exclude a nagging question from his mind. Who was this Miss Susanna Martin who had accompanied Lady Carlisle on the morning's expedition to view the king's collection? Somewhere, he knew, he'd heard the surname before ... and now the memory came back to him ... Surely it was the surname Maggie had whispered to him when he had visited the Brewsters' little house in Oxford? It was not an uncommon name, but was it possible that Martin had spent the morning in the company of a blood relation – perhaps his half-sister? Perish the thought if the lad was going to grow fond of her. Meanwhile he could only hope that Martin would spend his leisure hours with the train bands to whose command the City had just appointed the renowned old Norfolk soldier, Philip Skippon. That, at least, should help the lad to avoid the company of the dangerous Lucy Carlisle and her charming attendant.

At dinner that night neither Henry Ireton nor Martin Dowdswell disclosed his private thoughts. They were content to tell Joe and Hannah of the glorious pictures they had seen and of the splendour of the Banqueting House.

'So you saw the Banqueting House and Rubens' painting?'
Joe asked.

'Ach, Meister Shipley,' Martin replied in a passable imitation of the Surveyor of the King's Pictures. '*Si, si*, Meister Shipley, vee see great masterpiece. It voss *magnifico* . . . But Meister Ireton and I know something *di novo* – how you say, fresh from horse mouth? Our king iss truly vaary small man – much smaller, *capito*, than he shows in Sir Antony's *pittori*. Dat iss vork of vaary clever Dutchman, *hein*?'

15

Henry was glad to be back with his mother in the family home at Attenborough. He disliked London, and he'd heard and seen enough during his stay with the Shipleys to assure himself that the conflict between the king's Privy Council and John Pym's Parliament must come to a head very soon.

Being the man he was, he knew exactly where he stood and where the Ireton family ought to stand. They would, of course, remain loyal both to the Reformed religion and to the monarchy. The family had served the King of England over many generations – had not an Ireton fought with distinction at Agincourt? But how long could these two loyalties continue in twin harness? That was the fearful doubt he discussed at length with Jane Ireton and the rector.

His personal faith was straightforward and honest. Like his family, he was an Independent – his Christian belief based on bible truth, but ready to let other men worship God according to their own lights, provided only that their first allegiance was to England and not to some foreign power beyond the seas. Neither he nor his mother nor the rector of St Mary's would accept for one second the near-Roman rituals of Archbishop Laud. As a trained lawyer he would implacably oppose the archbishop's plans to revive the jurisdiction of the ecclesiastical courts. It followed, inevitably in his view, that Laud must cease to advise the king. He must go. So too must Laud's devoted friend, the Earl of Strafford, recently summoned back from Ireland to solve the royal problems with Parliament. Clearly the king must find new advisers in closer sympathy with the people of England and the people's representatives in Parliament. In short, King Charles had to be rescued from his friends, and perhaps from the sinister Medici influence of his French queen and her Papist entourage.

He'd heard enough from Mr Pym and Lady Carlisle – not to mention his friends in the Middle Temple – to know that Parliament, which represented the people of England, was determined to be predominant in government. It was equally clear that the Laudian Church must submit to a new Reformation if it was to be acceptable to the people. So far, so good.

But every intelligence from the capital suggested that His Majesty would refuse to accept these two conditions. Indeed, the king had recently returned from a war in Scotland undertaken with the sole purpose of foisting Laud's prayer book and the Rule of Bishops on the fiercely Presbyterian Scots. Could one imagine a greater folly? Especially when war was waged so ineptly that Leslie's Scotsmen had swept aside the rag-tag army of the king as if it were chaff – and occupied Newcastle and the border for good measure! It was even reported that men in the City of London rejoiced in the victory of Scotland over England. But this, too, was folly in Henry Ireton's view. What England and the king needed was not a bogus accommodation with Scotland, but a new and efficient government backed by the people of England.

Henry's personal opinions, discussed so earnestly with Jane Ireton, were soon to be reinforced by his brother John, who was now beginning to make his way in the City. In John's view, civil war might not be far away. Within a year the City was likely to elect a lord mayor and Common Council loyal to Parliament. The way ahead looked increasingly clear and increasingly dangerous. This very day Henry had heard in Nottingham that John Pym had ordered Lord Holland to seize Hull for Parliament – and with it the military stores assembled for the Scots war. Was Parliament itself on the warpath?

Events began to move with incredible speed. By the end of 1640 Laud was confined to the Tower. Within a few months Strafford was executed after a farcical trial. What worried Henry was not so much the illegality of the trial and the subsequent Act of Attainder, as the failure of the king to protect his greatest servant from Pym's vengeance. Young Martin, who had joined the City apprentices screaming outside Westminster Hall for Strafford's death, had later seen the tall, black-bearded, bowed figure of the great earl walking to his execution, murmuring the words of the Psalmist: 'Put not your trust in princes, nor in any son of man.' That was a terrible indictment of the king.

Could such a man be trusted to work within the constitutional limits defined by John Pym in his so-called Grand Remonstrance – copies of which were now circulating in Nottingham and the other great cities of England?

Jane Ireton listened to her son's growing fears. And when he sought to amuse her with memories of his visit some years back to the king's pictures, she put her own interpretation on the story. You cannot inflate a man above his real size, even though he be the annointed King of England. Those great canvases by Van Dyck might marvellously portray the long thin features of the king with the prominent eyes under the heavy lids. To the charitable, the eyes might suggest gentleness and charm – or even the longing of a boy who had never quite grown up. Others, more critical, might see in those same eyes the fire of a fanatic priest. But the little Dutchman had surely dug deeper into the truth with his double-edged words: 'Our king iss truly vaary small man.'

The rapport between mother and son continued to grow through the shortening November days of 1641 – those dull days in the farming calendar when fences are repaired and hedges trimmed and Englishmen find time for hunting.

But suddenly, the peaceful farmlands of Nottinghamshire were startled out of their yeoman complacency by terrible news from Ireland. In Ulster, settlers and their wives and children had been brutally massacred by the Catholic Irish. Fifty thousand murdered, one hundred thousand, half a million – who could say? Protestant England – over the whole spectrum of its variegated shades of religious loyalties – was united by anger. Many citizens who had invested in the new Irish settlements would lose their money as well as their sons and daughters. All would be speculating whether the king, returning from another visit to Scotland, would use the crisis to raise an avenging army. And – worst fear of all – would such a force be used to quell the Irish Rebellion or be turned against the Commons of England?

Great issues were at stake. Henry Ireton rode over to his friend and neighbour, Francis Thornhaugh, to make doubly sure that their well-drilled, well-uniformed troopers were ready for action – in whose service neither man could yet decide.

* * *

At nineteen years of age young Martin Dowdswell felt little concern for the great issues that troubled the mind of his guardian in Nottinghamshire. The schoolboy had grown into a strongly built youth, with broad shoulders, a spring in his step and a twinkle in his eyes which suggested that he was unlikely to take the problems of life too seriously.

In fact, he was increasingly bored by the political excesses of his fellow apprentices, though he enjoyed their company at work and during their *sub rosa* visits to the Black Eagle in Bride Lane where they told the most irreverent jokes about the pomposity of their masters. On the other hand he had discovered two new and distinct interests of his own in the persons of the soldier, Colonel Philip Skippon and the girl, Susanna Martin.

He never tired of singing the former's praises. The Earl of Essex might hold command of all the train bands south of Trent, but in Martin's eyes Colonel Skippon was the man who mattered.

'He's changed everything up at the Artillery Garden,' he told Joe Shipley proudly. 'He knows each of us personally, expects us to be as swift as the Swedes at priming the musket, and as well-practised in the postures of pike as the Dutchmen he's been commanding in the Low Countries.

'But that's only the half of it,' he added. 'Drill? Uniform? Why, he says we carry the standards of the old Guild of Archers and Handgunmen. And as such he means us to drill better than the Royal Guards in Whitehall and look equally smart in our uniform. I reckon that Henry will love the colonel, Joe – a man's man, Norfolk-bred, speaks his mind plainly and, although he doesn't boast much book-learning, you can't catch him out on the Bible – which, he says, is the best companion a man can have.'

The boy's hero-worship was infectious, and Joe and Hannah clapped their hands when Martin paraded before them in his all-scarlet tunic, breeches and hose – surmounted by his pot-helmet and ostrich plume – the whole effect set off by white linen collar and cuffs. 'See what I mean?' he said to the Shipleys. 'Real soldiers, eh? And ready to take command and fight if the call comes. The colonel spoke to me specially the other day. I might be posted, he says, as an officer to one of the London regiments – could be the one which covers London west of the Fleet River. So you see, dear Hannah, I might be called to defend your honour.'

Martin drew his sword and lunged at an imaginary opponent on the other side of the room. 'Madam,' he said, 'the villain is dead – stone dead.'

Hannah, half-serious and half-laughing, told him not to talk so big, sheath his murderous weapon and take off his uniform before she had to launder his white cuffs. But behind her light-hearted reply she realised with something of a shock that the boy she'd cared for through his schooldays was a boy no longer.

She was, perhaps, the more flattered when he invited the Shipleys to attend a forthcoming parade at which the lord mayor would be presenting new colours. Nor was she greatly surprised when he asked if Miss Susanna Martin might be permitted to join them.

His acquaintance with the girl had started with that first visit to the royal pictures, and taken a step forward when he had received a further invitation from Somerset House to accompany Lady Carlisle and Miss Martin on a second tour of the galleries.

On this occasion there were no new jokes at the expense of Mr van der Doort, for the poor man had recently taken his own life. Lady Carlisle said, somewhat heartlessly, that this sort of thing could often happen when a man took his responsibilities too seriously. But Martin and Susanna were both angry at her tone of voice. They'd liked the little man and his theatrical asides, and were very sad that he was no longer there to guide them. However his successor, Jan van Belcamp, conducted them most efficiently through the pictures by Dutch and German masters which Martin and Susanna found much more pleasing than the big Italian canvases seen on the previous visit.

'Marvellous paintings,' Martin told the Shipleys, 'some of them would look fine on your parlour walls – *A Boy Looking through a Casement Window*, self-portraits by Rembrandt, Rubens, Dürer and Holbein – Susanna said she could feel them stepping out of the pictures. And then there was Bruegel's picture of *The Three Soldiers* and *A Bass Viol Player* by Terbrugghen – all of them truly memorable. Afterwards we fell to wondering whether the king and queen might not prefer Titian's *Jupiter and Antiope* for their bedroom – they are making love, you see. And Susanna laughed and said it was strange to think how clever Their Majesties were at choosing pictures and how silly at choosing people. Odd, wasn't it? But Susanna has no use for those drunken sots who swagger around the court, scraping and bowing before the queen and then laughing behind her back.'

Joe looked up sharply and said in a slow, firm voice, 'Stop that talk, lad. If you've learnt anything at school, you'll tell Miss Susanna to keep her thoughts to herself. Watermen learnt long ago to be as wise as owls – the more we hear, the less we speak. These are dangerous times, Martin, with spies where you least expect them. You keep the wisdom of the owls in mind, or you'll find yourself in trouble.'

Martin took the point, but Susanna continued to tell him of Lady Carlisle's indiscretions. One Saturday, on a day of late October sunshine, the pair took the boat to Greenwich. After eating at a riverside inn they were walking on the high ground of the park which looks down towards the royal palace when Susanna returned to the subject of Lady Carlisle. 'I can't understand her, Martin. She attends the queen and jokes happily enough with Wilmot and Jermyn and their friends, as if to the manner born. But all the time she is listening to the palace tittle-tattle with hostile ears.'

Martin laughed. 'You mean with Pym's ears?'

'That's not what I said.' The girl blushed. 'But Lady Carlisle *did* make a strange remark about you the other day.'

'And what exactly was that?'

'Well, it was really a question – but rather complimentary,' Susanna conceded, squeezing Martin's hand. 'Lady Carlisle asked how far I could trust the young man introduced to her by Mr Ireton.'

'The Devil she did. And how did you reply?'

'I told her that Mr Martin Dowdswell and Mr Ireton would both be true to their word at any time of the day or night – which is more than I'd say for the courtiers and foreign priests who surround the queen.

'Lady Carlisle looked at me very hard and asked me to

confirm that you were still lodging with Joe Shipley – that trusty old waterman, she called him, who lives hard by Somerset House. She seemed to be hinting she might need you to act as a messenger. It may have been another of her little plots, so I told her again that I would trust you to do anything I asked but' – and here the girl looked up boldly into Martin's eyes – 'but I thought you'd expect to know the nature of any message you were asked to carry.'

'Quite right . . . a very good answer to Lady Carlisle and exactly what Henry Ireton or Philip Skippon would have said in your place.'

Here was praise indeed – and Susanna knew it.

They turned easily enough to inconsequential talk about the Christmas holiday which Susanna would be spending at her family home in North Cray – only a short ride into Kent from Greenwich, you know. Perhaps Martin would pay them a visit in the spring – it was good to get away from stuffy old London and Susanna was sure that Martin would like her father.

After Christmas Susanna returned to Somerset House for the queen's great masque on New Year's Eve. On the second day of the New Year she came hotfoot to the Shipleys' house: She had a message for Martin, she told Hannah . . . must see him this very day . . . yes, before nightfall. Still at work? Well, let him come to the glove shop in the Strand . . . she'd be there at five o'clock . . . No, there was nothing more that Hannah could do . . . But if Martin asked questions, she should tell him to remember Greenwich . . . Those were the words she should use – remember Greenwich. Thanking her, Susanna hurried away unnoticed.

When Hannah greeted Martin on his return from work the effect of her words was immediate. He was out of the house within seconds of entering it. He actually reached the shop ahead of Susanna and was examining a pair of French gloves when she arrived.

'Let the lady try these,' he told the attendant. 'If they please her, I will buy them.' A few minutes later they were out of the shop and into the dimly lit street – with Susanna in proud possession of a new pair of gloves. The two young people of fashion turned conspirator.

'Thank God, you've come,' Susanna whispered. 'Now here's the message, Martin – there's not a moment to lose, for I must return to her Ladyship without delay. But tomorrow, you go to John Pym's lodgings in Westminster, you understand? Find him and tell him, with Lucy Carlisle's compliments, that he should be absent from the Commons on the fourth of January. He is to pass this same message to Hampden, Hazelrig, Holles and Strode . . . Got it? It doesn't matter what business is in progress in St Stephen's Chapel – he and his friends are to be out of it – and out of sight, too, if they value their lives.

'One other thing. Ask Joe Shipley if he and one of his mates can be at Westminster Stairs from eight o'clock onwards on January fourth. They might pick up a fare or two – you never can tell. And if you happen to be around, you could perhaps steer the fares Joe's way.

'Quite clear, Martin? I don't like Lady Carlisle's way of doing things any more than you do; but I think she has reason to fear for Mr Pym's safety. We'll meet again soon. But now, please let me make my own way back to Somerset House.' And off Susanna went into the night, waving her gloved hand in farewell.

The following day, by order of the king, the attorney-general preferred a charge of treason against the five members named by Lady Carlisle. Simultaneously, Martin found Pym at his Westminster lodgings and gave him Lucy Carlisle's message. Pym graciously thanked the young man for his early warning, which evidently confirmed previous messages from his spies in the City. He and Mr Hampden, he solemnly assured Martin, might well have a little business to transact in the City on the following day, and on these visits he preferred to make the journey by water. So . . . The leader of the Commons paused dramatically, and Martin thought he looked older and heavier than the man he'd seen at Sir Theodore's party, though the bright eyes under the shaggy eyebrows still radiated a lively feeling of strength and dominating driving power. And so . . . would Martin convey his gratitude to the friend who had instigated this message? Then with a broad smile, he turned to Martin. 'And thank you too, Mr Dowdswell, for your service. My old legs don't move as fast as yours these days so I'm doubly grateful for this early notice. But my eyes are good and I pride myself I never forget a face. I do not doubt but we'll meet again.'

On the fateful morning of fourth January 1642 Martin was present at Westminster pier to hold Joe Shipley's boat steady while Mr Pym lowered himself ponderously into the thwarts, assisted by his young colleague, John Hampden. A second waterman took the remaining three members on board. Together the two boats headed for midstream and moved on the tide towards the comparative safety of the City.

The operation was timed to perfection. That same afternoon the king travelled in his carriage to the House of Commons, accompanied by four hundred armed men, only to find that the five members he had come to arrest were no longer present.

Never had a King of England appeared so foolish. Not only did his appearance in the House call forth a polite rebuff from Mr Speaker Lenthall but, worse still, the high dignity on which Charles' conception of kingship depended was shattered in the eyes of the people's representatives.

Neither Martin nor Joe Shipley found any joy in the king's humiliation. They were sure that his action had stemmed from stupid advice wished on him by the queen and her French entourage – a view which seemed to be confirmed when, some six weeks later, the queen sailed from Dover for the continent and the king headed north. Rumours streamed out of Somerset House: Off to Holland with all the Crown jewels. Just in time to avoid a charge of treason against the State. And no one to mourn her going save the king and her two older sons.

Some of these rumours reached Henry Ireton and Francis Thornhaugh as they rode south towards the capital, charged to present a petition on behalf of the people of Nottingham against a villainous act of local land seizure. They found their progress to London impeded by the gigantic retinue conducting the king to Newmarket and the north. Courtiers, ushers, sergeants-at-arms, gentlemen-waiters, sumptermen, bottlemen, coachmen, the waymaker, the knight marshal – not to mention the young Prince of Wales, his brother the Duke of York and the king's German nephews, Rupert and Maurice – all contributed to halt the movement of other road-users, whether they were of noble birth or beggars. The King of England still held right of way, and the young men from Nottingham rode cross-country until they were clear of the royal progress.

Neither Ireton nor Thornhaugh was the type of man to accept delay. They, too, had work to do – with the House of Commons, not the king.

16

John Pym had made no secret of his City connections, nor yet of his house in Coleman Street. Nevertheless, the five members who had avoided royal arrest remained discreetly hidden until they were assured that the king had left Whitehall and was escorting his queen and younger child to Dover en route for France.

It was only then that Pym and his companions returned in triumph to Westminster, accompanied by a flotilla of watermen with Joe Shipley at their head and the cheers of London's citizens ringing in their ears. It was a public acknowledgment of the dominance achieved by Parliament over the Royal Council during the past year.

The capital was *en fête*, believing that some great prize had been won on its behalf, though unable to define the reason for joy or the possible consequences of Parliament's victory. It was also a splendid excuse for the City apprentices to claim a holiday, but Martin Dowdswell was not to be found among the cheering crowds.

His part in the action had ended most abruptly some days before the members' return to Westminster, with the arrival of a very angry John Ireton at the Shipleys' house. What on earth did young Martin think he was doing, carrying 'secret' messages from Somerset House to Mr Pym? Secret? Why, nothing could have been more public. According to John's friends in the City, Martin had been seen at the door of Pym's house in Westminster. He'd been seen again close to the House of Commons when the five members were making their escape downriver. The cloth merchant to whom Martin was apprenticed had put in a complaint about his absence from work. Colonel Skippon had no time for politicos in the men he commanded. As for Henry . . . well, John was not his brother's keeper, but he recommended Martin, if he had any regard for his guardian, to get out of London at top speed before the king's men caught up with him. John Pym might have won great parliamentary successes in the past year with the abolition of the Court of Star Chamber and the winning of pardon and compensation for Prynne and Lilburne, but he wasn't King of England, was he?

When Martin protested that he'd acted in good faith as a messenger for Lady Carlisle, John Ireton replied with a sneer that nobody in their senses would trust that particular lady or get involved in her foolish plots.

'I'm giving you the City's views, Martin, as simply as I can. Yes, I know you are your own man now, and I'll do my best to keep your job open, but . . .'

'But, but, but . . .' Martin's anger exploded as Henry's brother left the house. 'I don't want your help and I've no use for your fat friends in the City. Just leave me to go my own way.'

The boy slammed the door and slumped into a chair in the parlour with Hannah Shipley tut-tutting round the room.

'Now, now, Martin,' she said. 'Don't you get fussed about Mr John Ireton. He means well, but I guess he's got his own fish to fry. We'll talk things over with Joe when he comes home for supper. He knows a thing or two, does our Joe. At any rate, he'll surely agree you were right not to mention Miss Susanna. That's your affair – not John Ireton's.'

That same evening Joe gave his weighty consideration to the problem. 'Let's take it step by step,' he said, puffing at his clay pipe. 'Point one, Mr John Ireton means to get to the top as fast as he can – nothing less than lord mayor for him, I'd say. Clever . . . hard-working . . . but very ambitious for himself. Quite different from our Harry. *Ergo*, he don't want to be associated with this young stripling, Martin Dowdswell, who gets involved with Lady C.

'Second point. Mr John Ireton keeps his ear to the ground . . . knows Mr Pym isn't everybody's friend . . . expects His Majesty to make things difficult for any poor chap who may have played a part in forcing the queen to flee for refuge in France.

'Third point. Mr John Ireton has a genuine respect for his elder brother – something he shares with you and me, Martin. That's a point we must also bear in mind.

'So where do we go from here?' Old bearded Joe looked as

wise as Solomon, sitting at ease by the fireplace. He paused and carefully cleared the ash from his pipe. Then he looked at the boy sitting opposite. 'I'll tell you what I'd do in your place, Martin. Hop it. Disappear quietly, see? And when you come back, you forget the cloth trade and seek a job with Colonel Skippon.'

'But, Joe, where do I go?'

'Well, lad, what about a fourteen-day visit to your mother in Oxford? I reckon she'd love to see you again. And so would your grandad and his new wife. You like the idea? Right. I'll have a word with some packhorse men I know who travel the Oxford road – good companions, all of them. I reckon you can do with a change of air, and you can leave me to tell Harry all about it when he next comes to London.'

Four days later, as the sun was setting over the spires and towers of Oxford, Maggie Brewster held out her arms to welcome her handsome son at the door of the little home in Holywell.

'My darling boy,' she cried, 'it's lovely to see you. But how you've grown.' The fact that her rounded figure showed she was carrying a child seemed to increase Martin's stature as he leant down to kiss her. But nobody could have mistaken the pride in the mother's eyes as she stood back and looked him up and down before hugging him again. Here was the son of her first love, her soldier son, her yeoman son, the Dowdswell heir. Excited words tumbled over each other.

'And what brings you to Oxford, Martin? How goes your work in the big city? And how are the Shipleys? We've not seen you since Harry told us you wanted to be a soldier. And that was every bit of three years ago, wasn't it? So what's new?'

There were so many questions to be asked and answered. But Martin assured his mother that the news from London must wait until he'd been introduced to his small brother, and for the next hour Maggie and Martin played upstairs with little Tom Brewster.

The sturdy six-year-old had just been tucked up in bed

when his father returned from Trinity with a worried look on his face.

'The old man's not well,' he called out to his wife. 'Simon's real worried. Thinks he may need help, lifting him . . . may want me to sleep over there, just in case . . .' Then he caught sight of Martin coming down the stairs and, for the moment, dropped the subject of the president's health. Soon they were enjoying supper together and Martin was bringing them up to date with events in London – the king's abortive attempt to arrest the five Members of the House of Commons; their escape to the City and triumphant return to Westminster; the king's departure from Whitehall and the queen's voyage to safety in France; and finally, John Ireton's anger over his own involvement in the affair. But how, they wanted to know, was Martin concerned with the great John Pym?

'It was through a girl, you see, who persuaded me to convey to Mr Pym an early warning of the king's intention.'

'And who is this girl?'

'Oh, her name's Susanna, if you really want to know, Mother. . . Attends the queen's court at Somerset House . . . met her by chance with Harry Ireton . . . she's fair-haired, blue-eyed: I think you'd both like her . . . we see each other as often as we can . . . wants me to meet her father who owns a stretch of land in North Kent, the Cray valley or some name like that . . .'

'And the girl's surname, Martin?'

There was an abrupt urgency in Maggie's question which did not escape Tom Brewster's notice.

'Her surname? Oddly enough, it's the same as my Christian name. A pair of Martins, we often laugh about it.'

Martin looked up and stopped in embarrassment. Was his mother going into labour? She was gripping the table as if for support. Her knuckles were white and there was a desperate look on her face.

Somehow she managed to regain control. No, she said, it was nothing. She thought she'd heard movement upstairs. She'd better see that little Tom was in bed and asleep. Perhaps, while she was settling the child, Tom would consider where Martin could best be lodged since there was no room in the Holywell cottage.

The two men settled for a room over the Trinity College stables, which was kept available for the grooms. Tom conducted Martin to the college before returning to his distraught wife in their Holywell cottage.

He found Maggie lying on their bed upstairs, crying her heart out. 'Tom, love, I'm so worried. That girl Susanna must be Martin's half-sister. I'm sure of it. What are we to do ? It would be wicked to keep him ignorant. Someone must tell him, but who? Tom, tell me what to do. It's Martin's future I'm thinking of.'

Tom looked down at his wife. There was a sort of instinctive sympathy about him. Perhaps he understood the hurt in Maggie's eyes as he understood pain or fear in animals. He suddenly recalled that day, so many moons ago it seemed, when he had comforted a tearful Maggie in the stables of the Mason's Arms at South Leigh.

As then, so now. He said little, but he wiped away her tears, quietly helped her out of her dress and snuffed the guttering candle. He lay on the bed beside her, his arms around her body, her head resting on his chest: Sleep on the problem – that would be the best course, Maggie; sleep on it. Tomorrow, they'd decide how best to tell Martin. Meanwhile, Maggie mustn't worry. Since little Tom's birth, one baby had died of plague, and one had miscarried. No, she mustn't worry. They needed to think of their own future, not only Martin Dowdswell's. Who knows? All their tomorrows might be linked with the precarious health of the old gentleman nearing the end of his long life in the President's Lodgings at Trinity.

The president was sitting beside a window which commanded an excellent view of his beloved garden and the stables beyond. He had been dressed and helped to a chair by the faithful Simon who had left his master in reasonable comfort – his back propped upright with cushions and a heavily bandaged foot gently resting on a stool about the same height as the chair.

But Dr Kettel's thoughts were neither reasonable nor gentle. Gout's the very Devil, and he knew no good reason why God should have visited him with such an abominable affliction. At least he was sure of one thing. Neither God nor the Devil would stop him ruling Trinity College so long as there was breath in his lungs. He stuck out his jaw aggressively, prepared to fight his corner against the whole world.

The intermittent pain in his foot, however, kept him in a vile temper, and when he saw a man he didn't know emerge from the college stables he rang his hand-bell in a fury and ordered the ever-attendant Simon to apprehend the stranger who was trespassing on college property.

A few minutes later Simon reported in some trepidation that the stranger claimed to be related to Tom Brewster.

'I don't care whose son he is,' roared the president. 'Bring him here at once and I'll send him about his business.'

'And now, young man,' he began in a threatening voice as Martin Dowdswell was ushered into the room. 'What the Devil do you think you are doing, trespassing on my college property without my permission? What's this I hear about you being related to my head groom? Is that correct?'

'Not exactly, Sir. I'm really Mrs Brewster's son from an earlier marriage.'

The president's anger subsided. His mood changed. He looked very hard at the boy. No, memory hadn't failed him yet.

'So you're Miss Maggie's boy, are you?' he muttered, speaking more to himself than to the young man standing before him. 'The boy for whom I bought baby's clothes . . .' He began to number each point of recollection on his long bony fingers: Maggie's love-child, eh? The boy I used to see playing in Sam Dowdswell's stables at Osney . . . the boy his mother insisted be brought up a gentleman . . . and persuaded that quixotic Harry Ireton to give him a start . . .

'And now,' his voice rang out clearly, 'let me think. You are Maggie Dowdswell's son and you were christened Martin. Would I be right?'

The keen old eyes looked at the boy for confirmation 'So I am right. And what happened to you, Martin, after you left your mother? Nottinghamshire, first, and then St Paul's School? A fine school, too. And after that? So, you want to be a soldier? Then, what on earth are you doing, spending the night in my stables?'

It was a long story. But, as the president outlived his contemporaries, so he found it easier and easier to attend to the views of the student generation. He could always find time to listen to the young, and Martin felt increasingly at ease as he explained his distaste for trade and John Ireton's anxieties concerning his mission to John Pym. So here he was in Oxford – out of work, with no love for the City of London but a firm determination to become a soldier.

'And you hope Colonel Skippon will employ you at his headquarters?'

The boy hesitated.

'But he won't approve of you soiling your hands in politics – that's your worry, is it?' The president paused. He thought he had all the facts at his fingertips. Then his old face was transformed by one of his rare smiles. He liked what he saw of Martin Dowdswell – well-built, honest, straightforward. He looked at him more closely. 'I think,' he said, 'it might be wise for you, Martin, to stay around here for a week or two – in Oxford, if you wish. Or better, perhaps, with your grandfather out at Osney who can always do with an extra hand in the stables. Meanwhile, I will consider how I can help you on your way. But first I must have a word with Mr Brewster.'

Martin hurried away, somewhat overawed but also grateful for the great man's offer of help, while Dr Kettel ordered Simon to bring him writing materials. He was laboriously sharpening a quill pen when Tom Brewster appeared in answer to the president's summons.

'Ah, Tom, come in.' The president had a great affection for young Brewster whom he regarded as a personal friend. 'Come in – and for Heaven's sake man, stop staring at my foot – you can't cure the Devil's work that way! Now, about this boy of Maggie's. Does she know he wants to be a soldier?'

'Yes, Sir.'

'And does she approve? Soldiers don't always return, hale and hearty, from these continental wars, you know. Sometimes they don't come back at all. There are one or two I could name from this college who have taken leave of life investing some silly little Dutch town – all of them too young to die . . .' The president's thoughts began to stray; but after a shake of the head he returned to the point. 'About this boy's wish to be a soldier – what does Maggie say?'

'No doubt about it, Sir, Maggie approves. She knows what the boy wants, but . . .'

'Go on, man. What's she worried about?'

'It's the girl, Sir – the girl, Susanna who got Martin involved with Mr Pym. She thinks he's sweet on her.'

'Tom, you're talking in riddles. Is there anything wrong in a boy taking an interest in a pretty girl? Heavens, man, isn't that the way you felt about Maggie? Came all the way to Oxford for her sake, not mine, eh?'

'Yes, Sir. But this girl, Susanna – this girl . . . Maggie thinks she may have the same father as Martin . . .'

'The Devil she does.'

'And Maggie says someone's got to tell Martin the truth – but who? It's not good for Maggie to get worried when she's expecting another baby. You understand, Sir?'

The president examined his pen with extreme care. Suddenly, as his manner was, he jerked himself back to life. 'Women – I've said it many times before – are the very deuce. They're always making trouble, and the prettier they are, the more trouble they cause.' The president seemed about to expand on one of his more familiar themes. But seeing Tom's worried face, he returned to the practical problem which Tom had posed.

'Maggie's right, of course. If her supposition is correct this love affair has to be stopped. And the girl, Susanna, must also hear the truth. She mustn't be allowed to stray into forbidden territory – forbidden by the laws of God and man. What's her father's name?'

'Martin, Sir. Or so I believe. Maggie is a little vague, but from something she said, I think Mr Henry Ireton knows her secret.'

'Henry Ireton?' The name induced a new bout of speculation in the old man. Was Harry getting dragged into this political nonsense at Westminster? Was he still fuming with rage over that gas-bag Prynne and the Court of Star Chamber and the iniquity of bishops' power? Or was he busy with his estates in the County of Nottingham? The president looked out of the window – far beyond the stable, far beyond the towers of Oxford . . . Suddenly, he returned to the needs of his head groom.

'You'll do best to leave the matter in my hands, Tom. Tell Maggie not to worry, and keep Martin occupied. He'll be a better soldier if he learns a bit about horses from you and Sam Dowdswell. All I need is a little time.'

Later that evening Simon was entrusted with a letter addressed to Mr Henry Ireton and with orders to have it forwarded to London – and a second copy to the family home in Attenborough – by the quickest possible means of despatch.

17

While Martin remained with his family in Oxford, Francis Thornhaugh and Henry Ireton completed their journey to London, having circumvented the king's entourage that was making its ponderous, disruptive progress towards the royal hunting lodge at Newmarket. While they waited at the Shipleys' house for an official appointment to present their petition on behalf of the citizens of Nottingham, the two men speculated as to whether and when the king would return to his capital.

In due course the summons from the Commons was delivered. Now, in the third week of March 1642, the two friends stood facing some twenty Members of Parliament in a small room adjoining St Stephen's Chapel in the Palace of Westminster.

They were a striking pair, these two Nottingham landowners: Thornhaugh fair, palpably honest, still an undergraduate in appearance although the senior of the two representatives (probably owns more acres, whispered the cynical Denzil Holles to his neighbour); and Ireton, dark-eyed and dark-haired, his beard neatly trimmed, soberly dressed, but in bearing every inch the aristocrat. It was Henry who had been deputed to present the case in detail, and in a calm unhurried voice which carried an unmistakable note of legal authority, he developed his argument as a two-fold brief.

First, he expressed Nottingham's anxiety over His Majesty's absence from the capital at this time of national crisis caused by the rebellion of the Catholic Irish.

Secondly, he presented to the committee a detailed refutation of a sergeant-at-law's claim to land in which the citizens of Nottingham held traditional common land rights. This second case was supported by documents and ancient charters couched in precise legal terminology. But Henry Ireton's exposition was as clear as crystal. Not a word was wasted and the committee was clearly relieved and impressed.

Wisely, Henry had kept his two themes separate. But now, as he neatly laid to one side his law books and documentary precedents, his deep-set eyes scanned the faces of the men he had been addressing.

'Gentlemen,' he concluded, 'I would wish to end our exposition by thanking you for your most patient attention. You will have noted that the latter part of my case rests on local law and precedent and requires a legal judgment. The former part may be construed as no more than an expression of national concern which the people of Nottingham wish to be conveyed to Members of this House. But for me and my friend and neighbour, Mr Francis Thornhaugh' – and here eyes and voice seemed to compel the committee's attention – 'for me and my friend, the two cases are linked by a passionate conviction that we speak for the people of England as well as our County of Nottingham. We stand before you as champions of the inalienable right of an Englishman to freedom of speech as well as just government under the Law.'

Oliver St John, as chairman, after thanking the petitioners for the lucid presentation of their case, announced that the committee would retire to consider its verdict, and the members shuffled to their feet. Some were easily recognisable – among them, the red-faced Holles, young Henry Vane from Hull, Edmund Waller the poet, the wealthy Chiltern landowner John Hampden, who had led the stand against ship money, and Colepepper from Kent. But for Henry Ireton the audience had been reduced at an early stage in his speech to one man seated in the back row of the semi-circle of chairs.

This one man had asked no questions as others had done. But once he had caught Henry's eye, and made a pretence of clapping his hands. Once he had smiled and Henry knew he could be sure of at least one supporter on the committee. And once – or did he imagine it? – one of those piercing blue-grey eyes definitely winked at him.

And now Mr Oliver Cromwell, the member for Cambridge, who had remained seated while his fellow members left the room, crossed the floor to join Francis and Henry. His praise was positive and held no qualifications.

'As fair a presentation as ever I heard,' he said, shaking each man by the hand. 'May I be permitted to offer you my sincere congratulations? I hope you may win a favourable verdict for your common land problem. But, as Mr Ireton will know, lawyers move all too often at the pace of the tortoise, so that you may have to wait a day or two in London before judgment is pronounced. Should you be free this evening, I would be most happy to offer you a little hospitality at my house in Drury Lane. I'm not sure where Mr Thornhaugh is lodging, but Drury Lane is only a step or two from Temple Stairs.'

'Thank you, Sir. We'd gladly accept your invitation, would we not, Francis?' Ireton was again the spokesman. 'But how . . . how did you . . . ?'

Mr Cromwell stopped Henry in mid-sentence. 'Let me explain, Sir. I find I have come to prefer the company of the young. They talk to me without the subtlety practised by my fellow Members of Parliament. Truth to tell, I like the company of men and women who give straight answers to straight questions. So when, some years ago, I had the pleasure of sharing a chicken pie in Sir Theodore Mayerne's garden with your young *protégé*, Martin Dowdswell, I not only learned where he lodged in London but also received a very fair briefing on the Iretons of Nottingham.'

Oliver laughed and clapped the two younger men on the back. 'So, we meet in Drury Lane at six o'clock this evening? Excellent. Forgive me for leaving you so hurriedly. I have to join my learned colleagues as they ponder their verdict. Pity me, too. The splitting of legal hairs is not my favourite pastime.' And Oliver Cromwell moved away with that loping country- man's walk which seemed to distinguish him from so many of his fellow members.

That evening the Member for Cambridge proved himself a most convivial host. His conversation ranged over a variety of subjects which he thought might interest his guests, moving easily from hawking and hunting to the climate of the Cam- bridgeshire fens and the character of the Fenmen. Oliver's geniality was supported by an excellent dinner served by his housekeeper and accompanied by a robust Burgundy.

It was not long before Henry realised that his host made a point of seeking his guests' views before expressing his own.

In matters of religion, for example, would Cromwell be right in thinking that Francis and Henry were of the Independent persuasion? Not much use for bishops, eh? Leave men and women to study their Bibles and find Christ in their own way? Yes, that was his thinking and Mrs Cromwell's too. But his guests would agree, would they not, to some restriction on any Church which worked in alliance with a foreign power against the interests of England? It seemed an important point.

Oliver moved across to the political scene. Had the people of Nottingham received and studied John Pym's Grand Remonstrance? Not every one of its two hundred clauses, for Heaven's sake!

'But you say you *have* read it, Harry, from beginning to end? I stand amazed and humbled. Still, would you both agree with the gist of it – that good government can only be assured in England if the king and his advisers act in accordance with the will of the people as expressed by Parliament?'

Francis Thornhaugh was happy to agree provided he wasn't asked to read the whole document. He did not pretend to share Henry's legal appetite, and Oliver laughed.

'Nor have I that sort of appetite. But tell me, Francis, do you not hold command in the local militia? Right, am I? And under whose command do you place yourself?'

'I suppose, Sir, the Lord Lieutenant of the County, who is the king's representative. But recently all train bands, south of Trent, have been placed under command of the Earl of Essex. So I require notice of the question.'

'A bit of a problem, eh? Needs thinking over.'

Oliver changed the subject by asking about the state of the equipment carried by Thornhaugh's troop.

In fact, he never allowed the conversation to become too serious or too political. Yet somehow, when the young men left Drury Lane at midnight, they were both aware of a new dimension in their lives. They had, perhaps, told their host too much about their families and aspirations; but what about their host? He'd revealed a lot about himself too, laughed about the idiosyncracies of Members of Parliament and let them see the inside of his family life, as well. 'Ruled by Grandmother, you know. As I told John Milton the other day, it's the only common ground the Cromwell family shares with his beloved Italians.'

The two men kept repeating to each other snatches of Oliver's conversation: sometimes the boisterous humour of the countryman, sometimes shrewd comments on a political scene dominated by conflicting religious beliefs. But always they returned to the man himself. Very attractive – yes, attractive like a magnet. They felt they had been greatly privileged to be his guests. They were starry-eyed as they reached the Shipleys' house.

And Oliver? He climbed into bed a very happy man, knowing he'd met two men after his own heart.

Henry Ireton had no difficulty in identifying the author of the letter which Hannah Shipley laid before him on the morning following his dinner with Mr Cromwell. The eccentric handwriting of Trinity's President was unmistakable, even though it had become rather shaky with the passage of the years.

But he was hardly prepared for its contents. Not only did the president's letter confirm the half-feared blood relationship between Martin and Susanna which Henry had put from his mind. It also suggested – nay virtually commanded – that he, Henry Ireton, had a duty to save the young people from committing mortal sin. It even suggested – without any justification – that Henry should be acquainted with Colonel Skippon of the London train bands and with Mr Thomas Martin of Cray Valley in the County of Kent.

'Look at this absurd request,' he exclaimed, throwing the letter across the table to Francis Thornhaugh. 'What on earth does the old man expect me to do? I suppose I have to do something, if only because the orders come from the president.'

Francis laughed. Normally you could expect Harry to take decisive action on any problem confronting him, even if it meant a decision to do nothing. Nobody in the County of Nottingham was more self-reliant. Yet here he was, uncertain and seeking his friend's advice. Right, he should have it. 'Why not call on our friend in Drury Lane?' he said.

It was meant as a joke, but Henry was delighted. 'My dear Francis, it's a brilliant idea. Of course you're right. That man has some sort of link with everybody who matters round here. He'll tell me, if anyone can, where and how to act.'

Within the hour Henry was travelling upriver to Westminster Pier in search of the Member for Cambridge.

Oliver proved easily approachable. He listened carefully to Henry's dilemma, and then in his slow-speaking, thoughtful voice dealt with Martin. 'Leave that young man to me,' he told Harry. 'I've met Philip Skippon – a fine soldier of great experience, who enjoys the complete confidence of Parliament and the City fathers. I've seen enough of Martin to believe he'll appeal to the old warrior. In fact, I shall be surprised if Martin does not get a posting within the next few weeks.'

'As to the girl, that's not so simple. But I doubt if Thomas Martin would consider a boy of Martin's age and position to be an eligible suitor for his daughter's hand. So we can agree, can we not, that time is on our side, assuming your aim is to keep the boy and girl apart. Maybe the young lady should be encouraged to follow the queen to France . . . that is no more than speculation. But why not take a ride into Kent, Harry? See how the land lies in the Cray Valley, and then . . .'

'I know your conclusion, Sir. Pray to the God we both serve that the right words may come to my mouth at the right moment.'

'Yes, Harry.' Oliver's eyes were fixed on the younger man as he spoke. 'That would have been my final suggestion. And I promise that I too will remember you in my prayers.'

Mr Thomas Martin was pleased to receive the two gentlemen from Nottingham who had ridden from London and spent the night at the inn in Bexley village. A relief to escape the noise of the capital . . . he could well understand . . . and to see how farming prospered in this cut-off corner of England . . . we're lucky with the soil round here . . . a layer of chalk just below the ploughland . . . absorbs and holds water, you see . . . helps us in the drought years and, in good times, yields a surplus which we move upstream to London where we find a ready market. As a matter of fact, I own a few ships that operate from Erith – north to Yarmouth and round the Forelands to Sandwich and Dover, and sometimes across-Channel to Antwerp and Dunkirk.

Thomas Martin rambled on . . . 'You ask about my family gentlemen? Well, we don't pretend to great distinction in the county, though many of my forebears have fought in the French wars. But we've lived in these parts a long time, farming our own land, and we have children who will, I hope, continue the tradition. To be exact, our family comprises one son and two daughters though the older girl, Susanna, has been away from home in attendance at Somerset House.'

Henry had listened to Mr Martin with exemplary and unwonted patience. Now, like the swordsman who sees a sudden opening, he seized his chance.

'Susanna, Sir. Would that be the charming young lady who accompanied me and my ward, Martin Dowdswell, on a recent tour of His Majesty's picture gallery in Whitehall?'

'Did I hear you correctly, Mr Ireton? The name of your ward – Dowdswell – Martin Dowdswell?'

'Yes indeed, Sir. His mother came of a yeoman family which suffered some misfortune . . . I met her many years ago at her father's livery stables when I was an Oxford student . . . It was at her behest that I arranged for Martin to be educated under the care of my family.'

There was a long awkward pause in the conversation. Then Thomas Martin recovered his composure and suggested that Henry might enjoy a tour of his rose garden before riding back to London. Once alone with Henry, he came quickly to the point.

'You know the father's name, Mr Ireton?'

'I do, Sir. But rest assured that Maggie Dowdswell has kept her secret well.'

'And your object in meeting me today?'

'I understand that Martin and Susanna have become very good companions. I think you will agree that they should be encouraged to travel different roads.'

'Perhaps I should permit my daughter to follow the queen to France?'

'And Martin to follow a military career?'

'And Maggie, Mr Ireton . . . She was a lovely girl . . . tell me how she fares.'

'She's very happy, Sir: married to a fine man – name of Tom Brewster – who works at Trinity College. She has one child and is expecting another. Her only anxiety concerns Martin and Susanna; and, between us, I hope we can allay her fears.'

A little later Henry took leave of Thomas Martin and returned with Francis to London where they were delighted to learn that the Nottingham petition had been approved by Parliament. But before returning triumphant to their homes, they felt it courteous to report to Mr Cromwell on the outcome of their journey into Kent.

They found him in a state of deep depression – totally different from the genial Fenman who had entertained them so well in Drury Lane. It was as if he were carrying a burden beyond his strength.

'Grim news from all sides,' he told them. 'The king's moved north to York. He's rejected totally some very reasonable proposals from John Pym for resolving their differences. I fear that the first part of your Nottingham petition may prove more significant than the victory in the matter of common land and the people's ownership.'

'You mean, Sir?'

'Simply this.' Oliver's voice had a sharp edge to it. 'Time is running out for His Majesty. The Commons won't take "No" for an answer. I suggest you take your good news with all speed to the citizens of Nottingham, and spend the summer in equipping and training your local militia. You understand me? I fear greatly for this kingdom.'

Suddenly Oliver's face was transformed, his eyes sparkled and his voice was full of life. This man of many moods was smiling as he turned to Harry.

'Just one more point: I've arranged for young Dowdswell to be posted to the London Train Band Headquarters. Colonel Skippon assures me that he can turn Martin into a first-class soldier – but there'll be no time for politics or hanging about the royal court. That must be clearly understood.'

'And to make assurance double-sure, Mr Cromwell, I think Mr Martin of the Cray Valley will encourage his daughter to follow the queen to France.'

The two men looked at each other, suddenly burst out laughing and then solemnly shook hands. Already a bond of friendship had been formed between the thirty-year-old Ireton and Oliver Cromwell, twelve years his senior.

18

Martin really enjoyed his three-week break in Oxford – or rather in Osney where he stayed for the whole period with Sam and Betsie Dowdswell in their new stone-built house. There was no further mention of Susanna on the few occasions when he visited his mother, and time passed all too quickly in the Dowdswells' company.

One point was plain for all to see. Sam's affairs had greatly prospered since his marriage to Maggie's friend from the Mitre. Not only had Betsie given birth to two lovely children – a boy and a girl – who were a source of much joy to their father. In addition, she exercised a benevolent but effective control over her easy-going husband which he happily accepted. In short, she was endowed with sufficient tact and skill to manage Sam's life as well as his home.

Sam was a small landowner once more, having purchased four acres of good pasture behind his enlarged stables. His reputation as a breeder extended beyond the Oxford borders – northward to Banbury and Warwick, and east to Thame and Aylesbury. And at Northampton – reputedly the greatest horse fair in England – he was held in high respect as an expert and honest judge of a horse's quality, whether he spoke as buyer or salesman.

Sam, for his part, was delighted to have the companionship of his grandson whom he best remembered as the bright little boy Maggie had brought to Osney after the death of his first wife.

'So many years ago, Martin. D'you remember those early days when I relied for business on the young gentlemen from Oxford? I reckon it was a lucky chance that led Harry Ireton our way, wasn't it? Lucky for both of us, I mean. Shall I ever forget the time he knocked old Sanderson out of the Witney Chase? Courage, skill, understanding – what a rider he was!' Sam smiled at the memory of that triumphant day. 'But now, I suppose, he engages himself in more serious affairs. Do you see much of him, Martin?'

Conversation between grandfather and grandson had quickly become the easiest thing in the world. Here in Osney, Martin felt himself part of his own Dowdswell family – no longer the adopted boy who chanced to have fallen among kind and caring people.

One evening in June the pair were riding back from Banbury. The lowering sun lit up the contrasting colours of the rich countryside with a painter's perfection and Sam was cock-a-hoop over the prices he'd obtained for a couple of geldings he'd put up for sale. They had been bought by a member of the local Compton family, acting for the Earl of Worcester who was the richest landowner for miles around. But why should a knowledgable buyer like young Compton be so ready to pay above the market rates? That is what puzzled Sam Dowdswell; not least because at Aylesbury, a few weeks earlier, he had enjoyed the same good fortune. Could there be some link between the two transactions?

Sam posed the question to the green fields in general and to Martin in particular. Both Aylesbury and Banbury, he reminded himself, had witnessed a recent flare-up between parties of landed gentry pitching into each other about the rights and wrongs of King Charles and his Parliament.

'But what's that got to do with the price of horses, eh? There are not many people that worry about politics round here, Martin. Most of them rest happy so long as they have food and drink and a girl to love. I wonder how prices compare further north, up Nottingham way?'

Martin agreed to consult his guardian when they next met. He hadn't seen Harry for some time, he told Sam, not since he'd had this blazing row with his brother, Mr John Ireton. Still, he knew Harry had been entrusted with some parliamentary petition from the citizens of Nottingham, and Joe and Hannah Shipley were busy preparing for Harry's visit to London even before Martin had made his hurried departure. So he'd soon be able to find out the state of the market in the Ireton country.

'Matter of fact, Grandfather, the last time we met Harry was very interested in my military career. He's spending a lot of time, these days, with the Nottingham militia, you know and he's borrowed some of my military manuals about the new methods of warfare in Europe.'

Sam and Martin were still discussing these matters when they reached Osney. Betsie listened carefully to their talk about the inflated prices for horses in Aylesbury and Banbury: It seemed to have a bearing on rumours she'd brought back from Oxford. The local carrier had taken her early to the city, and after leaving the children with Maggie Brewster she'd made a duty call on Mrs Wotherspoon at the Mitre. That great lady was full of news that lost nothing in the telling: 'The Mitre's packed with strange gentlemen she told me. Not a room to spare . . . must hire more staff. (Hey, don't look so anxious, Sam . . . Mrs W. knows my days in the dining room are done.) But why this sudden rush, I ask her. And then she gets very confidential . . . very mysterious. It's none of my business,she says, nor yours, Betsie Dowdswell. But if the gentlemen guests drink too much and talk too loud, you can't help hearing, can you? And it seemes as if a very important personage may be coming our way very soon. This gaggle of grandees is spying out the land – the 'forlorn hope' as the military gentlemen call it. There's talk about it all over the city . . . enquiries for spare accommodation . . . requisitions of vacant halls . . . Goodness knows what the university's coming to!'

Betsie, with finger to lips, was giving a splendid imitation of a flustered Mrs Wotherspoon imparting the latest gossip 'in confidence'. 'So heigh-ho and up go the prices. It seems as if Mrs W. and you, Sam, are about to enjoy a season of plenty.'

But the shrewd Betsie had also been making her own deductions. Suddenly she said, 'If I were you, Sam, I'd scour the country and buy every decent horse you can lay your hands on.'

'So you would, would you, my love?'

'Yes. And you want to look sharp about it, or your dear friend Mr William Sanderson will get there first.'

'You're joking, Betsie.'

'I don't think so, Sam. In fact, I'd advise you to go for animals strong enough in the backside to carry a man-at-arms. I smell trouble though I don't know what it is or where it comes from.'

Martin joined in the conversation. 'If I hear the lady correctly, it sounds as if it's high time I returned to my soldiering in London. But those packhorse teams move a bit slowly,

Grandfather, for the train bands of London and Colonel Philip Skippon. Do you think I could possibly borrow a horse to carry me the whole distance?'

The following morning the Dowdswells and their two small children waved farewell to Martin as he rode down the Oxford road to say goodbye to his mother before heading for the capital. Sam Dowdswell had done his grandson proud, mounting him on a magnificent four-year-old bay, strongly built and easy of movement, with white socks and blaze which disclosed his breeding to anybody familiar with Lady Jane's markings.

'Good luck, Martin, and remember your instructions,' Sam shouted. 'On arrival in London you present the bay with my compliments to Mr Henry Ireton. As a lad, he thought he got the better of the bargain when he and Tom Brewster accepted a couple of good horses in exchange for Lady Jane. But for once in a way Harry was wrong and I was right. Tell him Lady Jane's offspring is not a gift – but a repayment of a debt I owe to one of the finest horsemen in England.'

On receiving Parliament's favourable verdict on the common land case, Francis Thornhaugh had hastened north to report the success of his mission to the Mayor and Corporation of Nottingham. But some sixth sense kept Henry Ireton in London.

It was not his custom to waste time in self-analysis. His mind worked with a simplicity and clarity which cut through the secondary arguments so beguiling to his contemporaries. Some process of reason would guide him to a point of decision – he often thought of it as divine guidance in answer to prayer. And when that point was reached he would act with lightning speed.

Did he really need to wait in London for Martin's return from Oxford? Why should he make Martin an excuse for calling on Colonel Skippon? Or for expressing his gratitude to the Member for Cambridge for his help in getting Martin posted to Skippon's Headquarters Staff at Finsbury? Was he justified in spending so much valuable time in listening to the great preachers in the capital? Who should say? All Henry remembered of those doom-laden days in the early summer of 1642 was that, contrary to his natural inclination to enjoy high summer amidst the greenery of the Trent valley, he remained in dirty, insanitary London.

When Henry Ireton eventually did head north in early July he was mounted on a superb horse whose every stride reminded him of his beloved Lady Jane; and he rode by way of Ely in the company of Oliver Cromwell.

The night was spent at the Cromwells' Ely house in the shadow of St Mary's Church – a house which was almost a replica, he realised, in shape and situation of the Ireton house at Attenborough. It was Henry's first introduction to Mrs Cromwell, the older Cromwell children and the grandmother whom Oliver treated with marked deference. But on this occasion he saw little of the family, for after dinner he was conducted to a room where he remained closeted with Oliver for the rest of the evening. The only other person present was the eldest surviving Cromwell son – a good-looking lad about the same age as Martin Dowdswell, who also carried his father's Christian name.

In Henry's eyes Oliver appeared to have undergone a complete transformation. He had emerged from the gloom of doubt and hesitation which had marked their second meeting in Drury Lane. His changed demeanour had become increasingly obvious on their journey from London. First, Oliver had admired Henry's mount, already nicknamed Witney. Then, he had spoken of Colonel Skippon with unequivocal approval: A fine soldier, Harry, born to command, and just the man to set young Martin on the right path. He had also made Henry laugh with a host of stories about the good people of Huntingdon and St Ives and the conservative dons of Cambridge. In short, Henry's travelling companion was a man completely at ease. And now, in the privacy of his Ely home, he was pellucidly clear about the immediate future.

'There is bound to be war,' he told Henry bluntly. 'Let's face it, there's no way it can be avoided. His Majesty has rejected Parliament's very reasonable proposals. Titled courtiers are despatched in droves to Westminister with proposals and counter-proposals whose only purpose is to confuse and delay the issue. Meanwhile, our agents report that the king is working on grandees like Newcastle in the North and Worcester in the West Midlands to muster their dependants for a *coup d'état* against Parliament. So, I warn you, Harry: be prepared. I am assured there will be no more overtures from Parliament to the king and his advisers in York. The shilly-shallying is over.'

'And what does all this mean in terms of action?'

Oliver seemed totally prepared for Harry's leading question. 'Each of us must answer your question by his own lights,' he replied. 'But, as an immediate step, I plan to arm my supporters in Cambridge. I shall also use my parliamentary status to neutralise the plots of that toady, the Bishop of Ely, and some of the college principals. And as a Cambridge graduate, I shall ensure that the university's plate is not handed over to the king in place of the financial support he would normally receive through a parliamentary vote.'

'And your longer-term policy, Sir?'

'No doubt about that, either. Rid the king of his evil and dissolute advisers. And, as an act of insurance, persuade my connections in East Anglia to present a solid military defence against any army advancing on London from the north.'

Harry was staggered by Oliver's certainty and his grasp of essentials.

'And London, Sir. Where does London stand?'

'That's another good question, Harry. To be truthful, I'm never quite sure of London. One day the crowd welcomes a hero – and next day it howls for his execution. Speaking personally, I put more trust in my Fenmen. But I fancy the king has trifled too long with the City's loyalty. You can pay too much, you know, for monopolies and knighthoods.'

'And the other ports of entry?'

'Solidly behind Parliament, as are the big wool towns in Yorkshire and the Midlands. I reckon the king will find his chief support among the great hereditary landowners who control the extremities of the kingdom – the Scottish Borders, the Welsh Marches and the West Country. But what about your county, Harry? Pig-in-the middle, eh? Sorry, that's not a fair question at this time of night. Think it over when you're back home. It's time for bed.'

Next morning Henry completed his journey on Witney, travelling through Peterborough and Grantham. On his arrival at

Attenborough old Brewster fussed over the horse and led him proudly to the stables while Henry rushed into the house to find his mother.

So much had happened since he and Francis Thornhaugh had left for London. He hardly knew where to begin his story, but in the end it all hinged on his meetings with Oliver in Drury Lane and Ely.

'It's not easy, Mother, to explain Mr Cromwell's attraction. First I meet a friendly MP with a marked interest in the traditional landed rights of the Englishman. Then, I happen upon a man beset by doubts and forebodings. And now – hey presto – a born leader shows himself, a man certain of his course of action, totally committed and totally prepared.'

'Prepared to fight against his king, Harry?'

'No, Mother. Oliver Cromwell's quarrel is with the wicked men who surround the king and persuade him to flout the will of the people's representatives at Westminster.'

'And you, Harry. Where do you stand?'

Henry Ireton looked at his mother in great affection. She understood him so well. 'Mother, I declare you knew the answer before you asked the question. Of course you did. But to clear any doubt which others may entertain, I'll give you my answer loud and clear. I intend to follow Oliver wherever he leads me – in peace or, if God so wills it, in war.'

In August everything happened as Oliver had foretold. The king and his counsellors received no further proposals from Westminster, and it was, perhaps, in sheer frustration that he decided to move south from York to Nottingham.

There, on 22 August 1642, the terrible truth was disclosed. The king had decided to call on his loyal subjects to fight against their own elected representatives. On a rain-swept square in the centre of Nottingham, the Royal Standard was duly raised. It was planned as a dramatic gesture to impress the people, but the weather was terrible, and few of Nottingham's citizens attended the ceremony. Perhaps it was just as well, for the royal herald muffed the lines of the proclamation which King Charles had re-drafted at the last moment. And even as the trumpets sounded, the flagpole swayed and toppled ingloriously to the ground.

Within the hour, two of his loyal subjects, Major Francis Thornhaugh and Captain Henry Ireton, disobeyed their king and clattered into the city at the head of a finely disciplined troop of horse, fully armed and uniformly dressed: their immediate objective to secure and mount guard over the magazine at Nottingham Castle in the name of Parliament.

Here, in the centre of England, civil war had been joined. And no man on either side could fully comprehend the grief of it.

19

Civil war in England – the thought was hardly conceivable to men and women who had enjoyed the Tudor peace. Was time to be retraced two hundred years back to the Wars of the Roses? But that was a mere squabble between the noble houses of York and Lancaster. In this year of grace 1642 new and greater principles were at stake – freedom of speech and freedom of worship; the right of the people's representatives to make laws and authorise taxation; a sharing of power between the King of England and his subjects. Such issues concerned every family in the land.

The women of England wept, or prayed, according to their lights. At Attenborough Jane Ireton prayed – prayed that Henry's life might be spared; prayed that John would not be in conflict with his family. Would Mary and her children in Leicester be involved? Would Sarah in distant Sussex support her Catholic husband against her beloved brother? Would happy-go-lucky Tom, who hated nobody, follow Henry into battle? And please, dear God, could she be allowed to retain the companionship of Clement and her youngest daughter until this dreadful war was done? Early each morning Jane Ireton knelt in supplication at the little desk in her own room before rising to direct the household and manage the Ireton farms.

At Ely a more leisurely Elizabeth Cromwell conducted the family prayers as her husband would have wished. Her thoughts, too, centred on her children – especially her eldest surviving son, already embodied as cornet in the Parliamentary Horse. But since her husband had delegated to good men the running of the Ely tithes and Fenland farms, she had time to plan on a wider front. Dear Bridget, praying at her side, was already eighteen years of age, and should be finding a husband. Young Oliver and even Richard should be looking for girls with dowries as splendid as the one she had brought to her husband. And how she wished that husband of hers would not be so foolishly indulgent with the younger children, Henry and Betty. The thought brought her back to this man of many moods. Again and again she prayed for Oliver's safety, giving thanks for the restoration of his health after those earlier years of religious doubt and constant fever. Elizabeth Cromwell wondered what the future would hold.

In the Hague where the king's agents hoped to interest the shrewd merchants of Amsterdam in the purchase of the queen's jewellery, Henrietta Maria also prayed daily for her husband – for his safety and success in defeating the insolent men at Westminster who questioned his God-given right to rule. She asked fervently that she might be allowed to stand by his side and lend him her strength with or without the European help she was seeking in Denmark, Holland and France. In time of war the daughter of Henri Quatre was a very different character from the immature bride who had so signally failed to warm the hearts of her husband's subjects.

Jane Ireton, Elizabeth Cromwell and the Queen of England were typical of many women of high and low estate who, in their various fashions, prayed for the safety of their families. In this fiercely religious age the fighting men were no less conscious of their need for God's blessing. But both sides assumed with supreme confidence that God would be in full support of their particular cause. The God of Battles might indeed inspire the combatants to supreme acts of heroism. But only the professional soldiers of the continental wars, who now rushed to enlist in the rival armies, appreciated that God tended to favour the better-armed soldier, the more disciplined regiment and the commander who understood the art of war as well as the lie of the land.

Meanwhile the harvest was still to be gathered and the barns filled with winter feed for the cattle. Trade must continue through the ports of England, and the little ships ply their business with Europe, including the modest fleets owned by Mr Robert Martin of Erith and Mr Edward Ford of Hastings – indeed, it was an Erith ship that had carried Susanna Martin to join the queen's household at the Hague.

Back in London, Joe Shipley would continue to transport London's citizens up and down river to their several appointments, and even find time to tell Hannah not to bother her head about young Martin. And at Oxford the Dowdswells would see their business flourish and the Brewsters would worry what the future might hold for them when the Trinity President died. In these small homes in Oxford and London Maggie and Betsie and Hannah all prayed for the safety of Martin Dowdswell.

As to that young gentleman, he was in his element, chiefly engaged in bearing General Skippon's messages to and from John Pym and the lord mayor. But he also accompanied his general on all parades and official visits to the City aldermen so that Hannah Shipley was constantly washing the cornet's linen and brushing his uniform. 'The general seems mighty fussy about dress,' she told Martin. 'I wonder what happens when you go to war.'

Martin laughed at the old lady. She was much more efficient, he told her, than Mrs Skippon who had come from Norfolk to Hackney specially to keep the general in trim. Life for Martin was full of excitement, so full that he had no time to think of Susanna though he knew she was in the Netherlands with the queen. He also knew – and he kept the secret well – that at any moment the lord mayor would order full mobilisation for the train bands of London.

After the fateful call to arms at Nottingham, King Charles moved swiftly towards Shrewsbury where he intended to draw support from Wales and build up a powerful force under the command of officers trained in the Dutch wars. His Palatinate nephews, Rupert and Maurice, regarded this as an essential first step. They had been appalled by the ignorance of their uncle's closest advisers who seemed to regard the art of war as a glorified extension of the royal craze for hunting. This was a recipe for disaster. The king's first need was for men like Hopton and Skippon's old friend, Sir Jacob Astley, who could polish up the skills of loyal county militias and impose discipline on the feudal retainers whom the old nobility was bringing to the king's service. It was no small feat that by October a fighting force of fifteen thousand men was ready to take the field.

Inexperience was no less a problem for the Parliamentary army being mustered at Northampton under Robert Devereux, third Earl of Essex. His noble status and record of parliamentary service were regarded as important qualifications. But his knowledge of tactics was limited and he had shown no decisive powers, the hallmark of every successful commander in the field. Once again, much would depend on his officers, largely drawn from the yeoman class, who might possess a firmer sense of purpose than the blindly loyal nobles flocking to the king's colours.

The cheers of his home village were still music to his ears as Captain Ireton rode into Northampton at the head of his sixty Nottingham troopers in the second week of September. Francis Thornhaugh had rightly decided that only a small detachment could be spared from the troops required for the defence of Nottingham and its castle. And so, from the Nottingham militia, it was Henry who was given the first field command.

For a few weeks, in miserable weather, the Parliamentary army moved ponderously towards Worcester. It was almost by chance – for the reconnaissance Intelligence of both sides was deplorable – that the two armies, some fifteen thousand men on each side, found themselves facing each other near Banbury.

Fifteen miles south of Warwick, Essex had ordered the Parliamentary army forward from Kineton village, the movement completed in full view of the king's forces ranged defensively on the Edgehill escarpment. Throughout a dreary October morning, brigade and regimental commanders had been receiving and giving orders and counter-orders. To Henry Ireton it seemed impossible that order could emerge from the confusion. But at last Meldrum's infantry was established on level farm land as the centre of the line of battle, pikemen and musketeers standing six deep in Swedish formation. The artillery pieces took up position between the infantry brigades, and the cavalry stationed themselves on either wing. It was, Henry recognised, the classic 'Battalia' layout: and it came as no surprise when the Royalists moved to take up a similar formation on the level ground at the base of the escarpment. The rival commanders might have been preparing for a game of chess.

Waiting for the first move, Henry's imagination could not

be stilled. He was almost sick with excitement as his sixty sabres took up position on the right wing beside Sir Philip Stapleton. When would battle be joined? How would his Nottingham troopers perform? He was so proud of them – their horses in superb condition, their red tunics a splendid patch of disciplined colour. But there were doubts too: they were only a tiny part of this vast battle array. Who could tell how others would react, most of them like his own men facing death in battle for the first time?

His mind ranged willy-nilly over little things – his mother and the younger children at home, his sisters in Leicester and Sussex. Then, back to the battlefield – to his right, the Wiltshire horse with Edmund Ludlow unrecognisable in a heavy cuirass; far away, on the left wing, young Oliver, Cromwell's son . . . John Hampden's regiment in their Foresters' green miles back on the Warwick road . . . and where were Oliver Cromwell and his regiment from Cambridge?

Trying desperately to occupy his mind, Henry began to analyse the situation of the two armies. It suddenly dawned on him that the cross-country march from Northampton had been made to no purpose and without adequate reconnaissance – tiring the troops and straining the chain of supplies. And now – let the sun be his witness – Essex had ranged his forces to the west of the king's army – blocking the road to Warwick rather than London! What a ludicrous mistake! Harry shrugged his shoulders. All fighting men are fatalistic on the eve of battle. Throughout the history of war the common soldier has been involved in correcting the mistakes of his commanders. Harry repeated the prayer he'd made before his troopers earlier in the day: 'Dear Lord, we fight for Thy honour and glory. Grant us the courage to do Thy will.'

As if in answer, cannon boomed their challenge, trumpets sounded, standards were raised: and in the centre of the line the foot inched tortoise-like towards each other. Away to the left Harry saw Prince Rupert's cavalry galloping headlong into the fight. Through the dust of battle could be heard fearful cries and the scream of dying horses. And then, to his right a similar Royalist charge was unleashed. But Stapleton remained unmoved. Wilmot and Digby had directed their assault on too narrow a front, as if they were only familiar with the tactics of the hunting field. They ripped past the extreme right of the Parliamentary line and would encounter a lively defence from the reserves at Kineton when their horses were tiring.

'It's our turn now, gentlemen.' And Stapleton's front-line sabres advanced, stirrup to stirrup, quickening pace as they wheeled left into the hard-pressed Royalist foot. A strange exaltation possessed Henry Ireton. He raised his sword high, yelled, 'Yeoman of Nottingham, strike home', and spurred his horse into the fray. His fury seemed to take charge of the animal he was riding. They killed and trampled on the terrified enemy without mercy. No quarter was asked or given. Poor devils – they had no time to change formation and meet the furious flank attack of the Parliamentary horse. At that moment Harry knew neither fear nor pity. But years afterwards he would be haunted by the bewildered helpless young face of the first man he killed that day.

The slaughter was terrible, the casualties beyond counting. As evening fell the exhausted armies drew apart, too tired to resume battle. Only the dead remained in the fields below Edgehill.

So heavy were the losses and so great the damage to the Parliamentary baggage train that Essex felt bound to regroup his forces. But the Royalists were equally hard hit. In particular, the loss of experienced officers had been appalling. Yet the salient fact remained that the road to London lay open to the king.

Why, then, did Prince Rupert move so slowly down the Thames valley towards the capital? Had the loss of officers affected discipline? Did the forceful requisitioning of food and horses, which earned Rupert the *soubriquet* of Prince Robber, indicate a supply problem? Or was there dissension in the high command where Rupert's personal courage and battle experience were counter-balanced by a fatal capacity for enraging the king's closest friends?

The fact remains that while the Royalist advance on London was still short of Brentford three regiments of Parliamentary horse from Edgehill, including Ireton's Nottingham troopers, reached the capital by the longer northerly route through Dunstable and St Albans.

*   *   *

The aldermen and wealthy merchants of London were quick to disguise their loyalties and hide their plate. But the sergeant-major-general of the Train Bands of London was made of sterner stuff. Skippon's long experience of war told him all he needed to know about long marches and hurried journeys.

'I tell you, Martin, lad,' he addressed himself to Cornet Dowdswell, his newly appointed aide-de-camp, 'Rupert's men will be tired out long before they reach London. Face 'em with a show of strength and I guarantee they'll run to their burrows like rabbits. So, with the agreement of Mr Pym and the lord mayor, we call out the train bands. You understand, Martin? All twenty thousand of them. And we put up such a show that the citizens will cheer us to the echo – an echo, lad, which will reach Rupert's ears in spite of his finely dressed locks. Early to bed, Martin. I want you at Finchley tomorrow at five a.m., with your horse watered and fed and three days' rations in your saddle bag. We've a long day ahead.'

It was a fine sight indeed that Philip Skippon offered the citizens of London as the six volunteer regiments, Red, White, Yellow, Blue, Green and Orange converged on the muster ground at Chelsea Fields. Hard by Somerset House, Joe and Hannah Shipley waved and cheered as, company by company, their local regiment, the Orange, streamed westwards down the Strand with drums beating the rhythm to marching feet and Alderman Pennington heading the column just ahead of the regimental standard of Argent and Trefoil.

And moving easily along the column rode the old bible student Philip Skippon – his skin tanned by thirteen years' service in the field, his strong features and dark curled moustache and beard immediately recognised by the cheering crowd. It was marvellous what the old soldier had achieved in five years, turning these unruly apprentices into a disciplined force, proud of their uniform and properly equipped.

'Fight hearty and pray hearty – that's what old Skippon expects of his men,' said a knowledgeable fellow standing in the crowd next to the Shipleys, 'and, by God, he'll hold 'em to it – even that stripling riding close behind him.'

'No need to worry about that one, Mister,' shouted an affronted Hannah. 'Our boy's no baby.' She might have said more, but at that moment Martin espied the Shipleys and with a broad smile saluted them as he passed by.

'Sorry, Madam, didn't mean no offence,' said the knowledge-able fellow. But Hannah heard nothing. She was shouting herself hoarse with excitement and her eyes were filled with tears.

The march of the Train Bands of London ended as the old general had predicted. At Brentford on 12 November Rupert brushed aside a small force hastily assembled by Denzil Holles, but his advance guard reported that his tired men had no hope of passing Skippon's army of twenty thousand men, reinforced by three regiments of horse, which opposed his advance on London at Turnham Green. There was no alternative but to retire to winter quarters in Oxford where the king had now established his court.

Philip Skippon returned to his family at Hackney, but not to rest. Essex had appreciated, as had Captain Cromwell and Captain Ireton of the Parliamentary horse, that Skippon commanded the most efficient infantry force under Parliament's control.

Martin Dowdswell returned to the Shipleys, reporting daily to his general. Oliver Cromwell and Henry Ireton also returned with their troopers to Ely and Attenborough. Both men were acutely conscious of the failure of a campaign which had aimed to separate the king from his advisers.

Before them lay a longer, harder struggle which might well depend on speed of movement and, therefore, on the use of cavalry. As a disillusioned Cromwell remarked to his cousin, Hampden, 'You must get men of a spirit that is likely to go on as far as gentlemen will go, or else I am sure you will be beaten still.'

20

By a strange coincidence of time and place Sam Dowdswell was one of the first men to reach Oxford with reliable news of the Edgehill battle.

In the last days of October the citizens and colleges of Oxford were at first regaled with extravagant rumours – a mighty victory for King Charles, God save the King! Prince Rupert had the Roundheads on the run. Triumphant Royalist commanders were chasing the rebels back to London and meant to teach Mr John Pym a lesson he'd never forget!

Then came more muted, grimmer news, filtering through the villages north of the university city – of the slaughter of pikemen and musketeers, of regiments decimated, of officers lost; and certain great ladies were to be seen praying for the safety of their men in college chapels and St Frideswade's Cathedral.

But Sam Dowdswell of Osney brought first-hand news – not a doubt of it. At the time of the battle, and in the company of Tom Brewster and a couple of grooms, he was taking eight horses to Bridgnorth to sell to the Marquis of Hertford for his Welsh levies. Two miles west of Warwick the small party had learnt that Parliament's army was re-grouping at the town. Walking back there to find out whether it was safe to continue their journey, Sam Dowdswell and Tom Brewster had been challenged by road sentries and taken for interrogation before Captain Ireton of the Nottingham Horse.

'Sam . . . Tom . . . what in Heaven's name brings you here? Spies, are you? Or short of horses, like a lot of gentlemen I could mention?'

Henry Ireton embraced them like the old friends they were. Soon he was firing question after question at them. How were Maggie and the children – two of them now, eh? And was Betsie behaving herself? And what of the old president? Keeping the college clear of unwelcome visitors? Good. You doubt if anybody would dare to cross the old man's wishes? Good. May it continue that way.

The two men answered Henry as best they could and, in their turn, plied him with questions. What had really happened at Edgehill? Why was he here in Warwick with his Nottingham troopers? Had many horses been killed in the fighting? And was Witney safe? Was it sensible for them to proceed to Bridgnorth?

'Oh, dear me, no,' Henry laughed, as he eyed the two men. 'Bridgnorth? That would be sheer madness. And quite impossible since you are now prisoners of the Parliamentary horse. It's just lucky that you've fallen among friends, not thieves like the poor merchant on the road from Jericho! But let's make a bargain: I will buy your horses. My only trouble is that I've no immediate need of them. So I want them delivered to Tom's father who can hold them in Attenborough for Major Thornhaugh's inspection. How do you say?'

Quickly a plan was agreed. Tom, the grooms and horses would leave Warwick in the company of Henry Ireton's troopers and, after a few miles, peel off north to Dunchurch and so to Nottingham by the familiar route that Tom and Henry had first used on their ride to Oxford sixteen years previously. Sam would make his own way to Oxford and allay any anxieties which Betsie and Maggie might have concerning his unusually long absence.

'As for Edgehill' – a hard note crept into Henry's voice as if he was seeking to keep a grip on his emotions – 'don't ask me about it . . . the blood, the slaughter, the cries of wounded men, the writhing horses, the churned-up fields . . . it was terrible . . . I see it all still. We came through safely, thank God. But don't be deceived. Nobody won the day. The war goes on – and I believe Oxford will be in the centre of it.

'As for you, Sam, you may find yourself riding on the same road as the king's friends. So, if you value your safety, lie low and keep quiet about our meeting. Understood? When Tom completes his mission and returns to Oxford, it will be time enough to convey to the president and your lovely wives and children the compliments of Captain Ireton and his family. And I trust Tom will also be able to confirm,' Harry added as an afterthought, 'that Witney is in safe hands and first-class condition!'

On the day that Sam returned to Osney, the king began to establish his court and royal council at Christ Church, Oxford. Before the year's end he was joined by his nephew Prince Rupert, who had returned to Oxford with a bedraggled army, weakened by heavy desertions after the failure of its march on London.

A new military plan had to be devised by the king. But so long as his titled friends continued to dispute their respective rights to high command, his professional soldiers, like Rupert and Sir Jacob Astley, could do no more than strengthen the perimeter of Oxford's garrisons – Wallingford, Abingdon, Banbury, Brill and Farringdon – and so establish a defendable enclave with the university city as its centre-point. Trained in the continental wars, such men were accustomed to long campaigns and interminable sieges! It was a form of military life they fully understood.

Sometimes, looking ahead to the summer campaign, they would ponder on the possibilities of a three-fold advance on London – the Marquis of Newcastle from the north, Hopton from the west and Rupert in the centre down the Thames valley. But their pipe dreams were weak on Intelligence. They took too little account of General Skippon and his volunteer train bands in London. They did not understand the peace-loving preference of the southern counties of England. Nor did their knowledge extend to the activities of a certain Colonel Cromwell, governor of Ely, now building up a formidable force to stop any northern army from approaching the capital.

Meanwhile, as the first months of 1643 passed into high summer, the university city was transformed into the seat of the king's government – its dubious legality bolstered by the summons to a skeletal parliament in Christ Church Hall.

Other colleges were requisitioned. Merton, where the warden had declared for Parliament, was seized for the king's use. St John's, Archbishop Laud's old college, was made available to Rupert and his brother Maurice, and their dependants of both sexes. Jesus College was reserved for the officers commanding the loyal Welsh levies. New College became a depot for military stores. And Port Meadow, the four hundred acres of pasture to the west of the city, was commandeered for the accommodation and training of new drafts reaching Oxford from the west and north.

Secretary Nicholas, devoted and industrious as always, established a Mint at New Inn Hall to which each college was asked to donate its silver. Some gave willingly, in marked contrast to the delays of wealthy townsmen ordered to pay tribute at the Penniless Bench. Yet some tradesmen prospered. The tailors of Oxford, for example, formed a co-operative to cut uniforms and have them finished by seamstresses in the surrounding villages, though they soon began to complain that they had to wait longer for payment than the innkeepers – Mrs Wotherspoon of the Mitre among them – who made pre-payment a condition of occupancy.

Citizens less well-placed were forcibly impressed to repair the city's defences, the old walls and the Castle, now filled with prisoners of war. Among the most notable of the Brentford captives was the rebel pamphleteer, John Lilburne. He would be hanged for high treason, hung as high as Haman – or so it was rumoured: but before this public spectacle could be staged, he was freed under an exchange of prisoners agreed with Westminster. Would Members of Parliament have worked so hard for his release had they foreseen the endless trouble that Honest John would cause them in the years ahead?

This, then, was Oxford, over-filled with common soldiers and men of title and almost empty of students, to which Sam Dowdswell and Tom Brewster returned. The latter might dwell safely under the protection of Trinity's famous president, but there were spies at every street corner and much treasonable talk in the ale-houses. Any man or woman who supported Parliament could be in mortal danger – not least Sam Dowdswell whose friendship with Ireton of the Nottingham Horse was well known to his old enemy, William Sanderson of Witney.

Oxford was also the city into which Queen Henrietta Maria made her triumphant entry around mid-summer.

From the moment she decided to leave The Hague – the hateful place of exile where the Puritan burghers referred to her as 'the Popish brat' and Charles as 'the man of Sin', the daughter of Henri Quatre behaved with all her father's legendary courage. In order to hasten the supply of arms and money to sustain the royal cause, she insisted on setting sail for England in gale conditions with the North Sea in its most hostile mood. Her squadron of Dutch ships was scattered and driven back by adverse January winds when within sight of the English coast; but on a second attempt in February she landed successfully on a deserted stretch of coast near Bridlington.

With a few ladies in attendance (and her favourite dog, Mitte) the queen scrambled to land over the rocks and lived rough with a posse of soldiers under bombardment from the Parliamentary guns until they were silenced by fire from the Dutch ships off-shore. From the coast she moved inland across the moors to Royalist York, and after a three-month stay assembled sufficient force to risk a journey through the rebel-infested country to the south. Crossing the Trent at Newark, she completed her hazardous journey to Oxford without further incident, skilfully avoiding Sir John Meldrum and his Parliamentary forces who seemed unwilling to face the three thousand men-at-arms escorting the queen.

Her courage and endurance had been truly remarkable. Prince Rupert welcomed her at Stratford-on-Avon where she spent the night in Shakespeare's house, and the king rode from Oxford to greet her at Kineton close to the site of the Edgehill battle. And at last, accompanied by her devoted soldiers from the north and one hundred and fifty wagons of supplies, she was escorted through cheering crowds to the lovely precincts of Merton College where she and her ladies hoped to reside until the king returned to Whitehall.

One of the few ladies who had braved the fearful journey from Holland to Oxford was Susanna Martin of North Cray, Kent. However great the risk of the voyage, she had been only too happy to get back to England and away from the censorious Dutch burghers who made the queen so bad-tempered. For Susanna, the stay in York and the hazardous march through enemy country had been exhilarating as well as exciting and had clearly won her the royal favour. By the queen's express wish she was now installed in Merton College with a room of her own which overlooked the Fellows' charming walled garden and its splendid mulberry tree. She was even allowed to exercise the queen's spaniels in Christ Church meadows, and was often summoned to the queen's lovely light room with its mullioned window facing south over the great Quadrangle. There she would be asked to converse in French and so provide a little innocent amusement to Her Majesty.

Sometimes Susanna would be ordered to hurry down the fine carved-oak staircase and open the door to the king who liked to visit the queen by a private way from Christ Church which brought him to Merton Chapel by way of the Corpus garden. Susanna grew accustomed to King Charles' small stature, his long Stuart face and his strange, expressive eyes. To her he was invariably courteous and charming; and when she and the queen sang a little *chanson* together with the queen providing a lute accompaniment, his cares seemed to fly away. The king loved music as he loved the work of the great painters.

But Susanna also noted the king's dependence on Henrietta Maria. They were lovers in the fullest sense, but the queen's word was dominant. As her attendants knew, Henrietta Maria was at her most imperious and the king most vulnerable after they had made love. Immediately on reaching Oxford, she persuaded King Charles to create Harry Jermyn Baron Jermyn of Saint Edmundsbury – a fair reward, many would agree, for the faithful service of *le favori* during the queen's exile.

Sometimes the queen's feminine intuition proved right, as when she persuaded the king to commission James Graham, Earl of Montrose, to raise the Highlands for the Crown. She had conceived a great admiration for this gallant Highlander when, at York, he had sworn loyalty to the queen after hearing that Parliament had named her traitor. But it was a different matter when her personal opinions obtruded into governmental and military decisions, for she was jealous of anybody who might challenge her influence over the king. In Oxford, she disliked Prince Rupert as she had once disliked Laud, the seventy-year-old archbishop, still languishing unmourned in the Tower of London. The hero of the Oxford Royalists was, in her view, an insufferable young German princeling, far too big for his riding boots. In no circumstances would she wish the king to give overall command of the army in Oxford to his twenty-three-year-old nephew, though Rupert's pre-eminence as a victorious commander in the field was beyond dispute.

To win the royal favour, you must make the queen your advocate. And the rule would hold so long as the queen remained in Oxford.

Outside the enclave of Royalist Oxford small sporadic battles continued, with victory and defeat more or less evenly shared, and all of them to no purpose.

In the North, at the start of the year, Newcastle's Royalist Whitecoats recovered most of Yorkshire from the tired, outnumbered forces of the Fairfax family, only to find that no move south was feasible while Hull remained in Fairfax hands.

The defence of Hull was not unconnected with a series of meetings held by local Parliamentary leaders in Nottingham to which Henry Ireton had returned after Rupert's retreat from London. Henry had led his battle-weary troopers home for rest and re-equipment and formally handed them over to Francis Thornhaugh, now promoted Colonel. For the moment, Henry was free to relax at the Ireton home in Attenborough.

But somehow the art of relaxation escaped him, and his home held no charms. Jane Ireton was the first to sense the change in her son. There was a harder, sterner look in eyes that reflected the burden as well as the horror of war. Gone was the happy warrior who had proudly led his troop of sixty men to the muster at Northampton. Gone was the optimist who had foreseen a swift campaign and the return to Whitehall of a king prepared to rule in concert with the people's representatives rather than in defiance of them. A mood of impatience and frustration overlay all his thoughts and actions.

Francis Thornhaugh also noted the change in Henry Ireton. So did Henry's young brothers. So did old Brewster and his wife who had received no hint of it from Tom when he had delivered the Dowdswell horses a few months previously.

What's troubling Harry, they all wanted to know. Why the sadness in his eyes? What have they seen?

'I'll tell you what I've seen,' he told his mother bitterly. 'I've seen stupidity in high places – a civilian committee in London giving contradictory orders to an army in the field; and an army wasting its men by setting up garrisons here and relieving them there. Men in garrisons don't win battles, do they? Of course not. They merely prolong a war and make new enemies by plundering the countryside.'

Henry's black mood persisted through the winter months. Often he might be found praying in St Mary's church. Often he would have Witney saddled and ride to consult Francis Thornhaugh or Colonel Hutchinson and his wife, Lucy, in Nottingham Castle. He could not stand inaction, even though common sense told him that, while the king held Newark, every available soldier in Nottingham was required to guard the city against Royalist marauders.

Not even the spring flowers and the early mating calls of the birds could bring joy to Henry Ireton. The fresh colours and sounds of the countryside he loved continued to mock his aimlessness until a glorious morning dawned at the end of May, and with the dawn a message from his cousin John Hutchinson at Nottingham Castle.

Colonel Cromwell, fresh from his successful fight at Grantham, had arrived unheralded in the city. He would like to meet Francis Thornhaugh and Henry Ireton, and would hope to stay with the Iretons if that could be arranged. Arranged? But of course. Jane Ireton had observed the change in her son as he read his cousin's message. She too would like to meet this man, Oliver Cromwell, of whom she'd heard so much.

Officially, the colonel came to Nottingham with plans for building up a Midlands force modelled on the Eastern Association which he had helped to create. Unofficially, his presence in Nottingham brought fresh inspiration – a re-creation of confidence. With the ladies – young wives of Lucy Hutchinson's generation, as well as anxious mothers like Jane Ireton – he radiated the charm and good humour of a man totally unaffected by success or rank. With Henry's close friends – Thornhaugh and his father, John and George Hutchinson, Gervase Pigott of Thrumpton, Tom Charlton and the rest of them, mostly linked by ties of marriage as well as friendship – he inspired an extraordinary sense of purpose.

There was something about this broad-shouldered, stocky Fenland farmer that cast a spell over all of them – young and old. One evening Jane Ireton watched him amble off to the stables, led by her younger sons and hand-in-hand with her teenage daughter. He'd like to take a look at Henry's horses, he said. And next day old Brewster was singing Colonel Cromwell's praises to all his friends in the village: A fine man ... yes, a fine man, Madam, and knows a good horse when he sees one. Mark my words: we could travel a long way with Mr Harry's new friend.

But Oliver brought reassurance too to those immediately concerned with holding the Trent crossing against a Royalist thrust from Yorkshire. Don't worry, he told John Hutchinson. Parliament would meet his request for reinforcements. And don't shed any more tears about the failure to capture the queen on the road between Newark and Oxford. That little affair was all over and done with. Anyway, her capture might have been very embarrassing. Indeed, she might well prove a serious embarrassment to His Majesty in Oxford. Oliver's laughter burst out as if he already knew the trouble the queen and her ladies would cause by their presence in the university city – and the young men laughed with him.

Meanwhile, would not Thornhaugh's regiment benefit from some service in the field? If it could be spared to strengthen Cromwell's cavalry from the eastern counties, they might combine to relieve the dangerous pressure being exerted by Newcastle's Whitecoats.

Early in July Colonel Thornhaugh and Major Ireton rode eastwards past Nottingham's cheering citizens at the head of a re-equipped regiment of horse to join Oliver's Cambridge regiment. Though the combined force was not strong enough to threaten Newark, they surprised Gainsborough and then conducted a masterly withdrawal in the face of Newcastle's superior forces. Thornhaugh was made prisoner but escaped to Lincoln, and this feat helped to boost their confidence sky high.

At Winceby, where Oliver escaped death by a miracle, they went forward to win a significant victory which led to the crossing of the Humber and the relief of Hull. So the pressure from the north was reduced and Thornhaugh's regiment returned with honour to its home base in Nottingham. In December Colonel Thornhaugh was duly appointed High Sheriff of the County.

But Henry Ireton did not return to Attenborough. He and his war-hardened troop became a squadron in Oliver's own cavalry regiment that was soon to become the *corps d'élite* of the Parliamentary cavalry. To mark his new allegiance Cromwell appointed him as his Deputy Governor at Ely, while the relief of Hull also led to the first meeting between Harry and the heroic Tom Fairfax.

Oliver, who had persuaded Henry to stay with him in Ely, now watched the start of a remarkable partnership with great personal satisfaction. Here were two men with whom it would be a joy to work: men fearless in battle, superb horsemen, tolerant as Independents in their religious stance, men whose word was their bond. At the age of thirty-one Oliver judged each man to be qualified for leadership by experience as well as by character – Black Tom's tactical skill as a soldier being matched by Henry Ireton's logic and dialectical skill. Together, they would be his greatest source of strength.

Jane Ireton learnt of her son's advancement from Francis Thornhaugh. It came as no surprise to her. Ever since Henry had first reported on his meetings with Cromwell at Westminster and Drury Lane, his mother had been waiting for this moment of separation. She knew in her heart that something far more powerful than opportunity had impelled Harry to follow Cromwell's star. The future must be in God's hands – not hers. In the silence of her own room she knelt at her desk and prayed for the safety of the Governor of Ely and his deputy.

As the months passed, the hopes of the Oxford high command gradually vanished into thin air. In the west, the great port of Bristol fell to Rupert, and his brother Maurice enjoyed some success in Wiltshire. But the experienced Hopton, though he registered a series of victories over Waller, could not persuade his Cornish army to move beyond the borders of their native county. Gloucester, the gateway to Wales, was besieged but held firm for Parliament until relieved by the Train Bands of London. Skippon marched across England to the city's rescue, displaying powers of endurance hardly less remarkable than the queen's on her journey to Oxford. The courage of the London Train Bands was further tested when Essex's army, of which they were part, began its return march to the capital.

At Newbury they were challenged by Rupert who deployed a considerable Royalist force to block the London road. There ensued a furious battle, with casualties as heavy as at Edgehill. The Royalists' losses were so serious that Rupert had no option but to withdraw to Oxford and allow Essex free passage to London.

Among the wounded on that autumn day outside Newbury was Martin Dowdswell. He was in the thick of the battle, close by Philip Skippon, when his horse stumbled and he was felled by an enemy halberd. The old soldier saw the boy's plight and stood between him and his assailants while he ordered some soldiers to carry Martin to the rear and get his wound properly cleaned and dressed. Later that evening the general saw Martin again. His orders were clear-cut, as usual.

'You've got to rest, Martin, until that wound heals – and no "ifs" and "buts" about it, young man. We'll find a safe lodging for you, never fear. Goodbye for the present. I must see these Londoners safely home. They've done me proud today – the finest men I've ever commanded in battle. And that includes you, lad, though you're only half a Londoner. Join me again when you're fit for battle. And may the good Lord be with you.'

That was all the old man said, but it was enough for Martin: he had passed the soldier's test. Taken to a safe house, the fine Tudor mansion of Littlecote near Hungerford, he was tended by the Popham household. A month later he moved in civilian clothes up the Vale of the White Horse. He was dressed as an itinerant bookseller, but he carried a warrant with a forged seal which authorised him to carry despatches between the local garrisons round Oxford. To be on the safe side, he by-passed Farringdon and Abingdon and late one night crept into the Dowdswells' house in Osney. Sam and Betsie were staggered – indeed horrified – by his arrival. There was no doubt about their welcome, but they reckoned they had sufficient problems on their hands without the presence of a rebel soldier in their spare bedroom.

21

At his stables in Osney, Sam Dowdswell was acutely aware of the danger of his situation. All his life he'd taken risks to gain and keep his independence, and in wartime there was no shortage of risk in running a business like his, dealing in a commodity of prime importance to both sides. But the presence in his house of a wounded refugee from the Parliamentary army was more than he'd bargained for.

Luckily, Martin's thigh wound was healing excellently, and he was actively plotting a return to his regiment. It was simply a question of choosing the moment and the method, and both would need Sam Dowdswell's help. Meanwhile, Martin was careful not to be seen in Osney. He would leave the village early and spend the daylight hours unnoticed in the crowded streets of Oxford, only returning to Sam and Betsie after darkness had fallen. From time to time he stayed in the rooms above the Trinity College stables to which Tom and Maggie Brewster had been moved after their Holywell cottage had been requisitioned for the military.

But he was far from idle on these city visits, taking careful note of the Royalist dispositions: the magazine of arms and gunpowder in the little cloisters at New College, the victuals store in Guildhall, the clothing in the Music School and the artillery train in Magdalen park. Philip Skippon had trained him well.

He was reasonably sure he had escaped recognition until he heard from Tom that the eagle eye of the old president had spotted him leaving the college; and on the same day, as he later confessed to his mother, he only just avoided his old flame, Susanna Martin, who was strolling with another lady of the court in the college gardens. When Sam Dowdswell's children also reported that a nasty man had been asking questions in Osney about the identity of their lodger, Martin knew it was high time for him to make his escape.

But even if Martin's departure lessened the danger, it would not solve Sam Dowdswell's dilemma. A false move – or even a lickspittle policy – could ruin the future of Betsie and the children as well as his own. Which side should he serve? Or should he supply both sides? All said and done, he felt no hostility to King Charles, though he trusted Henry Ireton and felt an almost fatherly interest in Martin. What would his wife advise?

Betsie was sick of Sam's questions – she'd been listening to them ever since the king had established Oxford as his wartime capital. 'It's clear enough,' she replied with some asperity. 'Martin must get away at the earliest possible moment. And then, Sam, you'll do well to be honest with yourself. You *know* you are going to back Parliament, not because of Harry Ireton or young Martin, but because you loathe William Sanderson like the plague. And you know that he and the Pope family have declared for the king.'

Having settled the question of allegiance, Betsie projected her tactical plan. It would be wise, she thought, to appear hand in glove with the Royalist administration; and, with a cunning use of recommendations from pre-war clients, Sam managed to win for himself a licence to supply horses for the King's Lifeguards and Prince Rupert's Horse. On the strength of this royal appointment he obtained from the city governor a licence to purchase remounts for the Oxford army outside the perimeter forts. His forays would be on the king's business, with no questions asked at the city gates when he returned with a string of horses for His Majesty.

Sam Dowdswell's business flourished as never before, yet he was too honest to be happy. Deep in his innermost being lay an inescapable stratum of Puritan belief, dating back to his childhood days at Witney. After the queen's arrival in Oxford, this distaste for double-dealing was fanned by resentment over the pomp of the court and, more especially, the behaviour of the titled non-combatants lording it in the city.

Nor was he alone. Other citizens, whose lives were being turned upside down by intolerable demands for accommodation and priority treatment, were equally unhappy. So, too, was the President of Trinity College whose uncertain temper had become totally unpredictable.

Like other heads of colleges, the old man had accepted the

king's airy promise of eventual repayment and allowed the college silver to be melted down in the New Inn Hall Mint. But Mr Secretary Nicholas had been almost blasted out of the college when he'd made a tentative request for accommodation. He'd been only too glad to accept the eccentric old man's reluctant concession that Trinity's chapel and gardens be made available for courtly worship and leisure. Thus the college grounds in the heart of Oxford became by day the Hyde Park of fashion for the court ladies and their gallants, and a place for romantic meetings after dark.

Against this strange, studentless background, the eighty-year-old president insisted on maintaining his accustomed state – his diminished staff reinforced by the presence of Tom and Maggie Brewster and their two children. Day after day the faithful Simon would, with Tom's assistance, help the gout-ridden old man to the chapel, while Maggie worked in the kitchen. All of them were liable to suffer the president's sudden bursts of ill-humour, save for the little Brewster boys whom he treated with surprising patience and affectionate generosity. It was as if they took the place of the students he missed.

One day a curious idea possessed the president. Maggie Brewster was summoned to his study and ordered to buy serviceable clothes for the children, and something for herself to match the dresses of the ladies promenading in the college gardens. The old man was chuckling at some private joke as he spoke. 'It's a long time, Miss Maggie, since I bought a set of clothes for your first baby.' There was a warmth of affection in his eyes. 'Don't look so surprised, my dear. You've as good a right to fine clothes as any of those so-called ladies who come half-clad to the chapel as if they aped the angels. Get along with you. Consult Mistress Wotherspoon, should you need advice, and then show me what you buy.'

Simon, whom Maggie rushed to consult, assured her that it was always best to gratify the president's whims, even when they sounded crazy; and a week later Maggie made a deep curtsey to the president, wearing her new finery. She had bought herself an over-dress of rose-red satin cut low on the shoulders and drawn in at the waist to show a confection of grey-blue material embroidered in pink, above and below the waistline. She looked superb and the president was delighted.

'Splendid, Miss Maggie, splendid. Spare your blushes, and take the boys to the garden this very day. These so-called gentlewomen are going to die of envy, I'll be bound.'

Nobody ever knew what was in the president's mind. But Maggie and the children were close to the cushioned garden chair in which Dr Kettel had been installed by Simon and Tom when she heard him shouting furiously at two of the court ladies, one of whom had apparently thought to make fun of the eccentric old scholar.

'I've never seen him so angry or heard his voice so harsh,' Maggie told Tom later. '"I will not call you whore," he shouted, "but get you gone for a very woman." The two ladies were terrified. I swear the doctor's eyes burnt holes in their bodices. They won't make sport with him again, I can tell you.'

The humiliation of Lady Isabella Thynne and Mistress Fanshawe was, indeed, the talk of Oxford for weeks to come, but it had a charming sequel. Hardly had the ladies fled from the gardens in blushing embarrassment when the president beckoned to the well-dressed lady with the two little boys and allowed them to play with his Dutch watch. The eyes of the giant ceased to blaze. They positively twinkled as peace returned to his garden.

He was a strange, unpredictable man, but Maggie Dowdswell, who had come to understand his moods, knew instinctively that this was the moment to tell him of her renewed anxiety over the relationship between Martin and Susanna. The moment she spoke, the old man seemed to realise how hard the young woman found it to raise this personal problem with him, for his reaction was immediate and positive.

'Thank you, Miss Maggie, for trusting me,' he said. 'You may find it hard to believe, but ever since I saw young Martin in the college gardens I've been worrying about my part in this extraordinary business. Truth, Miss Maggie, hates being concealed. It has a way of peeping, when least expected, through the hedge of lies or silence we build around it. Now that your boy has seen his half-sister again, I think it will be best for him to hear the whole truth. Will it help you if I enlighten him?'

Maggie found it hard to hold back her tears, and the old man patted her hand in reassurance.

'Don't worry, my dear. Martin is old enough now to face the truth. It won't be the first time I've helped young men of his age to meet the unexpected chances of life. And I promise that, however he reacts, his love and respect for you will not be diminished.'

Next day Martin met the president. Nobody knew exactly what passed between them, except that, according to Simon, the president treated the young soldier as if he were a gentleman-commoner of the college. He might have been the last undergraduate to whom the president would ever address himself.

Afterwards, Martin went straight to his mother. He was smiling and quite composed. 'Susanna is my problem, not yours,' he said, and kissed her affectionately.

Dr Ralph Kettel might appear formidable and eccentric to the outside world, yet within the college he loved, he often revealed to those about him a mind of deep understanding. But death was very near. He would gossip increasingly with Simon about the old days: the state of the college when he'd been appointed president under Queen Bess, the college buildings he had repaired and built, the young men he'd sent out into the world.

For a brief interlude he was jerked back to the present by one of his old students in the person of Edward Ford. A Sussex man, true to the king by birth and inclination, Edward had been captured at Chichester by Waller and Hazelrig and only regained his freedom in the exchange of prisoners earlier in the year. He had now made his way back to Oxford to receive the accolade of knighthood from the king and with it, orders to hold Arundel Castle until relieved by Hopton's Royalist advance from the West Country. Before taking up his new military duties, Colonel Sir Edward Ford thought it courteous to pay his respects to his old president.

According to Simon, the president unloosed a barrage of questions at the new knight, as if he were still of undergraduate status: A colonel, are you, Edward? And a knight to boot? Strong in the Old Faith – but no bar to advancement, eh? Well . . . well . . . well. Now tell me about your family,

Edward. Didn't you marry Harry Ireton's sister? Yes, yes, I remember now. Her name was Sarah . . . a charming girl too. And where's Harry? No, of course you can't say for certain, but you hear he's serving this Cambridge man, Oliver Cromwell? And already appointed Deputy Governor of Ely? Well . . . well . . . well. He was always going to the top, you know. Always. Tell your lady to keep in touch with him, if she can. I see nothing but trouble ahead, terrible trouble for all of you. But I say to myself, Ford and Ireton were always good friends . . . Sarah's a good wife to you, Edward, and a good sister to Harry. Perhaps, between you, you can find the right answer for England. Who knows? I urge you, keep in touch with Harry Ireton . . . keep in . . .

Those were the last words he spoke that night. Suddenly, the old man slumped in his chair, his breathing coming in rasping jerks. It was all they could do to move him to his bed on the ground floor before Edward Ford departed, leaving Simon to watch over the sick man through the night. But next morning the president seemed to draw on some hidden reserve of strength. His breathing was more even, and in slow, measured words he gave Simon his final instructions.

'I want you to stay here, Simon, when I'm gone, and see my successor into office once the Visitor makes up his mind about the new appointment. But get the rest out of the college – especially Tom and Maggie and the two boys. Get them away from this plague-ridden city. Let them take my horses, too . . . Sam Dowdswell may be able to help . . .

'And that reminds me, Simon. Get me that scroll you witnessed for me last week.'

Simon hurried to the president's study and returned with a legal document signed by William Sanderson as agent for the Pope family and signed and sealed by Ralph Kettel, President of Trinity College. It authorised a party of two persons and two children to travel with the president's horses to a farm near Banbury bequeathed to the college by its founder, Sir Thomas Pope.

'That's all they need, Simon my old friend. Leave the rest to Sam Dowdswell. He may be a bit of a rogue but he's never let me down . . . I can't say I trust that fellow, Sanderson . . . but I pray that God and the college's pious founder will bless the venture . . . And now to bed. There's no more for me to do.'

The old president died next day. After his stormy career the most colourful character in seventeenth-century Oxford passed quietly out of this mortal life. He had no more to give. He'd seen his beloved academic world collapse about him; but the college buildings he had repaired and raised as his memorial rested on sure foundations. He had been loved by those who served him, and in the centuries to come he would be well remembered.

There had been few to mourn the president's death, for he had outlived his generation. The world of scholarship on which Ralph Kettel had bestowed his eccentric genius had disappeared. In the lanes of the city soldiers brawled, and in the colleges and cloisters students had been replaced by courtiers and their ladies. As a mark of respect the gardens of Trinity had been temporarily closed to visitors and, deprived of the president's pervading presence, it seemed as empty of life as the littered desk in his study and the curtained four-poster in the bedroom where he had died.

But his final orders had still to be carried out by the faithful men and women who had cared for him in his last days, and on a dull December morning Tom Brewster carried the president's instructions to Sam Dowdswell in Osney.

Sam, as his custom was, turned to his wife for counsel. Betsie, he assured Tom, would know best how to carry out the president's wishes. She would devise the safest way for the Brewster family and the president's horses to leave Oxford. Betsie always came up with the best ideas. She might even know how to combine the Brewsters' departure with Martin's escape from the city.

For Sam and Betsie, Martin was the paramount problem. For weeks past they had become increasingly nervous about his presence in their house – a nervousness intensified after their children had been questioned about the lodger. They believed their house was being watched; and Martin, already impatient to report the Royalist dispositions, was dangerously overconfident about his ability to avoid detection. They had a horrible feeling that the net was tightening about them.

But, after a little consideration, Betsie made it clear that a two-fold escape depended on timing as well as planning. Not before Christmas, she said. And why not? Because a fine lady – an enigmatic smile played on her lips as she used the words – a fine lady would be unlikely to take her children from Oxford until the conclusion of the Christmas festivities on Twelfth Night. Nor would a Royalist agent, such as Sam Dowdswell, tour the country for horses during the festive season.

They all agreed that Betsie knew best – but what was this talk about a fine lady? The conspirators laughed as Betsie unfolded her plan. Why, Maggie, of course. Mistress Dowdswell would be the fine lady. She would be taking her two children to Banbury to avoid the plague-ridden humours of this overcrowded, low-lying city. She would wear her new clothes, though protected against mud and cold by a fashionable over-mantle and riding boots. 'A fine lady upon a white horse,' somebody said 'and riding to Banbury Cross.' Correct, said Betsie: Except that the president's horse is grey. And being a fine lady, she would naturally be accompanied by a faithful serving man to act as her bodyguard and carry the two children – the baby in a special satchel and the elder boy astride in front of him.

Betsie was warming to her theme. But Tom and Maggie, she emphasised, would also need time to practise their respective roles and teach the children to remain silent until clear of the city gates. And then, there was Sam – he'd need a few days to procure a suitable side-saddle for the fine lady and her grey horse.

'But wait a moment, Betsie love. Is that all I have to do?'

'Certainly not,' Betsie told her husband. 'But your expedition to buy horses for His Majesty's Lifeguards will be a separate operation – quite separate, even though it will take place at the same time. You will leave Osney with a groom, as you always do, but the groom will be young Martin.'

'And where do we link up with the others, Betsie?'

'Ah-ha! But that's a secret,' said Betsie, putting a finger to her lips. 'Tom and Maggie may have a little surprise on the journey. Only one thing is certain: they will never get as far as Banbury Cross.'

That was the size of it, Betsie would say no more for the moment. But Sam, Tom, Maggie and even Martin were all convinced that Betsie knew best. As old Simon confirmed to Tom Brewster, the president had a high regard for her ability. 'He told me once that if you wanted to know what was happening in Oxford, your best intelligence would come from the dining room at the Mitre. And for Dr Kettel that meant Miss Betsie. So, I says to you, Tom: don't worry about tomorrow. Just follow Miss Betsie's plan. She's a very clever girl.'

And with that, Simon retired to his small private room in the President's Lodgings to clean what remained of the college silver. Dr Kettel would expect him to keep everything neat and tidy for his successor. Simon shared his late master's pride in the college. He, too, was part of it.

22

Major Henry Ireton, newly-appointed Deputy Governor of Ely, paused on a street leading down from the Cathedral Close to the low-lying fields surrounding the high ground on which the town is built.

He was in the process of completing a survey of the domain for which he was now responsible. Southwards, he had ridden the Cambridge road with Oliver – and incidentally picked up expert tips on the characteristics of the Fenland people: Tough, Harry, that's what they are . . . Tough. Loyal and God-fearing, but slow. No good trying to hurry them . . . they don't like change . . . and yet, when it comes to a fight, they can be as cunning as they are tough . . . a bit like Hereward the Wake, I'd say.

After this tutorial Henry had made his way to the Ouse riverside on the east of the city. Standing on the quay, he stared across the endless flats of East Anglia, speculating as to what lay beyond his range of vision: centres of population like Norwich and Ipswich, and small rivers peacefully me-andering towards the hostile sea. It was an unfamiliar horizon.

Close by the river he had seen his Nottingham troopers safely settled with their horses in regimental quarters. Indeed, he'd meant to live there with them, as he had always done on campaign, but old Mrs Cromwell had told him very firmly that, as Deputy Governor of Ely, he was expected to live at the top of the hill. He smiled as he thought of the old lady: her age was well into the seventies, he reckoned, but she'd a mind of her own and a clear voice to which all the Cromwell family listened. Even in her old age it was easy to see in her strong open features the trace of her son's prominent nose and wide-set eyes.

So Henry had turned back to his house on the hill, hard by the remains of the former Benedictine Priory; and was now looking west over acre upon acre of flat fields, similar in every way to the dismal landscape he'd seen to the south and east of the city, the bridle paths from the dwarf farm buildings joining larger tracks leading to this central height of land, this Isle of Ely where long ago men had chosen to honour God with the greatest building Henry had ever seen. In the dim light of the December afternoon his eyes picked out the boundaries of the Fenmen's peat-workings and the rectilinear design of the drainage system planned by Vermuyden and the Dutch engineers. What a contrast with the twists and turns of the river that brought the water of middle England past St Ives and Ely to the Wash and the open sea. He must presume – and he smiled again – that God, the creator of the world, had no use for straight lines.

Looking towards the setting sun, he knew that somewhere, beyond the grazing meadows and the waterways lined with sedge and willow, he would come upon Ely's sister landmark, the great Cathedral of Peterborough. To the north he would find Lincoln, Gainsborough and Hull – the country over which the autumn battles had been fought. And somewhere, between the compass points of north and west, would lie his own county of Nottingham. Out there to the north-west lay the land he knew and loved.

He fell to wondering how his troopers would take to the damp bleakness of the Fens. Would they stay with him or seek a return to the fields and woods they'd known from infancy? Indeed, he began to wonder how soon he himself might expect to return to his farming at Attenborough, and thanked God for a mother who was proving such an efficient deputy in his absence. Henry Ireton pulled himself up with a jerk. When you're fighting a war, nostalgia is out of place and a waste of time. It's better to concentrate on today's tasks and pray that you will see tomorrow.

That evening he dined with the Cromwells in the governor's house beside St Mary's Church. The family was at full strength except for young Oliver who was serving in a garrison at Newport Pagnall. What a lively lot these Cromwells were.

At the head of the table sat Oliver, just promoted Colonel of Horse under the Earl of Manchester, with his old mother in the place of honour on his right, and on his left fourteen-year-old Betty with the sparkling eyes and happy smile.

Henry Ireton found himself at the other end of the table,

placed beside Mrs Cromwell who accepted the vagaries of life with a look of humorous resignation, but who was capable, as he was soon to discover, of exercising firm authority over her large family, including her husband.

The two little girls, Mary and Frances, were giggling together at some joke of their own. Between them was the fair-haired Henry Cromwell, already showing, at fifteen, something of his father's broad-shouldered physique. Then there was Oliver's unmarried sister and Richard who was known in the family as Dick. Although he was two years older than his brother Henry, he seemed less mature – a more sensitive type whose features gave a hint of the family's Welsh ancestry.

Henry Ireton's immediate companion at the dinner table was the eldest Cromwell daughter. Bridget was a girl of nineteen, already occupied with her mother in running this busy household. One day Henry meant to see more of this rather serious young woman who, in a curious way, appeared to be a feminine version of her father – with the Cromwell nose and strong hands and the wide-set eyes that suggested an inner depth of understanding. Tonight she was reserved, taking little part in the conversation, as if her chief concern was to see the meal efficiently served. The talk was of a general nature such as Henry would have heard in the Ireton home – inconsequential local jokes about the Fenmen's offerings of eels or wildfowl in place of tithes, and some pawky reference to the liturgy still being used in the cathedral.

'Patience, Mother,' Oliver was gently teasing the old lady. 'I'll sort out the clergy one of these fine days. But first things first. Meanwhile, I'll leave you to tell the world that the disappearance of the cathedral's Popish decorations was not my doing, but the work of some chancellor of Henry VIII who was clever enough to retain his job and his bishopric under Queen Mary. A man, you might say, of considerable intelligence and no principles. He might even find himself at home today in the royal court. But that, dear Mother, is only your son's personal opinion!'

The following day Henry found that Oliver had thrown away the role of *pater familias*. He was back as a field commander in the Eastern Association Army, making plans for the 1644 campaign. Henry Ireton's first task, he was informed, was to fit the Nottingham Horse into the great cavalry regiment, eleven hundred strong, now training at Ely.

'I'll help you,' said Oliver, 'and so will my brother-in-law, Desborough. All you need know at this stage is that, unlike your Nottingham Militia, your fellow officers are not all of ancient lineage. They come from every station in life – chosen like you, Harry, because they know what they're fighting for. Some need more battle-training. None of them knows as much about horses as you do. But I promise that by mid-summer this regiment of ours will be capable, with God's help, of driving this German Prince Rupert out of our English fields and back to the Rhineland where he belongs.'

Oliver's confidence was as compelling at Ely as it had been in London and Nottingham, and Harry was again conscious of certain qualities in this man of many moods which made him so much more than a soldier. There was, above all, an emotional commitment which he never attempted to hide. He needed to share his grief over any personal loss he was called to face. Henry knew that Oliver had been heart-broken when his eldest boy, Robert, had died of some mysterious illness at the age of eighteen, and a few months past had wept for the loss of his cousin John Hampden at Chalgrove Field. 'It should never have happened,' he kept saying, trying to control his emotion. 'A skirmish without purpose and England's finest leader in Parliament dead . . . It should never have happened.'

The loss of Hampden led Cromwell to consider the greater political void caused by John Pym's death from cancer, the news of which had just reached Ely. 'A great man and a great leader,' Oliver told Ireton. 'But in his last days I fear he made a terrible mistake. He should never have signed this so-called Solemn League and Covenant. Oh yes, I know that the arrival of the Scots can solve our manpower problem in the north. I know the Scots are a martial race with many professional soldiers trained in the continental wars under the Swedish king. But tell me, Harry, have you ever known a Scotsman give his service to England for nothing? You mark my words. The Scots will claim their pound of flesh as surely as Shylock in the play. And if, as I fear, they force Parliament to adopt rigid Presbyterian rules to regulate our worship in England, they will split this country as certainly as did King Charles and the red-faced Laud. I see a very ugly prospect on the Scottish border. Personally, I prefer to solve our English problems by ourselves.'

The following day Cromwell gave his sixteen troop commanders their orders: In the next three weeks they must be ready to move cross-country in small commando groups – objective, the Oxford enclave. The task – to harry the enemy. Hit and run. Collect all the horses you can. Round up cattle. Disrupt roads. Destroy bridges. But no pitched battles: is that understood? Think of the expedition as a training exercise in cavalry tactics or a reconnaissance in sufficient force to cause an attack of nerves among the Oxford courtiers and their ladies.

One final point. Strict discipline must be maintained. No plundering of peaceful citizens. No booty or theft except from known Royalists. If some stray soldier surrenders, take his horse, his arms and boots and let him walk home at his own pace. We don't want to be slowed down by a trail of prisoners. But should any troop commander – and here Oliver burst out laughing – should any troop commander happen to meet the king out hunting . . . why, conduct him here with all haste! I'm sure the Governor of Ely will be proud to provide His Majesty with the finest accommodation our Fenmen can make available.

At Oxford Betsie Dowdswell's double escape plan had taken more time to evolve than she would have wished. It was not until first light on a damp morning in late February that a lady of quality and her attendant finally mounted the president's greys and rode out of the Trinity stables on to the Banbury road. Maggie played her part to perfection. Somehow or other, Betsie had acquired a fashionable riding surcoat and felt boots to protect the lady's clothes, and she had topped the outfit with a velvet hat and a stylish feather to give it a touch of distinction. The lady riding on a fine horse was, for all to see, a person of importance, concerned to take her young family away from the health dangers of this overcrowded city.

At such an early hour the streets were virtually deserted. The riders passed a group of Welsh soldiers blearily returning to Port Meadow after a night in town. At the Lamb and Flag an ostler was cleaning up in front of the inn, but he was too busily occupied to take heed of the travellers. Thus unnoticed, they passed the church of St Giles and reached the city gate without incident.

Their luck also held at the guard post. A sleepy sentry briefly examined the imposing 'pass' which the great lady ordered 'her man' to produce in a voice which carried a nice blend of authority and asperity, and within a few minutes Maggie and Tom Brewster were on their way, encouraged by a parting salute from the guard who wished them a safe journey thought them lucky to be leaving Oxford. Soon they were quietly riding abreast along the high road to Banbury, not expecting to be 'surprised' by Sam Dowdswell and Martin until they reached the neighbourhood of Shipton-on-Cherwell.

Sam and Martin, however, were not so fortunate. In accordance with Betsie's plan, they had ridden westwards out of Osney, intentionally moving in a different direction from the Brewster family. Sam, accompanied by one or more hands, was a familiar figure up and down the Witney road and was duly recognised by friends who knew him to be employed in the purchase of horses for the king and Prince Rupert. As Sam crossed the Thames at the Swinford toll-bridge he told his old friend the toll-keeper that he had orders to proceed to the big house fortified by the king at Blessington, and would travel there via Eynsham and Woodstock. He gave no hint that the road he had chosen would also make it easy for him and Martin to intercept the Brewsters on the Banbury road.

But the two men were less than a mile past the toll-bridge when they were challenged by two troopers from a detachment of Royalist horse. In vain, Sam flourished his royal warrant and assured a dim-witted corporal-of-horse that he was making for Blessington on the king's business. The corporal remained suspicious. Marauders, it seemed, from the Parliamentary forces had been raiding the neighbourhood for horses and cattle. But Sam must have made some impression, for the man decided to leave an armed trooper with Sam and Martin, while he obtained further instructions from his commanding officer.

Sam thought fast. Interrogation and delay could prove fatal.

He gave the guard's horse a terrific whack on the flanks which caused the animal to buck and all but unseat its rider. Long before the trooper had recovered his stirrups, Sam and Martin were away at a gallop across fields that Sam knew like the back of his hand. But what should be their next move? The hue and cry would be raised along the length of the Eynsham–Woodstock road. Their only chance was to move at top speed to a point nearer Oxford in the hope that they could intercept the Brewsters earlier in their journey than originally planned.

It was a close-run thing, for when Sam and Martin emerged on to the Banbury road near Kidlington, spattered with mud and cut with briers, their hard-ridden horses almost winded, they saw Maggie, Tom and the children riding towards them.

'What on earth . . .' Maggie began. 'We were expecting you miles further . . . what's happened?'

But Sam had no time for talking. 'We cross the Cherwell here,' he said, 'I've friends at Islip.' They crossed another small stream and, threading their way up Islip's narrow main street, halted for a break in the shelter of Islip Church tower.

A loiterer asked them where they were heading.

'Escorting the lady and her children to her home at Bicester,' Sam replied.

'You'd best stay here, Mister. There's danger out there. They say Cromwell's Horse are scouring the countryside, seizing horses and driving away the cattle. That's no place for a lady, Mister! And they say them troopers eat children for supper!'

What idiotic stories these idle fellows invent, thought Sam. But say what they like, we'll make for Bicester, just the same. His party would stand a better chance with the men ahead than with the men behind him; and if there was trouble with these Parliamentary raiders, Martin could act as spokesman, and the royal warrant could go in his boot.

In fact, their progress was soon halted. Beyond Islip the road was blocked by a herd of cattle incompetently handled by a bunch of Parliamentary troopers who were clearly new to the job. Any countryman could have told them that if you round up cows before the morning milking, they won't move anywhere fast!

The same thought came to a neatly dressed officer who appeared at the far side of the herd to find out what was causing the delay and the noise. Abruptly the silly shouting ceased. Men were ordered to borrow milking pails from a neighbouring farm. Some cattle strayed off the road and the officer was able to make his way towards Sam's party, who suddenly recognised Henry Ireton. When the mutual cries of joyful astonishment ceased it was Henry and Sam who were the first to collect themselves.

'I think you'd better join us,' Henry said, drawing away from his devoted troopers who were straining their eyes to identify the major's friends from the enemy's country. 'My orders are clear. Take horses and cattle from any known supporters of the king, but avoid fighting and take no . . . er . . . prisoners. And now, by Heaven, we've collected four of them and a couple of small children for good measure.'

Henry was in great spirits. 'Now, look here, Sam,' the major continued to his leading prisoner, 'we've done enough to put this part of the world in a panic, so I suggest we move north into safer country. Agreed? Right. Then, when we reach the Leicestershire border, Tom can conduct Maggie and the children to my sister Mary's place at Lockington – there's plenty of room in Bainbrigge's big house. As for Martin, he can travel with Tom and Maggie; or if he's fit enough to rejoin his unit, he can ride with us to Ely, and in due course report to General Skippon in London.

'But Sam, what on earth do we do with you?'

A smile spread across the older man's tanned face – he'd always enjoyed a special friendship with young Harry, as he still thought of him. 'May I suggest, Sir' – and Sam mockingly touched his forelock – 'that, for once in a way, you disobey your orders and take me prisoner. My poor young stable lad is brutally killed before my eyes . . . a terrible sight, Major . . . but in the confusion I escape . . . You take my meaning? Yes, I'd prefer to keep my boots, if I may. But you steal my superb horse, and I get away on one of those wretched animals you've just stolen, knocking out my guards in the process . . . Your men are amazed at my courage . . . shout "good riddance" as I spur the old crock into a gallop . . . lo and behold, Major, you've successfully lost your embarrassing prisoner.'

Sam's imagination was running away with him but he returned to practicalities just in time. 'One point more. It would be wise for me to escape in the Aylesbury area, if you've no objection, Major. Thence I shall struggle back to my poor wife and babies by a road which nobody would expect me to take. I have, of course, been disgracefully handled and my bravery will be the talk of Oxford. Only Betsie will know the truth. But then, I've never been able to deceive her, anyway! Now, how's that for a story?'

There was no more to be said – Sam had summed up the risks. After a quick meal, Ireton's raiders , moved away in small detachments to a rendezvous near Northampton. Thence the Brewsters would travel north to Lockington, a mere twelve miles short of the Ireton territory round Attenborough. Martin would ride to Ely with the bulk of Ireton's Troop. And Sam Dowdswell would take his leave near Aylesbury to return to his wife in Oxford and, maybe, risk his life in the enemy's stronghold.

23

In due course Sam Dowdswell completed the final lap of his uncomfortable journey from Aylesbury, and urged the old jade over Magdalen Bridge after clearing his entry to the city at the guard post. The men on duty knew him well – they did not even ask to see the pass with the royal seal on it. But they listened open-mouthed to the story of his terrible experiences, and Sam's story lost nothing in the telling. Soon the guards at the gate were repeating it to a mixed audience of friends and strangers in half the ale-houses of Oxford:

Terrible experience the poor man 'ad . . . lucky to be alive . . . some place east of Islip . . . Mr Sam Dowdswell of Osney, yer know . . . out there on the king's business . . . runs into a posse of Parliamentary Horse, well armed and well mounted . . . cattle-raiders, they say . . . and there, right before 'is eyes, they murder 'is companion in cold blood, take over the 'orses 'e's been collectin' for the king and make 'im prisoner . . . an' all that 'ardly ten miles from 'ere as the crow flies. What's our lot doin', swankin' round town an' molestin' our women? That's what I'd like to know!

'Sure: but 'ow did old Dowdswell escape the villains?'

'Ah . . h . . . seems as if they takes 'im to Aylesbury, meanin' to force 'im to tell about the army's strength in Oxford. But Sam Dowdswell – 'e's a wise old bastard – waits 'is moment, slips the guard while most of 'em are off for a drink, nicks this awful old animal and gets away . . . Clever old chap, Mr Sam Dowdswell, an' lots o' spirit too.'

'The clever old chap' had in the meantime continued his ride along the High as far as the Mitre where he hired a good horse to carry him home to Osney, but not before repeating his story to the gossip-greedy Mrs Wotherspoon and her team of kitchen maids and stable hands.

Put the local residents in a panic, Mr Harry had ordered. Tell them a good story and see it gets repeated. Well, Sam thought, he'd done the major proud: told his listeners enough to strengthen the rumours already flying round the town, enough to make the grandees jumpy and their fine ladies sleep uneasy in their beds. He had no love for these fancy young men and their women who strutted round the town as if they owned the place. Sooner Oxford got rid of them, the better.

Sam was enjoying his role as *agent provocateur*, but he knew he mustn't overdo it. For the moment it would be best to lie low at Osney and hope to hear no more of that wretched corporal who'd questioned him eight days earlier at the far side of the Swinford toll.

The reports of enemy raiding parties in the Oxford enclave spread like wildfire through the inns and ale-houses of the city. Very soon they penetrated to the Royal Secretariat in Christ Church and the queen's apartments in Merton.

But the king was receiving more disturbing news from further afield. In the north the Scots had crossed the border to support the Fairfaxes, father and son, so that Newcastle's Whitecoats were hard pressed to hold York for the king. Indeed it had been necessary for Rupert to make a spectacular dash from Shrewsbury to relieve the threat to the Royalist stronghold of Newark. In the south, Hopton's Western Army could make no significant progress against Waller and Hazelrig, with Kent and Sussex showing a marked unwillingness to rise in the king's support.

As to Oxford, so frequent were the movements of great lords' personal regiments and their dispersal to outlying garrisons that, in Rupert's absence, no concentration of force seemed possible. Somehow, the king must exercise stronger personal control over his argumentative commanders if any coherent strategic plan was to be devised.

But the poor king was overburdened with more personal anxieties. His joyful reunion with the queen had inevitably led to a new pregnancy. With Oxford under threat and no hope of an advance on London, as envisaged when the queen had joined him the previous summer, Charles decided that Oxford was no place for his thirty-five-year-old queen to bear their ninth child.

Henrietta Maria, who was having a very difficult pregnancy,

accepted the king's decision with her accustomed courage, asking only that Susanna Martin should be one of her travelling companions.

The latter was, in any case, tired of Oxford. While summer lasted, she had enjoyed the court plays and the al fresco entertainments which gave the queen such pleasure. But as the dark winter evenings closed in, she had begun to feel as claustrophobic in Merton College as a prisoner in Oxford Castle. She longed to escape from the captivity of the court and return to the open acres of her father's Kent estate – a desire increased by the certainty that she had caught a glimpse of Martin Dowdswell in the Trinity gardens. The sight of him had thoroughly unsettled the girl. She felt certain he'd deliberately avoided her. But why? Why? The mere sight of him had reminded her of those meetings in London and Greenwich in a more peaceful and innocent world, and she was distressed by the memory. Angry and frustrated, Susanna was in no mood to stay in Oxford.

So she was delighted to leave Merton College when, on 17 April 1644 within eight weeks of her confinement, Henrietta Maria left the city. Taking fond leave of the king at Abingdon, the queen travelled to Bath under the protection of a cavalry escort commanded by Lord Jermyn.

The heavy coaches in which she and her ladies were carried lurched most horribly in the rutted, ill-kept road through the Vale of the White Horse. It was a rough ride for Susanna and the other women of the royal party, but for the queen it was sheer agony. Uncharacteristically, she also developed a great fear of capture, and after a few days in Bath insisted on moving to the comparative safety of Exeter.

Letters bringing news of her sad state of health caused the overwrought king such anxiety that in desperation he called for support from the queen's old medical adviser in London: 'Mayerne, for the love of me, go find my wife.' It was a royal command which Sir Theodore could not refuse.

Accompanied by another physician, the heroic old doctor completed the one hundred and seventy mile journey to Exeter in record time. Arrangements were in hand for Madame Peronne, the most famous midwife of Paris, to attend the queen's confinement. Her sister-in-law, Anne of Austria, provided a complete layette. And in Exeter, on 16 June, the Queen of England gave birth to a living child.

It was a miraculous delivery but, sadly, the birth brought no relief to Henrietta. She was still in acute pain from puerperal sepsis, when she learnt that the Earl of Essex, approaching Exeter with a Parliamentary army, had refused safe conduct to the 'Traitor Queen'. She had no option but to leave the baby to the care of Lady Dalkeith and Susanna, and creep out of Exeter disguised as a country woman. Later, she was carried in a litter by loyal Cornishmen to Pendennis Castle, one hundred miles further west; and from Falmouth a friendly Dutch vessel conveyed her to Britanny, after running the gauntlet of the Parliamentary Navy. When the poor woman reached France, broken in spirit and her back bent double, it was scarcely possible to see in her the proud Van Dyck beauty who, twenty years earlier, had travelled with such high hopes to England.

From France she wrote to the king that her own death was very near, little knowing that she would survive the beloved man to whom she had lately said farewell beside the Thames at Abingdon.

The baby girl, however, lived and grew strong. Plans were soon being negotiated for the royal child to be moved through the Parliament-strong counties of southern England to the king's country house at Oatlands Park near Weybridge. In the years to come the little girl with the dark blue eyes, christened Henrietta Anne by her father's wish and known to her eldest brother as Minette, would add her own chapter to the Stuart story.

While the joy of a new baby and the suffering of her mother combined to stir the heart of the highly emotional king, a great Parliamentary victory near York finally broke his hold on the North of England.

In those parts, the chivalry of earlier battles had largely disappeared when Royalist levies from Ireland landed at Chester and massacred the inhabitants of Bartholomy village which had opted for Parliament. And while this terrible crime was swiftly avenged by John Lambert, feeling still ran high as

Lord Leven's Scots jointed the Fairfax Yorkshiremen to lay siege to the capital of the North.

It was then that Rupert, confused by contradictory orders from the king, decided he must move to the relief of the York garrison. By another remarkable forced march across the Pennines he succeeded in raising the siege: but he completely failed to read the military situation through underestimating the strength of the Parliamentary army moving north from East Anglia to reinforce the Scots.

His miscalculation proved utterly disastrous. Perhaps he hoped to attack the Scots and detachments of Cromwell's cavalry while they were making a tactical withdrawal to Tadcaster. Perhaps he hoped to maul the Scottish infantry before reinforcements arrived from the south. If so, he failed in both objectives. Not only did Rupert and Newcastle find themselves committed to a set-piece battle against a numerically superior enemy force surveying the battlefield of Marston Moor from the high ground of Braham Hill. They also made the mistake of thinking that battle would not be joined until the following day.

Indeed, the Royalist commanders were enjoying a leisurely meal behind the lines at seven o'clock in the evening, when Oliver Cromwell's Ironsides thundered into action with devastating effect. They routed the Royalists' right wing, and though there was hard fighting in the centre and Goring's Horse drove the Fairfaxes off Braham Hill, Oliver remained master of the battlefield. He ordered the Scottish Light Horse to pursue and destroy the Royalist fugitives in Wilstrop Wood. He then directed his troop commanders Ireton, Berry, Whaley and Desborough, to wheel across the moor past Rupert's abandoned command post and attack the enemy in rear.

Oliver's victory was total. York and the North were lost to the king. Rupert barely escaped with his life. The Royalist artillery train was captured. Newcastle and his family took ship to Hamburg. The gallant Whitecoats stood their ground and were killed. In the July days that followed, the villagers of Tockwith and Long Marston buried the earthly remains of four thousand brave men who fell at Marston Moor.

Surely, after so great a victory, it should have been possible for the Scots to return to their own country and peace to return to England. But peace is an elusive thing. How could Parliament's leaders agree on terms to offer the king, while Presbyterian and Bishop and Independent were locked in argument as to the form a new government should assume? And what earthly power could persuade the king to revise his fixed ideas about the monarchy?

Henry Ireton, returning from the battlefield by way of Nottingham, pondered these questions. He was filled with foreboding when he should have been elated by victory. Whichever way he argued the case to himself, he could see no peace until Parliament and the army were reconciled. He could see no peace until their joint power was united by a single voice. He could see no peace for himself until these matters were resolved. And he could see no peace for England until King Charles agreed to parley with the victor of Marston Moor.

24

After the victory Cromwell's men were ordered south with other units of the Eastern Association, and Ireton's Nottingham Horse was granted a week's home leave before returning to Ely.

Now, fourteen days after the battle, Henry and his mother sat side by side in the sunshine on a wooden seat in the rose garden which Jane Ireton had always loved and tended. The scent of full-blown English roses pervaded the air. Bees went about their business. Cattle moved leisurely in the meadows bordering the Erewash stream, and the lake was undisturbed save for the occasional plop of landing waterfowl. Behind Henry and his mother rose the tower of Attenborough parish church, watching as if on permanent guard duty over the Ireton home.

Jane Ireton was well aware of her son's growing reputation: it was already the talk of the villagers whose small houses were scattered in unsymmetrical clusters round St Mary's. Had not two of their number accompanied Harry to the wars? And returned in his company for a short break before rejoining the regiment at Ely?

Soldiers' tales tend to exaggeration, especially when told by men who have been in the thick of the fighting. For the survivors the grief and suffering of war are quickly forgotten and replaced by visions of courage and glory which invincibly remain to stir the heart. Edgehill, Winceby, Gainsborough and now Marston Moor – all were names of battle honours won by the troop of Nottingham Horse that had followed Henry Ireton to the wars. Each engagement provided its own heroic story, but to the two young soldiers in Attenborough village, one theme stayed constant. Harry – our Harry – was a captain without peer:

A great lad, sure 'e is . . . always out front, yet comes out of the trouble without a scratch . . . an' I tell you summat else: ours is the best-run troop in General Cromwell's regiment.

Somebody asked, 'Is that the lot they call Ironsides?'

Ay, that's the name Prince Robber gives us. But Oliver Cromwell . . . ah – h what a man . . . 'Old Noll' we calls 'im . . Remember 'im staying 'ere last year . . . talked with old Brewster about 'is blessed 'orses? You should just see 'im when the fighting starts . . . An' I tell you, 'e's got a soft spot for our 'Arry. A few weeks back, got 'im appointed Commissary General, with a special job procuring good mounts for the cavalry. But, knock me down, when 'Arry sees the enemy linin' up opposite, 'e's back with us, as if by magic, an' the boys ride be'ind 'im into the scrap with a sort o' certainty I can't rightly explain . . . Born lucky, I suppose. But, yer know, 'e's still the same lad we grew up with. No side to 'im, knows us all by name, always lives with us in the field, same as Old Noll. And now, they say at the big 'ouse, young Tom Ireton's set to follow 'is brother. We'll look after the lad, best we can; but I wonder what Mrs I. will be thinkin' . . .

In the village the young lads noisily celebrated their victory and the old gave thanks for their sons' survival.

In the Ireton garden the rapport between mother and son was so absolute that speech seemed superfluous. There, before Henry's eyes, stretched his family inheritance. His mother, he was sure, had asked him to join her in the garden so that he could feast his eyes on this peaceful Ireton world in all its loveliness. With a woman's intuition, Jane Ireton was equally sure that her son would turn his back on it. But one question perplexed her. Was it emotion or ambition that prompted Harry's choice? Would the beauty of this golden afternoon evoke an honest answer?

As if her companion had heard the unspoken question, Henry turned to his mother, his voice a strange mixture of reason and emotion. 'It's like this, Mother,' he said. 'I hate leaving you and the family, our friends and . . . this peaceful place. But we are all part of England, you see, and I have been driven to the belief that only one man can restore our land to the peace and harmony this garden symbolises. And this belief or instinct – call it what you like – compels me to follow Cromwell wherever he chooses to lead. Not because he's proved himself master of the battlefield. Nor because he shares your vision and mine of an England in which the king shares power with his people as represented in Parliament. Nor yet because he shares our desire to create a land in which men and women are free to seek God in their own fashion and are never compelled by the State to a single form of worship. But because of something which I find hard to explain ... even to myself.'

Henry paused for a moment and Jane Ireton's hand gently pressed on his long tapering fingers – the hands, surely, of a thinker rather than a fighting man. Sensing her encouragement, he continued, without withdrawing his hand from hers.

'I've prayed so long about these things, you know: here in St Mary's, and in London, and Ely, and beside the camp fire. And now God – you must believe me – has given His clear, unequivocal answer. Something in my soul tells me that my vision of England can only become reality if the task is entrusted to a leader of genius. Such men, they say, only arise in an age of revolution. All I know is that in Oliver Cromwell such a man has crossed my path, and I truly believe he is God's Englishman, demanding my total allegiance.'

Jane Ireton stayed silent for a moment. She had listened to a confession, prompted by intense spiritual emotion – something with which no mortal man may argue. Then, feeling his body relax, she kissed him. 'Thank you,' she said. 'You've told me all I need to hear. Bless you, Harry, and may God march with you and Oliver on your journey.'

Henry turned and smiled at her. 'I'll be back soon,' he said lightly. 'Never fear. But one thing more I should tell you, Mother. I might bring a wife back with me. You see, I've decided to marry the eldest Cromwell daughter, if she will have me. You'll love Bridget, I'm sure. But for the moment not a word to the family until the lady's given me her answer.'

Next morning Ireton's Troop assembled at Nottingham Castle. The citizens waved and cheered as the riders clattered away down the Grantham road; and Tom Ireton rode with them. But no sooner had they rejoined the Ironsides at Ely than Henry Ireton, in his new capacity as Quartermaster General, received orders to report immediately to the Earl of Manchester at Doncaster. News of the fighting in southern England was somewhat garbled, but it was clear that while Rupert was engaged in the North the Earl of Essex had missed a golden opportunity of capturing Oxford and the king. Worse still, he'd committed the folly of splitting his army into two parts, leaving Waller dangerously exposed near Oxford while he moved on a wild-goose chase into Cornwall. Henry Ireton was not pleased. He hated incompetence and he hated dithering. Why did Parliament allow these noble earls, Essex and Manchester, to continue in command when men of the calibre of Oliver Cromwell and Tom Fairfax, Skippon, Waller and Lambert, were available? The situation must be remedied. He, Quartermaster General Ireton, would make his own assessment and report to Oliver. Ruefully, he left Ely. He had found no time to tell Bridget Cromwell what it was in his heart to say.

Martin Dowdswell would have greatly preferred to remain in the company of Ireton's Troopers after escaping from Oxford; they were a happy band and had given him a splendid welcome. But General Cromwell, who in his strange way had never forgotten his long-ago meeting with the young man in Dr Mayerne's garden, would have none of it.

'I'd like you to stay with General Skippon,' he told Martin as they rode together from Ely to London. 'That doesn't mean that Colonel Ireton or I will forget you; but, for the moment, we need you as our vital link with the general. We are all equally responsible to Parliament and its War Council; but some of us have a private citizen's interest in a swift return to peaceful government. Our immediate purpose is to separate His Majesty from his wretched self-seeking advisers in Oxford – a purpose which, in our view, will best be achieved by a quick outright victory in the field. Time, Martin, is our enemy. The king must not be given time to strengthen his local garrisons or to call in mercenaries from France or Ireland. Otherwise, England will be plagued like Europe with marches and counter-marches *ad infinitum*, and with sieges and the maintenance of strong points which can only prolong the misery of war. Have a talk, Martin, with Philip Skippon. He knows the extent of the ruin that a long war brings to a land and its people.'

A week later Martin reported to General Skippon, now commanding the Foot in Essex's Southern Army. He found the old general fuming with anger at Essex's decision to leave a small force with Waller near Oxford and direct the rest of the Southern Army towards Exeter. Any soldier with clear eyesight could see that such a move must weaken Parliament's grip on Oxford. It was a negation of the policy that Oliver had spelt out to Martin.

But Essex's march into Devon and Cornwall had a strange sequel, for Philip Skippon decided to appoint Cornet Dowdswell to his first independent command. He detailed Martin to take charge of an escort which, by command of Parliament, was to conduct the royal baby from Exeter to the royal residence at Oatlands Park near Weybridge.

There should be no trouble, the old general told his protégé, in moving a baby and a carriage-load of women across southern England. Still it might provide a good test for a young officer's initiative and, even, his tact. As for the Earl of Essex and his refusal to guarantee safe conduct to the queen, the less said, the better. In his gruff monosyllabic way, Skippon expressed his disgust that any government should give such disgraceful instructions to its soldiers.

Still, that was in the past. For better or worse, the queen was in France; and Martin's troop of sixty mounted men would be responsible solely for the safety of the royal baby until the Parliamentary Commissioners took delivery at Oatlands Park.

'As to your own bearing,' Skippon began to laugh. 'Correct is the word, Martin. Correct – and perhaps a little distant. Ensure the ladies have all they need for themselves and the baby. Stay at friendly houses, giving the residents advance notice of your expected time of arrival. And don't be angry when you discover that all public sympathy is bestowed on the baby and none on the tough soldiers responsible for the little girl's safety.'

It was an exciting assignment and with a nice mixture of pride and assurance, Cornet Dowdswell reported to Lady Dalkeith who, at the queen's request, had taken charge of the baby princess. To his embarrassed surprise, he found himself confronted by Susanna Martin.

'Susanna,' he exclaimed. 'You . . .'

But the girl stopped him, her eyes blazing with anger. 'Yes, it's I, Martin, and this time you can't hide from me. Nor can

I be fobbed off with stupid excuses for your despicable general who orders a mother to be separated from her new-born child. Has Essex no pity in his horrid little Devereux heart? And do you so demean yourself as to serve such a monster . . . God, how could I ever have trusted you?'

This one-sided tirade might have continued indefinitely, had not Lady Dalkeith entered the room and effectively taken control. She intended to be just as correct and distant as any stripling captain in the rebels' army. She came straight to the point. 'Three carriages,' she stipulated. 'Not more than fifteen miles a day, and no moving on if the baby isn't well.'

Cornet Dowdswell would be equally correct. Milady was most helpful. Three carriages would be procured, as requested. The daily start would be at eight in the morning and the length of the journey arranged to meet her ladyship's wishes. Martin gave her a most professional salute and turned on his heel without another glance at Susanna.

But keeping one's distance was easier said than done. The English soldier is incorrigibly sentimental about children: they serve as a reminder of the home to which he longs to return . . . As the cavalcade moved stage by stage across Dorset and Hampshire, the order to keep one's distance soon became a dead letter. The young troopers all wanted to have a peep at the baby with the deep-blue eyes (something to tell mother or wife back home), and the wet-nurse could always count on willing help at the end of a day's journey. Lady Dalkeith took an immediate liking to Martin, and after the first day agreed that the day's progress might be doubled to thirty miles. It was also agreed that Martin and two of his men should ride ahead to arrange the night's accommodation, preferably in a great house sympathetic to Parliament's cause. But that was a small matter. Nobody had any quarrel with the king's children, and no family made difficulties about feeding and accommodating the royal baby's escort.

Even Susanna's anger subsided. Her contempt for Essex could hardly be directed against the young soldiers who accompanied the three carriages. They were as likeable and friendly as the lads who had guarded the queen and her entourage from York to Oxford. But she could not escape from the certainty that Martin Dowdswell was deliberately avoiding her: he remained distant even when taking the evening meal with her and Lady Dalkeith.

The latter quickly sensed the personal tension between her two young companions. One evening she came upon Susanna crying her eyes out, and decided to tackle Martin about it, when Susanna was not present. Was he still smarting over Susanna's angry words before the journey started? What was amiss? Could she help?

Martin listened gravely to what Lady Dalkeith had to say, thought for a moment, and suddenly decided to take her into his confidence. He began formally and correctly, then continued in a rush of words. 'You see, milady, before the war Susanna Martin and I often met in London. There was an excellent understanding between us: we loved to be together. We were angry when Providence separated our paths, mine to join an army in the field and hers to join the queen in the Low Countries. And now what I have since learnt must keep us apart and, by the same token, is something I cannot in honour tell her.'

Old Lady Dalkeith looked hard at the boy. She was a kindly person of wide experience. This boy was transparently honest. She admired the restraint he put on his emotion. Of course, she would respect his confidence. She smiled. What an absurd situation! Taking the royal baby, Henrietta Anne, across England was simplicity itself compared with the dilemma of the escort's commander.

The party reached Weybridge safely. At Oatlands Park Martin duly delegated his responsibility for the little princess to the Parliamentary Commissioners and took his leave of the royal party. Impulsively, he kissed Susanna's hand in farewell, and with a final salute to Lady Dalkeith he rode away to rejoin his regiment. He never looked back.

25

About the time that Martin was handing over the baby princess to the Commissioners at Oatlands Park, Colonel Henry Ireton returned to Ely. He was in a mood of despair, having been subject to recurring disappointments since reporting for duty in September to the Earl of Manchester.

First he had been furious at the news of King Charles' victory over Essex at Lostwithiel in Cornwall – a wretched affair which had been followed by the dishonourable flight of the earl after leaving Philip Skippon to negotiate surrender terms as best he could. People were saying that this reverse in the West Country had cancelled the value of Oliver's great victory at Marston Moor.

Then came a further blow. In Cromwell's absence at Westminster Henry had been in temporary command of the Eastern Association Horse and persuaded the Presbyterian tortoise, Manchester, to move into Hampshire and link with the troops that old Skippon had managed to bring back by sea from Plymouth. At Basingstoke the combined force had also been joined by Waller's men whom Essex had left in the lurch earlier in the year. But these wise moves had only ended in further frustration.

In a second battle near Newbury, Manchester had signally failed to press home the advantage gained by Waller's brilliant march encircling the Royalist defensive position which should have ensured decisive victory, and even the capture of the king.

Now, in January 1645, King Charles was holding court in Oxford, so cock-a-hoop of final victory that he had superciliously rejected a peaceful settlement suggested by the Presbyterians in Parliament. Henry, with his Independent stance, had little love for these proposals, but that was beside the point. His concern was the failure of the Parliamentary commanders to capture the king.

In his anger he had bitterly criticised Manchester's incompetence in a deposition to a Parliamentary committee which had clearly influenced opinion at Westminster. But what had been achieved? The passing of a Self-denying Ordinance which debarred members of both Houses from holding military command! It was small comfort to Henry Ireton to know that this decree would end the lack-lustre vacillations of the noble Lords Essex and Manchester. But where would the Member for Cambridge stand? Would he be forced to surrender his command? Henry was horrified. He'd lived with front-line fighting men continuously since Edgehill. He knew, better than most, how much Old Noll meant to these hardened soldiers. Oliver's presence on the battlefield could mean the difference between victory and stalemate.

It was old Mrs Cromwell who revived his flagging spirits. 'Stop wearing yourself out with worry,' she told Henry, treating the Deputy Governor of Ely as if he were one of her grandchildren. 'You don't know my son as well as I do. He possesses a subtle, flexible mind – some might call it devious. But you want to remember this, Harry. In the darkest undergrowth of politics Oliver never loses sight of his objective. So please leave him to steer Parliament the way he wants it to go, and stop looking as if Armageddon was dated for tomorrow. You'll do better to come and sup with us tonight. And for goodness' sake, stop brooding.'

Harry looked down at the quizzical twinkle in the little old lady's eyes. They were examining him most closely. 'Yes,' she added decisively. 'You're really quite handsome when you smile.'

For Henry, as for other Ely citizens, Grandmother Cromwell's words were more of a command than a request; very soon he became a regular visitor to the Cromwells' house beside St Mary's Church. Some people might consider the young Cromwells a little over-assertive. Old-fashioned residents might disapprove of the family's squabble with the cathedral clergy; but within the home the sound of laughter was often heard, and family arguments were always leavened with humour.

Of the four daughters born to Oliver and Elizabeth, Bridget was the most serious. Frances and Mary were still of school age, and Betty, the acknowledged beauty of the family, was mischievous and light of heart. But Bridget was the girl who appealed to Henry. Her wide-set Cromwell eyes and good-humoured mouth, which reflected her mother's Bourchier ancestry, combined to give her an air of calm dignity and patience which acted as a useful foil to Henry's impetuous temperament.

Moreover, she seemed to possess an intuitive understanding of his present preoccupation – an inner conflict between his duties at Ely and his wider anxiety about the affairs of the nation.

The civil war was causing many abnormal problems to the Governor of Ely and his deputy. The rent-paying Fenmen, for instance, had been exposed to a series of Royalist raids on outlying farms during the absence of Cromwell's Regiment on the Newbury campaign and were asking for compensation and better protection. The soldiers, back in their winter quarters, were demanding arrears of pay. The preachers among them were claiming the right to proclaim their particular beliefs from the church pulpits of Ely, and thereby giving great annoyance to the local clergy.

Such local problems would not, normally, have worried Henry Ireton's decisive mind, but they were irritating distractions to a man whose eyes were fixed on a wider and more distant horizon.

What, he kept asking, was keeping Oliver in London? Was it true that he was off to the West Country with Waller? Henry was sure something big was happening and, as always, he was impatient to be part of the action. Bridget, walking with him beside the river or in the Cathedral Close and listening to his ideas for reconciling the king and Parliament, began to realise how much her companionship meant to him. She was proud to be seen walking with this tall, commanding man. But how could they contemplate a future together while Henry was obsessed with the part he would be called to play not only in the fighting but, more significantly, in the eventual peace-making process with the king?

Henry Ireton's suspense ended abruptly when, late one February evening, Martin Dowdswell rode into Ely carrying an urgent Parliamentary despatch for the deputy governor. Henry hardly found time to acknowledge Martin's presence.

Impatiently he snatched the letter and broke the official seal. He read it once. He read it again. Then it seemed as if his whole being were transformed.

'Martin . . . Martin,' he shouted, flinging his arms round his ward, 'it's happened! Appointed commissary general in this new army that Fairfax and Skippon are forming. Tom Fairfax wants me to report immediately . . . First task to get the Horse mounted, armed, trained, disciplined . . . ready to take the field by mid-April . . . Whew, Black Tom's in a hurry, isn't he?'

He paused to peruse the letter again. 'Hey, Martin, what's this bit about being prepared to command a new regiment? Me? To be parted from my Nottingham men in Cromwell's regiment? And, anyway, what part is Oliver playing in this set-up? I don't understand.'

Far into the night young Martin held the floor. As General Skippon's confidential amanuensis, he'd been involved in the plans for the New Model Army from the start, but for the most part his replies to Henry Ireton's questions were deliberately vague: No, he didn't know whose idea it was . . . Parliament, he supposed, or something called the Committee of Both Kingdoms . . . Yes, Oliver and his MP friends of the Independent persuasion might have played some part in it . . . but he believed the MP for Cambridge was back in uniform and serving under Waller . . .

Could Martin please get down to a few facts? Henry had no use for ifs and buts.

But of course, Martin replied. The basic plan was cut and dried. All units of the Essex and Manchester armies – and some from Waller's command – were to be broken up and merged into an integrated force of twenty thousand men. Even General Oliver's double regiment of twelve hundred horse would be reorganised.

Philip Skippon had it all cut and dried. Twenty thousand men consisting of eleven regiments of Horse, each of six hundred; twelve regiments of Foot each of one thousand men; one regiment of dragoons also with a strength of one thousand men; and an artillery train with the usual additions for surgeons, chaplains and so on.

'And the generals, Martin? The other generals?'

Martin had left the best part of his story to the end. 'Ah, yes,' he said, 'five generals. Now let me see . . . Sir Thomas Fairfax will be commander-in-chief under the title of Captain General – a very good choice in every fighting man's opinion; and acceptable to both Houses of Parliament because he keeps his nose out of politics though I'm told he has the same Independent views on religion as you do. Apart from your appointment, Philip Skippon will command the foot and Thomas Hammond the artillery train. You couldn't find better men anywhere.'

'But hold a minute, Martin. You spoke of five generals. So far you've only named four.'

Martin gave Commissary General Ireton a prodigious wink. 'Ah, yes, the fifth general . . . I understand the appointment is still vacant. Sir William Waller must be considered, but he might be required for an independent western command . . . so, it's anybody's guess, isn't it?'

'However, our general, who is better acquainted than most of us with the political machinations at Westminster, has said that the Self-denying Ordinance for MPs does not officially come into force until mid-summer. So, Harry, the question mark is as big as you like to make it!'

Martin had enjoyed his little mystery about the fifth general. He concluded on a more formal note. 'I suggest, General, that you will do best to report personally to the Captain General and get your marching orders at first hand.'

Next day Henry Ireton made a quick visit to his own men, ensured that the governor's office in Ely would function smoothly in his absence, and said farewell to Bridget and the Cromwell family. In the afternoon he rode south with Martin Dowdswell – his eyes firmly fixed on the campaign ahead of them.

The two men spent a night in London with Joe and Hannah Shipley before moving to Windsor where Sir Thomas Fairfax had established the Headquarters of the New Model Army.

The captain general was clearly pleased to have Henry Ireton with him. The two men were exact contemporaries, each of them thirty-three years of age. They shared the same love of horses and the same delight in the English countryside.

Their family backgrounds were similar – the recently ennobled Yorkshire Fairfaxes wealthier than the Nottingham Iretons though the latter could claim a longer pedigree. They had indeed been good friends since the Winceby fight, Tom Fairfax appreciating the value of Ireton's incisive mind and Henry equally confident of the captain general's outstanding gifts as a commander in the field. Their qualities complemented each other, and they shared a record of courage in battle which gave them a special place in the eyes of the men they led.

Henry was immediately aware of a sense of order and confidence in the Headquarters Staff. He thought it was largely due to the experience of Philip Skippon and the brilliant organising ability of the Secretary, John Rushworth; but Fairfax's choice of officers for the New Model was also a good augury for the future. Officers of proven ability like Rich, Rossiter, Whalley and Rainsborough would hold regimental commands. Promotion would be by merit, not birth, so that the ship's chandler, John Okey and Pride, the drayman, would be colonels in the New Model Army. There would also be a welcome measure of harmony on the religious front, for the Captain General had braved the disapproval of MPs like Denzil Holles by ridding himself of four Scots officers who were too aggressively Presbyterian for his taste. Oliver would surely approve these plans; but where on earth was he? Henry was soon to find out.

For a month Martin and Henry were kept busy – Martin acting as Skippon's chief aide, and Henry re-equipping the regiments of Horse with uniforms of Reading cloth, arms and light armour and, above all, horses – Suffolk heavyweights for General Hammond's artillery train, lighter animals for Okey's dragoons and, for the cavalry arm, sturdy Fenland stock crossed, if possible, with Arab blood.

The army, though still under strength in the infantry, was almost ready to move when Fairfax gave Ireton new orders. 'I'd like you, Harry, to join General Oliver,' he said, and noted the joy with which his orders were received. 'The great man has been serving under Waller in Somerset keeping well away, you understand, from certain dear friends at Westminster.' Tom Fairfax laughed at this calculated understatement. 'But now I must have him and his six hundred troopers back with my army. You are to join him, Harry, as soon as you can – somewhere south-west of Oxford, I would imagine; and Philip Skippon wants you to take Martin with you.'

'You said Oxford?'

'That's right, Harry. Oxford is Oliver's objective, and ours. I can't tell whether or not he hopes to stop the king from joining Prince Rupert in Hereford; but I'm sure he'll give you a good run for your money. We should meet again in a month's time. Meanwhile, good hunting.'

Harry and Martin sighted Cromwell's troops on the familiar ground they had reconnoitred in the previous year. Oliver's small force had arrived too late to stop the king from leaving Oxford, but otherwise, his reconnaissance was brilliantly accomplished. The Ironsides took hundreds of prisoners and horses after a brief scrap at Islip. They bluffed Colonel Windbank into surrender at Bletchingdon House. They took more prisoners at Bampton and sensibly withdrew from Faringdon Castle when its defenders showed resistance. North and south of Oxford the raid caused total panic among the Royalists left in the city, with rumour converting small setbacks into major defeats.

When, on 20 May, Cromwell and Ireton rejoined the main army at Newbury, the news of their exploits acted like a tonic.

It was much needed, for Fairfax and Skippon had been depressed and confused by a succession of contrary orders sent by their masters in Parliament. First, make contact with the enemy in Oxford. Then the first counter-order: direct your force on Andover and Salisbury to relieve Taunton. On 8 May Fairfax was already at Blandford, ninety-one miles from Windsor, when yet another direction was received: turn north, after detaching a sufficient force under Colonel Weldon to relieve Taunton. So, with his army strength reduced, Fairfax changed direction yet again.

But contradictory orders from London were far from being the captain general's only problem. On the long march to Blandford his officers had encountered considerable trouble with some of the pressed men who were showing a marked aversion to the prospect of battle. Fairfax took swift action, having two deserters hanged at a point on the army's route where every marching man could see the fate military discipline decreed for desertion. At the same time he cashiered the commanding officer of the regiment concerned. But these actions do not help morale, and he turned to Henry Ireton as the best man to bring the regiment up to scratch.

With some trepidation Henry applied to his new command the rules learnt from Oliver and studied in Martin Dowdswell's textbooks: know your men by name, and see they are properly fed, paid, clothed and trained in the use of their weapons. Soon Fairfax noted a very positive reaction among these young Kent soldiers who were now known as Ireton's Regiment. The men of Kent and Kentish men might be more politically motivated than Henry's beloved Nottingham Militia. They might argue among themselves about every aspect of religion known to God or man. But they were quick to recognise an officer they could follow. Time was short; but as the New Model Army moved north in search of the king, Ireton's Regiment was ready for battle.

Fairfax's masters at Westminster were, however, continuing to send him the most contradictory orders. It was scarcely believable, but on 31 May, just as the New Model was preparing to invest Oxford, Lieutenant General Cromwell and his regiment were ordered back to Ely. Skippon and Ireton were furious.

'Why in God's name,' the old man shouted, 'can't these Presbyterian busybodies leave us to fight the battle? Every rumour in the King Street inns and ale-houses makes them shiver. Do they really think that Oliver is needed at Ely to guard against attack on London from the north?' Ireton would have put it differently: he was quite certain that the order for Oliver to return to Ely was a political move, designed by his enemies to keep him out of the limelight. But Black Tom laughed at both his colleagues.

'Don't worry, my friends,' he said. 'I've just ordered young Dowdswell and a companion to ride to Ely with a coded message for my Lieutenant General of Horse. There are moments, you know, when a field commander is bound to disobey the instructions of his civilian masters. Please don't worry. I guarantee Oliver will be back with us well before the enemy comes over the skyline.'

Five days after Oliver's departure Fairfax raised the siege

of Oxford and ordered the army into Leicestershire. You could feel a new excitement running through the column of march. Black Tom, they said, had the scent of battle in his nostrils. Another seven days passed, with Okey's dragoons ahead of the main force seeking contact with the Royalist Army, when the New Model Army reached the village of Kislingbury, a few miles south of the little town of Naseby in Leicestershire. Suddenly, as evening fell, Martin Dowdswell galloped into camp, handed his sweating horse to a groom and burst into Fairfax's tent where the Captain General was finalising his plan of battle with Skippon and Ireton.

The lad was so excited he stumbled over his words. 'Sir,' he gasped, 'he's coming . . . General Oliver is coming . . . promises he will arrive midday tomorrow complete with his regiment of six hundred men.'

A breathless rider bursting into camp at nightfall never passes unnoticed. In no time at all, Martin's up-to-the-second information was spreading to every corner of the camp: Have you heard? Old Noll is on his way. Have you heard? Have you heard?

Next morning the soldiers going about their duties in the camp could often be seen glancing towards the eastern horizon. One man climbed a tree and reported a cloud of dust in the far distance – a body of horsemen for sure, moving along the track from Kelmarsh. Within seconds the cloud of dust had become a reality. Yes, yes, it was Oliver riding at the head of his Ironsides – the *corps d'élite*. Yes, they could see him clearly now – every man and officer familiar with his gestures. They watched him steady the pace of the leading riders with a slight move of his hand. The cheers grew to a crescendo as he slowed to walking pace through the lines, recognising some old soldier in the cheering throng, smiling acknowledgment to another's welcome.

It only needed the presence of this one man to change the army's mood. Men and officers – every one of them – knew that Old Noll had come to see them through to victory.

But where exactly was the enemy? At nearby Daventry? Or further away at Market Harborough? Ireton was ordered forward to Naseby to seek more exact information. The afternoon sun was still high as Henry's small force approached the little town. 'Any strangers been seen round here?' The question was asked a dozen times, and time and again, typically non-committal replies were received from the men and women working in the fields. But on the outskirts of the town, a lad gave the countryman's stock answer, 'Nobody so far as I know, Colonel,' then added, 'But they do say there be some feasting at the inn down yonder.'

The hint was clear and the action swift. Henry Ireton ordered his men to guard all exits from the square in which the inn was situated. His troop captain was to secure all horses in the stables and scare the innkeeper and the kitchen staff into silence. Then, with six hefty lads from Kent, he entered the dining room to the shocked surprise of a party of dice-playing Cavaliers.

Idiotically, he was suddenly reminded of one of Dr Kettel's Latin tags – *Suaviter in modo sed fortiter in re*. 'My apologies, gentlemen, for interrupting your game. But please keep your seats until I permit you to rise. My men have their pistols loaded and are trained in their use.'

He smiled at the apoplectic faces of six Royalist officers who had clearly dined extremely well. 'Now, Johnny' – he turned to a young trooper beside him – 'collect the winnings on the table and see the landlord is paid for his excellent service. And you, Peter, collect the gentlemen's weapons but leave the two packs of cards and the dice with the high-ranking officer at the head of the table. And now, Sir,' he turned to the Cavalier dazedly clutching the dice and two packs of cards, 'you have my word that your companions, who will ride under escort to my headquarters, will be treated honourably as prisoners of war. But I will allow you, Sir, to retain your horse, though not your weapons, and ask you to inform your commanding officer that the New Noddles, as you are pleased to call us, will be ready to join battle should you wish to stand and fight.'

There was neither time nor place for argument. Harry apologised handsomely to the innkeeper, assured his wife and two girls in the kitchen that they had nothing to fear from his Kentish lads, and rode out of town with his prisoners.

There was much laughter in the camp that night. 'You should 'ave 'eard 'im' – Johnny was the man with a story to tell. 'Colonel 'Arry, 'e showed 'em up proper, treated 'em 'aughty but very polite if yer know what I mean,' and Johnny gave a very passable imitation of his new colonel's clipped, precise speech. 'Caw . . . you should 'o seen their red faces when I collects the money and 'ands the dice and the cards to 'is Lordship at the end o' the table. Quite a party, I'd say . . . You ask Pete and the rest o' the boys.'

Johnny sat back to enjoy his pot of ale. Morale had never been higher.

Meanwhile, Ireton's prisoners brought news of the king and Prince Rupert. After joining forces they had moved against the great city of Leicester. When its valiant citizens had refused to accept the offer of quarter, its old tumble-down walls had been stormed and, in accordance with the prevailing practice of warfare, victory had been followed by pillage and rape and all the horrors to which civilians are subject.

But now, it seemed, the Royalist army of some ten thousand men was moving south to offer the New Model Army its first trial by battle.

Fairfax was delighted, and further confirmation came from John Okey whose dragoons reported the enemy's movement south 'as leisurely as it was obvious'. In Fawley Park, His Majesty was said to be enjoying a few days' hunting!

It was Philip Skippon who warned his colleagues against complacency. 'Better get to sleep early,' he said, 'we'll need to be up at break of day.' The old soldier knew for a certainty that battle was very close.

26

In early-morning mist on 14 June 1645 the combat units of
the New Model Army moved to a stretch of open ground in
Leicestershire previously surveyed by Fairfax and his commanders as an excellent site from which to launch a set-piece
battle. It lay about one and a half miles north of Naseby, close
to the windmill beside the Clipston track. From this rise of
land, known as the Mill Hill Ridge, one could look down to
Broad Moor and across the valley to Dust Hill, and so to the
area round Market Harborough where the Royalist army was
lying. Here, on Mill Hill and Red Hill, it would be hard for
the Parliamentary army to be outflanked. Not only did it enjoy
numerical superiority over the Royalists, especially in the
cavalry arm, but the ground it occupied was confined by
woodland on one wing and, on the other, by the Soulby hedges
running at right angles across the valley.

Henry Ireton, commanding the left wing of the Parliamentary
horse, was more than satisfied with the prospect. Signs
and portents always interested him and he speculated on
the curious fact that the decisive battle of this terrible civil
war would be joined in the very centre of England, on high
ground from which the Avon flowed west to the Severn and
the Nene and Welland flowed east to the Wash. Surely the
right place as well as the right time had been reached for
decision.

For the newly-promoted general, only one question remained open. How would the New Model's ostentatious troop
movements influence the decisions of the king and Prince
Rupert who had been very slow to appreciate their proximity
to Fairfax's army? Would they continue moving north towards
the great Royalist stronghold of Newark? Or would they be
fooled into thinking that the New Model was withdrawing and
therefore vulnerable to attack while on line of march?

The squally rain of the past weeks had disappeared and, as
the morning sun cleared the mist, Henry soon observed enemy

troops moving from Sibbertoft and Clipston on to Dust Hill. His pulse quickened. It was certain, then, that the Royalist high command had decided to join battle.

He turned at the sound of a great cheer behind him, and there was Old Noll riding towards him, his horse surrounded by cheering troopers. His presence seemed to transmit an extraordinary excitement and confidence to the men surging round him. It was as if his light-hearted talk was directed to each man personally. 'Well, then, which of you has the best voice? You, Joseph? Let's try it out. Ready, Joe? The cry for today is "God our Strength". Got it? God . . . our . . . Strength. I'll join you. Right, all together now!' And as they shouted, they heard an echoing cry from Skippon's infantry in the centre and then, faintly from further away, the same words from Whalley's and Cromwell's horse on the right of the line. Hearts were beating faster as Oliver moved quietly towards Henry and his second-in-command, Charles Fleetwood.

'A quick word, Harry,' he said. 'You want to move the troops back behind the crest of the ridge. Rupert will know you are here, of course, but he won't be able to assess your strength if he can't see you. And here are two more points to keep in mind. First, our weakest point is in the centre. Don't worry if some elements of Rupert's horse break through to Naseby. They'll get a very hot reception, I can tell you, from the trained musketeers that Tom Fairfax has set to guard the baggage. And secondly, John Okey and his dragoons have now taken up position behind the Soulby hedges. They have orders to slow down any advancing cavalry with enfilading fire. That will be the moment for you to launch your own attack.' He clapped Ireton on the back. 'Good luck, Harry. Good luck, Charles.' Oliver's remarkable eyes looked straight at each of his chosen leaders. Then he waved to the men. 'Don't forget the words, Joseph. God our Strength.' And the Lieutenant General of Horse was away to his post on the right wing, as swiftly as he had appeared.

At half past ten the Royalists were seen advancing slowly towards Skippon's infantry, and Hammond's demi-culverins began to lob shot into the Royalist second line. The enemy cavalry – yes, Henry could see Rupert's great pennant waving in the light breeze – was edging slowly forward, keeping pace with Astley's infantry. They were still out of range of Okey's dragoons.

Henry could feel the tension rising. 'Draw sabres.' He moved to the crest of the ridge, backed by a thousand troopers, with Charles Fleetwood behind them in command of his reserve regiments. Random thoughts were chasing through Henry's mind – it had been the same at Edgehill and Winceby and Newbury: Mother, Bridget . . . be with me . . . Martin, stay close to Skippon, those lads around you will need you today . . . Tom, brother Tom, you are in good hands with Colonel Rich and Fleetwood . . . Oliver, Tom Fairfax . . . may the God we serve protect . . .

Suddenly Rupert's horse squadrons broke away, charging up the hill, apparently undeterred by flanking fire from the Soulby hedges. Dear God, had Okey's musketeers been too slow to react to Rupert's speed? Too late to worry. 'Charge!' yelled Harry, 'God our Strength!' and crashed down Red Hill into the opposing cavalry. The force of his charge halted the squadrons opposed to him. A few minutes of furious hand-to-hand fighting, sabres clashing, horses screaming, men falling: and Harry saw Prince Maurice bearing away to follow his brother. Pray God, Charles Fleetwood and the reserve line would stop the prince from wheeling and attacking him in the rear. Meanwhile, his own men were holding their own . . .

He looked to his right. The sight was desperately clear – Skippon's infantry were proving no match for Astley's experienced pikemen and musketeers. Harry's first priority must be to relieve the pressure on the centre. 'To the right,' he ordered, 'follow me . . . Right,' and spurred his excited horse into the Royalist foot. But with the knowledge gained from previous disasters at Edgehill and the Moor, these fine Royalist pikemen were ready to counter the manoeuvre. Henry's horse fell, instantly killed by a musket shot to the head. He shook himself clear of the stirrups, killed a pikeman with his sword, received a glancing pike wound on his left thigh, still sought to close with the enemy, but was struck by a halberd just under his eye . . . He fell bleeding to the ground.

Others were more fortunate. In the centre, Martin saw Philip Skippon badly wounded by a cannon ball, but managed to hold off the enemy while his general was carried to the rear.

He was fighting to steady his men when a tall helmetless man, with tanned skin and flowing black beard, appeared miraculously at his side. An encouraging voice – they said Tom Fairfax always lost his stammer on the battlefield – reassured him. 'Well done, Martin. Well done, lad. We'll soon be on top. We're closing in now from both flanks.'

The captain general spoke true. On the far wing Cromwell had handled his cavalry with supreme skill, crossing some treacherous ground to engage Langdale's Northern Horse and see them off the field before detaching his two reserve regiments to destroy Rupert's Bluecoats who formed part of the second line of the Royalist foot.

Meanwhile, Okey's dragoons had followed Ireton's move and launched a fresh attack from the left which proved as effective as Cromwell's on the right. As for Prince Rupert, he had received such a reception from the marksmen guarding the baggage train at Naseby that he had hastened back to Broad Moor, only to find a field of carnage such as he had never previously witnessed. With the regiment of horse he personally commanded he managed to get back to Dust Hill and the royal command post. But to rally the cavalry for a defensive stand was beyond his powers, and he had no option but to speed away with the king to Ashby de la Zouch and thence to the safety of Hereford.

Parliament's victory was decisive and complete: the main Royalist Army irretrievably smashed, its baggage lost, its artillery train captured and, worst of all, the unhappy king's cabinet papers seized and sent to Westminster. They only served to confirm the suspicions already aroused by the earlier capture of Digby's papers at Sherborne and the recovery of Henrietta Maria's correspondence from the sea at Dartmouth. There, in black and white, it stood revealed that the King of England was calling on Irishmen, Swedes and even the Duke of Lorraine in France to help him wage war against his own people. For the first time, Englishmen who had been fighting to save their king from evil counsellors began to doubt their sovereign's integrity. Men spoke of hypocrisy and deceit: of a man who might dismiss a sacred oath as a casual lie. Some were even whispering the dreaded word treason. Could such a man enjoy the trust of the English people?

Henry Ireton knew nothing of these developments. A triumphant Cavalier officer had seen him fall, made him prisoner and had him carried back to an isolated cottage where a woman from Sibbertoft was ordered to get him on to a couch and bathe and dress his wounds. He was still conscious – his face a ghastly pallor, his fingers gripping the side of the makeshift bed – when some triumphant members of his own regiment burst into the house. The Royalists were taken completely by surprise. It was the purest chance that Henry recognised one of the troopers as the lad who had collected the gaming money at the Naseby inn. 'Johnny,' he said, his voice scarcely audible, 'this officer and his men have treated me with total courtesy. They must now be shown the same mercy that they have shown me. I want one of you to return to Colonel Fleetwood or Colonel Rich and report my location and what I have said. The rest are to ensure the safety of the people in this cottage, whether they be enemy soldiers or peaceful civilians. You understand, Johnny? This officer and his men are to be given their freedom in return for my life. It is a matter of honour.'

Henry Ireton lay back exhausted. In the next two days a succession of visitors came to the cottage: the chief surgeon, Master Winter; Fairfax's chaplain, Mr Dale; Colonel Rich and Tom Ireton; and finally Martin Dowdswell with a message from the captain general, to the effect that Fairfax had received orders to recapture Leicester and then end all Royalist resistance in the West Country. He wanted Ireton as his deputy – but only when he was fully recovered.

It was the message that Ireton needed most of all. So he was wanted, was he, by Black Tom? He had not failed as a soldier. If the consolidation of victory required him to act as Fairfax's chief negotiator and treaty maker, so be it. He and Fairfax had only one objective: to use the victory of Naseby to restore peace to the whole of England.

As Henry was moved very carefully to his sister's house at Lockington and then, after another week, to the family home at Attenborough, the old impatience returned. Black Tom needed him. So, probably, would Oliver, but that might mean entering the world of politics. For the moment he was a soldier. As soon as he could get back in the saddle, he would move south-west to join the captain general.

But the enforced rest at least served to remind Henry of more peaceful pursuits. Martin Dowdswell had commanded the escort which brought him safely to William Bainbrigge's great house at Lockington, and there Henry had watched his sister Mary presiding without fuss over the three-tiered Bainbrigge family – the offspring of two previous marriages as well as her own. He also noted Martin's joy at meeting his mother and Tom Brewster who had remained at Lockington after the escape from Oxford. As Henry watched Martin playing with his little step-brother and step-sister, his mind moved to Bridget Cromwell and the Cromwell family in Ely. The domestic scene was something that he longed to enjoy.

But did the choice lie with him? He asked the question a hundred times as he joined his mother at Attenborough for his last weeks of convalescence.

It was very peaceful there. Jane Ireton was relieved to see her eldest son's wounds healing so well. She rejoiced to see him mounted on Witney once again and riding with old Brewster over the Ireton land and visiting Francis Thornhaugh and the local families. She brought him up to date with Ireton business; the children still at home – Clement and Matthew and Ann; she mentioned the possibility of selling some marginal land to the Charltons of Chilwell. She wondered whether Tom and Maggie Brewster should not be persuaded to move from Lockington to Attenborough. She speculated as to whether Martin Dowdswell would remain in the army when the war was over. Once she asked Henry about Bridget Cromwell: had he considered where they would want to set up home? But to this last question her son would only say that Bridget was as much concerned in the war as he was. Henry smiled almost self-consciously as he turned aside his mother's question. But Jane Ireton could read his mind as clearly as a book. Henry, she knew, was determined to return to serve with Fairfax at the earliest possible moment.

News from the West Country was increasingly exciting. Calling another Yorkshireman, John Lambert, to strengthen his command structure, Fairfax had won a series of victories, and taken Bath and Bridgwater and Sherborne in a campaign of lightning speed.

Henry returned to the New Model as Fairfax approached

Bristol. He was so happy to be back again as part of Black Tom's remarkable team. Oliver and John Lambert were there So, too, were other commanders of proven courage and ability like Okey and Weldon, Rainsborough and Rich. Only the seriously wounded Skippon was missing.

Prince Rupert, once again in the great city of Bristol which he had captured at the start of the war, made a show of resistance. But plague broke out, and when Ireton and the dragoons crossed the Avon to threaten the city from the north and Weldon and Rainsborough stormed the southern defences, Rupert wisely sued for terms. It was noted that the Articles of Surrender, drawn up by Ireton, were extremely generous. The prince, escorted by two regiments of Parliament Horse, was granted safe conduct to Oxford, only to be ignominiously cashiered by the king he had served so well. First, the great Earl of Strafford, and now his finest soldier. How poorly the king rewarded his best men!

Oliver was soon ordered to resume his duties as Governor of the Isle of Ely and as Member for Cambridge. But somewhere at Westminster the thought must have taken root that General Henry Ireton was something more than a fine soldier, for he was named MP for Appleby in Leicestershire, while continuing to serve as Fairfax's chief colleague in the West Country. Was the Self-denying Ordinance a dead letter now that Essex with his stupid Devereux face and meek little Manchester of the vacant features had been removed? Perhaps the pace set by Fairfax was too swift or his campaign too successful for Parliament to overtake him with further directives!

To ensure there were no further Royalist outbreaks in the west, the New Model remained at Exeter, though Fairfax spent a week's convalescence with his over-powerful wife in Bath. But during the bitterly cold winter the captain general and his commanders continued their mopping-up operations. Many gallant actions were fought including a brilliant move with packhorses through deep snow to storm Dartmouth at midnight.

Hopton, lacking reinforcements, conducted a masterly Royalist withdrawal to Launceston and Bodmin while the young Prince of Wales escaped from Pendennis Castle to the Scillies.

But final surrender could not be long delayed. At Truro terms were drawn up by Henry Ireton and John Lambert and duly accepted by Hopton. Once again the generosity of the terms reflected the high regard felt by the Parliamentary high command for a skilful and courageous opponent. On both sides loyalties were still respected and courage honoured.

The war in the west was over. As the cruel winter gave way to spring, Henry Ireton was ordered to move on Oxford, taking with him his own regiment and Colonel Rich's. Fairfax and Lambert would follow with the artillery train and the Parliamentary foot.

By the beginning of May 1646 the full strength of the New Model Army lay before Oxford. It was twelve months since Fairfax had left the muster ground at Windsor, and his objective remained unaltered: to capture the king.

27

In Oxford confusion reigned. The king, it was true, still held court at Christ Church; but he was only monarch in name since he had lost all effective military support. Eternal optimist that he was, he still clung to the belief that he would win the final round with Parliament by playing off Presbyterian members against the Independents of the victorious army – and both of them against the Scots. But whatever the royal hopes, lords and ladies were leaving Oxford as fast as horses and carriages could be provided.

Within the city Secretary Nicholas still managed to keep a few administrative wheels turning, hampered as always by irresponsible advice from Digby and his friends; while the hated governor had been replaced by Sir Thomas Glenham, who had been honourably treated when surrendering York after Marston Moor. It was thought his appointment might make life more tolerable for Oxford's harassed citizens, while the presence of Prince Rupert, still held in honour by Fairfax and Ireton though not by the king, might cause the Parliamentary army to hesitate before mounting a full-scale assault.

But who could bring relief to the defenceless city? Rumour chased rumour with the persistence of a ferret. It was believed that an undetected spy within the secretariat was supplying information to the enemy. The captured papers revealing the royal plans for French and Irish reinforcements were the subject of gossip at every street corner. Citizens who favoured the cause of Parliament were no longer talking in whispers.

Among such men was the irrepressible Sam Dowdswell who was presently languishing as a prisoner in Oxford Castle. His arrest had taken place while Cromwell's raiding parties were rounding up horses at Islip and Bletchingdon prior to the great battle of Naseby. It seemed he had been voicing his approval of the raiders' action at his favourite Osney ale-house and, in a burst of alcoholic boasting, claimed some personal credit for the performance, foolishly mixing it up with the earlier raids at the time of Dr Kettel's death.

Betsie only learnt of Sam's stupid indiscretions when armed guards arrested him and marched him off to Oxford gaol. The elaborate cover-up of the previous year had finally proved of no avail. With William Sanderson acting as chief informer, Sam could expect no mercy. He would be strung up on the gibbet at Carfax as certainly as the other malefactors and deserters awaiting sentence in the overcrowded, stinking cells of the city gaol. Only by bribing the gaolers could Betsie see him or bring him food.

In her desperation she decided to take her troubles to Mrs Wotherspoon at the Mitre. That formidable old lady was full of sympathy. 'My poor dear Betsie,' she said. 'It sounds as if your Sam acts the same as the gentlemen who come here to dine. If they have been anywhere near the battlefield, they feel compelled to tell the world about it, and if they swallow a drop of brandy after the claret, they talk still louder. That's men all over.

'But you mustn't lose heart.' The shrewd old lady leaned confidentially towards Betsie. 'I hear that Colonel Ireton is commanding the enemy's advance guard at Waterstoke.'

'Not Harry Ireton?'

'That's the gentleman, my love. You know him of old, don't you? Well, I'll tell you something else' – and Mrs Wotherspoon put her finger to her lips as she dropped her voice to a whisper. 'Some of the court gentlemen know him too. There's our new city governor for one. I'm told he was a student under the old president a few years before Harry Ireton came to Trinity. And there could be a connection with Mr Ashburnham who, just at the moment, has the ear of His Majesty – or so they say. You want to know why Mr Ashburnham might be helpful? Very simple, my love. The gentleman is Member of Parliament for Hastings. So you see he'll be acquainted with Colonel Ireton's favourite sister. Remember Miss Sarah? There was a lovely girl. She came here with him before the war.'

Mrs Wotherspoon might have drawn further on her memories of the good old days, but she came back to the point as her eyes saw Betsie's anxious face. 'But it's your Sam we have to think about, isn't it? Now supposing His Majesty decides to make overtures to the ... er ... rebel general ... you see what I mean? It wouldn't exactly help his negotiations if any harm came to Harry Ireton's old friend Sam Dowdswell, would it?'

Back at Osney Betsie was puzzling how to use her knowledge when she heard an insistent wolf-whistle coming from the direction of the stables. She recognised it immediately: Martin Dowdswell giving notice of his presence. She hurried to the back door and gave an answering whistle. A moment later Martin and a burly companion he called Johnny were inside the house.

'What on earth ...' Betsie began, but a smiling Martin held up his hand. 'No shouting, or you'll wake the children, Mrs Dowdswell! And whatever you think, you haven't seen me or my friend! We're just a couple of strangers hoping for a bowl of Berkshire broth before we leave this unhealthy city where I've been showing Johnny some of my old haunts.'

Betsie had learnt long ago not to ply her menfolk with questions. Give them time to talk and they would generally tell her all she wanted to know. As she bustled across to the fire to heat the soup for her visitors her mind was concentrating on what her unexpected guests could do on Sam's behalf.

She glanced over her shoulder at the two young men sitting at the big kitchen table. What a fine-looking pair they made ... any girl would be glad to entertain them. When, a few minutes later, they were dipping hunks of bread into the hot soup, Betsie eyed Martin more closely. He was bearded now, tougher and heavier than when she'd last seen him – he must be twenty-four, she supposed. But the soldier she saw before her was still the boy of former days – ready for adventure, unconscious of danger, a twinkle in his eye. She waited for the inevitable question: 'So where's Sam, Betsie?' And very soon Martin Dowdswell was fully informed about her husband's grim situation.

He listened hard. When Betsie had finished her story he rose from the table and took his leave, saying that he and his friend must report back to their commanding officer before daybreak. But then he added: 'This commanding officer, Betsie. I think you'd like him. A very inquisitive type, isn't he,

Johnny? Wants to know how the university city is looking before he makes a state visit.'

'That's right,' Johnny took up the cue. 'Colonel Harry's very interested in prisoners, Madam. And thank you for the soup – just what we night-riders needed.'

The two spies from the rebel army crept out of the back door. As they left, Martin said to Betsie by way of clarification, 'We generally talk of our colonel by his Christian name – it shows we like him, see? Actually he's been known as Harry all his life: or at least ever since he was a hard-riding young fellow in his student days. He takes life more seriously now . . . reads the Bible every day . . . often quotes some verse from Isaiah about setting prisoners free. And he never forgets his old friends . . . never.'

He gave her a smacking kiss before disappearing into the blackness of the night, and Betsie slept better than at any time since Sam's arrest.

On 23 April 1646 some emissaries from King Charles presented themselves at the headquarters of the New Model Army at Waterstoke under flag of truce. They were received by Colonel Ireton, with Colonel Nathaniel Rich at his side and Cornet Dowdswell as aide-de-camp in attendance. For the most part the delegation consisted of officers granted safe passage to Europe under the terms of the Treaty of Truro which Ireton had negotiated. But Mr Ashburnham, acting as their spokesman, also brought with him a letter confirming that 'His Majesty would be prepared to live wherever Parliament should direct, if only he might be assured to continue king'. Colonel Ireton responded courteously, but very formally. He was glad to receive this most helpful communication from His Majesty; but Mr Ashburnham would appreciate that, as commander of the Parliamentary army's advance guard, he could do no more than forward the king's gracious message by fastest possible means to Parliament and Sir Thomas Fairfax. He would, however, make one counter-request and ask for an assurance that no action would be taken against any prisoners held in Oxford gaol while negotiations were in progress. He had, indeed, thought it right to make this request in a letter which he would like Mr Ashburnham to deliver to the city governor.

Meanwhile, he would ask to be excused in order to draft an immediate despatch to Westminster, and leave Colonel Rich to escort Mr Ashburnham and his party back to the city gates.

Henry Ireton was exultant. He could scarcely contain his excitement. Now he had to think fast and clearly. Martin and a companion were ordered to prepare for an immediate ride to London to deliver a letter from Colonel Ireton direct to General Cromwell at his house in Drury Lane, leaving the Member for Cambridge to decide when and how to present Ireton's letter to the House. Within two hours Martin was on his way, and Henry forced himself to relax, after arranging for a copy of his letter to be conveyed to Fairfax who was moving towards Oxford with the main army and the slow-moving artillery train.

For ten minutes Ireton remained in prayer. He asked for God's guidance in all that lay before him. Especially he prayed for an end to the fighting and for mercy to be shown to all prisoners and fighting men. Then, refreshed in spirit, he reflected on his own position.

Here he was, involved in the final military solution to this terrible struggle between the king and his people. He, a scholar and lawyer turned soldier, was taking his first step into the devious paths of politics. True, he had recently been elected Member of Parliament for Appleby, but the Naseby campaign, followed by convalescence from his wounds and the subsequent siege of Bristol, had prevented him from taking his seat in the House. Now everything he'd fought for was coming to pass, and he began to speculate whether the search for peace would take him further afield, or back to the green acres of the Trent valley. He smiled to himself, wondering whether and where his future days with Bridget would be spent, irrespective of the tasks assigned to him.

But back to the present. Somehow he must possess his soul in patience while Westminster decided on the next step. But patience was a quality that did not march in step with Henry Ireton's impulsive mind. Might he not hope to be entrusted with the peace negotiations? After all, his skills had been successfully employed by Fairfax in arranging the Treaty of Truro and the end of hostilities with Prince Rupert at Bristol. And while Harry had no ambition for success in this world, he had no doubt about the gifts that God had given him. Plans for a new Constitution for England began next to tumble over each other in his mind. Suddenly, he longed for Bridget to be at his side. Apart from his mother she was the only person with whom he had discussed his ideas for the government of England: a clear plan in which power would be shared between the monarch and his people, and a constitution in which the Law would guarantee to all its citizens freedom to worship God as their hearts desired. He slept the night through, and when he woke next morning he was still thinking of Bridget and England.

His euphoria ended abruptly with Martin's return from London with a letter addressed in Oliver's sprawling handwriting.

'You won't like its contents,' the young man remarked as he delivered it. 'No, I haven't opened it, but the general told me as much before I left London . . . Said something about going through the proper channels . . . and the danger of cutting corners. But he was very genial all the same, Colonel. Gave me a good meal at his house in Drury Lane and said he'd be writing separately about his eldest daughter.'

Martin watched Henry Ireton open and read the letter, saw his expression change from a sort of puzzlement to one of anger. Suddenly he turned to Martin. 'And you say the general was in a genial mood, Martin? By Heavens, you wouldn't know it from this reprimand . . . seems as if I should have reported to Sir Thomas Fairfax who would have felt bound to send it to those pottering Presbyterians in Parliament who in turn would have sent their reply at the pace of a Suffolk Punch dragging Hammond's artillery train! So now we waste three weeks and sit on our backsides, do we? I tell you, Martin: Black Tom, Lambert and I could settle this affair with His Majesty, as honourably and conclusively as we settled with Hopton at Truro and the prince at Bristol.'

Martin waited for the storm to pass. Fairfax and the main army, he quietly reminded Ireton, would be investing Oxford within the week. The second letter from General Oliver should arrive any moment. And, anyway, what about that conversation Harry had once had with Grandmother Cromwell? Something about a subtle mind, wasn't it?

Henry's anger gradually subsided. 'Of course you're right, Martin. Old Noll is playing the fish his own way which means, I suppose, leaving the negotiations to Parliament. But I don't like it, I prefer the direct hit, and the swift kill. You mark my words, Martin. We need to secure the king's person and negotiate with him and not with his lackeys. I have a horrible foreboding that this delay will allow His Majesty to escape the net.'

Ireton's fears were well founded. Some weeks before 20 June, when Oxford formally surrendered, King Charles stole away from the city in disguise, accompanied only by John Ashburnham and a chaplain called Hudson. He succeeded in reaching the Royalist stronghold of Newark where he surrendered to Lord Leven, the Scots commander. The Scots in turn escorted him north to Newcastle where they were on the point of opening negotiations with Parliament for handing over their captive in return for £400,000. Selling their king for cash – what a shoddy business!

Such matters were not yet public knowledge. All Henry Ireton knew was that he had been double-crossed by Mr John Ashburnham and his delegation. Still, his negotiating skills did not go unnoticed. It was he who, assisted by John Lambert, completed arrangements with Sir Thomas Glenham for the surrender of the university city; and in doing so he granted terms as generous as those at Truro and Bristol, allowing Prince Rupert and his brother Maurice to ride away over Magdalen Bridge with the honours of war and safe passes to the Continent. Again it was he who, accompanied by Fairfax and Lambert, signed the Treaty of Surrender at the City Hall. He also carried some responsibility for the strict discipline which set a guard over Bodley's library and ensured that no looting took place in the captured city. And, to the amusement of his three companions, it was Colonel Ireton who received a special ovation as the cavalcade passed the gates of Trinity. There, in the forefront of the crowd and spotted immediately by Henry and Martin, stood Sam and Betsie Dowdswell with old Simon beside them, shouting for joy and crying in gratitude. Henry had not forgotten his debt either to Oxford or his friends.

Yet the heady celebration of victory seemed very unimportant in the light of another event that took place in those overcrowded weeks. For a second letter from Oliver had reached Henry assigning the lease of an Ely farm as a marriage settlement for his eldest daughter; and this had been followed by Bridget Cromwell's arrival for a wartime wedding in the Chapel of Lady Whorwell's house at Holton where Fairfax had established Main Army Headquarters.

The marriage service, attended by Martin and a handful of fellow officers, was busily organised by the 'Generaless', Lady Fairfax, and would have been a short ceremony had it not been for a marathon sermon by Mr Dell the Fairfaxes' chaplain. But at last bride and bridegroom escaped to the privacy of their own room in the great house. There was a touching humility and no constraint in their love-making. Their companionship remained as easy and natural as it had always been at Ely. Bridie understood her man – his need for action, his hatred of cant, his innate modesty and his deeply religious nature. And Harry never had eyes for another woman.

First, they knelt beside the bed and prayed together that God who guided the lives of every living creature would bless their marriage and grant them the gift of children. Then they undressed, she from the heavy brocade she had worn in the chapel and he from a dark green civilian jerkin and breeches. And so they were united in love – God's own children naked and unashamed.

Theirs had been a strange courtship, marked by brief encounters and long absences; and Henry Ireton might never enjoy a married life free from the cares of State. But Bridie was beautiful to his eyes, her body strong and yielding to his touch; and for her he was the hero of her dreams – *un chevalier sans peur et sans reproche*. On this lovely night in June she gave herself to him, seeing no change in him save the small wound mark on his left cheek and the great scar on his thigh. In their loving, they experienced a miraculous release from care. And in their love of Christ and in their mutual constancy of purpose, they knew they would always remain united.

Part Three

The Army is King
1647–1649

Colonel Ireton was chiefly employed or took upon him the business of the pen . . . and was therein encouraged and assisted by Lt. General Cromwell and Colonel Lambert.

Bulstrode Whitelock, *Memoirs*

28

Although the fall of Oxford and the king's surrender to the Scots marked the end of the civil war, that young professional soldier, Martin Dowdswell, continued in active employment. Indeed, during the so-called year of peace in 1647, he had never been more active in his role of courier between the great soldiers who had built up and commanded the victorious Parliamentary army. His duties often brought him to London, where he stayed at the Shipleys' house by Temple Stairs.

Inevitably, he found himself answering the old couple's questions about his new-found heroes, above all the character of Oliver Cromwell.

'You're right to put him first,' Martin assured the old waterman. 'That's where we all place him. At the moment he has most of his family living with him in the Drury Lane house, having handed over his and Harry's responsibilities at Ely. But he doesn't really like London. You ask what he's like? That's a hard question to answer. He's a deep one, is Old Noll.' Martin was searching for the right word. 'Difficult to make out, you see. One day he's the cautious MP for Cambridge. Next day he's the confident victor of Naseby. One day he's full of religious doubts about Major Harrison and "the Saints" or political doubts about John Lilburne and the Levellers, so that I hardly know what he's talking about. Yet next day he's as jovial and carefree as any friend you might be meeting in a Thames-side ale-house. Or again, he's modesty itself in his dress and bearing, but unashamedly pleased with Parliament's reward for his war service – £2,500, they say, and the income from the Marquis of Worcester's forfeited estates. I don't know what to make of him, but I'll back him all the way to the top; and I think I know why. I tell you, Joe, the man is human – same as if he's one of us, despite his high position. For instance, when I deliver a message to General Oliver, he always finds time to ask about you and me. Only yesterday he was telling me of some of his family worries and about his old mother not enjoying London life. See what I mean? And talking of families' – Martin turned to Hannah – 'Harry and Bridget are expecting their baby in early summer: and that will be the Cromwells' first grandchild.'

Joe and Hannah Shipley loved Martin's visits. They had, after all, fostered him since his early schooldays and they never tired of hearing his tales about his grand friends.

Martin continued his analysis: 'Next comes Sir Thomas Fairfax from Yorkshire – the same age as Harry and his greatest friend: often in pain . . . suffers from the stone and a domineering wife who makes him take the cure at Bath. Still, he's a great man to have beside you on a battlefield . . . the army will go a long way for Black Tom. The same goes for General Skippon who has at last recovered from his Naseby wounds. And you'll be hearing more of John Lambert, I can tell you – another Yorkshireman and scarcely older than me. He gained a great reputation in the north after Black Tom came south, and now he is part of the high command working hand in glove with Harry. Like Harry, he's been to university and had legal training which comes in useful when you're negotiating with the king, or the Scots, or these difficult fellows at Westminster . . .'

'And what of Harry?' Hannah asked. 'Has he changed much since he married Bridget Cromwell last year?'

Martin laughed. 'He may be a bit more serious, but I don't think that's anything to do with Bridget. I'll leave you to judge for yourselves when he next asks for a bed. I guess he'll prefer to stay with you rather than brother John who has just taken a City heiress to wife. At the moment Black Tom is keeping Harry in Essex at Saffron Walden where he's very busy with his pen – doesn't like being disturbed.'

'I wouldn't be surprised,' said wise old Joe, puffing away at his clay pipe in the inglenook, 'if General Oliver ain't keeping Harry away from the Commons until his row with Denzil Holles blows over.

'Not heard about it, lad? Why, it's the talk of the town: every waterman on the river has a different version to tell. Anyway, it appears that Harry told this red-faced chap straight out that if he wanted everybody to worship after the Scots fashion he'd best take himself north of the Border. So Holles loses his temper, which he don't find too difficult to do, and challenges Harry to a duel, at which our man half draws his sword, then snaps it back and tells Holles that the Ireton family prefer to keep their swords for more serious encounters.

'Cor, love me, I can see Harry as clearly as if I was sitting opposite him in St Stephen's – his dark eyes blazing, his cheeks whiter than ever with the small scar under his left eye, his words clipped in an effort to keep his anger under control, yet every gesture showing his contempt for this ill-tempered snob. He don't like Holles one little bit – and that's not only because he's in league with the Scots, but because he sneers at colonels like Okey and Hewson and Pride who haven't enjoyed his education and social positon. Maybe Harry's not the right man for Parliament, eh?'

'You may be talking sense, Joe, but Harry's not the only one who is fed up with these Scots-led politicians. There are a lot of others too. You might include General Oliver among them, but of course he minds his words more carefully.'

Martin had his own reasons for gossiping with Joe and Hannah. In addition to enjoying their hospitality he also learnt much about Londoners' opinions and moods from Joe's well-informed waterman sources; and in due course passed the information to his army superiors. But he was very careful never to give any reasons for his frequent journeys between Saffron Walden and Drury Lane. Nor did he hint that Henry's next visit to the capital might be more than a routine appearance in pursuance of his parliamentary duties.

In fact, Martin was well aware that Henry had asked for an immediate conference at Cromwell's London house. Moreover, his knowledge of Ireton's mind convinced him that something dramatic was in the wind. Martin sensed and shared his guardian's pent-up excitement. He was sure that Ireton, now accepted by his fellow officers as the army's chief man of ideas, was planning some surprise – swift action perhaps – to break the deadlock between army and Parliament. And high time too!

Nearly a year had passed since the king's escape from Oxford and his surrender to his Scottish friends at Newark. They had taken him, for his greater safety, to Newcastle where he was permitted to hunt or play golf as he wished.

These days of leisure were an indication of the tempo which governed Parliament's negotiations with its Scottish allies. First, its commissioners presented the king with humiliating terms which he could not conceivably accept. Then they wanted to move him further from the Border and haggled with the Scots over terms for his repossession. They finally settled for £400,000 to cover their obligations for services rendered and to ensure the return of the invasion force to its native land.

It was only towards the end of 1646 that the king had begun to move south under Parliamentary guard: and then the royal progress was deliberately slow, resembling as nearly as possible His Majesty's spectacular pre-war journeys to Newmarket and Theobalds. A royal journey never fails to attract sightseers, and there were very few Englishmen who shared Edmund Ludlow's enthusiasm for a republic. Most of them – and that certainly included the Parliamentary army commanders – could not imagine their country without a king at its head, and the people of Yorkshire and Nottingham gave proof of this loyalty as they turned out in every town and village to cheer Charles on his way south. Near the city of Nottingham he was officially saluted by Sir Thomas Fairfax, supported by the county notables – the Thornhaughs and Iretons and their friends.

It was not until February 1647 that the king reached Holdenby Hall in Northamptonshire – one of the most spacious residences in England where hunting and other field sports could be enjoyed by His Majesty. Colonel Graves, to whom Parliament had entrusted the king's safe-keeping, appeared to have a most congenial task.

Meanwhile Parliament, which had shown so little urgency in its negotiations with the king and its Scottish allies, was even more dilatory in tackling the grievances of the fighting men who had brought victory to its cause. Making gifts to Fairfax and Cromwell and staging receptions in their honour did not absolve its members from meeting the serious arrears of army pay which were provoking intense anger at Saffron Walden where Fairfax had concentrated his main strength.

The officers still managed to maintain the discipline which had been such a feature of their citizen army. Faced with disaffection in Massey's crack regiment which had conducted the heroic defence of Gloucester, Fairfax and Ireton had no hesitation in disbanding it. But when Parliament ordered demobilisation without firm proposals for back payment to the troops – and even sought to make pay conditional on volunteering for service in Ireland – anger boiled over.

A petition from senior officers achieved nothing but more delay. When two hundred officers confronted the Parliamentary Commissioners in the nave of Saffron Walden's lovely parish church, nothing was gained beyond arid discussion on service in Ireland. All Parliament's proposals were turned down flat by six regiments of horse, including Fleetwood's regiment and a troop commanded by Tom Ireton. A fortnight later, following a conference at Saffron Walden's Sun Inn attended by Cromwell, Ireton, Skippon, Lambert and Whalley, a further meeting was held in the parish church and Skippon offered to take command in Ireland. But the troops would have none of it. Ireton was instructed to draw up a moderate but positive demand for pay, known as the Declaration of the Army, while all ranks were assured that it was lawful to delay disbanding until they were paid in full.

Still, Parliament remained obdurate; and Ireton, who had remained in Saffron Walden, came to London with his own solution. It was a typical Ireton plan, as bold as it was simple: seize the king and place him under the army's protection. With the army's position thus strengthened, Ireton argued, Parliament would be forced to meet its backlog of pay. Only then could the soldiers accept demobilisation and a return to their peacetime occupations.

On the last day of May, Fairfax and Cromwell learnt the details of Ireton's plan at the Cromwell home in Drury Lane. As experienced cavalry commanders, they appreciated the merits of speed and surprise: five hundred men, say a regiment of horse, to surround Holdenby, disarm Colonel Graves and his unsuspecting guards, and take possession of the house and its royal tenant.

Fairfax nodded approval, but Oliver voiced his doubts. 'What if His Majesty proves obstinate? If the plan fails and we are held responsible, we shall be arraigned by our enemies at Westminster – and deprived of power, if not our lives.' He saw the disappointment in his son-in-law's face and began to chuckle. 'Don't look so gloomy, Harry,' he said. 'Your excellent plan only requires two minor modifications. Let the five hundred men – that should be strength enough – be led by a low-ranking officer, and not by a regimental commanding officer. And let the expedition approach Holdenby by any route other than the road from Saffron Walden. If we win, well and good. If the plan goes amiss, we admonish those in charge of this irregular action. See my point?'

Thus it was arranged. A detachment from Fairfax's regiment set off on a routine journey to the Oxford garrison, commanded by a young tailor's apprentice, Cornet Joyce, who had been selected for the task by Fairfax. Martin Dowdswell rode with him in a very unofficial capacity – his single duty being to report the result of the mission to the high command at Saffron Walden.

In the event, the plan was brilliantly executed. Joyce's irregulars, turning north from Oxford, took possession of Holdenby without spilling a drop of blood. When the young tailor spoke directly to His Majesty and the king asked on whose authority he was acting, the cheeky lad pointed to his five hundred men. The king laughingly conceded that he knew of no fairer authority and moved under Joyce's escort to Sir John Cutts' home at Childerley near Cambridge.

On hearing of Joyce's coup from Martin, who covered the fifty miles to Saffron Walden in record time, Oliver Cromwell's cousin, Colonel Whalley, was ordered to take over the command from Cornet Joyce. But when it was suggested that the royal party might wish to return to the luxury of Holdenby Hall the king demurred, remarking that Sir John Cutts' garden provided an excellent venue for a meeting with the army commanders.

They were left in no doubt that the king preferred the army's company to that of his previous captors. Fairfax he had encountered briefly on his progress from Newcastle, but he now met Cromwell and Ireton for the first time. All three men – each stemming from the yeoman class of landed gentry – were most favourably impressed by the king's courteous reception. Though small of stature, he had a natural dignity and found it easy to exert his considerable personal charm over men and women whom he met in personal audience for the first time. In the delightful surroundings of this English garden he promised to do everything in his power to speed up payment to the army, and suggested that the process would be helped if General Fairfax would agree to move him closer to London.

At this point Henry Ireton was instructed to prepare the army's case for presentation to king and Parliament. He had, indeed, thought longer and more clearly than any other army leader concerning the settlement of the kingdom; and his earlier Declaration of the Army, sponsored by the newly-formed Army Council, had contained a memorable – and, as some would hold, a dangerous – phrase: 'We are not a mercenary army: we speak for England.' Friends and enemies were beginning to learn that Commissary General Ireton had a disconcerting habit of meaning exactly what he said or wrote.

His full plan for a revised Constitution was now drafted with exemplary clarity. Under his Heads of Proposals the king and queen would return to Whitehall, parliamentary seats would be redistributed to give better representation to the new centres of population, the legal system would be reformed, and Parliament would control taxation and the top civil and military appointments. Finally, an Act of Oblivion would cover the cases of Royalists prepared to be loyal to the new Constitution.

One day this Nottingham landowner's Heads of Proposals would provide a sound base for England's constitutional monarchy; but in 1647 three obstacles proved insurmountable.

First, the Presbyterians in Parliament, determined to force a uniform system of worship on an unwilling nation, suggested that the army (by which they meant 'the Independents') were posing a threat to the authority of Parliament. The charge was sufficient for the disgruntled Massey to stir up City opposition to the army proposals.

Secondly, the rank and file were increasingly exposed to the unpredictable but dangerous eloquence of Honest John Lilburne, who was demanding universal suffrage and an end to the king – 'that man of blood who must account for all the blood he had shed'. Such a creed was anathema to all who shared the property-owning background of men like Fairfax or Cromwell or Ireton.

But the greatest obstacle to Ireton's plan for the establishment of a constitutional monarchy lay with the king himself. As Charles was conducted south, moving from big house to big house in stages corresponding to Fairfax's step-by-step advance on London, Martin noticed the change in his guardian's feelings towards the king – his earlier optimism changing first to doubt and then despair.

Unlike Fairfax and Cromwell, Ireton had already been double-crossed, and he didn't like being fooled. He had good cause for wondering whether Ashburnham's mission at Oxford was anything but a ploy to gain time for the king to leave the doomed city. Believe Ashburnham if you like, but could the king really have been ignorant of the deception?

And now His Majesty was offering titles of nobility to the three army leaders! What foolishness! How could any man who aspired to leadership be so bad a judge of character? Was Charles, and not his queen, the foolish one who had sought to arrest the five Members before the war? Had he learnt nothing? Who, in God's name, could convince him that the only hope of regaining his throne lay in the hands of these honourable men in whose company he was travelling to London?

Clutching at straws, Ireton's thoughts turned to his brother-in-law, Sir Edward Ford, presently living in exile at the queen's court in France. Sarah Ireton's husband might be the one living Englishman who could convince the king of Ireton's high purpose. Edward Ford had always remained a king's man, despite a miserable war – captured at Chichester and freed; knighted by the king in Oxford and then made prisoner again at Arundel; escaped from the Tower of London only to be rounded up again at Winchester when Cromwell had returned last year from the West Country. And now an unhappy exile at the queen's court, separated from his wife by the English Channel. Hardly a record of success – but at least he would vouch to the king for Henry's integrity.

Arrangements were made for Martin Dowdswell to meet Ford at Dover and conduct him to Army Headquarters under terms of safe conduct. But alas for these high hopes. By the time Ford reported to the king, the latter was already in open negotiation with the Scots and in secret correspondence with the French.

With unbelievable obstinacy, King Charles believed he possessed the diplomatic skill to play off the Scots and Parliament against the army. Perhaps he was deceived by the fact that his charm and courtesy had gained for him a measure of freedom such as few prisoners can ever have enjoyed. When, on the journey south, he reached Caversham and was reunited with three of his children, Cromwell and Ireton were invited to witness a family scene which was worthy of a van Dyck canvas. The sentimental Oliver was moved to tears, but his son-in-law was less impressed.

Meanwhile, as Parliament continued to procrastinate, Fairfax moved his forces closer to London – from Newmarket through St Albans and Windsor to Hounslow Heath. Members at Westminster were quick to interpret the army's threat. Leading Presbyterians like Holles and Massey read the signs correctly and fled to Holland and the Channel Islands. The City of London rushed to make submission. Its citizens cheered themselves hoarse as Fairfax staged a display of strength which nobody could mistake – the fighting men of the New Model Army marching through the City and over London Bridge: nine thousand foot and seven thousand horse, drums, trumpets, colours flying; Hammond and Rich with the infantry; Old Noll at the head of the cavalry; and in a carriage, escorted by his own Lifeguards, Sir Thomas Fairfax with his wife, Anne, and Mrs Elizabeth Cromwell at his side. London had seen its new rulers and the lord mayor was quick to meet Fairfax's demand for £50,000 to meet the arrears of army pay.

But where was Commissary General Ireton in all this junketing? That was the question uppermost in the minds of Joe and Hannah Shipley as Martin returned from the great parade to the Shipley home by Temple Stairs.

'Oh, Harry doesn't hold with all this show,' Martin assured the old couple. 'He's happy to stand aside until the king is transferred to Hampton Court where he can sleep in the state rooms and enjoy his own pictures. Then Harry'll move to Putney where, for his purposes, he will be close enough to the king and far enough from Westminster. At the moment, his chief worry is what Lilburne will do next to upset army discipline.'

'Poor man,' said Hannah. 'When he last stayed with us, he

looked so worried, as if he carried all England's troubles on his shoulders. All those families separated, like his own sister and Sir Edward, I could have wept for her; and everyone else convinced they know the only road to salvation. It's a sad world we live in. As for Harry, I told him to return to his wife and baby.'

'Ay,' Joe chipped in. 'Hannah's right. Harry's more likely to get things sorted out with the king at Hampton Court if he spends a week away from his cares, with Bridget and the little girl. What's her name again, Martin?'

'Elizabeth,' replied Martin, 'Elizabeth, after Grandmother Cromwell and Bridget's mother. But set your minds at rest. Harry has acted on your advice, though he has only a temporary home at Windsor; I doubt if he and Bridget can settle down – worse luck – until the king has been persuaded to accept Harry's plan for the settlement of the kingdom.'

29

As Edward Ford boarded the small Dutch yaugh, lying at anchor in the Port of London, he was in a state of total dejection.

He was acutely aware that he had failed in the mission which he had undertaken. The king, it was true, had received him most kindly. His Majesty fully understood that Henry Ireton's proposals, if accepted, would ensure his return to the throne. He must have known, also, from his own observations as well as Edward's commendation, that Ireton was a man of his word, with the will and the strength to carry out what he promised to do. Furthermore, he must be aware of the military power wielded by Fairfax and Cromwell. And yet . . . and yet . . . ? Why had the king shown no positive reaction? What evil genius blinded him to the reality of power?

Edward had remained in England as long as his permit lasted. He had developed a happy relationship with his unobtrusive escort, Captain Martin Dowdswell. His friendship with Henry Ireton remained as firm as in their Oxford days, strengthened by Henry's promise that, in his proposals, toleration would extend to Catholics provided they did not make common cause with the nation's enemies. And for a few blessed weeks he had been reunited with his family. He had assured Sarah that he would soon rejoin her for good in their Sussex home . . . that her brother's plan would in due course win the royal approval . . . that His Majesty, newly transferred to his own palace of Hampton Court, was being treated by the army with marked respect . . .

But as he said goodbye to Sarah and their seven-year-old daughter – standing forlorn beside Hannah Shipley at Temple Stairs – Edward knew that his wife had detected the doubt in his voice. Soon, he supposed, she would discover from her brother the difficulties that were confronting him and his father-in-law at the army debates in the parish church at Putney. Martin Dowdswell had told him that the Heads of

Proposals, recommended with unanswerable logic by Henry and exemplary patience by Oliver, had so far failed to win the support of the so-called Agitators and other members of the officer corps. A day spent in prayer had done nothing to soften John Lilburne's demand for the cessation of all negotiations with the king. And Edward knew from Henry's own words that Oliver's support for the king's restoration had seriously undermined his and Ireton's popularity with the army.

His mission to England could do no more. The king's future lay in his own hands. Edward's only remaining duty was to report his failure to the queen in Paris where he must needs remain an exile till this triangular contest between king, army and Parliament was finally resolved.

He would be more profitably employed in studying the lines of this Dutch ship on which he was embarked. With the Channel calm and the wind constant, he was making the passage to Dunkirk in excellent time; and the Dutch crew were delighted to explain the new rig of mainsail and jib which had been perfected on the inland waterways of Holland. In Edward's judgment, this small ship would be much easier to handle than his square-rigged fishing fleet based on the old Cinque Port of Hastings. If life in England ever returned to normal, he could foresee a time when these ships, built on Dutch lines, would take over the complete coastal trade.

The return to France was a prospect that gave Edward no pleasure. The queen's court, moving uncertainly between the Louvre and St Germain, was a seedbed of intrigue. Quarrels daily: the lecherous Digby challenged to duels by Wilmot and Rupert; the queen's guards called out to separate the combatants; servants not knowing whether or when they would receive their wages; that holy fox, Cardinal Mazarin, protesting his support for Henri Quatre's daughter, but in fact delighting in England's weakness while he settled his quarrel with Spain; and the queen herself, preparing to sell the last of her jewellery to help the Prince of Wales finance an invasion from Holland. How ludicrous for loyalty to be so blindly committed! Had the queen's advisers no understanding of the strength of Parliament, when backed by the invincible army of Fairfax, Cromwell and Ireton? Had the king's correspondence with the queen so hidden the truth? Had she learnt so little of 'the liberties of England' during her fifteen years in Whitehall?

What he had heard in his brief sojourn at Hampton Court had filled him with foreboding. Even while the king was negotiating with Parliament and army, mysterious messengers were reaching His Majesty from his loyal followers in Scotland, Wales and Lancashire, and even from the previously unconcerned County of Kent. All carried the same message: 'When spring comes, we will rise again.'

But how, in Heaven's name, could the nobility of England have the face to launch their ill-armed peasants against the finest army in Europe? Not only were these Royalist plots ridiculous, born of arrogance and sheer stupidity. They were also being discussed so indiscreetly that Sir Thomas Fairfax must soon get wind of them. Young Dowdswell had made it clear to Edward that the king's entourage was virtually incapable of preserving secrecy or hiding its futile plans.

God help any of Edward's friends who now took up arms against Parliament! As his lumbering coach lurched its slow way to Paris along the rough roads of northern France, Edward recalled his conversation with old Dr Kettel on his last visit to Oxford. Had not the hope been expressed that he and Henry Ireton would one day combine to end the agony of England? Now, it seemed, that hope was as dead as the dear old president, confounded by the obstinacy of a king who trusted nobody and was mistrusted by all.

Bridget Ireton, like other army wives, had no hope of a settled home until hostilities were concluded; and being of an equable temperament, she would normally have counted herself lucky in having baby Elizabeth to care for and kind neighbours to meet in the pleasant market town of Kingston-upon-Thames. She had no desire to live in London.

But her husband! If only he were not so distressed by the turning fortune of politics! Day by day, he rode to St Mary's parish church in nearby Putney in order to gain the army's support for the king's restoration. Each night he came home with diminishing hope. His great plan, he told Bridget, was being slowly murdered as the Levellers, Lilburne and Wildman, bayed for the king's blood and redoubled their demands for universal male suffrage. If their ideas won the day, England would be ungovernable.

But, worse than this, Harry was beginning to doubt the strength of his father-in-law's help. Not that his general support was in question any more than that of Fairfax or John Lambert who had played some part in the final draft of the Heads of Proposals. But, in the event, Harry had been left to carry the burden of debate. Oliver's efforts to meet the wishes of army Agitators and Presbyterian Members of Parliament struck Harry as a dangerous compromise with principle. Such shifts as Oliver proposed were out of keeping with his true beliefs. Was he being persuaded by the Devil whose voice Harry heard clearly in every inflection of Wildman's voice?

Bridget, who understood her father's mind better than anybody in the world except his old mother, did her best to reassure her husband. Harry must remember, she said, that his hero was often unpredictable – hadn't Grandmother Cromwell told him so? And Oliver might be a sick man. As a girl she had lived through his earlier period of self-doubt – that illness of the mind which Sir Theodore Mayerne had done much to cure – and the same symptoms were showing again. Oliver, believing himself chosen of God to forward the Divine purpose, was questioning his source of motivation. It was not easy, she told Harry, for either of them to live in the shadow of a great man who was enduring the dark days of the soul. They must be very patient. Whatever the outcome of the debates in the chancel of Putney church, she and Harry must retain their faith in Oliver.

Meanwhile, what would Harry advise about the invitation just received from Hampton Court? Her father and mother had accepted an invitation to dine with the king. So had Sir Thomas and Lady Fairfax. She thought her father would wish them to strengthen their personal contact, and Anne Fairfax would help her to choose a suitable dress for the occasion. What did Harry think? She understood that apart from royal attendants like Ashburnham and Berkeley, the only other guests would be Colonel and Mrs Whalley – the colonel being charged by Parliament with safeguarding the king's person.

Henry smiled at his young wife's ingenuous attempt to take his mind off the Levellers at Putney. 'So, Bridie, His Majesty hopes to win the day by suborning the generals' wives, does he? He's a wily one, I tell you. But of course we join the party – that would certainly be your father's wish. But not a word, I pray you, concerning Oliver's *malaise* or these tedious Putney arguments – the king hears too much from Anne Fairfax about what happens at the meetings of the Army Council. We'll visit Hampton Court in search of knowledge, not to give it away. Promise?'

Henry kissed his wife. He loved her best of all when she had the solemn look in her eyes.

And what a splendid entry the Iretons made when they met the king in the great hall at Hampton Court. Bridie, in a full-sleeved dress of rich, ruby-red satin, round-cut from the shoulders, and serving to show the Cromwell pearls against her clear skin; and Henry, much taller than his royal host, his dark hair long and his small beard trimmed, dressed *en civile* – his dark green tunic, breeches and hose set off by the white lace of collar and cuffs. Henry Ireton and his young wife could have graced any court in Europe.

Clearly the king was determined to win Bridget's favour. He was so happy, he said, to be meeting her at last. Her father and husband were, of course, well known to him – a formidable pair indeed; honourable men after his own heart, but hardly forthcoming, Madam, about their private interests. Could not Mrs Ireton enlighten him concerning their homes and family backgrounds?

Leaving Henry in conversation with Ashburnham, the king led Bridget away from the other guests towards a cabinet filled with small *objets d'art*. 'Would you not agree, Madam, that these small pieces I have collected possess their own special beauty, independent of the troubles we mortals are heir to?'

Bridget was suddenly conscious of being in the presence of a connoisseur, not a king. 'When the light is good,' Charles continued, 'I would hope to show you the paintings we have brought to Hampton Court. But meanwhile, consider this small collection of mine. Each piece beautiful in itself, you see, but also expressing the nature . . . the personality of its creator.'

The king's long fingers withdrew an exquisite little silver goblet from the back of the cabinet. 'Please accept this,

Madam, for your baby,' he said. 'I'm so glad to know from Captain Dowdswell that the child prospers.'

Bridget turned to the king, holding the little gift and wondering whether her words of thanks successfully hid her surprise at the mention of Martin.

The king continued, 'Captain Dowdswell has won for himself a special place in our small household. Not only does he prove himself a rare hand at bowls. In addition I owe him a great debt for bringing our baby safely from Exeter to Oatlands Park – the baby daughter I've never seen since the day of her christening. A king, Madam, is not immune to grief.'

For a moment the king's expressive eyes filled with tears. Then an almost mischievous smile transformed his face. 'Remember, Madam, this present is for Miss Elizabeth Ireton. Let it never be whispered that the King of England attempted to influence General Ireton by a gift to his wife. In this corruptible world, the gesture might be misinterpreted. And I honour your husband for what he is – an Englishman as true as tempered steel.'

Less than a week after her visit to Hampton Court, Bridget was sitting in the bay window of the little Kingston house beside the Thames when Martin arrived hot-foot from Whitehall. 'I have a message, Ma'am, from your father. You and the baby are to move at once to Windsor Castle where a suite of rooms has been prepared for you.'

'But why the urgency, Martin? The general and I are very happy here. Has my husband been informed?'

'Yes, indeed. I come from Putney, and he asks that you be ready to move before nightfall. There has been, I understand, a threat to his life – wild talk, he assures you, but he will explain everything. Meanwhile, I must hasten to deliver a message to Hampton Court.'

Martin and his companion, Kentish Johnny, left in a flurry of dust to deliver a separate note from Cromwell to his cousin, Colonel Whalley, asking him to inform His Majesty that some sectarians were believed to be planning the king's murder. It would be wise to strengthen the palace guard; but above all, Whalley must warn the king of his danger, and also see that the danger was known to his three companions – Ashburnham,

Berkeley and Legge. Martin and Kentish Johnny were under orders to report the completion of their mission to General Cromwell in Whitehall as quickly as possible.

Neither the Iretons nor Martin Dowdswell ever fully understood the sequel. But the king informed that excellent soldier, Colonel Whalley, that in the circumstances he must be considered free of his parole not to escape. Within twenty-four hours His Majesty and his three companions were moving freely on the towpath of the Thames, having easily evaded the 'strengthened' guard. And following Ashburnham's advice, the king had made for Carisbrooke in the Isle of Wight under the strange impression that he would receive a warm welcome from Colonel Robin Hammond, the castle governor newly appointed by Parliament. Hammond, the younger brother of the New Model's artillery commander, may have been thought sympathetic to the king's restoration. But his first loyalty was to Parliament – hardly surprising since he was married to the daughter of Oliver's cousin, the great John Hampden. And there, as if decreed by Fate, the king's escape ended – in a castle on the Isle of Wight, where he was permitted every privilege except freedom. At Westminster it was observed that the king's new place of detention made correspondence with friend or enemy considerably more difficult than in the spacious plan of Hampton Court Palace. And the Iretons, as well as Martin and Kentish Johnny, noted that General Cromwell was once again in the best of health. The brooding melancholy which had so troubled Bridget Ireton a few weeks previously had disappeared as if by magic.

Martin and Johnny now began to act as couriers between Carisbrooke, Windsor and the new Cromwell home in King Street, Westminster. At Carisbrooke Castle, as at Hampton Court, they remained friendly with the royal entourage – Johnny in the kitchen quarters where he was very popular with the locally recruited servants, and Captain Dowdswell sharing apartments and entertainment with the king's special friends.

Neither man was concerned with the nation's day-to-day problems. These succeeded each other with staggering complexity: Fairfax and Cromwell sternly dealing with an army mutiny which involved the execution of its leaders bv firing squad; Parliamentary Commissioners travelling to Carisbrooke with a plan combining Ireton's plan and their previously rejected Newcastle proposals; Royalist disturbances by the City apprentices who were frightened off the streets and their leader killed by a cavalry charge led by Cromwell and Ireton.

But in their respective jobs the two young men kept their eyes and ears open, so that when a Scots delegation arrived at Carisbrooke, Martin made an immediate report to Windsor. Twenty-four hours later, Kentish Johnny reported news gathered from the kitchen quarters: namely that a French courier, recently arrived at Carisbrooke, would be returning to France the following day with messages for the queen. Letters would be carried in the Frenchman's saddle bag and he would be overnighting at the Blue Boar Inn in Holborn.

By chance, Cromwell was at Windsor when Johnny gave Ireton the man's description together with his time of arrival and stopping place in London. Within the hour, Generals Cromwell and Ireton, with Captain Dowdswell in attendance, left Windsor, disguised as troopers, for a drinking evening in London.

'Anybody know the whereabouts of this ale-house?'

Henry laughed as he answered Oliver's question. 'Know it? Of course I do. It's a most respectable inn. In my student days I often took a meal there – once, I remember, with my brother-in-law, Edward Ford.'

Before six o'clock the three troopers reached the Blue Boar, where they stabled and fed their tired horses. For an hour they sipped London ale waiting for their French quarry within the entrance of the hostelry. Were they on a fool's errand? Martin reassured them: Kentish Johnny didn't make mistakes.

Suddenly the waiting ceased. A man with a limited knowledge of English was asking the outside porter for overnight accommodation. There was the sound of a slight altercation – apparently the man insisted on bringing his horse's saddle into the inn. But the nature of his reception surprised the porter as much as it did the French guest. Martin blocked all further progress. Harry snatched the saddle. Oliver, ready with a sheath knife, slit the saddle bag and ripped out the letter they sought.

'That's enough,' Oliver shouted. 'Leave this Frenchie his luggage and the better part of his saddle.' Without a backward look, the three troopers jostled their way past the startled people at the Blue Boar, out to the stables, on to their saddled horses and away from Holborn at the gallop. Oliver was shouting and laughing like a schoolboy as the three riders turned south past Lincoln's Inn and along the Strand. He might have been an undergraduate on a night out. But as he reached his house, he recovered his dignity. Martin was ordered to care for the horses, with a pat on the back. 'Well done, Martin,' Oliver said. 'Nothing like mounted men, eh, if you want to surprise the enemy.'

Oliver and Harry greeted Elizabeth Cromwell who seemed to accept their sudden incursion as if it were all part of her daily routine. Yes, of course, there would be a meal for the three of them and a bed for Captain Dowdswell – she only hoped they would find a change of clothes before they supped.

She hurried away towards the kitchen, and Oliver turned to his son-in-law. 'Now, Harry, we will see what sort of urgent message His Majesty desires to send to his queen. Cut out the endearments – that's not our business. Go on, read it out.'

Henry was staring at the letter as if transfixed. Suddenly, anger took over. The dark eyes were blazing. His voice was unnaturally tense. 'Read it for yourself . . . go on, read it for yourself . . . Charles Stuart, the double-crossing traitor . . . tells *my* wife how highly he values our friendship . . . honour . . . integrity. And now he tells *his* wife that he prefers to entrust his cause to Lauderdale and the Scots rather than accept our English proposals for his restoration.' Henry pushed the letter towards his father-in-law.

Oliver read it for himself. His silence was no less menacing than the younger man's outburst. Nothing more was said. They changed from their troopers' uniforms. They ate. They slept. But there was no more laughter. Charles Stuart had sealed his own fate. The liberties of the kingdom would be recovered without the king's help.

30

The dying rays of the winter sun were still giving a little dim light to the Southwark riverside as Martin Dowdswell dismounted outside the Shipleys' house and looked across the Thames from Temple Stairs. He was back in London with orders to ensure that General Ireton could rely on accommodation with the Shipleys over the next few weeks; but he was also hoping for a bed for himself and a taste of Hannah Shipley's cooking. He would be glad to be clear of his makeshift quarters at Windsor.

Joe and Hannah showed no surprise as they opened the door, for they had grown accustomed to Martin's sudden arrivals and equally sudden departures. He was always welcome, and of course they would provide a room for Harry, as they continued to call their one-time student lodger, though proudly aware of the high place he now held in the nation's business.

'But what of Mrs Ireton and the baby?' asked Hannah. 'I'm longing to meet them, and Joe and I aren't getting any younger, you know.'

Martin laughed. 'You'll have to ask Harry about that,' he said. 'All I know is that another baby is on the way and Bridget means to stay at Windsor until the child is safely delivered.'

Henry wanted it that way too. For all his love of his two oldest friends in London, he was a countryman at heart, and shared his wife's view that children were best kept away from the big towns.

Joe's searching eyes were watching Martin carefully. 'Now come along, laddie. You can't tell me you've ridden twenty-two miles from Windsor on the late afternoon of a plaguey cold day just to discuss babies with Hannah. Something's been happening down there that's brought you to town, eh? From what I hear up and down the river, Harry won't be having much time to spare for his family.'

'Right as usual, Joe. At Windsor the grandees are all fully

engaged – Fairfax, Oliver and Lambert as well as Harry – and they spend most of the day in prayer!'

'Asking for guidance, eh? Well, they'll find they have a few problems up here too. Londoners don't take kindly to soldiers quartered on their doorsteps – though I grant you that, as soldiers go, this lot is mighty well-behaved. The trouble is they keep on shouting that they have no use for the king whereas His Majesty still has a lot of friends round here. The latest news is that the apprentices are starting to love him again, shouting "God save the king" in the streets and sporting the royal colours! There's something romantic, I suppose, about a king locked up alone in a castle. But there you are. The whole place is at sixes and sevens, and the silly fellows generally make trouble when business is rotten, as John Ireton will be quick to tell Harry when they next meet.' Joe Shipley spat his disapproval into the log fire.

'Sixes and sevens – that's a fair description of what life has been like at Windsor! But I've a bit of good news for you, Joe. Whether it's due to God or Old Noll, the grandees have sorted out their problems with the army Agitators. Believe it or not, Levellers like John Lilburne, Fifth Monarchy men like Harry's good-looking friend, Colonel Harrison, top soldiers from the north like Lambert and Hazelrig, are all singing the same tune. And here's something else, Joe. There's a Parliamentary Commission down there, which looks like accepting the army viewpoint. If that happens, God will in very truth have performed a miracle.'

'Let's hope you're right, boy.' Joe got up and stretched his legs. 'Time to find out what Hannah's cooking. If those Members of Parliament pray as long as they talk in St Stephen's, I'd say you're well clear of Windsor.'

Martin's forecast was right on target. Cromwell's and Ireton's reluctant conviction that the double-dealing king could no longer be trusted by anybody had made it comparatively simple for them to regain the leadership that had been challenged by the army extremists at Putney. With considerable diplomatic skill they had not only reunited army opinion, but also persuaded the visiting parliamentary delegation to call off their own negotiations with the king. To celebrate the new accord, a feast had been held in the Great Hall of Windsor Castle, and the Commission honoured with a twenty-five-gun salute before being escorted back to the capital. Those army officers who were also Members of Parliament had followed the delegation to Westminster and were present when the House resumed business in the New Year.

The outcome of the ensuing debate in the Commons was soon common knowledge all over London, spreading through the King Street ale-houses and along the Thames waterfront. Long before Ireton reached the Shipleys' house, Joe was retailing the news to his wife. 'Cromwell's settled the issue, they say . . . seems as if he let the other wind-bags do the talking. Then, when everybody's waiting on tenterhooks, wondering if he'll intervene, he gets up in that hesitating way of his, as if he's having an argument with his own soul. First, he assures the House that the king is "a man of great parts and a great understanding" but then – listen to this, Hannah – but then, playing on the word "great", he adds that, unfortunately, His Majesty is so great a dissembler and so false a man that he's not to be trusted any more. By all accounts, it was a fair knock-out blow. Never before had he spoken so clearly against the king.'

'And Harry – did he speak, Joe?'

'No, not a word. But outside the House, his name's on everybody's lips. Some blaspheming pamphleteer is writing of Oliver as God, and Harry as his son, Jesus Christ! What a scurrilous lot they are. But the army – and the people in the know – call him "the army's Alpha and Omega". That's the way it goes.'

Later, Henry returned and joined the three of them for some mulled wine. He seemed much happier than he'd been when he visited the Shipleys at the time of the Putney Debates. But he wouldn't say anything about his own part either at Windsor or Westminster, preferring to tell Hannah about Bridget and baby Elizabeth walking in the Great Park at Windsor. He was, however, full of praise for his father-in-law. 'You can't exactly explain his hold on the House, Joe, nor on the soldiers if it comes to that. He seems to have a gift for sharing the same worries that are crossing everybody's mind. And then, hey presto, he comes up with the only possible solution. He's no orator, mind you, but he possesses a unique sense of timing – an instinct for choosing the right moment for decision. Today, in the House, his was the only voice that mattered.'

'And what of his health, Harry?'

'Oh, he's quite his old self now he's got everybody singing the same tune; and he's full of laughter. I shared his carriage up King Street. Crowds were running alongside, all cheering and shouting. He leans out to wave to them, but then he turns and says to me, "Don't let their cheering turn your head, Harry. They'd cheer us just the same if we were being taken to execution at Tyburn." He has a great understanding of men, has Oliver.'

So, at long last, the irreconcilables were reconciled. Parliament, the army extremists and the army commanders were all agreed that they should break off their dealings with the king. And after the Commons debate, nobody was in any doubt as to who held the master card.

But how should Oliver use his new-found power? Like as not, he would seek his son-in-law's advice. And Henry Ireton, sitting with Martin in the Shipleys' first-floor room which he'd first entered with Sarah twenty years before, decided to use his companion as a sounding board. The young man, recently promoted Major in Fairfax's regiment, had proved himself not only as a soldier, but also as a highly intelligent gatherer of information for the army commanders. There was a disarming innocence about his approach to people which invited confidences.

Henry put the question bluntly: 'Time to turn your mind to politics, Martin. How is England to be governed without a king?'

Martin saw exactly what his guardian was driving at. 'No king and, therefore, no head of State . . . it leaves an awkward gap in the Ireton Constitution . . . that's the point, isn't it? I've no answer to your question, but I think you may be making the wrong military assumptions. Are you sure the war is over? According to my contacts, support for the king goes far beyond these trouble-making City apprentices. Kentish Johnny had a very mixed reception when he took a week's leave in Kent last week; and a friend in Lambert's regiment tells me his colonel's off to the North, but only when he has been issued with fresh equipment for six regiments – so there could be trouble on the border. Chatter-boxes at Hampton Court and Carisbrooke suggest that His Majesty may still have a few cards up his sleeve.'

'And you've passed your doubts to Fairfax?'

'Most certainly, and I'm sure he's alive to the military danger. But back to your first question, Harry. I'm no politician, but a master at St Paul's School once told me that you should stand at a distance if you want to see a picture whole. Why don't you get away from Westminster and take a look at the political picture from Windsor, or Oxford or Nottingham?'

Of course, Martin was right. How could a man think clearly in this highly-charged atmosphere at Westminster? The following morning Henry took leave of Fairfax and his father-in-law, and travelled to Attenborough by way of Windsor and Oxford.

He spent the first night of his leave at Windsor in accommodation within the castle reserved for him and his family. What a joy it was to be back with his wife and baby daughter and to find Bridie in such good health as she looked forward to an increase in the family.

They were well matched, these two – in quickness of mind as well as in religious conviction. In addition to her mother's domestic virtues Bridget possessed her father's shrewd common sense when it came to forming political judgments. Being fully acquainted with her husband's constitutional plans for restoring the king, she was alive to the new dilemma he now faced. Far into the night she and Henry discussed the problem. When he left for Oxford next morning, he was in general accord with his wife's view: 'Treat the king with respect, but hold him prisoner in Carisbrooke Castle. Consider whether he should not be replaced on the throne by one of his three sons. Above all, do nothing in a hurry.'

The final piece of advice might have been interpreted as a gentle reproof, for Bridget was well aware of her husband's penchant for over-hasty action. But she had certainly opened Henry's mind to new possibilities, and as he rode towards Oxford he found himself analysing the qualities of the king's sons. Charles, the Prince of Wales: a lad of spirit though hardly ideal if you believed the stories brought by Edward Ford from the queen's court in Paris. James, Duke of York, certainly not. gauche and obstinate and difficult to handle. But Henry of Gloucester, still young enough to learn from an understanding regent and, from what Harry had seen of him at Caversham, a most attractive boy. Yes, this third son might well prove the best replacement for the king.

But a further thought intruded as Harry crossed the Thames at Folly Bridge and rode towards his old college. Involuntarily, his mind reverted to those pre-war dinner parties he'd enjoyed with his old president. In particular, he recalled the evening when that stubborn undergraduate from Wiltshire had been his fellow guest. Since then, he'd seen much of Edmund Ludlow, grown up to be a reliable soldier and a good Independent MP for his county, but still totally committed to his republican views. True, they'd received short shrift from Dr Kettel. True, too, that in the last few weeks Oliver had slapped him down at a boisterous party in King Street. Still . . . one had to admit that Ludlow offered a possible alternative solution to the problem.

At the Trinity lodge Harry found his former college as static as a dead cat. Enquiries confirmed that old Simon had hardly outlived Ralph Kettel and that the president's successor was a more or less permanent absentee. With Tom and Maggie Brewster back in Attenborough, the college held no appeal, and Harry resolved to spend the night at Osney where Sam and Betsie Dowdswell gave him a great reception.

His old friends had certainly prospered since the Royalists had surrendered Oxford. Sam's old antagonist, William Sanderson, was dead. The life of the city, though not the university, had reverted to normal. Betsie's two children were strong and healthy. The money made by Sam during the Royalist occupation had been used to buy more land. Sam had even heard from America that the son by his first marriage was prospering in New England.

There was no restraint as Sam and Betsie Dowdswell entertained General Cromwell's famous son-in-law – no standing on ceremony. As Henry Ireton took the road to Nottingham, he marvelled at the ways of Providence – Sam Dowdswell restored to the world his father had known, and all because of two quirks of Fate which had brought him a second wife and a huge profit from the civil war.

By the time Henry reached home he felt wonderfully clear of the cares of office. His mother was delighted to find him so relaxed. Together they discussed the Ireton family affairs. Jane spoke of the younger children, of Mary's splendid management of the Bainbrigge ménage in Leicestershire, of the excellence of the preacher at St Mary's and the completion of a land sale to the neighbouring Charlton family. Henry told his mother of John Ireton's imminent promotion in the City to Mastership of the Clothworkers' Company and even to the mayoralty; of the success of brother Tom, just promoted Quartermaster General under Fairfax; of Bridget and the family at Windsor; and finally of Sarah and Edward Ford, and the latter's failure to win the king's support for the Ireton proposals for his restoration.

That reference to the setback to the Heads of Proposals prompted his mother to ask the inevitable question: 'What next?'

But Henry was not to be drawn. 'We wait upon the Lord,' he said.

Jane Ireton was too wise a woman to press her son further. She knew him so well. Impetuous in small things, in larger matters Harry would only speak when he was sure of his next step. Meanwhile his fame, in which Jane Ireton took great pride, would never be allowed to affect the special rapport between mother and son.

Spring came early in 1648. By mid-April the trees were showing new growth, the cherry was in blossom, primrose and anemone were bringing colour to the fringes of the woods, and his mother's garden was alight with forget-me-nots and pansies. The air was filled with the scent of wallflowers and the murmur of bees.

Each morning Henry woke to the call of the birds. Although he saw much of the Brewsters and found time to visit Francis Thornhaugh and the Hutchinsons at Nottingham Castle, he spent most of his leisure hours looking around the family property. Surely, he kept on saying to himself, this was the life he was meant to live. He could picture a wonderful future with Bridget in this chosen corner of England which meant so much to him and his family. Why not surrender his army commission and even his membership of the House of Commons? However great the success that had come to him through this terrible civil war, he had no worldly ambition such as his brother John entertained. Sufficient for him was the life waiting for him and Bridget in this unspoilt Nottingham village.

Harry's daydreams were rudely interrupted by an urgent message from Fairfax. General Ireton was required to report immediately to Advance Headquarters in Croydon, south-west of London. Kentish Johnny, who brought the message, was short on background information. There was trouble, he'd been led to believe, big trouble . . . nation-wide . . . Fairfax was back from his Yorkshire inheritance – his father had died and he was Lord Fairfax now . . . First thing he'd done was to order Ireton's Kent Regiment up from Salisbury . . . top priority for re-equipment, following a conference with Cromwell and Skippon in his house in Queen Street . . . Depot for stores and equipment already established under Quartermaster General Tom Ireton . . .

'Right, Johnny,' Henry broke in. 'I've got the message – so we leave here at first light tomorrow. But what has set off this state of alarm?'

Johnny only knew that things had begun to happen when Major Dowdswell suddenly arrived at the army headquarters in Whitehall and asked for an immediate audience of General Cromwell. Yes, he'd ridden direct from Colonel Hammond at Carisbrooke Castle. The trouble, he thought, must have started down there . . . could have been an attempt at escape. But he'd hardly spoken with Martin before he'd ridden north . . .

Henry took a last lingering look at the peace of the garden. Then he walked down to the stables to tell the Brewsters to have horses ready for dawn departure. At first light he took leave of his mother. With a heavy heart he set off for London with Kentish Johnny as companion. Suddenly he seemed far, far away from the earthly paradise he'd been planning for Bridget and himself.

31

Martin Dowdswell was the first man to greet Henry Ireton on his arrival at the army's Whitehall headquarters, and was quick to tell him how, during his recent routine visit to the Isle of Wight, he had uncovered a plot for the king's escape from Carisbrooke. The plan had come to nothing, largely through the indiscreet talk of the king's attendants; and Robin Hammond, who had previously permitted his royal prisoner an extraordinary measure of freedom, insisted on the immediate dismissal of those arch-conspirators Berkeley, Arbuthnot and Legge. But Martin, reporting the affair to Fairfax, had also passed on his suspicion that the planned escape might be linked with a network of Royalist risings all over the country.

'Suspicions? Might be?' Henry interrupted sharply. 'It's facts I want, not suppositions.'

Martin paused. His friend was clearly in one of his tough, cross-questioning moods. 'The facts, Harry, are that His Majesty's staff-work, luckily for us, remains as inept today as it was after Marston Moor and before Naseby. To be specific, the timing of the operation has not been properly co-ordinated. South Wales has prematurely declared for the king and the Book of Common Prayer. Next, our gallant old enemy, Marmaduke Langdale, has seized Carlisle and Berwick – and nobody knows why! Meanwhile, the Earl of Norwich (that's old Goring, remember?) has just turned up in Kent to cause as much trouble as he can, though Johnny tells me that the old rogue can't count on many friends in the county.'

'And Fairfax?'

'Oh, he's calm, as he always is when he sees a battle on the horizon, and so is General Oliver. They reckon that Wales can be contained easily enough west of the Severn; but it's possible that Langdale's seizure of Carlisle and Berwick may be the prelude to a two-pronged Scots incursion into the northern shires. Meanwhile, they take the news from Kent rather more seriously since any success in that quarter may threaten the capital and stir up these troublesome London apprentices. One way or another, it looks as if we shall have more fighting on our hands.'

'And you make no distinction between these uprisings and the war we've just concluded?'

Martin shrugged his shoulders. 'To a soldier all wars look the same, don't they?'

'That may be a soldier's reaction, Martin, but it's not mine. What you are talking about is rebellion, pure and simple – rebellion against the lawful government of England, as exercised by the nation's representatives in Parliament. In terms of law and politics, rebels can expect no mercy.'

Ireton hurried off to Fairfax's City residence in a state of considerable agitation and was only partly reassured by the army commander's review of the military situation. Evidently, on his journey to his Yorkshire estates after his father's death, Fairfax had met young Lambert and satisfied himself that, with six regiments under command, his brilliant protégé would be able to conduct a defensive but harassing rôle, should the Scots cross the border.

'As an extra precaution, Harry, we are sending Harrison north with his regiment and alerting the Nottingham Militia; but I've total confidence in John Lambert. He's a Yorkshireman, born and bred, with a deep dislike for all Scotsmen who cross the border into England, and he's forgotten more about the hidden ways across the Cheviots and the Pennines than the Scots will ever know. Meanwhile, Oliver will be moving across England with six thousand horse. He may have trouble if he has to invest Chepstow or Pembroke – but he'll know what to do. The moment he's clear of trouble, he can move north, if he's needed there.'

'And London?' Fairfax was quick to allay Henry's anxiety. 'No trouble at all,' he replied. 'Philip Skippon has all the strength he needs. Remember, the Londoners still look up to him in gratitude for his work with the train bands, and he has already moved a battalion of foot to hold the bridgehead at Southwark in case old Goring is so foolish as to advance on the capital.'

'So what about the Home Counties?' Fairfax clapped Ireton

on the back. 'That's where you come in, my friend. Remember our visit to the West Country after Naseby? Our journey into Kent could follow the same course. Mind you, I'm not expecting you to be working out a Truro Treaty or a Bristol capitulation; but Parliament must win and retain Kent's friendship. That's an imperative. My belief is that we shall best restore the peace if we appear in overwhelming strength, using the best-equipped and best-disciplined regiments at our command. Your Kent Regiment will be in the lead, Harry, spreading the idea that, although we are strong, we bring peace, not war. Whalley, Rich, Barkstead and Hewson will be there too. If our luck holds, we can avoid serious fighting and simply chase Goring out of the county. He doesn't belong there anyway, and you know as well as I do that the Kentish men and the Men of Kent have the same aversion to foreigners as my neighbours in Yorkshire.'

Fairfax left nothing to chance. In the City Mr John Ireton and the Clothworkers' Company were quick to meet the army's requirement for new uniforms. The Master of the Armourers' Guild was frequently in conference with Fairfax at his Queen Street house. At Croydon, Quartermaster General Thomas Ireton was assembling stores with exemplary efficiency. Foreign embassies were reporting to their governments on a military professionalism never previously seen in England – surely, the emergence of a standing army which, if provoked, would be capable of challenging the greatest military powers in Europe. And, in plain clothes and without advertisement, Martin Dowdswell and three troopers from Ireton's regiment were riding into Kent to study the course of the Medway and the lie of the surrounding countryside.

But where was the eldest Ireton during this period of re-equipment? He was known to have been in conference with Fairfax, Skippon and his father-in-law. On various occasions he had spent the night with the Shipleys, who expressed concern about his health. He had been in touch with Members of both Houses at Westminster. He was certainly present when Martin reported to Lord Fairfax on his reconnaissance of the Medway crossing points. But most of the spring he spent with Bridget at Windsor.

To the outside world it seemed entirely natural that Henry should wish to be with Bridget when the birth of a second child was imminent. But his stay at Windsor was also concerned with the preparation of a conference at the end of April to which senior officers and regimental commanders were to be summoned by Cromwell.

The conference turned itself into three days of preaching and prayer. Not prayers for victory in the battles ahead, but prayers of penitence from soldiers who could hardly believe that the God they honoured had permitted a second civil war to threaten England. What sin had they committed? Had they, who had been responsible for Parliament's overwhelming victory, made covenant with Evil? Had the January accord with Parliament been wrong in the sight of the Lord? Had they parleyed too long with 'that man of blood, Charles Stuart'? Was the King of England who had received Fairfax, Cromwell and Ireton so courteously at Childerley Hall and Caversham, and charmed them and their wives at Hampton Court, the proverbial wolf in sheep's clothing?

Henry and Bridget Ireton never knew whether Oliver's purpose in calling the conference was religious or political; yet they were fully aware of its importance in renewing the army's sense of purpose and unity. Bridget noticed that Henry had lost his depression. He and her father now seemed to know the path they had to tread. They and all these hardened soldiers left Windsor with a feeling of exaltation and certainty. God willing, they would scotch rebellion in England with the speed and certainty with which a man kills a viper. And in human terms, nothing would be left to chance.

Suddenly, movement orders began to circulate from Fairfax's headquarters. On 3 May Oliver, at the head of eight thousand men, left for Wales, and a chain of communications was established with John Lambert in Yorkshire. By 21 May the Kent force under Fairfax and Ireton was mustered on Blackheath, while the supply train was moving from Surrey into West Kent. On 30 May Advance Headquarters were operating from Eltham. Whalley was ordered to cover Watling Street from Rochester to Dartford, while Fairfax advanced to attack the rebel army in the Maidstone area. Ireton and Rich were held in reserve, though elements of Ireton's horse forded the Medway at unmanned crossings to spread alarm behind the enemy lines.

The plan worked like magic. The Earl of Norwich withdrew from Dartford when faced with Whalley's Naseby veterans. A small engagement took place at Farleigh Bridge when 'Shoemaker' Hewson's regiment routed the rebels and secured the Maidstone bridgehead. Away into East Kent moved Ireton and Rich at lightning speed. By 8 June Ireton had accepted Canterbury's surrender without a shot fired, and on the same day Rich had secured Dover after a brief argument with sailors at Deal. Most of the rebels hastened back to their peaceful farming occupations. Only Norwich and a cadre of professional soldiers managed to cross the Thames and join the Essex rebels.

The campaign in Kent had been a triumph of speed, organisation and public relations. Within three weeks all Kent had returned to its Parliamentary allegiance; and Whalley had crossed into Essex where he was joined by Fairfax and Ireton before Colchester.

Unhappily for the citizens of the old Garrison City, the Royalist commanders refused Fairfax's offer of quarter. The latter had no option but to lay siege to Colchester. All exits were sealed and the Mersea blocked to cut off supplies from the sea. Yet the citizens fought on and caused considerable casualties to Barkstead's regiment which had fought its way into the suburbs. But no man, however brave, can hold out against starvation, and on 28 August the defenders of Colchester surrendered.

In the seventeenth century the fate of a city which refused quarter was well understood. The horror of Tilly's sack of Magdeburg was known to every professional soldier; and in England only three years earlier the city of Leicester had been pillaged by Rupert's Royalist army.

The fate of Colchester was mild by comparison. Fairfax and Ireton exercised mercy as they had done in the West Country; their mission was to restore the peace which the rebels had sought to destroy. But the ringleaders of Colchester must pay the penalty for rebellion. Some were shipped to the West Indies, others to forced service under the Doge of Venice. Only Sir Charles Lucas and Sir George Lisle were shot. Unlike other

Royalist leaders such as Astley and Hopton, they had broken their parole. In the eyes of Fairfax and Ireton it was the unforgivable sin, and for them there was no mercy. No such charge could be brought against Gascoigne who was granted the freedom of exile.

Just before Colchester's surrender, news reached London of Oliver's overwhelming victory at Preston. It was a mixed force he and Lambert had defeated – Langdale's Northern Horse and Munro's Irish levies as well as the Scots invaders. But among the soldiers it was the presence of the Scots in the Royalist Army which caused the greatest resentment. It redoubled the determination of Parliament's army to bring the king to account. Nobody doubted that to call in a foreign power to settle an English quarrel was a traitorous offence, and in those days most Englishmen – and certainly General Cromwell – still thought of Scotland as a foreign nation.

But victory brought no joy to Henry Ireton. He was saddened by the news that his old friend, Francis Thornhaugh, had been killed at Preston. Tom Fairfax, too, was far from well. Oliver and Lambert were now engaged in negotiating a durable peace with the leaders of the Kirk in Edinburgh. That, and the cleaning up of the North, would be a long process. It could be months before Oliver felt free to return to the capital, and while the army commanders had been in the field Edmund Ludlow reported that the Presbyterian Members of Parliament were up to their tricks again, reopening talks with the king. The hard-won accord in January between the army and Parliament might never have taken place. In the midst of these preoccupations Bridget had borne a second daughter, to be named Jane after her paternal grandmother. Tried beyond endurance by political vacillation and despairing of any progress, Henry Ireton resigned his commission from the army.

For a few days at the end of September he enjoyed the life to which he loved to return. Bridget was in good health. Little Elizabeth was delighted with baby Jane. Trying out a new horse in the Great Park he was minded to visit Sam and Betsie Dowdswell at Osney. He had played what part he could in shaping England's destiny. His conscience was clear. But any idea of returning to a quiet life was shattered by a message from Fairfax delivered by Martin. Black Tom refused point blank to accept Henry's resignation. With Oliver remaining in the North, Fairfax must have Ireton at his side.

'What does this mean?' Henry asked Martin. 'He's surrounded by officers of first-class ability, isn't he?'

'I can't really be sure,' Martin replied, 'and you don't like me guessing, do you? But it may be that his Lordship is being urged by his wife to keep clear of the political scene. She's a very determined woman, is Lady Anne. Some say she's in the Presbyterian camp, but won't declare herself because she worships Black Tom. Others think she's really on the king's side and welcomes these talks at Newport between His Majesty and Parliament.'

'And do the negotiations make progress?'

Martin laughed. 'If my Isle of Wight sources are correct, the king is having the time of his life playing off Vane against Holles. By the end of the month he will make some counter-proposals to Parliament which in turn Parliament will reject.'

'And so *ad infinitum*?'

'Or until forces from France or Ireland land in England and change the balance of military power in the king's favour.'

Henry looked carefully at the younger man. This lad whose education he had sponsored had used his intelligence as well as his eyes and ears while on courier service between Carisbrooke, Windsor and Whitehall.

He put a further question. 'So you think it's time we intervened, Martin?'

'Certainly, Harry. But only if the army is united within itself *and* with Parliament.'

'And how can that be achieved when half the Members of Parliament are set to delay talks with the king in order to neutralise the army's strength?'

Martin had a ready answer. 'My military textbooks say that the good soldier chooses the simplest way to his objective. In other words, divide by two, Harry. Reduce the Members of Parliament to those who think the army's way.'

Henry began to laugh. 'And cut the Constitution in half too? Well, it's a nice simple thought to leave with me. I'll give you a letter for Tom Fairfax withdrawing my resignation, but tell him I must remain at Windsor until I have worked out a plan to settle this issue once and for all.'

Day after day – and far into the night – Ireton worked on a new plan based on his talk with Martin Dowdswell. Following meetings with army officers and certain Members of Parliament at the Nag's Head in London, the Garter in Windsor and St Alban's Abbey, his Remonstrance of the Army took final shape. In many respects it followed his earlier Heads of Proposals. But it set forth in long-winded legal phraseology why Parliament must be accepted as sovereign – *salus populi suprema lex*. It also accepted the united army view, recently strengthened by a petition from his own regiment, that the king must account for his actions before a properly constituted court of law. After considerable persuasion from fellow officers, Fairfax agreed that the Remonstrance was a proper document to present to Parliament. He shared to the full his officers' anger when Parliament, still theoretically in touch with the king, delayed an examination of the document – too long, they said; too complicated; must have time for consideration.

But the army was not prepared for a stalemate. On 29 November the king was forcefully moved from the Isle of Wight to the sterner confinement of Hurst Castle on the mainland. On 2 December Fairfax moved the army from Windsor to Kensington, with Hewson's regiment stationed at Whitehall and Pride's in St James. On 6 December, acting on Ireton's advice, Fairfax ordered Colonel Pride to march to the Commons with a register of Members and deny entry to those Members who were not of the Independent persuasion. Once again, Ireton had cut the Gordian knot.

The operation was carried out with perfect timing and without any regard to constitutional procedure. But the political objective had been achieved at last. Parliament and the army could now speak with one heart and mind. The people was sovereign. When the all-powerful victor of Preston at last reached London he accepted that his son-in-law had prepared the stage for the final act in the drama.

32

On the day of Pride's Purge, Cromwell had been away from London for seven successive months.

In late April he had set forth, on Fairfax's orders, to quell the South Wales rising. His mission completed, he had obtained new footwear for his men at Leicester and moved north to join Lambert. In August he had comprehensively defeated the Scots invaders at Preston, and his subsequent visit to the Kirk leaders in Edinburgh was, perhaps, a wise political and military decison. But why, in Heaven's name, should this man, whose formidable personality now dominated the English political scene, choose to delay his return to the capital by laying siege to Pontefract in Yorkshire when young Lambert was entirely capable of directing the operation?

It did not make sense. But at Windsor two people, at least, understood the reason for Cromwell's prolonged absence. Bridget and Henry Ireton knew he was keeping away from London because he was unsure of his next political step. In his own words 'he was waiting upon the Lord', convinced that his victories, culminating in the annihilation of the Scots at Preston, marked him out as the human instrument chosen by Almighty God to settle the affairs of the kingdom of England. And he had much to ponder, for already the army was demanding the execution of the king.

In London Fairfax was impatient for his return and sent Major Dowdswell north with a peremptory order for General Cromwell's immediate return. But the general was not to be found at his Pontefract headquarters and Martin was redirected, first to John and Lucy Hutchinson at Nottingham Castle, and thence to Jane Ireton's home in Attenborough.

There, he was surprised to find the great man discussing family affairs with Mrs Ireton as if there were no crisis at Westminster. Bridget's two little girls, he assured Jane, were really lovely . . . Luckily they inherited the Ireton good looks and showed no sign of the Cromwell nose . . . What a shame

that Mrs Ireton had not yet set eyes on her grandchildren . . .
If only lasting peace could be restored . . .

Oliver broke off to welcome Martin. He opened and read
Fairfax's message and turned with a smile to Mrs Ireton. 'It
seems, Madam, that I am required by my commanding officer
to return to London – a city for which I and my family have
conceived a profound dislike. It means, I fear, we must wait
upon another day to continue our conversation. But before I
leave your county I must pay my respects to Colonel
Thornhaugh's widow. What a fine man the colonel was. Whenever I look back on this rebellion, I grieve for the brave men
we have lost in a war that should never have happened.'

Both Jane Ireton and Martin noticed the change in the man
as he spoke – the concerned family friend suddenly extending
the dimensions of his compassion to embrace the whole of
England. The light in his eyes and the timbre of his voice
conveyed a sense of purpose, almost of personal mission, as he
said goodbye.

'But be of good cheer, Madam. We will meet again when
peace is re-established. Meanwhile, I promise that the life of
Francis Thornhaugh will be avenged, as surely as the lives of
all those others like my son, Oliver, and my cousin Hampden,
who have fought the good fight.'

While Oliver Cromwell made arrangements for handing
over his command at Pontefract, Martin was permitted to
stay for three days at Attenborough before accompanying the
general back to London.

The short break enabled him to renew his links with the
Ireton family and to enjoy his mother's company. He now felt
that Maggie was reconciled to making her home in Attenborough with Tom and the children. She saw much of Mrs Ireton
and was pleased that her husband had succeeded his father in
charge of the Ireton stables. It was a job for which he was well
suited, even if it lacked the explosive excitements of Dr Kettel's
Oxford.

But Maggie was also very proud of her soldier son. It really
seemed that in Martin she was seeing her early ambitions
fulfilled. 'A major now, are you? But not too high and mighty
to kiss your mother and play with the children.'

'Good Heavens, no,' her son assured her. 'Whenever I'm

here, I remember the thrashing Mrs Ireton gave me all those years ago – and that keeps you in your place, eh?'

'And what will you do when peace returns? Marry a pretty girl and settle down? Or go on soldiering with these fine generals of yours?'

'Who can say?' Martin was not to be drawn. 'As far as I can make out, the future of all of us rests with General Cromwell.'

Maggie was greatly impressed. 'That's right, Martin. General Oliver's the horse to back. This village has taken him to its heart. D'you know he found time to go down to the stables specially to see Tom's old father and mother? Remembered them from his previous visit, he said. Thought he'd like to see how the horses were keeping. And then the village children flocked around him, and he gave each of them a soldier's button as a keepsake. Yes, they think he's the greatest man they've ever met.'

Martin laughed. 'That goes for me and Harry Ireton, too.'

Yet even Martin was surprised at the ease with which Oliver took control of the Council of Officers as soon as he reached Whitehall. Nobody disputed his authority. All were certain that he would break the impasse they had reached.

During the past weeks events had moved at great speed – they always did if Henry Ireton was in charge, though he had been careful to see that everything he did was endorsed by Fairfax. If Oliver had been in London, he would probably have moved more cautiously – persuaded Parliament, for instance, to sanction its own dissolution rather than employ Colonel Pride's shock tactics which lost friends as well as enemies. He might have kept the king a little longer at Carisbrooke, and held back the army's advance on London until it received an invitation to do so from Parliament. He constantly reminded his younger colleagues that public opinion must be respected in Westminster and the City as well as in the army.

But Oliver was a realist as well as a visionary. What had been done could not be undone. He showed no displeasure at the over-hasty actions of the army officers, praised Fairfax for his wise moves and the colonels for the discipline of the regiments stationed in London, and sat down with Ireton to consider even at this late stage how they could save the king's life when the army was howling for his blood. That was the overriding question.

In wording the Remonstrance, Ireton had inserted a sentence which implied that the cause against the king must not be pre-judged. But could a public trial be avoided? Could the threat of it persuade the king to accept the rôle of constitutional monarch which Ireton had always envisaged? Could the prior conviction of Hamilton, Capel and Norwich – all peers who were guilty of rebellion against the State – make the king see that his very life depended on accepting the army's terms? Should the Army Council make plans for a regency with the attractive eight-year-old Prince Henry as the eventual successor to the throne? Or could Cromwell, Ireton and Fairfax see no alternative to the extremists' demands for the king's death? And if so, must they accept a republican Constitution such as Henry Marten and Edmund Ludlow had constantly propounded?

All these possibilities were considered, and even re-considered in the light of evidence from a poor Abingdon girl, called Elizabeth Poole, who claimed to be a prophetess, filled with the Holy Spirit. Using the imagery of the Old Testament, she told the high-ranking officers of the Army Council that it had been revealed to her in a vision that they should 'bind the king's arms and hold him fast under' but should not kill him. Her words were taken very seriously – not least by Ireton. In a strange, incoherent way the wild-haired crippled woman spoke the soldiers' language – the language of the good book. And after this incident, Martin and the Shipleys began to notice the strain in Henry Ireton's face.

But in all the army's doubts and uncertainties, one decision was crystal-clear: King Charles must be brought from the grim isolation of Hurst Castle to a point where the nation's leaders could have closer contact with him; and orders were issued for His Majesty to be conveyed to Windsor in a coach and four, escorted by a squadron of cavalry under Colonel Harrison, with Major Dowdswell acting as his chief liaison officer.

Martin never forgot that cross-country journey. At first the king seemed so pleased to be leaving the cold of the Hampshire coast in favour of the familiar surroundings of Windsor. He was fascinated by the outstanding good looks of the blond

Colonel Harrison, whose new buff tunic and bright red sash gave the lie to those who thought that every Puritan wears black. And he was pleasantly surprised to meet Martin once more. As to Cromwell and Ireton, the king recalled them as honourable gentlemen whom he had enjoyed entertaining with their wives at Hampton Court.

As the journey proceeded – the party took eight days to reach Windsor – Martin noticed again the contradictory elements in the king's character. One was conscious of his small stature in contrast to the tall figures of Harrison and Martin himself. His hair had turned grey and was flecked with white. His eyes held sadness in them, a hint of reproach to all who shared responsibility for his captive status. He carried an air of resignation.

Yet at each stopping place on the journey – Winchester, Alresford, Bagshot – the man was transformed. As on the progress south from Newcastle, the people received him gladly – and he came alive. Children were brought to him to receive the healing touch still associated in people's minds with a divinely appointed monarch. Wherever he stopped, men and women shouted 'God save the king.' At Winchester a mayoral reception was held in his honour. The Stuart charm and courtesy were manifest. In the eyes and hearts of country people, Charles was still their king. The sadness only returned when the crowds dispersed and the cheering ceased.

Martin reported his impressions to Henry and Bridget Ireton on his return to Windsor, emphasising the king's hold on the affections of the country people. But very quickly a more fundamental change became apparent in the king's thinking.

No longer was he interested in compromise or argument. In the loneliness of captivity he had found a new and sterner resolution. He refused to reconsider the plans for a constitutional monarchy as set out in Ireton's Heads of Proposals. And when, at Christmas, the Earl of Denbigh travelled to Windsor with a last appeal from Cromwell, the king refused him audience. The fact that Denbigh was brother-in-law to the Duke of Hamilton was of no relevance to Charles Stuart.

Old friends seemed forgotten though he enjoyed the company of his dogs. Denied converse with Dr Juxon, who had seen much of him at Carisbrooke, the king was seen to be studying sermons and reading the Bible constantly. He wrote to his sons and longed for letters from the queen in France, and asked to see the two children, Elizabeth and Henry, who were still in England. But his position as King of England and Head of its Established Church was not for negotiation. He held his Trust from God, not Man.

Those living in the precincts of Windsor – officers' families as well as those guarding the king – were baffled. Did the king's new obduracy signify a fatalistic resignation to the Will of God? Or a touching Christian humility, such as had never previously been seen in him? Or could it be that Charles Stuart was consciously preparing himself to meet the last enemy?

For the rulers of England there could be no further stay of action. Both the army and the Members of a diminished Parliament were demanding the king's trial with increasing vehemence – so trial there must be.

But Cromwell and Ireton were determined that the king's trial should be properly conducted by qualified lawyers in open court, and that those who sat in judgment must be drawn from every corner of England. Whatever the outcome, there must be no comparison with the assassination of Edward II or Richard II in the grim secrecy of medieval keeps. There must be no repetition of Fotheringay where the king's grandmother, Mary of Scotland, had been beheaded in secret on her royal cousin's orders. Justice must be seen to be done.

Yet this was no easy process. The rumour-mongers and the pamphleteers soon discovered that three distinguished lawyers – Selden, Whitelocke and Widdrington – had diplomatically left London. Cromwell's cousin, Oliver St John, refused an invitation to serve on the court. So did Sir Harry Vane who had always supported the Independents in Parliament. Joe Shipley and the watermen fraternity all had their tales to tell, many of them quoting extremist preachers like the army chaplain, Hugh Peter, who demanded death for 'the great Barabbas of Windsor'. Decent prople were horrified at the extravagant propaganda circulating in the City and the equally hysterical counter-cries against Cromwell and Ireton. London was alive with rumours . . . had Fairfax received a letter from the queen . . . had the Prince of Wales pleaded with Cromwell . . . foreign ambassadors kept seeking interviews. Even Martin was asked to plead with Ireton for the king's life in a letter from his old flame, Susanna Martin, now happily married to a Kent landowner.

There could, of course, be no turning back. The organisation of the trial proceeded with the speed and efficiency characteristic of the high-ranking officers produced by the New Model Army. Charges were agreed. Lacking legal precedent, Parliament passed a new law asserting that 'the Commons of England in Parliament assembled hold supreme power'. One hundred and thirty-five men were nominated for court service – were they judges or jury? John Bradshaw, soon to be Chief Justice of Cheshire, would preside over the court. John Cook, a clever republican lawyer from Gray's Inn, would lead the prosecution.

Westminster Hall, where Strafford and Laud had been indicted before their peers, would be the place of trial, and carpenters were already busy constructing stands for the public.

Henry Ireton was working at enormous pressure. The Shipleys, with whom he was staying, noted how strained he was. Reason and logic might dictate his actions, but he was still emotionally troubled by the warnings of Elizabeth Poole, and frequently sought guidance from the Scriptures. He also took very seriously the report that Martin had given him of the king's popularity outside London, and when they met at the Shipleys' house he made a special appeal.

'Look, Martin,' he said, 'you and Joe and Hannah have always acted as my eyes and ears in London. Today General Oliver and I need your help more than ever. I keep on repeating the old tag you must have heard at St Paul's – *salus populi suprema lex*. But how do the people – the ordinary folk, not the preachers and the soldiers and the MPs – how do they react to the court's proceedings? Will you and Hannah act as my observers in Westminster Hall?'

And so it came about that on 20 January 1649, only four weeks after travelling with the king from Hurst Castle to Windsor, Martin Dowdswell took his place, with Hannah Shipley beside him, to witness the trial of Charles Stuart in Westminster Hall.

The two of them stared around the hall, amazed at the

hundred-foot-high hammer-beamed roof and the vast size of the ancient building which jutted out at right angles from the miscellaneous buildings of Parliament.

The public galleries were packed with spectators, but Martin and Hannah were in privileged seats behind the commissioners, near enough to identify them as they arrived – Cromwell, Ireton, Harrison, Ludlow, Whalley and Hutchinson, Pride and Okey: men of courage, known to every soldier in the land, interspersed with civic dignitaries and recorders from the great cities of England.

Next their eyes focused on the raised chair in front of the commissioners on which President Bradshaw would shortly take his seat. Below the president's seat a table was already occupied by two learned clerks, and beyond them in the body of the court was a red velvet chair reserved for the royal prisoner. Lawyers were fluttering around as they would be in any court of law, but Martin also noted that armed soldiers were lining every wall and point of entrance. More obviously, he noted that standards captured at Marston Moor, Naseby and Preston were prominently displayed.

What sort of court was this? Civil or military? And under what law would His Majesty be prosecuted? And how soon would he be brought to court? In answer to Hannah's questions, Martin confirmed that few people had seen the king's arrival from Windsor – it was one of the coldest winters London had ever known. All he could tell Hannah was that on the previous day the king had travelled by coach over icy roads and, accompanied by a strong cavalry escort, had been conveyed to St James' Palace where he had slept. But he knew Colonel Tomlinson who was in command of the guard and he guaranteed that the prisoner would reach the court at the appointed time.

Just before two o'clock in the afternoon the chattering ceased in the public galleries. An awesome silence was broken by a clatter of pikemen pushing their way through the crowd at the south door. They were escorting a diminutive hatted figure, dressed in black relieved only by a blue ribbon at his neck and the silver star of the Garter on his cloak, and carrying a staff topped by a silver knob. The King of England had come to stand trial before his people.

Every eye was on him as he took his appointed seat and looked quizzically round the hall. He had been conducted in great secrecy from Sir Robert Cotton's Thames-side house close to St Stephen's Chapel where he would stay for the duration of the trial. He seemed surprised at the number of spectators accommodated round the hall.

A moment later a fanfare of trumpets sounded, and Bradshaw took his seat on the dais – an imposing figure in a red gown and wearing a high beaver hat. In a fine, sonorous voice he announced to all present that the court, before which Charles Stuart stood accused, was a High Court of Justice constituted by the Commons of England in Parliament. Without more ado, the president ordered the prosecution to read the charge.

Here was the moment for which the little Gray's Inn lawyer had been preparing himself for the past three weeks. From a long scroll held in front of him, John Cook began to read.

It was tedious, high-flown stuff but Martin and Hannah heard the relevant clauses easily enough. Charles Stuart was accused of assuming unlimited and tyrannical power to overthrow the rights of the people . . . to this end he had traitorously levied war against the people . . .

The king, who sat close to the prosecutor, tapped him on the shoulder with his staff and stuttered, 'By whose authority are you . . . ?' But the sentence was never finished and John Cook blandly continued: 'Moreover he had sought to procure invasions from foreign parts, and in this present year caused the said war to be renewed against Parliament and the good people of this nation.'

Martin listened intently to the charge. Yes, you couldn't argue with what had been said. Everybody knew the charges were well founded, and causing war to be renewed in the past year was nothing less than rebellion, as Harry had once reminded him . . .

But prosecuting council had a further clause to read. 'Charles Stuart,' he shouted, 'was therefore impeached as a Tyrant, and Traitor and Murderer and an implacable Enemy to the Commonwealth of England.'

Martin could hardly believe his ears. The old lady beside him was quivering with anger.

'Tyrant, traitor, murderer . . .' this could lead to nothing less than the executioner's block. There could be no hope of acquittal. In contrast to the dramatic legal jargon of Cook's recitation, Martin could only hear one voice, the prisoner's scarcely audible stutter:

'By whose authority do you act?'

33

The trial of the king proceeded on its inexorable course. But truth to tell, there was little to excite Martin and Hannah and the other men and women who crowded into the public galleries of Westminster Hall, once their eyes had comprehended the new appointments and colourful stage-setting within the ancient edifice. They took note of John Bradshaw, attempting to impart an aura of legal authority to the proceedings in his red robe and high beaver hat (the public did not know it was lined with steel as a safety measure). Each day knowledgable spectators recognised and counted the commissioners as they took their places behind the president – solemn-faced, impassive men, mindful of their responsibilities as the nation's representatives. Eyes returned again and again to the small, dignified figure of the king seated opposite the president, and by way of contrast, to the chief prosecutor dancing about in his lawyer's gown close to the prisoner, and calling witnesses to prove what was common knowledge, as if he was making his case against a common criminal before a circuit judge.

For four tedious days the king refused to plead before a People's Court whose legality he refused to accept. 'By whose authority?' 'By what right?' The words, spoken with the slight stutter that had always afflicted the king's speech, seemed to echo in the hammer-beamed rafters of the hall long after the prosecutor's shrill exaggerations had died away.

But the spectators were offered at least one dramatic interlude. While Cook was indulging in one of his more preposterous charges, Lady Fairfax (easily recognised by Martin despite her mask) jumped to her feet and shouted that not a half, not a quarter of the people of England wanted this trial. That could well be true, Martin reflected, remembering his journey with the king through Hampshire. But when the lady added that her husband was of too good a wit to join the commissioners, Martin shook his head in amazement. Fairfax, as all the Army Council knew, had accepted every step leading to the king's trial, not least the stationing of his troops in Westminster and Kensington.

'That woman really is a termagant,' he confided to Hannah. 'Philip Skippon says a wise soldier should never marry his general's daughter and Black Tom must rue the day . . . Lady Anne is always telling him what to do . . . that's the only reason why he's not sitting up there with General Oliver and Harry . . . The next we know, she'll be dragging him off to Bath for a cure. She's a natural trouble-maker, I tell you . . . always pushing her Presbyterian views . . . she even annoyed old Mrs Ireton by trying to have some preachers replaced by Presbyterians last time she was in Nottingham . . . But she met her match there – and no mistake.'

Hannah began to laugh. 'You're a wicked boy, Martin. You'll be in trouble if you talk like that.' But their words were lost in the uproar that followed Anne Fairfax's intervention. A few cries of 'God save the king' were overwhelmed by the soldiers' shouts of 'Justice, justice', as the lady was hustled from the court.

Next day she appeared again – this time to denounce Cromwell in the most violent terms, deliberately forgetting his exemplary loyalty to her husband and the major part he'd played in the victories on which the fame of Fairfax rested. But nobody took much notice of her. If she hadn't been 'the Generaless' as Oliver used to call her, she would have been removed more speedily and more forcefully from the public gallery.

On the third day of the trial there was an altercation between the president and the prisoner. The king started a sentence with the words 'I require', only to be silenced by Bradshaw's tart reply that it was not for a prisoner 'to require of a judge'. But the king's point of law seemed to carry considerable weight with the president of the court and the many commissioners who had enjoyed some legal training, for there was a day's adjournment and the charge of high treason was deliberately dropped. But that was no more than a legal sop. The court entertained no doubt that it must always be lawful to kill a tyrant; there was no shortage of biblical and historical precedents – consider Ahab and Saul or Julius Caesar according to your source of information! And, surely, by every known definition, King Charles had shown himself a tyrant. Moreover, the lawyers were prepared to argue that he had been proved guilty of breaking that sacred, though unwritten, contract with his people to which every ruler must always be subject. Either way, there was no doubt in the commissioners' minds that the only verdict for the king's crime against his own people was Death.

On 27 January the president solemnly read the judgment, unanimously agreed by the commissioners on the previous day, '. . . that Charles Stuart be put to death by the severing of his head from his body'. In dazed unbelief the king listened to a recitation of the fearful words which, in his hearing and with his agreement, had once been pronounced in this same hall on his servant, the great Earl of Strafford. He protested, 'I am not suffered to speak . . . expect what justice other people will have.' But there was no more to be said. There could be no reprieve for Charles Stuart.

Martin Dowdswell led a weeping Hannah from the court to the jetty at Westminster whence they were conveyed downriver to Temple Stairs. Later that evening, while they were discussing the day's grim events with Joe Shipley in the front parlour, they were surprised to receive a visit from Henry Ireton. He had walked from Westminster, he said, to get away from the suffocating atmosphere of the court. Here, at least, he could relax – or that was his intention – though his finely-etched features wore the tense, implacable look that had worried Joe and Hannah on a previous occasion.

Thank you, he said in answer to Hannah's enquiry, he would appreciate a glass of Bordeaux, though he had no stomach for food. He still had work to do and must hurry back to Whitehall and the room he was sharing with Colonel Harrison.

It was Joe Shipley who broke the strained silence and, appealing to their long friendship, asked whether Harry could not ease their minds by telling them how he viewed the future with no king in the Palace of Whitehall.

Henry seemed relieved to be asked such a leading question. Lacking the daily comfort of Bridget's sympathy, he felt a need to talk with somebody outside the close circle of MPs and army officers with whom he had kept constant company since coming to London from Windsor.

'That's a question,' he told Joe, 'I cannot answer with any certainty. I've never pretended to be a prophet, though it's clear that we are living in a day when we must all expect changes in our way of life and thinking. But, as I see it, there are two unchangeable principles that we should observe: first, that a nation's government is always answerable to its people: secondly, that it is always subject to the rule of Law.

'There is a great danger in this new state of England that the people will set themselves above the Law, so that tyranny of the people replaces the tyranny of a king. That is my recurring fear. And you know, as my family and fellow officers know, that whatever form our new government takes, Henry Ireton will stand firm for the rule of Law and the toleration of religious belief. I shall fight for those principles as long as God gives me life. It is, I believe, my God-given task.'

The old warmth had returned to Harry Ireton's voice – the certain note of a man of faith. Then he added, with an apologetic smile as if he had revealed too much of his inner soul, 'I'm sorry, Joe, not to give an exact answer to your question, but at least you know why that ranter, John Lilburne, has singled me out for his vituperation. I've been the chief object of his hatred ever since the debates in Putney Church. Not only does he hold that every citizen should have a vote irrespective of his income, property or education. He also considers himself free to do what he likes without accepting any legal framework for his activities. Honest John's concept of liberty is totally alien to me, as it would have been to St Paul.'

'So where do we go from here?'

'That is for the nation to decide. But General Oliver's aim and mine is to restore good government through a new Parliament, re-establish the rule of Law as the guarantee of our freedom and insist on toleration for religious belief.'

He smiled again as if to excuse himself for talking too much. 'But perhaps you will also play your part by praying for those who, willy-nilly, will soon be entrusted with the government of England.'

Henry Ireton stood up to take his leave, and Joe also rose from his seat in the inglenook. 'I think I'll row you back to Whitehall,' he said. 'You're a good man, Harry, and this is no night for you to be walking the streets alone.'

At Westminster orders for the king's execution had already been issued. Carpenters were to be seen building the scaffold outside Inigo Jones' Banqueting House in the Palace of Whitehall. The City cloth merchants were instructed to provide black drapery to cover the structure. The common hangman and his assistant had been engaged to carry out the sentence of the court exactly as they would have been, had the execution been a routine affair on Tower Hill; but on this occasion both men would, for their later protection, wear disguise as well as masks. The public would have access to King Street which ran past the Banqueting House, but the scaffold would be closely guarded by pikemen. Ten companies of infantry would guard the route and a squadron of cavalry be posted at each end of the thoroughfare in case of trouble. Execution would take place around midday on 30 January 1649.

As to the royal prisoner, he would remain in St James' Palace until the appointed day. Colonel Tomlinson would be responsible for the king's security until handing over his charge to Colonel Hacker in Whitehall Palace. During the intervening days every courtesy would be shown to His Majesty. He would be permitted to see the two royal children, Elizabeth and Henry, who had remained in England, living with the Northumberlands at Syon House. And Dr Juxon, Bishop of London, would have complete freedom of access.

There was a terrifying precision about the orders. They left no room for error. The army's staff work could not be faulted.

So the king's last days were spent in his own royal palace, surrounded by the trappings of majesty. Through Dr Juxon and Colonel Tomlinson the nation would one day learn how Charles Stuart spent his final hours. It was in St James' Palace that he took leave of the thirteen-year-old Elizabeth and the eight-year-old Henry. He told them he was to die a glorious death for Law, Liberty and the Protestant religion, and the children must ground themselves against Popery. It was hardly the words their Roman Catholic mother would have used and the little prince hardly understood the significance of his father's advice. But the princess wept bitterly as she left the palace, clasping a keepsake and memorising the king's last words to her: 'Keep trust and forgive.'

The morning of 30 January dawned grim and cheerless. The relentless winter weather remained unforgiving. Ice had formed on the Thames and the cruel east wind was blowing up King Street.

In his room at St James' Palace the king was roused at five o'clock. He dressed carefully – a black suit, white handkerchief and two shirts as protection against the cold. He took breakfast and at ten o'clock Colonel Tomlinson, to whom the king had taken a great liking, conducted him through the Tiltyard and over the Holbein Gate into the royal suite in his Palace of Whitehall. On every wall he saw the Dutch and Italian paintings in which he took a connoisseur's delight. Did he wonder, perhaps – this small grey-haired man of forty-eight – how Sir Anthony van Dyck had painted him so large?

During the morning he asked Tomlinson to stay with him while he received the sacrament from Bishop Juxon. Then at half past one, after taking a glass of red wine and some bread, he was conducted by Hacker through the galleries of the palace towards the Banqueting House. On this final perambulation he was more conscious of people kneeling in prayer than of the many canvases past which he was walking. Only when he reached Inigo Jones' great hall did his eyes look up to the ceiling which Rubens had painted. The brilliant colours depicting the Triumph of Wisdom made mocking silent answer to the man who had commissioned the artist.

With Juxon beside him he emerged to public view through the windows facing King Street. He stepped on to the black stage set for the final act. He surveyed the scene before him – the hooded executioners in tight-fitting woollen clothes, the axe, the block, the pikemen immovable around the scaffold, and beyond them, as far as the eye could reach, a vast crowd. Somewhere among the men and women stood Martin Dowdswell, drawn to King Street as if by a magnet.

At the king's appearance the chattering of the crowd

changed to awed silence. There was no noise save the fretting of the cavalry chargers. In accordance with immemorial custom, it was time for the condemned man to address the onlookers.

The king could hardly be seen above the pikemen's helmets and the cruel east wind drowned his voice, but those nearest to him heard his unrepenting statement: 'A subject and sovereign are clean different things.' Those words were quickly followed by a declaration of faith as confident and brave as any Christian martyr ever spoke: 'I go from a corruptible crown to an incorruptible crown, where no disturbance can be, no disturbance in the world.'

'An' it please Your Majesty,' said the masked man, and laying aside his hat and cloak, Charles Stuart knelt with his head on the block. The axe fell and the headsman's assistant held up the severed head to the people, shouting, 'Behold the head of a traitor.'

But there was no answering cry of triumph from the people standing in the street below – only a groan such as had never been heard before: the men and women of England weeping for their king.

The grief of that awful day spread to all the towns and villages where once people had welcomed the coming of the king. Only after many days did a courtier pluck up courage to impart the terrible truth to the poor, broken queen at her tawdry court of St Germain. And Henrietta Maria who, some twenty years earlier, had brought to the English monarchy an offering of French panache as well as folly, resigned herself to a life of sorrowing, inconsolable.

Part Four

An end and a beginning
1649–1652

General Ireton was so diligent in the public service
and so careless of everything that belonged to himself
that he never regarded what clothes or food he used,
what hours he went to rest or what horse he mounted.
The Ludlow Papers

We that knew him can and must say truly we knew no
man like-minded: few so singly mind the things of Jesus
Christ and of public concernment.

Colonel Hewson

34

As the grieving crowds scattered and cavalry rode the streets, Martin Dowdswell stood irresolute beside the Thames at Westminster.

The young soldier could not come to terms with what had been done that day. Long ago, as an apprentice, he had seen Strafford on his final journey at Tower Hill, but this was the first time he had been an eye witness to a public execution. The obscene ritual would have sickened him if the victim had really been 'a murderer more evil than Cain' as the prosecutor, in one of his wilder moments, had chosen to describe Charles Stuart. But if John Cook's language was grossly offensive to Martin, so too was the conduct of the trial which he and Hannah Shipley had witnessed during the previous week.

How could the king's death be justified? That judges should agree on a capital sentence without hearing the prisoner's defence was a travesty of justice; and there they were, passing sentence on one who should surely have received most special consideration.

Martin could not look at the matter objectively. Had he not glimpsed the king's domestic happiness when he had toured the royal pictures in the company of Lady Carlisle and Susanna? Had he not spoken with His Majesty at Hampton Court? Played bowls with him at Carisbrooke? Been commended by him for his care of the baby princess? Eaten with him on the journey from Hurst Castle to Windsor?

In no way could he escape a feeling of indirect responsibility for the king's death – almost a feeling of personal guilt. Had he – his thoughts were moving into dangerous territory – had he not ridden with General Oliver and Henry Ireton to intercept the king's incriminating letter at the Blue Boar in Holborn? Had he not, by gaining the confidence of indiscreet royal servants on the Isle of Wight, brought early news to Fairfax of the king's plans to escape from custody? Was he not, therefore, an accessory to murder? Martin Dowdswell was sick at heart.

Desperately he rehearsed the other side of the story. He knew the sequence of events by heart: the king's extravagance; his defiance of the Commons; his propensity for choosing bad advisers (or was this the queen's fault?); his inability to trust three men of honour and ability in Cromwell, Fairfax and Ireton who had offered him the clearest of plans for saving the monarchy; his continuing duplicity in negotiation; and, finally, his turning to the Scots and the Irish to help him defeat his English subjects.

Clearly he was unfitted for kingship in the way his subjects understood the word. But was his death 'the cruel necessity' that the new rulers of England held it to be?

Martin's hands, deep in his doublet pockets to guard against the cold, clutched the letter he had received from Susanna while the trial was in progress. He'd done nothing about it, not even acknowledged it. The thought increased his sense of guilt. He could not leave the matter there. He remembered the words of an army preacher thundering from the pulpit that repentance was the essential prelude to forgiveness. Right, Martin Dowdswell. Stop hanging about on Thames-side. Do something to rid yourself of your guilt.

Next morning he crossed the river to the south bank, hired a horse at the George in Southwark and rode out into Kent towards the Cray Valley in search of Susanna Martin.

The young woman saw him before he saw her. Accompanied by two small children, she was walking briskly towards a timbered farmhouse a mile distant from her father's house. She recognised him immediately, though he was much changed from the man she'd last encountered on that embarrassing ride from Exeter. As he rode towards her he seemed to have filled out, to carry authority with him, to be much more than five years older.

'Martin,' she cried, 'what brings you here?' Her voice was unforgettable. 'Come into the house, out of this perishing cold.' She told the children to find a stable boy to take the horse and sat with Martin before a blazing log fire in a low-ceilinged room with lattice windows, the severity of its heavy wooden furniture relieved by colourful rugs and curtains of patterned damask. It was clear to the girl that her visitor was greatly perturbed, as she asked what had brought Martin into Kent.

'Your letter,' he said. 'Your letter . . . I did not know how to reply . . . You see you were right. I had access to the army commanders . . . I should have spoken even if my words had been addressed to deaf men. But I did nothing . . . and now it's too late.'

'Too late,' she echoed. 'Yes, we know of this terrible deed that has been done. We've read about it in Samuel Pecke's *Daily Diurnal*.'

'But your letter . . . your letter reached me in time for me to make my protest . . .' Martin started to pour out words of self-reproach. But the girl stopped him.

'What's past is past,' she said. 'Neither your conscience nor mine can restore the king to life. Oh yes, Martin. I too have a sense of guilt. Long before this awful day I saw tragedy building up at the queen's court. I sensed it first at Somerset House just after I met you and your guardian and grew tired of the artificiality of court life. You don't believe me? Well, can you imagine a greater contrast than that between your Mr Henry Ireton and the people attending the queen? They were rotten, Martin, rotten to the core. They had no purpose in life but to seek their own pleasure and a place in the peerage, and they gained their ends by money and an unsurpassed gift for nauseating flattery. Since setting up our home in Kent, I've found myself wondering again and again why the king tolerated these sycophants. Like the rest of us, he possessed the power of choice. Perhaps, he felt himself inadequate – it was, after all, only the death of his elder brother that brought him to the throne. Do you remember the words of the Dutch curator when we were looking at the Van Dyck pictures in Whitehall Palace – "Our King iss truly vaary small man – much smaller than he shows in Sir Anthony's *pittori*"? Strange how the words stay in my mind.'

Martin Dowdswell relaxed. 'So we say goodbye to the past, eh? And what occupies you now?'

Susanna laughed. 'Just at the moment I'm talking to my handsome half-brother who once diverted me from the boredom of the court at Somerset House. Don't look so surprised,

Martin. I don't know what your guardian said to my father all those years ago, but after I returned from Exeter he was honest enough to tell me about your mother and his Oxford romance. I think she must have been a very beautiful girl.'

Susanna was looking Martin up and down, as if discerning in him a reflection of her father. With a little shake of her head, she applied herself once more to Martin's question.

'But you ask what I'm doing now? Well, you've seen my children, Martin, and I'm married to a good man who, like my father, has refused to take sides in this dreadful war. Would you not like to stay and meet him? He's inspecting one of our ships at Northfleet, but he will be back before nightfall.'

'No, Susanna, no. It will be better if I go. My mind is at odds with itself and I have other calls in London which must not be delayed.' He looked at her again as he rose to his feet. She'd lost none of her beauty. Her smile, her voice were just as he remembered them in those carefree days before the fighting started. Only now there was about her an aura of maturity, the poise of a girl who had found contentment in her marriage, her children and the peace of the Kent countryside.

But he must not linger. It was time to take leave of his half-sister. At the front door he stooped to kiss her. Then, with a wave of the hand which seemed to signal the sad conclusion to a story, he went to collect his horse and take the road to London.

All the way to Southwark he thought of Susanna and the home she had established. Had the time come for him to give up the soldier's life – return, perhaps, to the easy companionship of his grandfather at Osney?

It was a tempting thought. Yet soldiering was, he believed, in his blood. It was his chosen profession and his career had prospered. His thoughts jumped abruptly from Susanna to wise old Philip Skippon who had plotted his course during those same pre-war days that he and Susanna had been recalling. How would the old warrior react to the king's execution? He had, as all the world knew, refused to sit in judgment on the king. Would he, therefore, distance himself from the new rulers of England? Would they, perhaps, want to dismiss him from his London command?

Next day Martin journeyed to Hackney to put his question to the old man and received the clearest of replies.

'I can only give you a soldier's answer,' Skippon said in his broad Norfolk accent. 'So listen carefully, young Martin. A professional soldier gives his loyalty to the State that pays his wages. He may not approve of every action taken by the civil authority, but he will not withdraw his service unless his conscience tells him he is making covenant with Evil.'

General Skippon observed the young soldier carefully. 'See you, lad, are the new rulers of England good men or bad? How say you, Martin?'

Put that way, the answer was easy. The old general was also telling him, in effect, to stop worrying over the past; to start looking to the future. But the future . . . England a republic for the first time? No longer the king's head on the Great Seal or the coinage? An end to many familiar things? A revolution greater than any man had dared to contemplate except some crazy fellow like Lilburne.

It was, indeed, hard to contemplate the future. Still, in the centre of things, he could see a rock of stability. The new rulers of England had, in peace and war, given unimpeachable proof of their ability, their integrity and their devotion to England. And who was he to withdraw his service from his guardian, Henry Ireton, whom he would trust to the end of the world? Or to that extraordinary man he'd first met in a shady corner of Mayerne's garden, and who now, by force of character and the providence of God, found himself in control of the nation's destiny?

'So you think I should remain a serving soldier?' Martin put his question tentatively to his mentor.

'That is your decision,' Philip Skippon replied firmly. Then he added: 'Still, it may help you to know that today I have agreed to serve on the new republic's forty-strong Council of State. So, too, have others, including leading jurists such as Selden and Whitelocke who, like me, always disapproved of the king's trial.'

There was no doubt that the old soldier had a very soft spot for Martin. His young recruit had turned out well and the future lay before him. As they parted company Skippon said in his gruff old voice, 'In a long life I've served many masters and, for the most part, have served those I could trust. For myself I would have no hesitation about working with Harry Ireton. He may be over-hasty in action. He doesn't suffer fools gladly – he's earned Lilburne's undying hatred. But he has the clearest mind of any man I know, and he never dissembles Like Fairfax and Oliver, he has only England at heart; and in thought and deed, he's true as Toledo steel.'

The call soon came to Martin. A message reached the Shipleys' house asking that Major Dowdswell should at his earliest convenience report to General Ireton's office in Whitehall Palace.

The Shipleys had already told Martin that Henry was working round the clock and was, for that reason, sleeping in the palace and eating with the Cromwells in King Street. And now, on reporting to his office, Martin found his guardian seated before a large desk in a room overlooking the royal gardens, and reached by way of galleries still adorned with the king's Italian paintings.

On one side of the room stretched a long table with eleven sets of documents neatly partitioned and separated from each other. On the desk was a single sheet of paper headed Martial Law at Sea which Martin eyed curiously.

Ireton, dressed in civilian clothes, laughed as he saw his ward's astonishment.

'There's no cause for alarm,' he said. 'We're not asking you to go to sea with Admiral Blake – not for the moment, anyhow.' And then, as Martin's eyes ranged over the eleven dossiers on the side table, he added, 'Nor am I asking you to read the proceedings of the eleven parliamentary committees on which I have been condemned to serve. They range from selling the property of deans and chapters to a survey of the king's debts and the crown lands. If you want to know what keeps me so busy, you'll find the details in the parliamentary records!

'Now sit down and let me bring you up to date with what I want you to do for me. Briefly, the new government faces two major problems – one internal and one external. The first priority concerns the regulation and good order of civil government at home. That's what is presently engaging my attention.' Henry waved to the piles of documents on the side table. 'But the external and more serious problem concerns the possible invasion of England from Scotland or Ireland. Our Intelligence Service tells us that both countries have invited the king's son to lead their separate rebellions, and Scotland has already proclaimed him Charles II. But Oliver thinks that the more immediate military threat comes from Ireland.'

Henry Ireton paused for a moment, giving Martin time to wonder where the conversation was leading, before he continued, 'Now most of us – and that includes the Council of State of which I am not a member – are painfully ignorant about Ireland. We don't seem to go back in time beyond the terrible Catholic massacre of Protestants in 1641. And it's my view that if we are ordered into Ireland, we should know more about its people and its history.'

Henry handed an envelope to Martin containing a letter to Bodley's librarian in Oxford. 'Now, this is where you can be of immediate assistance. Will you please hand this letter to the librarian with my compliments, and seek his help. He's a delightful man and is indebted to me for the speed with which we set a guard on his storehouse of knowledge when we captured Oxford.

'You will do this for me? I'm so glad. You'll see that the letter comes with the authority of the Council of State, but I shan't expect you back before the end of March. That should give you time to take my greetings to Sam and Betsie.'

Martin appreciated that Henry Ireton was in a good mood. 'And when do we take ship for Ireland, General?'

'Not so fast, Martin, not so fast. Just enjoy a short spell of university life. But here's a promise. If I'm allowed to give up this pen-pushing and permitted to take command in Ireland, I would need a military secretary covering the same skills that John Rushworth provided for Tom Fairfax and me after Naseby. I have it in mind that Major Martin Dowdswell might fit the bill.'

He chuckled as he took up his pen to complete the drafting of new regulations for the navy. But as Martin left, Henry shouted after him, 'And don't forget my message to Sam and Betsie. You may assure them – and the Shipleys too – that

I am in excellent health as are my wife and daughters at Windsor.'

Martin's stay in Oxford was both pleasurable and productive. He slept with the Dowdswells in Osney and rode with Sam to the scene of Henry Ireton's first triumph at South Leigh. He also enjoyed a brief meeting with Fairfax and Cromwell who, after forcefully quelling a serious army mutiny at Burford, stayed in Oxford to be appointed doctors of Civil Law by a grateful university.

But chiefly he was seated beside an old spectacled scholar in Bodley's Library. All knowledge seemed to be at his disposal. Piles of books were found and consulted. Thus Martin learnt that over one thousand years ago Vikings had settled on the east coast of Ireland near Dublin; that in the twelfth century the Normans had established themselves in the Dublin Pale and seized land and cattle from the Irish; and that in the following two centuries a series of expensive expeditions from England had signally failed to stop a deep-seated hostility between natives and settlers.

Coming to modern times, the Tudors – and especially Elizabeth – had sought to reduce Ireland to uniformity of religion, speech and social customs – all to no purpose since the Old Religion had stood firm. And now the colonising policy of the Stuarts had culminated with the bloody massacre of Protestants in 1641.

It was a sorry tale. But at the end of his exposition the little old man had something more to say. 'I would not presume, Major, to advise military experts on the control of Ireland. Yet I recall that the late Dr Kettel of Trinity College, who had a high regard for your Mr Ireton, once told me that the past loses half its interest if it does not guide the present.'

'And what conclusion, Sir, should I draw from the president's statement?'

'Why, simply this, young man. The episodes I have brought to your attention prove that whoever invades Ireland is liable to forget his original identity. I cannot explain why this should be so. Perhaps each successive newcomer is so bewitched by this land of legend and music and poets that his former loyalties are obliterated by a new and passionate attachment to his new

290

home. The lesson of the history books is surely this: that ultimately the Irish remain invincible.'

On the same March day that Martin conveyed to Henry Ireton the words of Bodley's librarian, Oliver Cromwell accepted Parliament's commission to bring back Ireland to its traditional dependence on England. He would be expected to emphasise that Irish loyalty must no longer be given to a Stuart in exile or a Pope in Rome, but to the English Parliament in Westminster.

On 12 July, with trumpets sounding General Cromwell, newly-appointed Lord Lieutenant of Ireland, left London for Bristol, travelling in a fine coach drawn by six white Flemish mares, and accompanied by a Life Guard of eighty senior officers.

In mid-August he set sail from Milford Haven with thirty-five ships. Two days later he was followed by a fleet of fifty-six ships under command of his deputy, Lieutenant General Henry Ireton. By the end of August eight thousand foot, three thousand horse and twelve hundred dragoons had disembarked within the Pale of Dublin. Superintending the movement of men and horses in his capacity as Military Secretary to General Ireton was Colonel Martin Dowdswell.

35

Martin Dowdswell's promotion ensured his presence at the operational conferences at which General Cromwell briefed his senior commanders. At Bristol he was fascinated at the masterful way in which Oliver set out the objectives of the Irish expedition.

As soldiers, Oliver reminded them, their first duty was to obey the orders of the new Council of State. As to Ireland, government policy could be considered in three parts: first, to prevent any possibility of the late king's supporters mounting an invasion of England; secondly, to avenge the priest-led massacre of Protestant settlers in 1641; and thirdly, to bring back Ireland into a closer union with England so that its people might enjoy the same laws as the English – the same freedoms of trade, speech and religious belief, and finally elect their own representatives to the Parliament at Westminster.

The first two parts of the council's policy were the army's special task. If all went well, he expected to drive all Irish armed resistance into Connaught and County Clare, west of the Shannon river, within twelve months. The task was urgent and more than one hundred ships were already assembled at Milford Haven.

Oliver had not minimised the gravity of the situation in Ireland. The great Royalist commander, the Duke of Ormonde, had been allowed to capture many garrison towns in Leinster and Ulster and was even threatening Dublin, having achieved the almost impossible task of uniting Irish Catholics and Protestant settlers under the king's banner. Moreover, the irrepressible Prince Rupert was preying on English shipping with a fleet of privateers based on the Scillies, but also using Irish ports.

But at Milford Haven despatches from Dublin and London engendered a confidence in the general which quickly spread to the troops awaiting embarkation. From Dublin came the news that Parliament's brilliant general, Michael Jones, had routed Ormonde's superior force at Rathmines and so made it safe for the army to disembark within the Pale of Dublin. London also reported that a naval force under Robert Blake had blockaded Prince Rupert's ships in Kinsale Harbour. Best of all, Roger Boyle, Lord Broghill, had confirmed in writing that he would support the cause of Parliament in Ireland.

Oliver was cock-a-hoop at his diplomatic coup with Broghill. 'It means, my friends, that Cork, Ireland's second city, will declare for us at the strategic moment. You understand its significance?' He turned towards Martin. 'You can forget your history studies at Oxford and concentrate on the geography of Munster – from Waterford to Limerick inclusive. Have you provided Harry with all the maps he needs?'

'Certainly, Sir. Distances out of Dublin will suit us well – Carlow fifty miles, Kilkenny a further twenty, then south to Ross and Waterford or west to Clonmel. Just right for cavalry operations. And at that point we would expect the navy to ensure our supplies through the southern ports of entry . . .'

'Enough, enough.' Oliver was laughing as he turned to Henry Ireton and the other officers. 'This Skippon-trained colonel of ours is quite right. We shall require Waterford, Youghal, Kinsale and Cork before our forces in Munster move further west – so the ports become a prime objective. And now let's get on with the job and see what Dublin looks like.'

Not a single man to whom he was speaking had ever crossed the Irish Sea, and most of them thought of the Irish people as the ancient world regarded the Barbarians – poor people who would remain a source of trouble unless they were civilised by their richer and better-educated neighbours. Had the English ever thought otherwise of the natives of Ireland? As the fleet set sail only Martin – and Henry Ireton to whom he had reported his researches in Oxford – remembered the words of Bodley's librarian.

By the end of August a fully-equipped and confident army had been efficiently transported to the Dublin area. But Cromwell's fame as a soldier had preceded his arrival, and many Dublin citizens, mostly Protestant, assembled to hear the great man's plan for Ireland.

Once again Martin Dowdswell was impressed by the political skill – a mixture of modesty and authority – with which

Oliver reassured his audience. His soldiers, he promised, would be under the strictest discipline – no looting from peaceful citizens nor illegal seizure of property; Irish traders would be offered open market facilities at all army bases; and trading restrictions would be lifted. There could be no doubt that the newly-appointed Lord Lieutenant of Ireland made an immensely favourable impression on the citizens of Dublin.

To his officers he now disclosed his military strategy. Ireton would remain in the Dublin area to co-ordinate plans for the drive into Munster while Cromwell moved north to recover the garrison towns captured by Ormonde, and establish closer contact with Sir Charles Coote in Londonderry and Colonel Monck in Belfast. These objectives would be gained, it was hoped, with minimum loss of life. But any town offering resistance, or refusing his offer of quarter, would be punished with the utmost rigour. England, he reminded them, had never forgotten the 1641 massacre.

Within the month all Ireland was horrified by the wanton massacre of armed men and priests in the streets and churches of Drogheda and Wexford after the Royalist commanders in both cities had rejected Cromwell's demand for surrender. The hideous slaughter had been deliberately ordered by Oliver at Drogheda, and repeated at Wexford in a fit of temper over delay in negotiations.

Henry Ireton and Martin Dowdswell never knew whether Oliver's terrible orders were inspired by the manic anger of a man who believed he was executing the vengeance of God on a sinful people, or by a calculated military decision which could at least be understood by professional soldiers who had witnessed similar barbarities during the religious wars in Germany. Certain it is that, following the sack of Drogheda and Wexford, the Irish levies hurriedly relinquished their hold on Ulster and Leinster.

Oliver now directed Ireton and Michael Jones south-west from Dublin. By-passing Kilkenny, they met little resistance except at Waterford which had powerful land and sea defences, and by gaining Youghal and Cork they ensured the availability of ports of entry for reinforcements from England. But as winter approached, an enemy far more powerful than Ormonde's Irish levies appeared in the form of malaria and dysentery which caused heavy loss of life, including that of Michael Jones at Dungarvan; and the high command was happy to settle into winter quarters at Youghal.

Yet Oliver was determined not to lose the initiative. In January 1650 the English commanders, strengthened by further reinforcements, completed Oliver's master plan. Henry Ireton, Reynolds and Hewson captured Waterford's outlying forts. Broghill and Henry Cromwell, Oliver's youngest son, advanced from Cork, and after defeating a considerable Irish force, made contact with Oliver at Clonmel. By the end of March the Irish command had no option but to evacuate its Kilkenny outpost.

Oliver experienced some trouble at Clonmel before Hugh O'Neill withdrew from the town after inflicting considerable casualties on the assault forces, but by 26 May he felt free to obey Parliament's instructions and return to England to tackle the Scottish problem.

His campaign in Ireland had been carried out by the veterans of the New Model Army with the same speed and efficiency which had characterised the suppression of the 1648 rebellion in England. Oliver had no hesitation in leaving the final section of the government's policy to his son-in-law, who was now named President of Munster and Deputy Lord Lieutenant of Ireland.

Little did he know, as he waved goodbye at Youghal and boarded the new naval frigate, *The President*, that he would never see Henry Ireton again.

For the second time Martin watched his former guardian assume the responsibility of supreme power; and, like many other observers in Ireland, he stood amazed at the superhuman energy and dedication which Ireton applied to the task. The man thought nothing of a sixteen-hour day which, starting and closing with prayer, involved the study of documents and legal problems far into the night, after a hard day often spent in the saddle.

As commander-in-chief, Ireton directed his generals to push all armed opposition north-west towards Connaught and County Clare – Sir Hardress Waller advancing on Limerick and Coote returning to invest Athlone after a decisive victory in Connaught. Ireton's more personal concern was the capture of Waterford without further bloodshed, a task which he rightly regarded as a political necessity. In late summer he finally entered the city but only after protracted and tedious negotiations which conceded liberal terms to Waterford's doughty old commander, Colonel Preston.

Martin, knowing his friend's impetuous nature, was surprised at his patience over this time-consuming bargaining at Waterford. It seemed as if his whole approach to life was changing. Was the spirit of Ireland getting into Henry Ireton's blood? The thought came to Martin as he and Henry explored the woods and running streams behind Waterford when he noted Ireton's absorbed interest and delight in the Irish countryside. The same thought recurred when they were riding together through the rich pastures of Tipperary, and Henry turned aside to visit the Rock of Cashel. They reined their horses to gaze in wonder at the great rock dominating the surrounding plain and at the ancient ruins of castle and chapel crowning its green and grey summit. This hill, Henry told Martin, was the capital of the former kingdom of Munster, and Martin was ordered to wait with the horses while the new President of Munster climbed the hill on foot. Beside the chapel he was seen to kneel in prayer, a pilgrim at a sacred shrine, seeking the help of his God and Ireland's in the task of pacification that lay before him.

Before the end of 1650 Parliament recognised the magnitude of Henry Ireton's assignment. He was to be assisted by four experienced civil commissioners, a chief justice and a second-in-command in the person of Edmund Ludlow newly appointed to the rank of Lieutenant General of Horse.

But Harry's most welcome support came with the arrival of his beloved Bridget who, accompanied by their eldest daughter, reached Waterford in Ludlow's three-ship convoy just after Christmas.

What a joy it was to be reunited with Bridie who could coax him out of his black moods when he was overtired and talk with him at his own intellectual level. Bridget would have liked to come with her mother to Dublin twelve months earlier, had she not been expecting a third child. As it was, she left the two younger children, Jane and baby Bridget, in Mrs

Cromwell's care while she embarked for Ireland with her eldest daughter.

In her new status as First Lady, Mrs Henry Ireton naturally required servants and suitable accommodation, and Martin was deputed to make the necessary arrangements with the mayor of Waterford. This proved a simple matter since the latter saw much advantage to his city if it provided a residence for the deputy lord lieutenant. Indeed, Bridget's ménage with its Irish-born staff worked happily from the start, and her only unexpected problem centred on the disturbing presence of an eighteen-year-old girl entrusted with the care of the four-year-old Elizabeth.

Maire O'Sullivan seemed well qualified for the task. She was a Waterford girl who from an early age had helped her widowed mother to bring up the younger members of a large family. But at eighteen she had blossomed into a young woman of striking beauty. She was of medium height, dark-haired, with brown eyes excitingly alive . . . Martin, remembering his hours of instruction in Bodley's Library, thought her family origins might go back to the early Iberian settlers in south-west Ireland. Whenever he encountered her in those early Waterford days his heart beat faster. The girl's trim youthful figure – her firmly-rounded breasts and swinging hips – excited and delighted him. He was entranced by her small capable hands and the lightness of her step – surely Maire's feet and ankles were made for dancing. And when he first heard her singing a lullaby to Liza in her native Irish tongue, his eyes unaccountably filled with tears.

In brief, Colonel Martin Dowdswell fell in love with Maire O'Sullivan at first sight, and the girl was not fooled for a moment by the excuses Martin found for visiting Mrs Ireton's establishment. This handsome young colonel was much to her fancy, and the sight of him and the sound of his footsteps brought a corresponding thrill of excitement to Maire O'Sullivan.

In February Ireton decided to ease the work of civil administration by moving his headquarters to Kilkenny, which was more centrally placed than Waterford and closer to Dublin. Martin superintended the move of Bridget Ireton's household, acting as personal escort to the ladies and carrying Liza, to the child's delight, on his own mount.

At the midday break he handed the little girl down to her Irish nurse, and on resuming the journey it seemed entirely appropriate for Martin to help the ladies into the saddle. Only Bridget, humorously observing these small gallantries, noticed that Maire O'Sullivan's hand rested in Martin's for that extra second that lovers require of each other, while her warm smile of gratitude brought an unwonted blush to the young man's cheeks.

The following morning, when Martin reported to Ireton as usual, he found the general in his sternest, official mood. Clearly, it was going to be one of those mornings . . .

'You know what I was doing yesterday, Martin?' The commander-in-chief began without preliminaries and didn't wait for an answer. 'I was packing Colonel Axtell off to England because, contrary to my express orders, he had sanctioned the execution of some Irish prisoners of war. Not a pleasant job, Martin. You don't need me to tell you that Axtell was one of my best officers, running this Kilkenny area with exemplary good sense. I don't like losing good officers, Martin.'

'No, Sir. Of course not.'

'So, I ask myself, what am I going to do with Colonel Dowdswell who dallies with an Irish girl who is supposed to be looking after my daughter?'

'Are you implying . . . ?'

'You know exactly what I mean and you are acquainted with the orders issued on the authority of Parliament – no serving soldier, officer or other rank, is to marry or consort with an Irish girl unless she gives proof of having accepted the Protestant faith. In present circumstances, when priests are still taking orders from France or Rome, it would seem a sensible precaution.'

The President of Munster permitted himself the hint of a smile. 'I doubt very much whether your interest in Miss O'Sullivan has left you time to convert her to the Protestant faith.'

'That is correct, Sir. We have not attempted to hide our love for each other as Mrs Ireton can tell you, but . . .'

'You have not shared the same bed – is that the situation?' Martin nodded. 'But you want to marry her?' Another nod from Martin. 'And the girl wants to marry you?'

Martin had often heard General Ireton cross-questioning some other wretch who had disobeyed his orders, but this was the first time in the course of his army service that he had stood directly in the firing line. He decided to take it straight and simple.

'Look, Sir. I'm in love with Maire – deeply in love, you understand – and come what may, I'm going to marry her as soon as she agrees to be my wife. But we must first get her mother's consent, and meanwhile, she's happy to remain in Mrs Ireton's service. Liza is very fond of Maire and would be very sad if she was sent back to Waterford.'

Henry Ireton paused in thought. He generally knew when men were lying. This boy was patently honest. He switched to a new line of argument.

'So you think this girl will be happy in England? And be congenial to your mother and your other English friends, eh? Then, perhaps it will simplify the problem if I obtain Mrs O'Sullivan's permission for her daughter to proceed to England with my wife? She and Liza will be rejoining the family as soon as we enter on the summer campaign.'

Nobody ever knew what was said when the President of Munster made a courtesy call on the mayor of Waterford. Henry Ireton was a man who kept his own counsel. But the O'Sullivan family moved from its broken-down cottage to more commodious quarters on the town's outskirts near St John's Gate about the same time that Maire O'Sullivan travelled to Dublin. A week later, in the company of Bridget Ireton and Elizabeth, she crossed the Irish Sea in a fine square-rigged ship to take up residence at the Cromwells' house in King Street where the younger Ireton children were staying.

The two lovers said goodbye to each other in Kilkenny. It was there they kissed for the first time. Maire was sobbing. She could not bear to leave Martin's arms and the feel of his body so close to hers.

'Don't cry, my Irish darling.' Martin gently drew back. 'Before the year ends, we'll meet again. For a few months only we take separate roads, but each of us travels in good company.'

And the Irish girl left Martin wearing a gold chain necklace, its links curiously wrought by an Irish craftsman. 'A gift, my love, to remind you of Ireland and me,' said Martin as he fastened the gold chain round Maire's neck. 'May it be a talisman for the future.'

Henry Ireton piled more and more duties on Martin Dowdswell. Hard work, he reckoned, would at least divert the young man's thoughts from Maire O'Sullivan, though he doubted whether time or distance would weaken his resolve. Soon Martin found himself fully occupied in arranging an army conference at Clonmel where his commander-in-chief would unfold his plans for controlling the west bank of the Shannon and occupying the three strategic bridgeheads of Limerick, Galway and Athlone.

Meanwhile, Henry Ireton was working at white-hot speed, signing innumerable orders that ranged from the definition of new administrative precincts and the control of local courts to farming regulations for preserving hay and halting the slaughter of lambs and calves. Healthy agriculture, as his family in distant Nottingham had taught him long ago, was the surest guarantee of peace, and his expert eye could already see a prosperous future for the horse-breeding industry.

Time was the enemy . . . if only he could be granted more time . . . he even had to waste time appeasing Broghill's jealousy of Ludlow by appointing his Lordship Lieutenant General of the Ordnance . . . Was there to be no time for sleep?

He was very tired. He must leave for Clonmel in the morning. But before he snuffed the candles, he still found time to write a family letter to Bridget in London. With the letter he also enclosed a sealed note for his father-in-law. It was concerned not with high affairs of State but with the love of Martin Dowdswell for Maire O'Sullivan. That, after all, was also part of the Irish problem.

36

By the end of June Ireton's main army was encamped before Limerick. To his intense annoyance it was still there four months later.

The campaign, so carefully planned with his senior commanders at Clonmel, had started well. The passages of the Shannon had been forced at Killaloe and Portumna, leaving Ludlow and Coote free to roam at large through Connaught and County Clare. Broghill and Henry Cromwell had routed the last remaining Irish field force. The senior Irish commanders, Ormonde and Inchiquin, had fled the country, and Ireton, delighted with his troops' performance, had led his army in a great service of praise and thanks to God for the outstanding successes granted to them.

Only Hugh O'Neill, who had given Oliver Cromwell such a hammering at Clonmel in the previous year, stood defiant behind the mighty medieval fortifications of Limerick. The Irishman had rejected the very reasonable terms which Ireton had offered, and English guns had been brought up the Shannon with other essential supplies to batter the city walls to rubble. But it was a long, slow process. A carefully planned assault had been beaten back, and Ireton, remembering Colchester, concluded that only starvation would force Limerick's surrender.

It was an unnerving situation for a man whose mind was already directed towards the ordering of the country and its return to prosperity. The autumn days were closing in, and the low-lying land of the Shannon estuary was a most unhealthy place for men in tents. Nor could heavy reinforcements be expected from England, since the best available units had been pre-empted for Oliver's Scottish campaign, only recently brought to a triumphant conclusion at Worcester.

But at long last, on 29 October, the tight blockade of Limerick took effect. Cut off from all hope of relief and with an outbreak of plague decimating the starving inhabitants of the beleaguered city, Hugh O'Neill had no option but to hand Ireton the keys of Limerick. The two men agreed terms similar to those offered by Ireton in June – military personnel to lay down their arms and non-combatant civilians to be granted amnesty; but those leaders who had delayed capitulation would be brought before an army court for judgment.

Before presiding at the court, Ireton spent a day in prayer. Then, following the precedents set by Cromwell at Pembroke and Fairfax at Colchester, prisoners convicted of taking up arms again after earlier conditional surrenders were condemned to death or exiled to the West Indies.

Hugh O'Neill, however, was treated as a special case. The fact that Ireton had developed a respect, even a sort of affection, for his Irish opponent could not be allowed to affect the issue. With an incorruptible judge, friendship is a dubious blessing. But two points worked in O'Neill's favour. First, he had never given his parole when withdrawing from Clonmel; he could not be said to have broken his word. Secondly, he had been born in Spain. Ireton seized on this latter point. Was it not a similar plea, put to him and Fairfax at Colchester, which had saved Gascoigne's life? The panel of army judges jumped at the opportunity and Hugh O'Neill received an honourable discharge at Limerick such as Ireton and Fairfax had accorded to Hopton at Truro and Rupert at Bristol. Three Royalists, at least, would always remember Ireton as a merciful judge.

To all intents and purposes the war in Ireland was over, for Galway was there for the taking. It was surely time for Martin Dowdswell to be released from his service in Ireland.

Henry broached the matter at his morning meeting. 'I've been thinking about you and that Irish girl of yours,' he told Martin. 'Mrs Ireton writes that Miss O'Sullivan, who has proved a great help with our three daughters, often asks about you and certainly hopes to see you again. Do you still feel the same way about her?'

Martin's eyes lit up. 'So you're quite sure, are you?' Henry took an imposing envelope from his desk.

'Well then, here's a letter to be delivered to Speaker Lenthall – a full and fair account, I hope, of what we've achieved to date in Ireland. You'd like to make the journey to England, would you? Fine. Off you go then – and the best of luck. You'll see I've addressed the letter to Lenthall at his house in Burford since the House isn't sitting, so when you reach England you'll be riding in familiar country.'

Martin stammered his thanks and promised delivery at top speed. Then he asked, 'And what is my next assignment?'

Ireton had thought it all out. 'You proceed to London, report to General Oliver, present my compliments to Mrs Cromwell and my wife and, maybe, pay a visit to the Ireton nursery!

'But to be serious, Martin, I should add two points – one concerns me and the other concerns you.

'First let me say that I hate the idea of losing you. Not only because you've proved yourself a first-class staff officer, but also' – Ireton's eyes came up from the papers on his desk to look Martin straight in the face – 'because your companionship has saved me again and again from too great an obsession with this land of Ireland. You have – how shall I put it? – a sort of counter-balancing effect on me. Whenever I see you, I am reminded of England – the people and places we've both known and the adventures we've both shared: the lessons at Osney when I was an undergraduate, gallops with Sam and your mother on Cumnor Hill. Getting you into St Paul's School, warming myself at the Shipleys' open hearth, pulling you clear of that apprentice mob in the Strand . . . a living link, if you see what I mean, with the peaceful days before we were plunged into civil war.' Henry paused, seemingly lost in his memories.

Martin said, 'But didn't you have a second point you wished to make?'

'Ah yes – of course I have. It's about this Irish girl of yours. I can't help thinking, Martin, that if you marry Maire O'Sullivan you may find it difficult to settle either in England or in Ireland.'

'You mean because we've been brought up to respect different religious disciplines?'

'No, Martin, no. I pray that you and Maire can settle such problems as easily and happily as my sister Sarah and Edward Ford settled theirs. Your problem, I fear' – and Ireton hesitated for a moment – 'your problem will be with your neighbours.

I've seen too much prejudice in the people around me, in England as well as Ireland – Presbyterians, Catholics, Laudians, Levellers, Anabaptists . . . the lot! If only my father-in-law and I could have found in our little world the tolerance we've preached and practised, how different our lives and actions . . .' Again, Henry's voice trailed away – the voice of a man whose life had been ruled by the art of the possible, dreaming the impossible dream.

Henry seemed suddenly tired. Martin waited a moment.

'And should Maire and I be faced with this invincible prejudice, what would you advise?'

'If I were you, Martin, I'd go straight to my father-in-law. He's the wisest man I know and he understands these things.'

'So, one final question. If I may not return to Ireland with my bride, who will take my place?'

The dreamer was once again the man of action. 'That's a good question, Martin. I've been thinking about your successor for some weeks and instinct tells me that the man for the job is Henry Cromwell. I spotted him first when he was a boy at Ely, and here in Ireland he has surely shown his quality. If the choice lies with me, I would like young Cromwell to share my Irish responsibilities. You may, perhaps, have observed that this land of Ireland exerts a special charm on Henry Cromwell. He, above all my other commanders, has caught the vision of an Ireland restored to peace and prosperity.'

Martin rode eastwards over the green expanses of Tipperary and Kilkenny and north-east to Carlow and Dublin. Only once did he turn from the road, following in his guardian's footsteps and climbing the time-honoured rock of Cashel to entrust his future to God. But as he knelt beside the ruined chapel at the hill's summit his concern was less with Ireland than with his love for Maire O'Sullivan.

On from Dublin he went, crossing the Irish Sea on a naval frigate to Bristol. From that great city he took the road to Cirencester and over the Cotswolds until he came in sight of Burford. His journey, he realised, had taken him from the heart of Ireland into the heart of England. How great the contrast was – not only between green plains and rolling uplands but between poverty and wealth, the broken-down isolated shelters of Ireland and the neat stone-built Cotswold villages.

At Burford Priory he was well received by Speaker Lenthall. But Burford was no more than an overnight stop, for after reading Ireton's despatch, Lenthall asked Martin to deliver a copy of it to General Cromwell in London.

Two days later Martin reported to Oliver. The latter read Ireton's long report with enormous delight, slapped his knee – 'Well done, Harry. Well done' – and after calling a secretary to rush the news to the press, he clapped Martin on the back:

Great news, young Martin . . . The Lord be praised . . . Great news calls for a jug of ale . . . You must be tired, lad. Sit down and fill me in with the details of the story. How is Harry? What's the state of the army? Spared that rogue, O'Neill, has he? And what news of my son, Henry? His mother keeps worrying about the boy . . . but you know what women are. Here's a health to my son-in-law and deputy, the President of Munster.

General Oliver was in exultant mood. He swallowed his ale and, refilling his pewter mug, turned an amused eye on Martin.

'Women,' he repeated. 'Now that reminds me of a letter I received from Harry, way back in March and written from Dublin I fancy . . . That's right, it was about the Waterford girl you found for Bridie's children. A very pretty girl if I may say so, and a Godsend to my daughter. Now here's some up-to-date news. The Irish girl is to take charge of the little Ireton girls while their mother travels to Ireland. Let me see . . . Yes, today my daughter has left for Chester to join an army convoy for Dublin. Mrs Cromwell thinks it very unwise for Bridie to risk the journey, as she's expecting another baby in the new year . . . but this daughter of ours is a very determined young woman and greatly concerned that Harry is working too hard. I can't say Mrs Cromwell was ever so concerned about me!'

Old Noll was in one of his light-hearted moods. When would he come to the point? Martin finished his beer. He said, 'I'm not sure I'm following you, Sir. Where are General Ireton's children, did you say?'

'And where is the nurse with the dark Irish eyes, eh? I must not keep you in suspense. The situation is that the three little girls and their nurse, strictly chaperoned of course, reach London from Windsor tomorrow.'

'And can I visit them here in King Street?'

'But of course you're welcome, though nothing can speed their journey. Can we offer you a bed for the night? Or will you stay with your old friends by Temple Stairs?'

Martin was amazed to find Oliver remembering Joe and Hannah Shipley. What a prodigious memory he had! After a moment's hesitation the two men agreed that the Shipleys might be disappointed if Martin did not accept their hospitality; but Oliver promised that Martin would be informed as soon as the Ireton children were settled into the King Street house.

Old Noll was as good as his word. Two days later, Maire O'Sullivan arrived at the Shipleys' front door, dismounting from one of the new hackneys which were beginning to steal the London passenger trade from Joe Shipley and his Thames watermen.

With Bridget Ireton's help, the Irish girl had arrayed herself in a dress which showed her figure to perfection. Circling her neck was the little gold chain which Martin had given her in Kilkenny.

In Limerick the evening light was fading from the sky and in the tented camp outside the city men were preparing themselves for sleep. But Henry Ireton continued to work by candlelight.

On that particular day he had written to Parliament refusing their offer of £2,000 as a special reward for his work in Ireland. It could better be applied, he said, to meeting the army's arrears of pay. An orderly had just left Ireton's tent with this letter and a collection of papers and ordinances signed by him, when Henry Cromwell reported that a lady had been arrested, disguised as a shepherdess and driving a mixed herd towards the County Clare border. The animals had been corralled, but what should they do with the woman?

Tired as he was, Ireton was persuaded to see the lady. Half an hour later she emerged from his tent smiling broadly and carrying a permit to drive her animals across the county boundary – a very different person from the terrified and tearful woman who had been hustled into his presence a little earlier.

Ireton laughed as he told Henry Cromwell what had transpired. 'Believe it or not,' he said, 'the "shepherdess" proved to be Lady Glamorgan's sister attempting to escape from the wicked English with everything she and her family could get on the road. When she had dried her tears she became so talkative I decided we should never make an end of it unless we sent her on her way. Any more Irish ladies like this – and I shall gain a reputation for clemency.'

They laughed over the incident and parted company for the night, but Ireton was too tired for restful sleep. Dreams alternately charmed or tormented him. Pleasing thoughts came to him: Bridie and the three children; Martin meeting his Irish girl and introducing her – he was sure of this – to Joe and Hannah Shipley; his mother running the Ireton lands with the help of his brother Clement.

The thoughts of his family turned to exaggerated anxiety. Would John become Lord Mayor of London? Would Tom recover sufficiently from the fearful wound received at Bristol to enjoy married life in Derbyshire? Would Parliament grant free pardon to his beloved Sarah and her Roman Catholic husband? And out of his care for Sarah came the inevitable question: how could her co-religionists in Ireland be persuaded to give up their ancient overseas commitments to the Stuarts and the Papacy and join Protestant settlers in building a new and prosperous Ireland?

Then to his overtired mind came a host of personal recriminations. By what mischance or miscalculation had he failed to win the king's approval for a constitutional monarchy? Should he have stuck to his plan and retired from army service in 1648 rather than be over-persuaded by Tom Fairfax? Had his compromise with Lilburne and his followers in the army inevitably led to the king's death? Had he really over-influenced Oliver's thinking, as so many avowed?

He awoke from his fitful sleep with a high temperature, burning with the same marsh fever that was attacking the troops. He struggled with the day's work, insisting on the sick Ludlow getting into a warm house in County Clare. When it was reported that a colonel and his ensign had been responsible for the death of some Limerick prisoners, he ordered an immediate court martial and reduced both men to the ranks. So long as life remained in him Ireton's orders would be obeyed to the letter.

It was his last act before fever forced him back to bed. An army surgeon bled him but there was no easement. Henry Cromwell sat with him through the night. Once he was heard to repeat the words he had spoken at the Putney debates: 'The main thing is for everyone to wait upon God for the errors, deceits and weaknesses of his own heart.'

As day broke, his right hand tried to grasp Henry Cromwell's but fell back. There was a tiny sigh of utter exhaustion. The candle of life had been extinguished, and Henry Ireton was dead, untimely dead in a tented camp outside Limerick. He was only thirty-nine years old. But those around him reported a smile on his lips, as of one who had found peace in his own time. From the Bible beside his bed a sheet of paper fluttered to the ground. On it were inscribed some verses from Henry Vaughan's poem set out in his beloved sister's handwriting:

> My soul, there is a country
>   Far beyond the Stars,
> Where stands a winged sentry
>   All skilful in the wars . . .
>
> If thou canst get but thither,
>   There grows the flower of peace,
> The rose that cannot wither,
>   Thy fortress, and thy ease.
>
> Leave then thy foolish ranges,
>   For none can thee secure
> But One, who never changes,
>   Thy God, thy life, thy cure.

The news of Ireton's death spread through the land of Ireland and across the sea to England. Extravagant tributes were paid to his memory: by many senior officers such as Ludlow and Hewson who had served in Ireland; by the chief justice in

Munster whose hand Ireton had guided; and, most touchingly, by the Irishman, Hugh O'Neill. And in Ireland, law and order held firm.

Ireton's embalmed body was taken from Dublin to Bristol. From Bristol Castle guns thundered their salute and the mayor and many prominent citizens accompanied the hearse out of the city before handing it over to an escort of Cromwell's own regiment of horse. The procession moved across England to London where the body lay in state at Somerset House.

But the grievous news had far outrun this ceremonial home-coming. A distraught Bridget returned from Chester to Windsor to bear Ireton's fourth child. In the village of Atten-borough Jane Ireton, stricken by grief such as she had not known since her husband's death, sought comfort in the great parish church beside her house. Humble families in Not-tingham, Ely and Oxford mourned the loss of a very dear friend, while in London special plans were made to honour this great servant of the new republic.

Early in February 1652 soldiers lined the streets as the funeral procession moved, with muffled drums beating, along the Strand to Westminster. The great captains of the New Model Army marched beside the gun-carriage – Cromwell, Skippon, Lambert, Fleetwood, Harrison, Desborough and the rest. In Westminster Abbey the sermon, later to be sold by the thousand in pamphlet form, was preached by Dr John Owen, the new Dean of Christ Church, Oxford, who had accompanied the expedition to Ireland. Solemnly the body of General Henry Ireton, President of Munster and Deputy Lord Lieutenant of Ireland, was interred in Henry VII's Chapel – the resting place of kings.

Never in living memory had Londoners witnessed so great a funeral. To the leaders of the new State it had seemed right to honour the achievements and singular character of so great a man. Only those who knew Henry Ireton most intimately could imagine the half-cynical smile of amusement which would have crossed his face at the thought of all this fuss. Earthly honours were not of Henry Ireton's seeking. He was a very private man. Left to himself he would have chosen the peaceful serenity of St Mary's, Attenborough, to be his final resting place.

In the Cromwells' nursery in King Street Maire O'Sullivan was also weeping – but hers were tears born of a young woman's frustration. After her joyful reunion with Martin and many subsequent meetings at the Shipleys', her thoughts and passionate hopes were all centred on her marriage to the man she loved. She could hardly wait for the day of her wedding. Dreaming of the future, she found it almost impossible to accept old Hannah Shipley's counsel of patience: Martin may be finding it hard to persuade a minister to conduct the wedding ceremony . . . Martin is still shattered by the shock of his guardian's death . . . What comfort was this for a young Irish girl, alone in London, who longed to be her own mistress and make her own home as the wife of Colonel Martin Dowdswell!

And now – to see her small world undermined by a general's death in distant Limerick! With Martin engaged from dawn to dusk in making arrangements for this pompous funeral, and with Bridget Ireton back from Chester and herself under orders to accompany the Ireton children back to Windsor . . . The situation was intolerable.

Maire O'Sullivan wrote a good hand now – Bridget had encouraged her in this and many other ways – and she was tearfully engaged in writing to tell Martin of her forthcoming move to Windsor when Cromwell and his wife entered the nursery to visit their grandchildren. Surprised and flustered, Maire tried hard to conceal her tears, but when Mrs Cromwell asked if she was sad to be leaving London, she could control herself no longer.

'No, no, Ma'am, it's not that,' she sobbed. 'I love the children. I'm very sad for Mrs Ireton. I want to help her. But what of my marriage to Colonel Dowdswell? He's given me his promise, Ma'am . . . you know he has.'

It was, indeed, one of Oliver's most endearing characteristics that, however occupied he might be with great affairs of State, he could always make time to cope with the small domestic griefs and anxieties of his family and friends. It had always been so, and the same quality was manifest now in his concern for Maire O'Sullivan as he reassured her that Martin was a man of his word and would soon be with her again.

Immediately after the funeral Oliver had a word with him. He started the conversation in his usual hesitant manner, as if testing the ground for a sure foothold. 'This has been a very sad time for all of us,' he said, 'but there comes a moment, you know, when mourning has to end. We all live under God's Providence, and we must accept that you and I, Martin – yes and Bridie too – are fated to live in a world without the joy and comfort of Harry Ireton's presence.' Then he suddenly came to the point, as his manner was. 'So now I ask you, Martin, how and where do you and Maire O'Sullivan see your future?'

The suddenness of the question took Martin by surprise. He began to play for time . . . he'd been so concerned with the funeral . . . Maire must stay with Mrs Ireton, at least until the new baby was safely delivered . . .

Oliver broke in. 'But you still intend to marry this Irish girl, don't you?'

Martin was in no doubt about that, he said, but he was unsure about his job and he feared that living in England would be terribly difficult for Maire.

Oliver interrupted him again.

'Then, why not chance your arm, as Harry would have done, and see what New England holds for you? There's a land crying out for men like you and women like Maire O'Sullivan. And you'll be sure of a job as well as a welcome. Didn't Harry once tell me that your mother's brother had made a success of life in Boston? Did not a Brewster from Nottingham sail in the *Mayflower*? And I warrant there'll be no shortage of Irish people to greet your bride. But you'll break her heart if you go on brooding about the past and doubting the present.'

'So what do you suggest?'

'Why, get down to Windsor at once, man. Put the idea to the girl. Get married. Get on a boat.'

Oliver's enthusiasm was infectious, as it had always been with men preparing for battle. Fear was reduced to its proper size. Martin jumped to his feet. He was conscious of the exhilaration he had felt as a boy when meeting the unknown Cromwell in Sir Theodore's garden. Once more he felt the magnetic power of the man who had once drawn Henry Ireton from the peaceful obscurity of a Nottingham village to the service of the State.

Martin knew no further doubt. A new world was calling him forward.

37

Neither the memoirs of the day nor the later history texts make mention of Martin Dowdswell. But in the early spring of 1652, some three weeks after Bridget Ireton gave birth to a son, Martin and Maire O'Sullivan were married in the same City church in which Sarah Ireton had once made her vows to the Roman Catholic, Edward Ford, and once again Joe and Hannah Shipley signed the register as witnesses. There was only one unexpected visitor – none other than General Philip Skippon who limped into the church with a Bible he had personally signed for the bride and bridegroom and two letters which he handed to Martin after the ceremony. One of them, very official and resplendent with the House of Commons Seal, was addressed to Governor Roger Williams, founder of the City of Providence, New England. The second, much less official, carried the name of Captain Gatehouse, Master of the *Hope of Bristol* – this second letter to be delivered to the said Captain by Colonel Dowdswell before the last day of April. Both letters were addressed in the unmistakable handwriting of Oliver Cromwell.

A honeymoon journey took Maire and Martin to Windsor where they said goodbye to Bridget, her three daughters and the baby boy who was to be christened Henry. They moved to Oxford where Martin introduced his young wife to his grandfather and Betsie Dowdswell, and on to Attenborough to meet his mother and Tom Brewster.

Martin was apprehensive about his mother's reaction to his marriage, for he knew that, despite her grim early years at Osney, she had inherited a strong Puritanical distrust of all Papist connections. But he had reckoned without the massive good sense of Jane Ireton. The latter had quickly won Maggie's affection in the days following the Brewsters' move from Oxford, and the two women had become good friends. Now, choosing her moment, Mrs Ireton spoke to Maggie very firmly. Had not Sarah Ireton's marriage to a Roman Catholic prospered? Well then, why should Maggie fret about Martin's marriage to Maire O'Sullivan? As to New England, had it not brought wealth to Maggie's brother and fame to Tom Brewster's uncle who had sailed in the *Mayflower*? 'Come, Maggie, you are proud of your soldier son. You should trust his judgment, too.'

In the event, Maggie's fears were totally allayed by Maire's Irish charm and Martin's delight in his bride. After a stay of three days, Colonel and Mrs Martin Dowdswell departed from Attenborough, carrying the village's good wishes and Maggie Brewster's blessing. Martin also received a gift from Jane Ireton. It was a small wooden box with the Ireton arms carved on it by Henry Ireton in his schooldays as a gift for his mother. She now entrusted it to Martin as a memento of his links with the Ireton family.

And so, light of heart and happy in their love, Maire and Martin made their way to Bristol and delivered Oliver's letter to the Master of the *Hope of Bristol*.

Captain Gatehouse was blessed with a powerful voice and a pawky sense of humour, and he was immensely proud of his ocean-going vessel. 'The powers that be have chosen a fine ship for you,' he said as he conducted Maire and Martin to their cabin on the poop deck. 'I trust you'll enjoy the voyage and the company. Mind you,' he added with a laugh, 'while we do our best for the friends of generals and admirals, I should warn you that comfort at sea depends on calm seas and fair winds. You never know your luck, but I hope you'll find these quarters reasonably comfortable.'

The next morning the *Hope of Bristol* left on the tide, carrying a cargo of west-country cloth and bound for the southern Irish ports before making the long haul to Boston.

She was a fine ship indeed – far more commodious than anything Maire or Martin had known on their short journeys across the Irish Sea. The *Hope* was built on old-fashioned lines, three-masted and square-rigged, wide in the beam with a high poop and a beak bow. She also carried a spritsail forward and a lateen mizzen which Captain Gatehouse used when navigating the narrow waters of the estuaries where his ports of call were situated.

At Waterford Maire and Martin went ashore while the *Hope*

discharged her cargo and took on stores. They took a nostalgic last look at Reginald's Tower and the familiar streets within the walled city, and visited the new house by St John's Gate: where they attended a great O'Sullivan party – a mingling of laughter and tears and optimism. Who was to say when some other members of the O'Sullivan family would not want to follow the lovely Maire to this land of infinite promise?

Many hands were waving on the Great Quay at Waterford as the *Hope* sailed away down the Barrow estuary, past the outlying forts which Ireton had found so hard to capture three years previously, and set course on the eighty miles of coastal water to Cork.

At Ireland's second city – and as some would say its fairest – the *Hope* spent a further three days. More stores were loaded, and some Irish emigrant families (their papers and credentials carefully checked by Captain Gatehouse) accommodated below deck in the forward section of the ship.

At last, towards the end of May 1652, Maire and Martin Dowdswell found themselves standing beside the master as the *Hope* moved majestically towards the open sea. They took a last lingering look at Cork's lovely setting – the wooded hills in the background, and the placid water of the Lee reflecting the riverside buildings. The houses and the busy quays slipped slowly behind them. The estuary widened. Ireland, like England, was no more than a memory. As they sighted Barry Head to starboard, the *Hope of Bristol* sprang into new ocean-going life – men everywhere, hauling on the yards, more sail hoisted to catch the light easterly wind, the bow wave leaving a trail of white in the blue water astern and the ship's timbers creaking.

So the *Hope of Bristol* headed west, carrying Martin Dowdswell and his Irish bride to that tract of land in New England where Oliver Cromwell's friend, Governor Roger Williams, had guaranteed to all men and women in his state those freedoms of speech and worship to which Martin's guardian had devoted his life.

AUTHOR'S NOTE

Destiny Our Choice is a work of fiction. The Dowdswell family, the Brewsters and Shipleys and the women in their lives are creatures of my own imagining. But the events in which they take part are deliberately placed between 1611 and 1651 – the lifespan of Oliver Cromwell's son-in-law, Henry Ireton.

Ireton was born in the village from which my family stems and educated in the Oxford college of which I am a member. But I have made his life the framework of my novel because it poses the question endemic to my theme: 'How far does human choice decide a nation's destiny?'

I have rested Henry Ireton's character on the remarkable tributes paid at the time of his premature death, discounting the frustrated abuse of John Lilburne and the virulent criticism of Royalist pamphleteers which only serve to emphasise the strength of Ireton's character and the power he wielded with Cromwell.

As to his family, Tom Ireton's Will, still extant and filled with delightful bequests for his brothers and sisters and their spouses, gives ample proof of the happiness and tolerance of the Ireton home. Sarah and her Roman Catholic husband both figure among the legatees!

But Ireton's association with the white knight, Thomas Fairfax, is also significant. In the brilliant post-Naseby campaign and in the second civil war of 1648, Fairfax always chose to have Henry Ireton at his side; and although Ireton may have been primarily responsible for Cornet Joyce's capture of the king and Colonel Pride's 'purge' of the Commons, Fairfax gave these masterful 'illegalities' his massive support. Fairfax and Ireton, exact contemporaries in age, must have been very good friends.

At the Restoration Henry Ireton's body was, like Cromwell's, disinterred from Westminster Abbey and shamefully mutilated at Tyburn. But his family was left in peace except for London's Lord Mayor, John Ireton, who suffered long imprisonment. Bridget, who married Charles Fleetwood after Henry Ireton's death, died in 1662; but the three Ireton daughters married well and the posthumous son, Henry, rose to the rank of colonel in the regular army which was the linear descendant of the New Model.

I am left with the conviction that Henry Ireton was both a great and a good man. I believe that, in pressing his plans for a constitutional monarchy upon the king, the army and Parliament, he saw the future more clearly than any of his contemporaries. I believe that in Ireland he learnt the virtue of patience, the lack of which had been his great weakness in the critical year leading to the king's death. I think he would have found a certain wry amusement in the Royalist Clarendon's grudging praise: 'Ireton never dissembled.' Above all, I wonder whether English history would have followed a different course if Henry Ireton had not died at the age of thirty-nine in the fever-ridden army camp outside the walls of Limerick.

J. A.

3 September 1986

DINAH LAMPITT

TO SLEEP NO MORE

England at the time of Edward III — a time when marriageable daughters were welcome currency in the plans of ambitious men. In the Sussex village of Mayfield, young and beautiful Oriel de Sharndene has been forced into marriage with the Archbishop of Canterbury's brother though she loves a handsome Gascon squire. Yet all is not as it seems, for these are three people who have not only met in another life but are fated to meet again and again.

From medieval England to the witch hunts of the seventeenth century and the smuggling and highwaymen of the eighteenth, TO SLEEP NO MORE is an unforgettable tale of three characters whose souls cannot rest until their final destiny has been resolved.

A Royal Mail service in association with the Book Marketing Council & The Booksellers Association
Post-A-Book is a Post Office trademark

ALSO AVAILABLE FROM HODDER AND STOUGHTON PAPERBACKS